To Janice & Danny

God Bless You all!

From Your Friend
Michael Pope

OCT 6 2011

The Life and Times
of
Gloria Bunker

by Michael Pope

RoseDog🐾Books
PITTSBURGH, PENNSYLVANIA 15222

The contents of this work including, but not limited to, the accuracy of events, people, and places depicted; opinions expressed; permission to use previously published materials included; and any advice given or actions advocated are solely the responsibility of the author, who assumes all liability for said work and indemnifies the publisher against any claims stemming from publication of the work.

All Rights Reserved
Copyright © 2010 by Michael Pope
No part of this book may be reproduced or transmitted in any form or by any means, electronic or mechanical, including photocopying, recording, or by any information storage and retrieval system without permission in writing from the author.

ISBN: 978-1-4349-9955-9
Printed in the United States of America

First Printing

For more information or to order additional books,
please contact:
RoseDog Books
701 Smithfield Street
Pittsburgh, Pennsylvania 15222
U.S.A.
1-800-834-1803
www.rosedogbookstore.com

CHAPTER ONE:
Heading to the House

Traffic on the Van Wyck Expressway in Queens going to and from JFK was horrendous, but that wasn't bothering Gloria. Her mind was preoccupied. She sat in the back seat of the taxi with her dark glasses on, trying to prevent anyone, especially the taxi driver, from seeing the now-smudged mascara that covered her tear dripping red, swollen eyes. Every now and then she would sniffle and take a dab at her nose and eyes. That would give it away that something was definitely wrong. She was still in shock and in denial, not believing what had happened. Just a few hours ago, everything was normal in her life. It's amazing how things change so abruptly that it sends your mind into a tailspin. Deep down inside, she knew it was coming before it happened. She tried not to think about it at the time. "If you don't think about it, nothing negative is going to happen," she had kept telling herself. But it did happen. To Gloria, it seemed like only minutes before that she was in California working as a realtor, showing that huge 3-bedroom, 2-story loft to some very interested buyers when she got the dreaded call. When her cell phone went off, and she looked at the number, she had already known. She had stared at the number for what seemed like forever as her heart began racing and she started to sweat heavily.

Gloria had excused herself from the prospective buyers and told them to feel free to look around on their own, which they did. Once she was alone and out of hearing range from the prospective buyers, she took a deep breath, then answered. Before she even had the opportunity to say hello, she had already heard sobbing on the other end of the phone. She knew who it was coming from immediately.

"Gloria!" a crackling voice cried as it tried to gain composure through the sniffling.

It was Stephanie, who had moved back into the house once Archie became too overwhelmed with running the restaurant and maintaining the house alone. She continued doing her successful singing and voiceovers while tending to Archie's needs, which really weren't many. Most of the time, he wasn't home. It was recently that he had begun looking different and would come home tired and out of breath from working in the restaurant.

As Stephanie continued trying to speak, Gloria braced herself as her knees began shaking uncontrollably.

"U-uncle A-Archie! H-he's, h-he's ....!" The words that Gloria had feared to hear were manifesting themselves loud and clear in her ear. Her daddy had died.

Her mind brought her back to the present as she sat in the back seat shaking her head and sobbing ever so slightly. "This can't be happening. This is just a dream. No, no, a nightmare. Oh God! Will you please wake me up?!"

Unfortunately for Gloria, she was awake and no matter what she tried to do or try to deny, she would never again have the pleasure of hearing her father, Archie, call her his little girl. Her source of support was now gone forever. First it was her loving and caring mom, Edith, who died in the 80s, and now her daddy, Archie. One thing Gloria was happy with was the fact that even though they died 20 or so years apart, they died the same way: at peace and in their sleep. "Now you are together for eternity," she said to herself as that comment brought a slight smile to her face. The smile quickly disappeared once she realized that she had no more parents.

But in reality, Gloria wasn't a little girl. She was a beautiful, mature woman with a family. She was far from being alone. Gloria had Joey, who was in his late 20s. She had him with her first husband, Mike Stivic, whom she had been civilly divorced from for decades, and she had the twins. Zoe was the girl and Matthew the boy. They were in their teens. She had them with her second husband, Raymond Shaw, who she buried two years after the twins were born. She had thought that she would have a long-lasting and loving life with him till he unexpectedly died of a heart attack, so very young. They had said that he died quickly.

Gloria started thinking about who would be there for her kids if anything happened to her when all of a sudden, she was startled by a loud horn from the car that was behind the taxi. She jumped a little out of the seat and made a gasping noise, causing the driver to look at her through his rearview.

"You okay, Mom?" Zoe asked lovingly as she laid her head on her mother's shoulder. She also had her hands wrapped around Gloria's arm for comfort.

Matthew took hold of Gloria's trembling hand and squeezed it gently. He was sitting on the other side of her. He glanced toward her and smiled. "Don't worry, Mom. It was only a car horn," he assured her.

Zoe and Matthew were both very concerned for her. Gloria put a feigned smile on her face and nodded slightly. "I'm fine, you guys. The unexpected sound of the loud horn spooked me a bit, that's all."

The twins both looked at each other, then at Gloria. When they were satisfied with the response, they resumed being preoccupied with their own sad thoughts.

The twins really did love their grandfather, Archie, very much. Gloria knew by the expressions on their solemn faces what they were thinking. This was really the first death experience that they ever had to deal with. They weren't born when Edith died and they were too young to remember when their father died. She could only imagine what was going through their heads.

Gloria glanced over towards Zoe, who was comfortable and snuggled on her shoulder as her hands wrapped around her arms like she was holding onto an anchored tree in a windy snow storm, trying not to be blown away. Oh, how she looked so much like her when she was a teen: petite, ivory complexion, dirty blond thick wavy hair, big almond shaped eyes with the color to match, along with long doll-sized eyelashes. She even had her nice hips, small waist and big perky cheerleader's breasts. Zoe had also inherited Gloria's feisty temper, her strong will and her "go get them" attitude. Gloria then glanced over towards Matthew, who was staring out the window, slightly bopping to the music and moving his mouth, mimicking the singing on the taxi driver's radio, which was being played very low. Even though they were twins, they weren't identical. They did favor each other, but to Gloria, Matthew looked more like Raymond and even had a lot of his qualities and mannerisms. Just like Raymond, Matthew loved music—all different kinds of music, from opera to rap—and he could play almost any instrument by ear. Unlike Zoe, Matthew was tall, just like his father, with an athletic build. He also had an ivory complexion covered slightly with acne and peach fuzz facial hair. His hair was also dirty blond naturally, but when he was in a 'rocker mood,' he would dye it. At the present time, it was white blond and cut short and spiked up in the front. He was quite a handsome young man and was considered very popular at the school that he and Zoe attended. Besides the same attributes that Zoe had, Matthew was very curious about how things work. Gloria and Zoe were opposite of Matthew in that category. Neither even knew how to program the clock on the VCR/DVD/CD player. Matthew also liked to be alone and do a lot of writing of songs and poems. While Matthew was independent, Zoe tended to be needier.

After she finished looking at the twins, she then started thinking about her firstborn son, Joey. He would be making a later flight into JFK. He had last-minute things that he had to do. Even though Joey and the twins had different fathers, they all resembled each other because of Gloria's strong genes. Joey had Mike's hair color, and it was long. Sometimes he would just put it into a ponytail. He was ivory complexioned, with Gloria's eyes and lashes. Everything else was Mike's. He had Mike's Polish straight nose and thin lips. He even had Mike's appetite. The only difference was that Joey was still thin. Joey was a brainiac who loved to read all kinds of books. He went to college right after high school—free tuition and all—and now, after very hard work, he was a teacher. Just like Mike, Joey wanted to teach and save the world.

All three siblings loved each other very much, and they all loved Gloria. Even though Joey had moved out a few years back, the siblings still spent a lot of time together, visiting each other frequently.

Gloria was concerned about Joey because he had experienced so much death in his short life. He remembered the divorce between her and Mike. Even though they stayed mutual friends all his life, Joey never liked the separation. He also remembered when his grandmother died. Even though Raymond was not his real father, he loved him and Raymond loved him like he was from his own bloodline. Joey had experienced another separation. Now his grandfather, Archie, was dead. Gloria could easily read the twins when there was a problem, but Joey had always been different. He kept so much inside that she never knew how he really felt. She did feel, though, that he threw himself into his teaching, his studies and whatever else he did. She thought that was the reason he could never stay in a long-lasting, meaningful relationship. He changed girlfriends the way the average male changed his briefs. Gloria had stopped asking Joey how his girlfriends were doing, because by the time she blinked her eyes, those girlfriends would be history.

As the taxi made its way through the traffic, heading to the house on Hauser St in Astoria, Queens, Gloria glanced toward the driver's identification, which was posted in the middle of the dashboard. She thought that he looked familiar. No, he resembled someone that she knew. When she realized who it was, she started to smile.

"Lionel. Lionel Jefferson," she said to herself. "A young Lionel Jefferson." Gloria began nodding her head, as she was positive that she was correct. The only difference that this young driver, by the name of Kenneth Reed, had from Lionel Jefferson was that his hair was corn-rowed like Latrell Spreewell wears his hair when he plays basketball. Gloria remembered that Lionel used to wear a huge afro, so big that he could've hid Jimmy Hoffa inside it. Even though they hadn't seen each other in ages, Gloria and Lionel and Lionel's wife Jenny had remained friends and sent holiday and birthday cards to each other every year. Even though he was very rich and living up in Bel Air, whenever he was in NY checking on the Jefferson-Willis Help Center, which was named after his mother and mother-in-law, he would always stop by and visit Archie. Not too many people understood Archie, but Lionel did, and Gloria always got a kick out of the way every time Archie would make a racist comment in front of Lionel, Lionel would always turn it around, causing the joke to be on Archie. Archie was none the wiser. Even though Archie never came straight out and told Lionel how he had felt about him, he really cared a lot for him and was very proud of him. The last time she had seen Lionel was at his mother Louise's funeral. She made a mental note to give him a call and let him know what had happened once she caught her breath and got settled. She was then reminded that her father was really gone. She started sobbing lightly again, as she dabbed at her nose and eyes.

While driving, the taxi driver noticed Gloria's expression, even though she had the dark glasses on, and he also heard her slight whimper and he became concerned.

"Ma'am, excuse me for asking, but are you all right? I mean, that's a stupid thing for me to say. Obviously you aren't. What I am trying to say is that if there is anything that I could do, like stop at a store and get you something before we reach your destination, I can do that for you if you would like." Kenneth looked sincere and talked very kindly.

He looked at her through his rearview mirror and when Gloria looked toward him to respond, she noticed that Kenneth's flawless bronze complexion was smooth–looking, like a baby. She also noticed that he had a pair of warm and sincere hazel eyes.

"Oh, thank you so much for your concern, but you do not have to stop. We should be reaching home," Gloria thought for a moment. "Home"— she hadn't said that word in such a long time. "We should be reaching home shortly." Gloria had gotten a chill up her spine when she said home.

"I hope you didn't just come from a vacation," he said in a joking manner. The comment caught Gloria by surprise.

"What do you mean?" she asked.

"Well, you have suitcases and you are heading home, but you've been crying ever since you got in the taxi." Kenneth was still smiling.

"Well, we are not actually going to our home. We are going to the house where I grew up. See, the reason I have been crying is because I have returned home to bury my father." When Gloria finished speaking, the driver's flawless bronze complexion turned ashen.

"Oh, I am so very sorry. I-I-I didn't mean to..." But Gloria cut him off before he had the opportunity to finish.

"Oh, it's okay. You didn't know." Gloria tried to assure him that no harm was done, but the driver had continued apologizing, which showed Gloria that the impression that she had about him was correct.

The driver was coming up on the Astoria Blvd. exit to get off the Van Wyck when Gloria asked him if he would take that exit which he did. There were different ways to get to Hauser Street, but Gloria thought that maybe

Astoria Blvd. wouldn't be as crowded as the other streets. Usually a ride from JFK would take only 20 minutes, but today it seemed like it was taking an eternity.

Once they reached Astoria Blvd, traffic was flowing smoothly. They would be at 704 Hauser Street in just a few minutes.

About a mile or so traveling down Astoria Blvd and past LaGuardia Airport, Gloria started asking the driver if he would turn down certain blocks—a left here, another right a few blocks later. The twins knew what she was doing, but the driver didn't.

"Ma'am, I know a quicker way to get us to 704 Hauser St from here."

"Oh, I'm sure you do, and there are many ways to get to 704 Hauser Street from here quickly," Gloria said as she nodded in agreement. "I just wanna see something very quickly, that's all." Gloria was looking out the window as she talked to the driver.

The driver didn't complain. He just nodded and continued driving. He figured that as long as she had the money and was paying for the ride, he would drive her to the moon if she wanted. The longer the ride, the better it was for him.

Once the driver got on the block that Gloria wanted to see, she asked him to slow down. The twins perked up, and all three began looking out the right side of the window. The driver looked, too, but didn't know what he was supposed to see. "Are you looking at the sales in the store window?" the driver asked.

"No," she smiled slightly. "I just want to see my daddy's place, that's all."

"But ma'am, I thought you said that your father's house was on Hauser? We are not on Hauser yet."

"Oh, the house is definitely on Hauser Street, but my daddy had a bar and grill over here."

When they finally reached the place from the street, she patted both of the twin's legs. "There it is, guys," she said in a very low and solemn voice. The twins nodded with proud smiles on their faces, then they started to tear up.

In the midst of all the Chinese food takeouts, 99 cent stores, discount stores and so on, stood 'Archie Bunker's Place.' The building had its gate down over the windows and doors, and there was a big cardboard sign taped on the gate that covered the door. There were cards and candles—some looked to be lit—and even flowers leaning up against the building. They couldn't see what the sign said because they weren't that close to the building. As the driver continued looking, he asked if he should stop but she said no.

"Ma'am, are you the daughter of Archie Bunker?" he asked with an energy level that seemed to turn up a notch. "Are you telling me that Archie Bunker passed away?" This comment piqued her interest, especially the way that he said her father's name.

"You sound like you knew him."

"Knew him?" he said loudly. "Everyone knows Archie! Man, I come here often to eat. As a matter of fact, I come here maybe three days a week. Archie Bunker's Place is a staple in this community. Yeah, I knew him," he said proudly. "We were on a first-name basis. He knew most of the cabbies and even gave us discounts because he used to moonlight back in the day as a cabby. That was way before my time, though. Archie Bunker is gone. What an awful surprise." The driver's face became sad as he sucked his teeth then shook his head back and forth. "He definitely will be missed. Please be sure before I drive off to give me all the funeral arrangements. I have to let everyone know down at the garage. Everyone is going to be shocked."

Gloria couldn't get over the fact that her father was so well known. She had forgotten that her father had been running the place for 20 years and it had been very successful. With his name hanging above the entrance, everyone was bound to know him or know of him. This made Gloria feel proud. She also realized that Kenneth had been the first adult that she had spoken to since finding out that her father had passed away, and she didn't mind hearing kind words about him. Kenneth even started telling her stories about things he had witnessed concerning Archie, and everyone in the taxi began laughing. Kenneth asked her if she was offended by him talking, but she quickly told him no and was eager to hear more. The twins wanted to hear more, also. They knew that Archie was quite a character. Kenneth continued talking as he made his turn onto Hauser Street.

"Yeah," he said as he laughed, nodding his head as he remembered him fondly. "Archie sure was an outspoken, opinionated S.O.B." When he realized what he had said, he wiped the smile off of his face and became apologetic. "Oh, I'm sorry for my language, ma'am. I didn't mean to be so disrespectful."

Gloria and the twins continued laughing. "Oh, no offense taken; in fact, that's probably one of the nicest things I ever heard concerning him."

When Kenneth saw that Gloria wasn't offended, he relaxed, nodded and smiled again.

"Yeah, my father definitely was a one of a kind," she added. "You had to get to know him to love him. Daddy was... was..." Gloria was thinking of a word to describe her father, when all of a sudden everyone including the driver shouted in unison.

"A character!" They all started laughing louder, with Gloria joining in.

The reminiscing continued for a few more blocks till next thing Gloria knew, Kenneth was pulling up to the curb in front of 704 Hauser St. He was lucky. There was no other car parked in front. Once Kenneth parked, he apologized to Gloria and the twins again for their loss. Gloria dug down into her purse so she could give Kenneth the funeral information. He promised that he was going to be there as she handed him the info. Gloria then introduced herself to him and told him to call her by her first name. The twins did the same, then Kenneth after. He popped the hood of the trunk from inside the car so he could take out their luggage, but before he had the opportunity, Matthew told Kenneth that he didn't have to worry about taking the luggage out of the trunk and that he was going to do it himself.

Gloria didn't realize that Stephanie was standing on the porch looking towards them. Once she did notice, she noticed that Stephanie was standing there with a smile on her face, but Gloria was able to see that she had been crying because her eyes were red and puffy. "She must've heard us when we pulled up in front of the house," she thought to herself. She only realized she was standing there when she heard Matthew greet her. Stephanie greeted him back with a smile and a wave. While that was going on, Zoe got out on the opposite side of the taxi, while Gloria and Kenneth continued talking inside. Zoe then yelled up towards the porch to greet Stephanie, who in turn greeted her back. They both smiled at each other. The twins quickly got the luggage out of the trunk, closed it, and then headed up to the house after giving Stephanie a hug and kiss.

While Gloria continued talking to Kenneth, she looked at the meter and dug again into her purse to take out money to pay for the fare. She handed it to Kenneth and told him to keep the change. He nodded appreciatively with a smile. Before Gloria got out of the taxi, Kenneth gave her his card and told her to call him if she needed.

"If you need help moving back, just give me a call, too. I don't live that far from here. I live in Woodside over by Queens Blvd. It's just a hop, skip and jump from here," he said with a smile.

Kenneth's comment caught Gloria off guard. The farthest thing from her mind was to move back to NY, so she quickly responded.

"Oh, Kenneth, I don't think that I'll be moving back here to NY." Gloria began to shake her head. "I have my job and apartment back in California, plus the twins are comfortable in their school and with their friends. Yeah, New York is a chapter that I closed many a moon ago," she said with a chuckle. "I just got used to the smog and traffic, and now you are talking about me moving back here. Thanks for the offer but I don't see it happening anytime in the future," she replied graciously.

"So, what are you going to do about the bar?" Kenneth asked sadly.

"Oh Kenneth, right now, I don't know what I am going to do. I don't know anything right now. I'm just playing everything by ear. I'm just going to take it one step at a time, and it will probably be baby steps."

"I understand," he said as he nodded. He then extended his hand to her and she shook it with a smile. She made her way out of the taxi. A few seconds later, she watched as Kenneth drove away, then she turned to face

The Life and Times of Gloria Bunker

Stephanie and the house. Stephanie smiled and waved at her cheerfully. "Hi, Cousin Gloria!" Stephanie said enthusiastically.

Gloria looked up towards her and smiled back. "Hey, Steph." She quickly glanced up to the right and left of the house and noticed that the block looked so much different from the last time that she was there. She hadn't noticed it before, but Archie's house and her old house next door, which had once belonged to the Jeffersons, were the only two houses on the block with their porches still opened. All the other houses had enclosed their porches, which made their front door be at the top of the stairs and on the sides of the door were windows. How long had it been like that? she wondered. Most of the people that she knew had moved, like her. They had all either retired and moved or passed away. Only a few still remained. Across the street, old houses had been demolished and co-ops went up in their places. Gloria could see that there was a lot of foot traffic walking up and down that block. The days of everyone knowing their neighbor were long gone. She just chalked it up to community renewal. She didn't like it, not at all.

As she also quickly glanced at the old house she once had shared with her ex-husband, Mike, she noticed that the grass wasn't cut and the porch didn't look clean. There were leaves and garbage mixed together and scattered all in the front and on the sides of the house. She didn't like that, either. She heard music coming from inside of that house and saw some lights on, too.

There was no reason her old house should look like that. She wasn't quite sure if that should be her concern at that moment. She had so many other things to worry about. She started heading up the front stairs slowly, thinking to herself that her parents would not be greeting her once she walked through the door. Oh, how she missed her mother's joyous and loving smile, and how she was so willing to please Gloria in every single way. Gloria started to remember how her mother would always greet her as if she hadn't seen her in ages, even if it had only been a day or just a few hours. She also started thinking about her father when he used to greet her with his, "Hey, little girl!" Oh, how she prayed to hear those words or to be able to see them just one more time. It was too late for her to turn around and head back down the stairs. *Come on, girl. You can do it.* She willed herself to continue walking up the stairs, even though her legs were wobbly and unsteady. *You have to be strong, if not for yourself, for the family.* Gloria didn't take off her dark shades till she was to the top of the front steps and walking towards Stephanie to give her a kiss. "No need to be too emotional out in front of strangers. That's what closed doors were made for," she thought quickly to herself. Stephanie kissed her back as they walked inside—so far, so good.

CHAPTER TWO:
Gloria is Introduced to the Past

One of the first things that Gloria noticed about the house was that it was filled with flowers and cards. Without turning to Stephanie, she made a comment as she took off her jacket and put it in Archie's chair along with her purse. "My God, Steph. The place looks like a flower shop!" Her eyes were wide with amazement. Stephanie closed the front door and walked into the living room near her.

"Yeah, I know. They've been arriving all day. Some came yesterday. Word just spread so very quickly." She was nodding her head as she looked around herself. Gloria then turned and looked at Stephanie. She went toward her and began rubbing her shoulders with a smile.

"Hello there, beautiful. Let me stand back and get a good look at you!" Stephanie smiled modestly and started turning around as if she was modeling her outfit. Stephanie was taller than Gloria. She stood about 5'7" with a slim, athletic model-firm frame, long shiny black hair, naturally long eyelashes, a nice smooth thin nose and pouty lips. She still had the dimples that she had as a little girl, but they were more prominent now. She was wearing a long white t-shirt that said 'Proud to be a New Yawka' and black spandex leggings. She also had a pair of slippers on, but no socks.

"You are absolutely gorgeous. I haven't seen you in ages. How old are you now? With beautiful skin like that, you must be about 16, huh?" Gloria teased as she looked at her up and down.

"Oh, stop it, Cousin Gloria," she said bashfully. "You know that I am 25."

"The only time that I get to see or hear you now is on television or the radio."

"Oh, I haven't made it yet. Just some bit parts here and there and maybe some background vocals on some tracks. Nothing major yet, but soon, I hope." She then stuck both hands out to Gloria, as if to introduce her.

"And what about you? You are still beautiful, too!" Gloria put her hands through her long blond hair, then she looked at herself, feet to head.

"This ole thing?! Not too bad for a single middle-aged mother of three, huh?"

"Not at all, Cousin Gloria. Not bad at all." The comment made them both chuckle.

After a few minutes of making light conversation, their eyes met. They couldn't contain the anguish, pain and hurt any longer. They ran towards each other, held one another tightly and just started crying hard for what seemed like forever. They both cried on each other's shoulder so loud and hard, that their shoulders were soaked and wet.

"Oh, Cousin Gloria, he just wouldn't wake up! He was fine before he went to bed. Nothing was unusual. He ate a big dinner, talked on the phone for awhile while he smoked his cigar, and played me a game of Scrabble while lecturing me on finding a good all-American husband." The two were slowly releasing each other's embrace as they sat on the couch. "I got up yesterday morning as usual and made a big breakfast, which he devoured. He then went to the television and watched Maury and Jerry, cursed and yelled at the screen while making me crack up laughing. I think that was the reason why he was making those comments—just to see me laugh" She started smiling through her tears as the two held each other's hand for comfort and support. "After all of his morning shows were over, he told me that he had some work to do upstairs. I thought nothing of it. At lunchtime, I prepared some sandwiches with potato salad, then called for him to come down and eat. I waited for him for awhile but he never came downstairs. I kept calling for him, then finally I went upstairs and he was lying peacefully on his back with his hands and feet crossed on his bed. At first I wasn't going to try and wake him, but as you know, Uncle Archie snores loudly. I didn't hear anything from him but he looked so peaceful….So relaxed… I called him softly at first then I went into the room." Stephanie was losing her composure again. "That's when... Th-th-that's when…" Stephanie's eyes welled up and started to overflow with tears as she began to cry hard.

Gloria leaned over and pulled Stephanie towards her as they both hugged and wailed more. Once the two were able to get their composure, they resumed talking.

"Listen, you guys must be hungry. When you called me from JFK and told me that you were safely here and waiting for a taxi, I started preparing something for you to eat."

"Oh, that's great. I am starving but first I want to freshen up." Gloria sniffled some then wiped her nose. "I must look like a mess with all my mascara running, nose running, and eyes all puffy, clothes wet and sticking to my body. I must look like Tammy Faye Bakker on acid!" When she said this, Stephanie chuckled, as the mood was lightening up slightly. Stephanie got off the couch and headed towards the kitchen.

"Okay, good. Go on upstairs and freshen up. Pick any bedroom that you will feel comfortable sleeping in; your old room or your parents' room. You know that the twins are going to want to sleep downstairs in the basement. Ever since Uncle Archie remodeled that basement and made it into a two bedroom apartment with TV, DVD and CDs, along with the kitchenette and bathroom for them and Joey, they spend most of their time down there anyway. You and I will stay upstairs." That was ok with Gloria.

Gloria got off of the couch and began fixing her clothes. She got her jacket and purse off the chair, then started up the stairs slowly. Once she reached the second floor, she saw that the twins were considerate enough to bring her suitcase up and leave it in the middle of the hallway. They didn't know what room Gloria was going to sleep in. Gloria heard Stephanie open the basement door to the sound of loud music. She heard her yell down to the twins that she had prepared something for them to eat and for them to get ready to come upstairs to eat. They yelled back up to her in acknowledgement. Gloria then heard Stephanie close the basement door and head through the kitchen door.

Gloria picked up her suitcase and automatically headed toward her old bedroom, the room she grew up in, though it had been remodeled a few times since she moved out. Archie had first made it a den, then for a while Teresa Betancourt rented it out while she studied to become a nurse, then once Stephanie moved in as a young girl, it was changed back into a little girl's bedroom.

Gloria stepped into the room and stood by the entrance staring. Even though not the same furniture she had as a little girl, the new furniture was in the same location. The big bed was between the two big windows, along with the two end tables with lamps. Opposite the bed was the long dresser with the mirror on top of it. The television set sat next to the closet and opposite that was the desk. This brought memories back of when she was a little girl. She was remembering an incident when she was about five or six years old and she was very ill. She remembered that she was lying in her bed swamped with all different sized dolls to keep her company. Her mom, Edith, had just gone upstairs to check her temperature and to keep her company for awhile. "Mommy was so beautiful," she said softly as she fondly remembered.

She remembered that Edith's hair was very long then, and it was very thick, flowing luxuriously down her back. Gloria remembered that Edith was slim and had a house dress on. She didn't wear jewelry. Only her wedding ring was on her finger, and she remembered that Edith wore just a tad of makeup. She remembered that her mom came into her room and sat on the edge of her bed, smiling lovingly, and then reached out and touched her forehead. "Sweet lavender," she said. "Mommy always smelled like a lady, even if she just stayed in the house."

Edith had touched her forehead so gently that she wanted to melt. "Oh, Gloria, it's still a bit high but you are getting better. Hey, I got a great idea!" she said excitedly. "How about I go downstairs and bring you up some ice cream, huh? Would you like that?" When Edith asked that, Gloria's eyes tried to light up as much as possible as she nodded her head weakly, but she was excited to be able to have the ice cream. As Edith was leaving, she heard the front door open from downstairs. "Oh, Gloria, your father must have come early from work," Edith said excitedly.

During those younger days, he didn't walk up the stairs. He was doing two or three steps at a time back then. Archie had met Edith in the hallway on the second floor as she was headed down the stairs, and gave her a kiss.

"Hey Edith there," he said cheerfully. "A little birdie told me that my little girl there still wasn't feeling good." She remembered how happy she had felt that her daddy was home and that he was concerned how she was feeling.

"Yeah, your little girl is still lying in bed but she has her dolls to keep her company. She has been such a good little girl that I am going to get her some nice ice cream from the fridge." With that, Edith zoomed past Archie as she headed to the kitchen downstairs.

"You go and do that there, Edith, while I check on my little girl."

Archie started towards Gloria's room but briefly stopped and called out to Edith before she made it to the kitchen. "Oh, by the way, Edith, there..."

"Yes Archie?"

"Get me a beer while you are at it, will ya?" Gloria remembered that it wasn't really a question when he asked for a beer. It was like a friendly order, the way a patron would order one from a bartender. Edith didn't have to respond to it because he had always requested it when he had come home early or late from work.

Gloria remembered seeing him when he walked through the entrance to the bedroom and towards her bed. How gigantic he looked. Back then he had a full head of hair and it was cut short. It wasn't gray. It was light brown. He was also thin then. Back during this time, she thought that her daddy was the most handsome man in the whole wide world and could not imagine ever leaving him. She loved her mother with all of her heart but she definitely was her daddy's special little girl.

When Archie came near the bed, instead of sitting down, he knelt at the side of the bed and took hold of her little hand.

"Hey, little girl. I hear that you still don't feel too good, huh?"

"No, Daddy." Little Gloria responded with a pout. "My twote hawts bad and I keep cawfin. My head hawts, too."

As Archie held her little hand, he noticed that it was burning up.

"Hey, little girl, your hand is on fire. Maybe when mommy comes back with your ice cream, it'll cool you off, huh?" he joked with a smile. She nodded back as she smiled, too. Gloria remembered that she wanted Archie just to pick her up and hold her in his strong arms to make the pain go away.

"Daddy, I rather have you here next to me than have that ice cream." The young Gloria replied. "I even rather have you here next to me than have all of these dolls." Archie just smiled lovingly and fatherly at her. Gloria remembered saying that and wondered what was going through his head when she did say it.

"Well, you know something, little girl? I am glad to be here next to you. I wouldn't want to have any other daughter than you. I just wish that I could make you feel so much better. I don't like to see my little girl sick or hurt. You are very special to me."

"Why, Daddy?" the young Gloria asked as she coughed and winced in pain as she touched her throat.

"Cause you are my little girl, forever and ever and ever." Archie had exaggerated the 'forever' as he shook his head back and forth causing Gloria to smile widely. "You know what?" he asked, taking his finger and touching her nose.

"What, daddy?" Gloria was now laughing. Next thing she knew, Archie began singing his special song to her.

"You're my little girl. From heaven above, God sent you to us with love,
There'll never be another angel like you.
You're my little girl. From in the sky,
You shine brighter than the sun in July,
You know that you can change the gray sky to blue.
But there will come a day when another man will take you from me, I want you to know that you will always be…"

"What's that?" the young Gloria added her little part to the song

"You'll always be my little girl." Archie was developing a tear in his eye as he smiled.

When Archie finished singing, he stood up, kissed her on her forehead then sat at the edge of the bed, patting her little hot hand.

Gloria watched the images of her past slowly disappear as the tears began to flow down her face. "Oh, Daddy, how much I love you. I'm going to miss you, oh so very much!" Gloria started wiping away the tears as she stepped out of her old bedroom. She then made her way to the master bedroom where both of her parents had drawn their last breath. Archie had never rearranged the room or changed the furniture since Edith passed. Out of all the years of Gloria's life, she never slept in her parents' room for the whole night. As a little girl, she might have fallen asleep on the bed while watching television with them, but they would later carry her to her own bedroom. Gloria had made up her mind. She was going to sleep in the master bedroom to feel closer to them.

Fifteen minutes later, Gloria was heading back down the steps, nice and refreshed. She threw on one of Archie's shirts and she also had put on spandex and sandals. No socks. As she reached the bottom stairs, she heard light talking and laughter. Everyone was at the table waiting for her to arrive.

"I hope I haven't kept you guys waiting too long." She pulled out a kitchen chair to sit.

"No Ma, we just came upstairs too." Zoe said as Matthew nodded.

"Just in time to get everything while it was nice and fresh. I even had time to boil up some soup to go along with the food." Stephanie had removed all the flowers and put on the table a stack of sandwiches, potato salad, soup, soda, coffee and cake, along with paper plates, cups and bowls for the soup. When Stephanie sat down, they all said grace, then Stephanie told everyone to dig in. Gloria stared at the food then nodded. The twins had no problem in serving themselves the well-prepared food.

"Stephanie, it's simple but it looks so filling, and that's good because I haven't eaten anything, not even on the flight. I am so hungry I could eat a horse!"

Everyone started passing plates and food around, then Gloria went for the soup. She scooped some into her bowl then picked up her spoon and began stirring it. The next thing everyone knew, Gloria burst out laughing, which caused everyone to look at her strangely.

"What's so funny, Ma?" asked Matthew who was biting into his sandwich.

Gloria took a sip of the soup then put down her spoon. "I remember when I was younger and married to Mike. Daddy was sitting here..." she pointed to her spot. "Mike and I were sitting where you two are sitting right now." Nodding to Stephanie, "And Daddy, unbeknownst to him began eating some horse meat that Mike and I had gotten, but before he had eaten it, he had said that he was so hungry that he could eat a horse. I hadn't thought about that story in such a long time. I don't think that I thought about it since it first had happened." Gloria began laughing again. "Oh, how Mike and I laughed!" As she laughed, she shook her head back and forth with tears in her eyes. They were happy tears. Gloria's fond memory caused everyone at the table to start howling with laughter.

"Gloria, you gotta be kidding me! Did you ever tell him what he was eating?" Stephanie's eyes were wide with surprise.

"Are you kidding? He would've killed us!" Her voice went up an octave as she opened her eyes wide. This made everyone laugh even more.

"How did this all come about?" Zoe was holding her sandwich and staring at Gloria as if she was waiting to hear the punch line of a good joke. Gloria began telling them the whole story, and the laughter just started all over again. For some reason, everyone looked over at Matthew's expression as he held his sandwich. He looked at it suspiciously then looked at Stephanie through the corners of his eyes as if he was thinking that Stephanie used horse meat in the sandwich. Instantly everyone was howling with laughter once again.

"Don't worry, Matthew," Stephanie assured him once the laughter calmed down and she was able to speak without choking on her food. "It's not horse-meat" When it got quiet and Matthew felt comfortable to continue eating,

Stephanie finished her sentence. "Or is it?" Stephanie made her eyes look suspicious, raising her eyes up and down and causing everyone to start laughing once again.

While everyone ate, they continued telling stories that they remembered about Archie. Everyone had something interesting to say that the others had never known or had known but just wanted to hear again. They sat at the table for almost an hour just talking, eating and laughing. The little bit of soup that was left by then was now cold and all of the sandwiches were gone, thanks to Matthew, who showed no shame in his greediness. The soda had disappeared, along with the coffee. There were only a few more pieces of cake, but Gloria was sure that it wouldn't last too much longer. They would've continued sitting at the table chatting up a storm, but someone was ringing the doorbell. Gloria was the closest so she headed towards the door to see who it was.

"Be prepared to answer the door all day, Cousin Gloria. The doorbell rang three times while you were upstairs freshening up." Stephanie then stood up and looked at the table. "Maybe that's my cue to start cleaning up the table."

When Gloria got to the door and opened it, she saw that there were three teenage girls standing on the porch with flowers and cards in their hands. One girl on her right was a black girl with a beautiful almond complexion. Her hair was braided up, with a bandana tied around her forehead. She was taller than the other two girls and had nice, attractive hips and breasts. The girl in the middle was white with red hair, curly and flowing down her back. She had cute freckles on her button nose. She was petite with a nice, firm body. The third girl who was to her left was a girl who either was Spanish or mulatto with a nice healthy, tan complexion. She had thick black kinky hair which she parted in the middle then let it bounce onto her shoulders. Her eyes were huge and had soft features. She wasn't fat but she was heavier than the other two. All three had tight jeans on, with white sneakers and sweatshirts, one pink, one blue and one s red. They greeted Gloria with a hearty hello and smiled.

"Hi, girls, how are you all doing? I haven't seen you in ages," Gloria commented happily. She opened the door wide to invite them to come in, which they did.

Once they came in and Gloria closed the door, the redheaded girl was the first to speak as she extended her flowers and card toward her.

"Ah, Ms. Gloria, this is for you and your family from me and my family. We are so very sorry for your loss." she said sincerely as Gloria took the flowers and card, then kissed the girl on her forehead and gave her a hug.

"Thank you so very much, Melissa." Gloria began making room on the coffee table to put the girls' flowers.

The black girl was the next to give Gloria flowers and card. She had her head bowed slightly as she welled up with tears. Her voice cracked a few times as she tried to speak.

"We all are going to miss him so very much." She gave Gloria a hug after she put the flowers and the card down.

"Oh, thank you so much, Janee." Gloria hugged her back then kissed her on her forehead too. "You are so very sweet."

Last but not least, the third girl did the same thing and after Gloria put the flowers and card on the table, she went to hug her too. Gloria responded by doing the same and also kissing her on her forehead. All three girls had tears in their eyes.

"Thank you so much, Beatrice. I appreciate this so very much. I know that my dad would've appreciated it also. Please, when you go home, tell your parents that I said thank you. I will make sure to give you the funeral information before you all leave."

Once the flowers and cards were taken care of and the tears stopped flowing for a minute, one of the girls began to speak again.

"We saw you all arrive by taxi but we didn't want to bombard you as soon as you made your way into the house," Janee commented.

"Yeah" replied Beatrice. "We thought that this would be a good time to stop by." Melissa nodded in agreement.

"This was very thoughtful of you three. I know that you all want to see Zoe. She's right over there." Gloria turned toward the dining room table and noticed that it was empty. "Oh, they started cleaning off the table. Everyone must be in the kitchen."

Gloria yelled into the kitchen to get Zoe's attention.

"Hey, Zoe, Destiny's Child is here to see you! They also brought flowers and cards!" When Gloria said that, the three girls started laughing. Zoe came zooming out of the kitchen as she was drying her hands and ran right into the three girls' embrace. They all started talking a million words per mega second, and what amazed Gloria was the fact that they each understood what the other was saying. One second, Zoe was touching one's hair, then they checked out her outfit, then they laughed, cried, touched each other's shoulders then laughed more. Gloria just watched in awe at the four in their own little huddle. She was blown away by the fact that the three only saw Zoe maybe three to four times a year for certain holidays, but when they got together, the four were the closest and best of friends. You couldn't separate them once they were all together. Gloria tried to say something to the four girls but they were so busy chattering away that they had forgotten that Gloria was even standing there. All of the focus was on Zoe.

Gloria walked away from the mini–crowd, shaking her head with a smile on her face. She then picked up the three cards on the coffee table. She headed for the kitchen to give Stephanie a hand in cleaning up. She was passing by Edith's chair when Stephanie came out of the kitchen.

"Hi girls," she said with a smile. Stephanie started wiping down the dining room table. The girls smiled and waved at her as they greeted her back.

"Have a seat while I bring you all some cake and soda." Before the girls could even respond, Stephanie pivoted back through the kitchen door to retrieve the goodies. The girls said thank you then sat down and continued their blab-a-thon.

By this time, Gloria had made her way into the kitchen behind Stephanie and noticed that Stephanie and Matthew had already cleaned up everything. Matthew was putting a fresh garbage bag in the bin while Stephanie was putting the three cups for the soda and the cake on a little platter.

"Wow! You already cleaned everything up. I came in here to give you a hand."

"Gloria, remember that everything was on paper plates. I only had to wash the soup pot and the ladle. Everything else went into the garbage." Stephanie opened up the fridge and took out soda and began pouring it into the three cups for the girls. When she was done, she headed out the kitchen door, but Matthew stopped her and opened the door for her. Stephanie smiled at him when he did this, then she headed out the door and towards the girls. When the three girls saw Matthew, they flirtingly and teasingly said hello to him, then they burst out laughing. Matthew began turning crimson red then shook his head at the girls. This made the girls cackle even more. Matthew rolled his eyes as he smiled bashfully. The girls stood up and took a cup of soda and a paper plate with cake on it from Stephanie and said thank you to her. They also gave Stephanie their condolences which she appreciated much. Once she started back towards the kitchen, the four didn't miss a beat. They were chatting up a storm and picked up right where they had stopped. Matthew headed downstairs quickly while the women, young and old, mingled and talked in separate rooms.

The Life and Times of Gloria Bunker

By the time Stephanie made it back through the kitchen door, Gloria was putting away the bottle of soda. Only thing that Stephanie could do was chuckle and shake her head. This caught Gloria's attention.

"What did I miss out there?" She asked as she turned around and walked toward the kitchen table to sit down. She pulled out a chair so Stephanie could sit down too.

"It's just so amazing about those four girls out there. Zoe knows what's happening here in New York and in this area more than I do and I actually live here. You should hear them talking out there. I wonder how they are able to breathe!" The comment made Gloria laugh.

"Or understand one another," she added. "I know what you mean. They met Zoe at the Hauser Street block party ten years or so ago and they all have been close ever since. Even though we live in Cali, they call all the time and she calls them. Needless to say, my telephone bill is almost as much as my rent!"

Now Stephanie was the one who was laughing.

"Oh, Steph, I don't mind. I have the best kids in the whole world. No one could ask for better than what I have with them. I wouldn't trade them for the world plus ten million dollars. They don't give me any problems, thank God. They are very smart in school and they don't like to hang out. That is not easy to say for some parents, single or together, raising a child or children in California." Stephanie just nodded as Gloria talked. "It wouldn't bother me so much if everything wasn't so expensive. The traffic is hideous, along with the smog. Sometimes the smog is so thick that I couldn't see an albino being followed by swans."

"Oh, I know. I remember when I came to visit you all in Cali for the holiday season a few years back. It was just terrible."

"It is even worse now." Gloria was sucking her teeth and shaking her head. "But the kids like it, plus everything is close for them. The school is close and the stores are even closer…Not to mention…" When Gloria said this, she and Stephanie looked at each other with a smile then shouted in unison, "…the mall!" They continued chatting until the phone rang. There was a telephone in the kitchen, hanging on the wall. It was closer to Gloria's side so she reached up to answer it.

"Hello, Bunker residence…" she said casually. "Oh, Mr. Bunker is no longer here. He passed away yesterday. This is his daughter, Gloria. Can I help you? Oh, thank you. I do appreciate that. Oh, is that so?" Her eyes got wide as she stared at Stephanie. "Well, I didn't know that," Gloria continued. "Well, I don't know what I am going to do right now. Yes, I am the one who is making the decisions. Well, I think that we can arrange that. Well, I haven't made any plans for later tonight. Sure. That will be fine. Oh, nice talking to you too, Mr. Kindred. Oh, I am sorry. Yes, my name is

Gloria. That's Gloria Bunker Shaw. No, that's Ms. Can you give me that number again slowly?" Gloria was reaching for the memo pad that hung on the wall next to the phone. Gloria began writing down the number as she continued making facial expressions to Stephanie, who wanted to know what was going on and who Gloria was speaking to. "I will call you. Goodbye for now." She hung up the phone.

"Well, who was that?" Stephanie asked excitedly.

"That was a Mr. Kindred. A Mr. Daniel Kindred from a real estate company called 'Maximum Properties.' He said that he had made Daddy an offer to buy the house and that Daddy was going to be getting back in contact with him. He wants to come over tonight to discuss it with me. He didn't want to talk about it too much over the phone. That is why he wants to come over."

"Wow Gloria, I didn't know anything about that." Stephanie looked surprised.

"Me either, but you know something, as I think about it, it makes a lot of sense."

"What makes a lot of sense?"

"Well when I called Daddy a while back to see how he was doing, he was in a real good mood. He said to me, 'Woopty doo, there, little girl...'" she started imitating Archie. "'Woopty doo. I got a big surprise to tell you.' I was so excited that I asked him what it was, but he kept telling me that he would tell me when the time was right. No matter how much I asked him, he wouldn't tell me. I think that this was it. He just didn't have a chance to finally tell me. I guess that he thought that he had a lot of time left. I am so sorry that he didn't have a chance to tell me in his own words," Gloria replied sadly.

"Do you really think that this is what he meant?"

"What else could it have been? Oh Steph, I am so confused. I never had to deal with stuff like this before. All of this is such a shock and everything is happening so very quickly. Daddy always had a plan B concerning everything. He was so organized that I am embarrassed. He could plan anything. Me, I am the total opposite. I like to stay in my little comfort zone. I don't like dealing with surprises. I don't know how to handle them. I usually end up making the wrong decisions. You know, Stephanie, after Ma unexpectedly died, he immediately planned everything that he wanted done if anything was to happen to him. He would say, 'Little girl, I ain't getting any younger.' I remember how much it had bothered me even back then when he had made this comment. I didn't want to think about him dying but he was one step ahead of the game. He would say, 'Remember, if anything happens to your ole man, you know who to call and you know where all my legal stuff is.'"

"Yeah, you are right. He gave the same speech to me when I was young, and he would say it often. He even reminded me again once I moved back into the house." After Stephanie said this, she jumped in the chair as if lightning went through her body. "That reminds me. I almost forgot. Archie's attorney, Mr. Rabinowitz, called. Remember I told you about the doorbell ringing while you were upstairs freshening up? Well, the phone rang too."

"Oh? What did Mr. Rabinowitz want?"

"Uncle Archie's will. He wanted to come by today and read it but he said that he had to cancel because there was an emergency that he had to take care of. He said that he will try to be back by tomorrow. This emergency would be taking him out of town and he was leaving that very moment, after he hung up with me."

"Oh thank God this emergency happened after he took care of Daddy's funeral arrangements. He worked fast. He had everything planned quickly. He has been Daddy's attorney for as long as I can remember. As a matter of fact, he wasn't just Daddy's attorney, but he was also his friend.

"Yeah, he took it pretty badly when I called him to tell him what had happened. He cried like a baby. I was quite surprised. I didn't know that they were that close. But once the tears dried, Mr. Rabinowitz sprang into action. He knew what to do. He was talking a mile a minute what he was going to do and what had to happen. He already had copies of Uncle Archie's legal papers and he began to get Uncle Archie's stuff in order. I'm sure that Uncle Archie drilled it into his ear too," she said with a smile.

"I'm sure that Daddy did the same to the Reverend Felcher." Gloria said jokingly, but the comment caused Stephanie to jump again.

"Oh, Gloria, I am so sorry. I should have written down these messages but I was just so bombarded with things that I forgot to tell you that he called also, almost immediately after Mr. Rabinowitz called."

"It is okay, Steph. I understand. What did he want?"

"He just wanted to check on us. He wanted us to know that he and his family were here for us, plus he wanted to see how we were doing and holding up. He wanted to assure us that he was ready to do the service on Saturday. He also wanted us to know that he spoke with the funeral director and that he was giving us the biggest room. Everything is good to go."

"Oh, Steph, that takes a big load off of my shoulders." Stephanie nodded and Gloria started laughing. "Hey, Stephanie, remember when Daddy used to refer to Reverend Felcher as the Reverend Fletcher? We would say, 'It is Felcher, not Fletcher.' Then he would say, 'Whatever.' Daddy always had a name for everyone."

Stephanie just smiled and nodded again. "I think that Uncle Archie would always say things like that just to make us laugh. He always had something to say, just to say it."

"He loved to keep us on our toes." Gloria added. "Oh, Stephanie, I remember this one time when Daddy..." Gloria went on to tell her some of the crazy antics that Archie did that had everyone in an uproar. She just couldn't stop the memories from flowing through her head, and she really didn't want to stop it. She didn't want to forget her father. She wanted to remember everything about him, good or bad.

Gloria and Stephanie sat in the kitchen telling stories for what seemed like forever. When talking about Archie, there was never a dull moment. They laughed and cried and smiled as they recalled fond and not so fond memories that they could laugh at now but couldn't at the time they were happening. This went on till Zoe came into the kitchen.

"Ah, excuse me, Ma and Steph, but I'm just coming in to let y'all know that I'm going outside for awhile to hang out with the girls, unless there is something that y'all need me to do around here." Zoe's mouth was speaking sincerity but her body motions were saying that she really wanted to go out and be with her friends. The two grownups knew this and decided to put her mind and body at ease.

"Oh, no, honey. Go right ahead. Go spend time with your friends and have a good time." With that, Zoe nodded with a smile, then quickly turned around and left the kitchen, skipping. A few seconds later, Stephanie quickly jumped out of the kitchen chair to catch up to Zoe.

"Wait a minute, Zoe!" Stephanie shouted. Zoe stopped in the dining room near her three friends, hoping that Stephanie didn't decide that there was something that she wanted her to do. Zoe turned to face Stephanie as she came out the kitchen towards her. "Let me give you some change to line your pocket." Stephanie began reaching into the drawer near the stairs to take out some change, but the three girls protested quickly.

"That is not necessary, Stephanie. This is on all of us." Janee said.

"Thanks anyway, Stephanie." Zoe said as the four girls walked towards the front door and started to make their way outside.

Stephanie nodded then followed behind the girls to lock the door once they left, but before she closed the door, the four girls and she saw someone across the street that they all knew then they shouted across the street to give their greeting.

"Hello, Mr. Barlow!" they sang in unison. Gloria was still sitting in the kitchen daydreaming when she heard them sing the name.

"Mr. Barlow? Which Mr. Barlow? Please, don't let it be...be..." She was acting the way a dog does when it hears the master in the distance.

"Hey Chris, how ya doing?" Gloria heard, as Stephanie was the next to greet him. Gloria's palms began to sweat as she blushed like a little school girl. She sneaked to the kitchen door then stuck her head out. She saw the girls head down the porch. Stephanie didn't see Gloria do this because she was way too busy talking to Chris Barlow.

Gloria then sneaked over by the basement door, hunched low, and peeked over the corner, trying to see if she could get a glance at him. She couldn't see anything, so she tried to get closer by making her way quickly to the steps leading upstairs. Once she made her way to the third step, she peered over the corner in her quest to catch a glimpse of him.

"Yeah Chris, Zoe is getting to be a grownup." Stephanie yelled back.

"He must still be far off because I can't hear him or see him yet," she thought to herself. She was trying to get Stephanie's attention but she was too busy focused on the conversation that she was having.

"Psst! Psst! Steph, what does he look like?" Gloria was still blushing and had a schoolgirl curious look on her face. "Does he have gray hair? Is he fat? Oh, is he still cute?" Gloria asked as she began poking Stephanie in her side and her back.

Gloria's sound caught Stephanie by surprise, not to mention all of the poking, and caused her to stumble over her words.

"Ssshh, Cousin Gloria. I can't answer you and talk to him at the same time." She was trying to whisper out the corner of her mouth, but kept her smile towards Chris Barlow. "Plus... stop poking me...It tickles." Stephanie wanted to laugh but she was trying to stay cool and not embarrass herself in front of him.

Despite what Stephanie told Gloria, Gloria continued grilling and poking Stephanie which almost made Stephanie burst into laughter.

"Listen, Chris, why don't you come over for a moment..." When she asked this of Chris, Gloria's eyes bulged out in a panic as her heart began racing.

"No, no, Stephanie!" she whispered, then she pinched her in her back, causing Stephanie to thrust her stomach forward. "Don't invite him in! I don't wanna see him!"

Gloria began pulling the back of Stephanie's shirt. Stephanie really wanted to burst out laughing but she was really trying to play it cool.

"Matthew and Gloria are here. I'm sure that they wouldn't mind seeing a friendly face during this tough time. Oh, no, it would be no problem," Stephanie assured. Gloria started hearing sounds of footsteps drawing closer to the house, causing her to panic.

"I'm gonna kill you, Stephanie!" she exclaimed as she sucked her teeth then zoomed up the stairs two at a time so Chris wouldn't have a chance to see her until she was ready. This time, Stephanie did laugh. Chris didn't pay any attention to it. If he did, he never said anything about it.

Once he arrived on the porch, he held his arms out to Stephanie and gave her a hug and a kiss.

"Oh, Stephanie, I am so very sorry to hear about Archie's passing. The neighborhood won't be the same now that he is gone," he said in a very soft, comforting tone.

"Thank you so much, Chris. Please come in." She moved away from the door to make room for him to come in. "Have a seat anywhere. I'll go let Matthew and Gloria know that you're here." She was now closing the door. "Gloria!" she sang by the stairs. "You have a visitor!" Stephanie couldn't help but laugh again. "You won't believe who the cat dragged in." Chris didn't catch on to what was going on or what had happened to cause her to act this way.

"Okay! I'll be down in a moment!" Gloria yelled back to her, acting like she was busy and had no idea who was downstairs. Gloria was furious with Stephanie for inviting Chris over. Gloria's skin broke out in a cold sweat and her stomach tightened. What was she going to say to him and why was she acting like a…a… giddy little school girl? She hadn't seen Chris in decades. She had a long history with Chris. They were boyfriend and girlfriend decades ago, way before she had married or even knew Mike. They were childhood sweethearts. She wasn't a child anymore, but all of those exciting tingly feelings were coming back stirring up emotions that she hadn't felt in ages.

Gloria began pacing back and forth, occasionally glancing at herself in the full length mirror. She stood sideways and sucked in her stomach.

"Well, I am not a size four anymore…" And then she took both hands and grabbed her breasts. "But I still got these." As she modeled in front of the mirror, she heard three voices downstairs, then she heard some laughter. "Matthew must've come up from the basement," she thought to herself. When she looked back at the mirror, she decided that she wasn't going to let Chris see her in the outfit that she had on. She ran quickly over to her suitcase then threw the contents on the bed as she tried to find something nice that Chris would like.

Gloria took off Archie's shirt and put on something that was more fitting. She had a yellow T-shirt that said on the front, 'Welcome to Sunny California' and the back said, 'Make sure that you leave before the sun goes down.' She thought that it would lighten the mood. She contemplated about changing the black spandex pants and putting on a pair of jeans, but decided to keep the spandex on. It hugged her all in the right places, especially the butt area. She kept the sockless sandal look as she began fluffing up her hair. She was so nervous but very excited at the same time. Why was she so concerned if he liked the way that she looked? He might be married or have a girlfriend. Hey, nowadays, he might have a boyfriend. She was going absolutely nuts.

After awhile, she decided that she better head downstairs. She didn't want to be rude. She was not supposed to know that Chris was downstairs, so she began to psyche herself up to get going.

As she started heading downstairs, she heard Matthew head back to the basement. Stephanie and Chris were sitting in the living room chatting up a storm. Stephanie was on the couch in one corner and Chris was sitting in Archie's chair. Gloria stopped for a quick second then held her breath as she continued down the stairs. Stephanie looked up when she heard the sound of footsteps coming down the stairs.

"Oh, here she is." Stephanie was now staring at her.

"Stephanie, you said that someone is here?" Gloria was acting totally oblivious to who could be there to see the family.

As she reached the bottom step, Chris stood up, all six feet one inches of him, and smiled his pearly whites at Gloria as he looked at her with his still jet black bedroom eyes, from head to toe.

"Oh my God, it is Chris! Chris Barlow!" Gloria didn't need to pretend to be surprised, because she was. He looked exactly the way he had looked when she had last seen him decades earlier. He was still tall, and his body was still physically fit. He still had a full head of thick, dark, curly hair which was ever so slightly receding in the front. His face had no wrinkles and he was clean shaven; no beard, no mustache, no nothing. He was ruggedly handsome to her. He had a pair of nice fitting jeans on. "He is a size 32," she thought as she stared at him. "But look how muscular his legs are."

He had a plaid long sleeved shirt on. No jacket. "Gloria, he definitely has a wife or girlfriend." She thought and said all of this to herself in less than two seconds.

Before Gloria even had an opportunity to make it into the living room to greet him, he walked quickly behind Archie's chair and met her by the steps.

"Hi, Gloria," he said, smiling as he checked her out from head to toe. "You look absolutely beautiful!" If looks could talk, he was feeling the same way that Gloria was feeling. "You haven't aged a bit," he added sincerely.

"Thank you so much for the compliment, Chris." She was beet red by this time. That was when he reached across to her and gave her a hug and kiss. Oh, how she didn't want him to release the embrace. She thought that he smelled good. His hug and kiss was done in the very respectful way that a person would do when they hadn't seen an acquaintance for a spell.

Gloria noticed that he had taken the smile off of his face and become serious. "Gloria, I am so sorry to hear about Archie, really I am."

"Oh, thank you, Chris. I do appreciate that." Gloria nodded and smiled.

They both stared at each other for a long time, remembering times that they spent together holding and kissing one another, holding hands, long walks in the evenings, cuddling and sitting on the porch at night looking up into the sky at the stars. Just being so much in love. Gloria didn't want to break the spell that she was under, and neither did he. Stephanie was sitting there, watching them as they stared at each other, looking like a Polaroid photo. She cleared her throat, which broke the spell between the two, then they both came and sat down in the living room, Chris in Archie's chair and Gloria in Edith's.

After they sat down, they started staring into each other's eyes again and smiled, but the quietness was killing Stephanie.

"Ah, Chris, would you care for a piece of cake or some coffee?" Chris kept looking at Gloria as he responded to Stephanie.

"Oh no thank you, Steph, I cannot stay too long."

"He has a girlfriend," Gloria immediately started to think. "He has to see his girlfriend."

"I'm doing a carpentry job a few blocks down the street."

"Looking like that?" Gloria was looking up and down at him with her eyes wide. "You look like a model for Brawny paper towels!" Everyone laughed as Chris smiled modestly and blushed.

"Well, I have men who work for me. They are actually doing the work. I am going to make sure that they are doing it correctly. Often, I get in there and mix it up too, but today, I am just checking on them."

"I remember years ago when you remodeled the basement for Daddy. Daddy had invited us to come and spend the Easter holiday, and he said, 'Woopty do, there, little girl…' she was imitating Archie in an exaggerating manner making them laugh. 'Go downstairs in the basement and bring up those old Perry Como and Sinatra albums. I am in the mood to be cheery. You cannot have Easter without Perry and Old Blue Eyes. They're in the box up against the wall by the boiler.' I didn't wanna go down there because I thought it would be all dusty and dirty and covered with soot and stuff, not to mention the spiders and bugs. I never liked going down into that basement. Not even when I was younger. I didn't want to argue or complain, either. Daddy wanted Perry Como and Sinatra; I'd get Perry Como and Sinatra. I remember reluctantly opening up the basement door. The first thing that hit me was an airy smell. I remember that as if it was yesterday. The basement had always had a damp and musty smell to it. I just figured that he had cleaned it or something, but when I turned on the light switch by the stairs and looked down and saw carpet, I was shocked. I was like, "what is going on here!" As I slowly continued walking down the steps, I saw a bright lit, wall-to-wall carpeted, wall paneled two bedroom apartment; you had even installed a bathroom with a shower, and hid the boiler room behind a removable shelf; so ingenious. At first, Daddy didn't tell me that you were the person who had remodeled the basement till after I finished raving about it. When he told me that you were the person and that you had done it so quickly, I was amazed. Everything is so detailed, so precise." She was sounding like she was promoting a commercial for Chris's company.

The Life and Times of Gloria Bunker

"Your dad had taken a chance on me back then and trusted me to do a good job. I couldn't let him down."

"Oh, Chris, Daddy always liked you, ever since we were little tots. You were like, one of the only boys that he wouldn't mind having in the house. You two got along great." Gloria was nodding her head

"Yeah, I always liked him also. The way you and I were so close and he and I so close, he thought that I would have been his…"

Quickly Chris stopped his words because he was feeling uncomfortable to say what he really wanted to say. "Son-in-law," he said to himself. "He thought that I would have been his son-in-law. Oh Gloria, where and why did things go wrong between us?"

Those were words that Gloria and Stephanie would not hear. What Chris would say is, "He thought that I could be the son that he never had." Gloria smiled in agreement, but she knew what he had meant the first time.

The telephone rang as the three talked in the living room. Since Gloria and Chris were doing most of the talking, Stephanie got up to answer the phone.

"Hello, Bunker residence. Oh, hi, Jerry." She pointed to the two and told them that the phone call was for her. "Hold on, Jerry. I am going to switch phones so I can talk to you in private." Stephanie headed into the kitchen and picked up the kitchen phone, then Gloria got up and hung up the phone in the living room. "Thanks, Gloria!" she yelled.

Gloria noticed that when she got up to hang up the phone, Chris was trying to be casual as he looked at her butt. She also noticed through the corner of her eye that he nodded and smiled. She figured that he liked what he was checking. She liked it and she liked the attention she was getting from him. After she hung up the phone and headed back to where she was sitting, she continued talking to Chris.

"That was Jerry. That is Stephanie's agent," she said casually.

"Gloria, I just can't get over how young and great you look!" As she was about to sit down in the chair, she noticed that Chris was feeling more comfortable talking now that Stephanie was not in the room. He was leaning over Archie's chair to be closer to her side. "How long has it been?" Gloria wanted to reach across the chair and touch his hand. The urge was very strong, but she was trying to hold on to her feelings.

"It has been over 20, 25—oh, Chris, it's been way too long."

"It is funny how fate works, huh?" he commented. "You are in the passenger's seat while fate is driving on cruise control, then when you least expect it, when you think he was going to continue going straight, he makes an unexpected turn. You never know what direction fate will take you in."

"Yep, you got that right." Gloria was nodding in agreement. "Sometimes fate heads for the guardrail and goes off a cliff." This comment made Chris laugh.

"Well, you've done great with your life. Archie told me that Joey got his MBA and was doing a lot of activist work and that he is a teacher, and I already know that the twins are straight A students in school. Hey, speaking of Joey, isn't he here?" Chris was now sitting up in the chair and began looking around for any signs that Joey was there.

"Oh, Joey will be here soon. He had last minute things that he had to wrap up before he leaves. He is supposed to be coming with Mike and his wife."

"Oh, so Mike did get remarried?"

"Yes, to a wonderful woman. Beth is her name. She is very sweet and I like her a lot. We are good friends and even hang out with each other on occasion. I figured that if she was going to be in my son's life and help raise him when he was young, I better get to know her. When I did, I found out that she and I had a lot in common and once I did, we just hit it off well. Joey loves her, too. Chris, I really must admit that it was hard to accept that there would be another woman in my son's life besides me, but I couldn't have asked for a better stepmother than her."

"Gloria, I must say that is absolutely commendable."

"Thank you, Chris. Well, speaking of commendable, you didn't do so badly yourself, Mister business owner."

"Yeah well, I can't complain concerning that." Chris chuckled a few times.

"Your wife must be very pleased with you?" Gloria was now the one who was leaning over in her chair towards Chris anxiously hoping to hear that he wasn't married.

"Oh no Gloria, I am not married." Chris was shaking his head with a nonchalant smile on his face.

"Well then, your girlfriend must be very proud of you..." she eyed him closely, still waiting to hear what the answer was going to be.

"Nope..." he was still shaking his head with a smirk on his face. Gloria sat back in her chair. Her expression had changed drastically. She almost looked disappointed. Chris noticed the change instantly and became concerned.

"What's the matter, Gloria? Is there anything wrong?"

"I should've known, Chris. Those big, rugged, youthful features, that muscular physique, those nice tight jeans to hug your butt and thighs..."

"What, Gloria? I don't understand." Chris was shaking his head, confused, as if he had done something wrong and didn't know what it was.

"You are gay!" Gloria was now crossing her arms across her chest in a disappointed manner. Her look caused Chris to burst out laughing, a big, knee slapping kind of laughing that caused Gloria to look at him. "What is so funny?" Chris wiped the tears from his eyes and tried to get his composure back before he began to speak again.

"Gloria, I am not gay. As a matter of fact, I am far from gay." When he said this, Gloria unfolded her arms, smiled in relief, and leaned back towards him. "Listen, Gloria, I was married at one time, a very long time ago, but it didn't last. Thank God that we separated then divorced as friends. I've had many girlfriends since then."

"But I don't get it, Chris. You are every woman's catch. Every woman's dream and even every woman's fantasy. You are absolutely gorgeous. I don't see any reason why you are still single."

"Well, I know why. Mostly it has been my fault. See, I just never found that special person that could even come close or measure up in any way to my first love."

Gloria's heart just dropped to the floor and her face was burning like fire.

"Oooh, Chris," were the only two words that were able to come out of her mouth. She was so blown away by the comment. She thought that if she had looked into the mirror, she would have looked like a blond plum, a blond plum with tears welling up in her eyes.

"It is okay Gloria. God has blessed me immensely. I've had a wonderful life, I assure you." Chris smiled at Gloria but she could see that he didn't look very sincere.

"Chris, that's one of the nicest compliments that I had ever heard." She was overwhelmed by his words. She began talking very sincerely. She couldn't help it; she reached over and took hold of his strong masculine hands.

"I'm vibrating," he said as he looked into her eyes. The comment caught her off guard, causing her to freeze as she stared at him.

"I beg your pardon?" she said, letting go of his hand quickly. He started laughing and shaking his head to let her know that she misunderstood what he was saying.

"I'm sorry. I meant to say that I am being beeped. I have my phone on vibrating mode."

"Oh, now I understand." She chuckled in relief as he dug into his pocket to see who was calling. A look of disappointment crossed his face as he stood up.

"Oh Gloria, I am so sorry, but I gotta go. My men are calling me over to the job site." Chris was putting the phone back into his pocket. Just as he stood up, Stephanie was coming out of the kitchen.

"Oh? Gotta leave so soon, Chris?"

"Yep, my guys are beeping me. Hopefully there isn't a problem."

"Chris, I'm so happy that you decided to take me up on my offer to come in."

"Yeah, Chris, I'm so happy that you decided to come in also. It's really been my pleasure to see you again." Gloria was now standing up, also.

"Well, maybe I'll be seeing more of you now that you are back. How are you going to get all of your stuff here from Cali?"

"Oh no, Chris." Gloria was shaking her head. "We aren't moving back. We'll probably be going back after I get everything straight around here."

"Oh? That's a shame. So, what is going to happen with the bar?"

"I don't know anything yet, Chris. Everything has been a shock to all of us."

"I truly understand." Gloria could see that Chris was disappointed. "Well, let me give you my home number just in case you might need me for anything."

Chris began digging into his pocket, then he pulled out a business card and handed it to Gloria. "Maybe we could go out and have a bite to eat or something before you leave. We could talk about old times…uh, unless your boyfriend or sig-nif-i-cant other would mind?"

"Chris…" Stephanie responded quickly, before Gloria had the opportunity. "Gloria is single, more single than Abraham Lincoln on that dollar bill." Gloria playfully slapped Stephanie on the arm.

"Don't you have to meet someone on the corner of 'Mind your business' Avenue, Stephanie?" When Gloria said this, Chris chuckled. Gloria playfully cut her eyes at Stephanie then turned back to face Chris.

"I wouldn't have said it like that, Chris, but I am single and I would love that." Gloria was looking at him with a warm and sincere smile.

"Well, I better get going. I'll see you all in a few days at the funeral home."

Chris made his way to the front door with the two women following behind him, checking him out the way he was checking Gloria out earlier.

Chris had been in the house millions of times. He knew how to open the front door. Once he unlocked the door, then opened it, he turned to the women seriously.

"Once again I wanna give my deepest sympathy to you." After those kind words, he turned around and zoomed off quickly. Gloria watched intently as he headed down the porch and off down the block. She liked the way that he walked, so tall and upright like a soldier, so self assured, so confident. She imagined walking beside him and holding his hand again, like she used to when they were so very young. Gloria didn't realize that she was staring that long or that hard till Stephanie took hold of her chin and pushed up.

"Close your mouth, cousin, you might have some uninvited guests like mosquitoes."

CHAPTER THREE:
Remembering Chris

Gloria snapped back to reality then backed away from the front door and closed it as she watched her ex-boyfriend Chris slowly disappear out of her sight, but now she was staring at a closed door.

"Well? Well? Tell me everything. What did I miss?" Stephanie sat back down on the couch excitedly, like a school girl waiting to hear all of the latest tales and gossip.

Finally Gloria pulled herself from the door and headed to Archie's chair. "Stephanie, I could just kill you! How could you have done that to me?" Gloria scolded her as Stephanie sat up straight and put her hand on her chest.

"What I did! You started it. You knew you wanted to see him, peeping around the stairs hiding, asking me all those questions. In my whole life, I've never seen you act like that before. Look at that glow that you have on your face" When Stephanie brought this to Gloria's attention, she touched her face and smiled.

"I am, aren't I?" She then started giggling. "My God, Stephanie, he hasn't aged a bit."

"Apparently his eyes said the same about you."

"He was exactly how I remembered him. So well spoken, good manners…" Gloria began sitting back in the chair fanning herself with a smile.

"Yeah, I guess he is kinda handsome. I see him all the time. I never looked at him any other way than maybe like a dad figure or something. He is very respectable in the community and everyone knows and loves him." Stephanie made herself comfortable back on the couch, smiling excitedly.

"Okay, I wanna know everything. Uncle Archie told me a long time ago that you two used to have a thing for each other. If he had all these nice qualities and he could still make you melt after all these years, what happened?

Where did everything go wrong?" Gloria sucked her teeth and rolled her eyes and shook her head back and forth.

"Oh, Stephanie, If only I knew where to start. You know, I've known the Barlows my whole life. They've been friends of the family forever." Gloria was looking up as she remembered. "My earliest memories of Chris and myself together were when we used to play in the sand box at the playground. I didn't think anything of him then. He was just a friend. We played tag and we would chase each other, both of us laughing at the top of our lungs and screaming too." Gloria was now smiling as she thought back. "My earliest memories were only of Chris and myself. Oh, of course I had girlfriends and all that, but Chris was the only boy in my life. When we got a tad older and outgrew the sand box stage, I was becoming more feminine and he was becoming, well, well…Prehistoric, like boys normally do!" This caused Stephanie, who was listening as if she was waiting to hear what the winning lottery numbers were, to start laughing. "I wanted to play with dolls and have tea parties and dress up. Chris on the other hand wanted to climb trees, mud wrestle and play tackle football, but we were getting feelings for each other and didn't know how to express them. I remember I would be walking with my girlfriends to school and he would bounce the basketball to hit me lightly in the shoulder, then he would laugh and run away after he got the ball back, or he would take my books and make me chase him. Oh, Stephanie, he was doing things just to drive me crazy, but that was his juvenile way to tell me that he liked me. My way was to have my hair done nicely, a pretty little dress, smelling good, you know, being a little lady. Well, one day—I remember this as if it was yesterday…" She said, being more animated than before.

"We were having co-ed gym in school and I was doing flips on the gym mats with my girlfriends when Chris playfully came over to me and pushed me onto the mat. He then ran off laughing, but for some reason, I just sat there on the mat, then I started crying. Don't ask me why I started crying. It didn't even hurt or anything like that. He pushed me and I fell on a mat, for God's sake! Well anyway, when Chris saw that I wasn't chasing after him and that I was on the mat crying, he came back over to me and gently helped me up by my hand and walked me over to the gym benches. Boy, did I milk it, Stephanie." Gloria began laughing as she remembered the incident. "I started crying harder, then he took my head and laid it on his shoulder while he patted the side of my head. 'I'm so sorry, Gloria,' I remember him saying ever so softly and soothingly. 'For the rest of my life, I will never lay my hands on you to ever make you cry again. I promise. Could you ever forgive me?'" Stephanie could see that Gloria had tears in her eyes but they were happy tears as she remembered the incident.

"Oooh, Gloria that is so sweet." Stephanie felt like she was going to tear up too as she put her hand on her chest and sighed.

"Well, Stephanie, all through elementary school, Chris and I were together all the time. We were like the two most noticeable kids in school. We ate our lunch together, did recess together, were in the same class together—Stephanie, not once did I ever get tired or bored with him. I only had eyes for him and he always and only had eyes for me. JHS, our relationship was stronger than in elementary school. We started going to the movies alone, holding hands, kissing—all things adolescents did. When HS came, still, Chris was my first love. We went to parties and dances, and double dates—everything those late-teenagers did together. We talked about getting married and having children and where we were going to live and spending our lives together. Stephanie, my life with Chris was like a fairytale. I was a princess and he was my knight in shining armor. He treated me so well. While other friends our age had already been in and out of relationships, Chris and I still were together. It was like magic. Our friends envied our special and unique relationship. Some even resented it, but it was what it was. I was for him and he was for me. We cared deeply for each other. For sure, everyone thought that we were inseparable and would definitely get married after school. Our school year book even said that we would most likely be married and would have more kids than any other students in the history of the school. We were that much in love."

Gloria became quiet for a moment as she sat there, frozen in time. Stephanie had her eyes wide as if she was watching a great movie. "Well, don't leave me in suspense at the best part of the story!" Stephanie shouted, as if she couldn't hold on any longer from the anticipation. Stephanie was moving to the edge of the couch, as if she would hear better by doing this. "What did he do to cause the relationship to fall apart?" Gloria began shaking her head back and forth in disagreement.

"Stephanie, don't assume that it was anything that he had done. On the contrary, it wasn't him at all. It was me. He was Samson and I was unfortunately his Delilah. I was the one, the guilty one to cause everything to tumble down, destroying our relationship, leaving him crushed." Gloria was almost speaking in a sad and haunting whisper.

"Oh, Gloria what happened? What did you do?" Gloria hesitated before she started to speak again then she breathed in and out deeply.

"Someone told me about this young hippie rebel. When I saw him and heard him speak, I had to see and hear more of him. His name was..." Stephanie was nodding in understanding and finished Gloria's sentence.

"Michael Stivic!" Stephanie had the enthusiasm of a contestant on a game show, and when she got the answer right, she began clapping and jumping up and down in her seat as if she was getting points to win the game.

"You just won Jeopardy's daily double!" shouted Gloria as if she was an announcer. "See, Stephanie, my whole life up to then was only Chris and me, not to mention my family. I had never experienced anything other than Chris. Yes, Chris was tall, dark, handsome, intelligent, and respectable, and so on and so forth, but I wanted to be daring. I wanted to try something different. I wanted to be a little bit of a rebel, too. When I tried it, I liked it. I liked it a lot. I had been such a good girl, not causing my parents any hard times, any troubles. I wanted to be a little bit adventurous, and in a way, I wanted to piss Daddy off too, I guess. Even though I loved Daddy with all of my heart, I didn't believe in his views. I guess getting involved with Mike was my way of standing up to Daddy, I don't know. But what I did know was once I wanted to see and be around Mike, I just left Chris out in the cold. No reason, no explanation, no nothing."

"Gloria, that was just awful!" Stephanie began sucking her teeth angrily.

"Stephanie, it wasn't just awful; it was downright selfish. I only thought about my feelings and didn't care about his. I was so scared and such a coward then. I didn't know how to break up with him. One minute, he and I were walking arm in arm, then the next thing he knew, I wasn't calling him or returning his calls when he called me. I quickly withdrew from him to spend all of my spare time thinking about or being with Mike. He was really worried about me. He thought that I was sick or something. But I wouldn't tell him what my problem was. When he would call the house or even come by, I would tell Mommy or Daddy to make up some excuse. They didn't like that idea at all. They loved Chris and knew that he didn't deserve what I was doing to him. Mommy kept telling me to let him know how I felt, but I just couldn't. When he finally found out that I wasn't sick, he asked if it was something he had done. He wanted to know if he was the reason why I was suddenly avoiding him. I told him that I just needed some space. He tried for awhile to speak to me and even tried to get back with me, but after awhile, he just gave up and stopped. Our parents still continued seeing each other, but Chris no longer accompanied them. His family stayed cordial to me but you could tell that they were hurt that Chris and I were no longer with each other. They never said anything but you could definitely feel it. Before they had even met Mike, Mom and Dad were both disappointed that Chris and I weren't together also. Mom wasn't that bad but Daddy definitely let me know how he felt. I don't know how long it was before Chris found out about me and Mike, nor do I know who told him, but what I do know was once he saw me, and believe me, I did try to avoid him as much as I could, he approached me with a sincere smile on his face. At first, he was reluctant to approach me, but he did. I thought that he would be furious and I'm sure he was when he first found out. Surprisingly, he was nothing but a gentleman. He said, 'I'm glad that you are happy now and this is all I'll ever want for you.' Then he just walked away. When I got home, I cried like a baby. I treated the first love of my life so coldly."

Gloria's voice was quivering as the tears fell down her face. Stephanie was feeling her pain as she let the waterworks come down, too.

"He didn't deserve that. He was too good a person to be treated like that. I must've seen him from afar maybe twice after that…till now."

Stephanie stared at Gloria for a few seconds then just started crying hard.

"Ooh, that is the saddest story that I have ever heard in my whole life! Gloria, how could you have been so cruel?" Stephanie was talking in a high voice while the tears flowed.

"Easy. I was young, stupid and immature—you name it, I was it. Oh, Stephanie, it killed me for years. I don't think that I've ever forgotten what I did to him. There were many times while married that I secretly wondered how my life would've been if I'd married Chris." Stephanie was trying to get her composure but was having a little difficulty.

"Well Stephanie, that's the whole story and the truth, the whole truth and nothing but the truth." Stephanie was now rubbing at her eyes and wiping away the tears with her hands.

"Now I understand why you were hiding from him and didn't want to see him. You were going to be a coward now, like you were a coward years ago."

"Stephanie!" Gloria was shocked by Stephanie's honestly and tact.

"Well, come on now, Gloria. It is true, right? If I hadn't invited him in, you would've still tried to avoid him." Gloria just stared at Stephanie guiltily, not really knowing what to say. She was speechless, but then she looked at the card that he had given her and nodded with a smile.

"Yeah, Stephanie, you are right. I can't undo the past, but I can definitely make up for it. Even though it has been decades since Chris and I were together, he still deserves an explanation. It is better late than never."

"So, when are you going to tell him?"

"The next time he and I are alone." Gloria was now standing up but was still staring at the card that Chris had given her. "I'm going into the kitchen to hang his number up on the bulletin board next to the wall phone." Stephanie got up after and followed her towards the kitchen. As they were walking, Matthew came out of the basement. He then began looking around.

"Wassup?" he said to everyone cheerfully.

"We're going into the kitchen," they replied in unison.

"Where is C.B?" Matthew was now following behind the two of them into the kitchen.

All three made their way into the kitchen as Gloria made her way to the bulletin board. Stephanie sat down by the table and Matthew stood near the kitchen door.

"Did you say C.B? Who is C.B?" Gloria turned from the bulletin board and stared at Matthew curiously.

"Chris, Ma!" he replied in a laughing manner as if she asked him a silly question.

"Why do you call him C.B?"

"Gloria, those are Chris's initials. Chris Barlow, C.B."

"How long have you been calling him C.B?" For some reason, Gloria was feeling left out that she didn't know about this nickname business. When Gloria asked this question to Matthew, he and Stephanie stared at each other.

"Well, Ma, I think it has been about twelve years."

"I think that it has been longer than that, but twelve is playing it safe." Stephanie added quickly as she nodded then looked at Gloria, who was staring at the two of them as if she missed the punch line of a joke.

"Anyway, Matthew, he couldn't stay long. He had to get to work." Matthew sucked his teeth in disappointment.

"I hope that he didn't think that I was being rude by only chatting for a moment with him. It's just that I was on the computer fighting space aliens with my partner from England and I had to get back to assist him. I had the game on pause to chat with C.B., but I had to get back."

"Don't worry, Matthew. He understood. He knows how important those computer games are to you, especially when you and he play them for hours on end," Stephanie said as she tried to reassure him.

"Hey, Ma, C.B. is a whiz at these games. He is like the Terminator, unbeatable. I'm still trying to beat his score but I just can't. I've came close when I play him but he is just too good. It is as if he designed the computer games himself and knows all the hidden points and secret dimensions. You should play him one day. Oops! I forgot that you don't like computer games."

Gloria couldn't believe what she was hearing. Matthew had a nickname for Chris and she hadn't known anything about it. For twelve years Matthew had been calling him C.B. and they play computer games together.

"Wow, it seems like you and Chris have become pretty close, huh?"

"Well Ma, not really," he said nonchalantly. "No more than usual."

"Gloria, Matthew has known Chris his whole life. And so has Zoe. They like Chris a lot. Heck, we all do."

"Yeah Ma, Chris is mad cool!"

"Yeah Gloria, when the twins came for the holidays and you stayed in Cali, sometimes Uncle Archie would need certain parts, like electrical or plumbing parts, for the house or the bar, and he would send Matthew down to Chris's shop. Matthew would stay there for hours and Archie would have to call down there to get Matthew back." Stephanie and Matthew both started to laugh. Gloria started to feel jealous over their relationship. She wished that she had been doing things with Chris also.

"You would've known about this if you weren't always trying to hide from him," she said out of the corner of her mouth so Gloria could hear her and that it would sound like gibberish to Matthew, which it did.

Matthew didn't respond to Stephanie's gibberish comment. He just looked at her strangely and shook his head back and forth with a smile. "Well, will he be coming back?" Matthew asked the two women anxiously.

Gloria then patted her hand over his card on the bulletin board as she stared at it, thinking about the two of them seeing each other after so many decades.

"Matthew I'm almost certain that he will be coming back," she said with a smile.

"That's what I like to hear, Cousin. That's what I like to hear," Stephanie said in encouragement.

CHAPTER FOUR:
That Strange House Next Door

The three continued talking in the kitchen till Matthew realized that he had left the full garbage bag still sitting on the floor next to the empty garbage can.

"You guys keep talking. Let me take that garbage bag out into the back. I had forgotten all about it." Gloria went to open up the door for him but was still talking when she glanced out over towards her old house.

She noticed that there was a lot of garbage scattered all over the yard. This sight really made her upset. She was so upset that she had to comment on it. She stopped right in the middle of her conversation with Stephanie to mention her disgust.

"You know what, you guys. This really ticks me off! Look how our neighbor over here leaves the house. Garbage is everywhere! It never looked like that when I was growing up here. The Jeffersons kept the backyard so clean, and so did Mike and I. I have never seen this house looking the way that it looks right now!"

"Let me see what you are talking about, Gloria," Stephanie said as she got up to see what Gloria was looking at. When she saw what made her upset, she shook her head.

"You know, this is the first time that I have noticed that. You're right, Gloria. That looks pretty bad."

"It looks like that in the front of the house too and especially on the sidewalk in front of the house. Who lives there now, Stephanie?"

"Oh Gloria, I don't know. So many people have moved in and out of that house. For the last few years, it's been renters. I don't know if the owners are still the Warners."

"I remember them—the older couple. They went into a nursing home but the daughter and son who had moved away earlier didn't want to sell it, so they rented it out instead. They weren't the friendliest neighbors that God had allowed to live on this block. That's what I do remember. They never wanted to speak when someone waved or smiled to them, or even say hello to them. They stayed to themselves."

"Well, Ma, maybe no one lives there." Matthew interjected.

"No, someone definitely lives there, all right. I heard noises coming from inside the house when I was coming up the porch, plus there are lights on in the house."

"Yeah, Matthew, someone lives there. I don't know who they are but Uncle Archie did. I've seen him over there a few times coming out of the house. They must be his friends"

"Do they know that Daddy died?"

"Gloria, I don't know. I didn't tell them, but that doesn't mean anything. I hardly told anyone, but from all of the telephone calls that we've received and flowers that are being brought to the house, everyone knows."

"Matthew, honey, would you do me a favor? When you take out the garbage, would you go over next door just to see who is living there and let them know about your grandfather?" Matthew nodded and headed out the back door with the garbage bag in his hand. When he left, Gloria closed the door then turned to face Stephanie to continue talking about what she was saying before she had seen the mess next door, but she noticed that Stephanie was looking at her in a peculiar manner.

"What's wrong, Stephanie? Why are you looking at me like that? Do I have drool hanging from my chin or something?" Gloria chuckled after she made the comical remark.

"Gloria, I haven't seen you and Matthew together at one time in it seems like forever."

"Yeah, he is getting big, isn't he...or either I am just getting shorter."

"No, no, Gloria, I am serious. That's not what I'm talking about. He also looks like you, no doubt, but I can definitely see a lot of Raymond in him."

"Well, of course, silly. We are his parents, you know." Gloria said as she rolled her eyes, surprised that Stephanie would even say such a thing.

"Oh, Gloria, wait a minute. I'm not finished. I have just noticed this. Just hear me out on this, okay and follow me. How tall was Raymond?"

"Six feet two, why?" Gloria was now sitting back down at the table. Stephanie held her hand up as if she didn't want Gloria to interrupt.

"Okay, he is six feet two. Now, can you describe the type of body structure that he had?"

This comment caused Gloria to put a big smile on her face as she reminisced. "Oh, Stephanie, he had a beautiful body. His body was very athletic looking. He had big ole muscular legs and a nice butt, not to mention that he had a big ole chest and arms. You would never think that he was a veterinarian's assistant. You would've thought that he worked a lot outdoors."

"Like a construction worker even?" Stephanie sang as she looked at Gloria through the corner of her eye slyly.

"Yeah," Gloria quickly answered.

"Maybe even a contractor? Hey, maybe even a carpenter?" Stephanie's voice went an octave higher, causing Gloria's mouth to drop. She looked at Stephanie with confusion.

"Stephanie, what are you getting at?"

"I don't know, Gloria. I'm just looking at you while you describe Chris."

"Why are you saying this, Stephanie?" Her voice was getting louder and began to sound a tad frustrated.

"Look, Gloria, same height, same body structure. I remember Raymond from when I was younger. They have the same complexion, same cleanshaven face, same color of hair and eyes, very friendly and caring. He liked me and I definitely liked him, he was well mannered and Raymond even worked with his hands just like Chris, plus he even loved to fix things. Raymond fixed and repaired animals while Chris fixes and repairs buildings, and most importantly over all that I just described, they loved you so much that they wanted to spend the rest of their life with you."

Gloria was frozen in her chair. She looked like she was in a trance. Her mind was racing. Was Stephanie right in what she had just said? Were they really that much alike? It seemed like everything about them was the same.

"Subconsciously when I fell in love with Raymond, was I really thinking of Chris, and when I married Raymond, subconsciously was I finally marrying Chris?" Part of her wanted to deny the similarities, but she couldn't. But why would she or should she deny it? She loved Raymond and she loved everything about him because he was so much like Chris. She had married Mike because she thought that was what she wanted. Yes, she was happy that he gave her a beautiful son, Joey, but she really wasn't happy in the relationship. The only difference between her and Mike was that Mike realized this before she did. How many times did she purposely walk by Chris's house just to hopefully get a glimpse of him? How many times did she see him from afar then try to catch up to him, just to slowly back off some then walk a safe distance from him without him or anyone else knowing? How many times when Mike was making love to her had she thought about Chris and felt like calling out his name? How much happier she would have been if she had married Chris? But she HAD married Chris in a way. She married Raymond, who had all of Chris's qualities and strengths. He even had his features. That is it! She admitted it! It was true! But as usually happens in life, sometimes all good things must come to an end. Raymond died.

The Life and Times of Gloria Bunker

Gloria snapped out of her trance and came back to reality.

"My life hasn't been fulfilled or really happy since Raymond died. Yes, he gave me two beautiful children, but as a woman, having that special need met in the bedroom late at night, that shoulder to cry on or to lean on, to have that feeling of being protected and cherished hasn't been there. It died with him."

Gloria then looked over towards Stephanie then nodded her head.

"Stephanie, I think that you are right. Everything that you said makes total sense. How did I not know that? You know, Stephanie, he said to me in private that he hasn't had a successful marriage or a lasting relationship because he was trying to find a woman like me, but my life had become fulfilled when I met a man just like him."

"Yeah Gloria, but that man died ages ago. Chris is here and he is single and available."

"Oh Stephanie, I don't know. I hurt that man too much."

"He didn't look too hurt when he saw you. As a matter of fact, the way he kept his eyes on you and the way that he was smiling, I would say that he looked quite, quite well."

Gloria stood up and started pacing the kitchen floor in confusion.

"Oh, Stephanie, it just wouldn't be fair to try and start something now. I'll only hurt him again. Look, I'm going to be heading back to Cali eventually."

Stephanie stood up and patted Gloria on the back. "Look, I know that you have a lot on your mind. I'm sorry that I even brought it up. I would hate to add anymore pressure on you than you already have, but if I were you and I knew that I would be going back to California, who knows when you'll see him next? I would tell him everything. Let everything out. Tell him about the past and spend as much time with him as possible. You might not have another chance to do it. None of us are guaranteed a tomorrow." Stephanie then gave Gloria a kiss then left the kitchen. Gloria stood there absorbing what Stephanie had said then she yelled toward Stephanie, who was making her way up the stairs.

"You should've been a counselor or something instead of a singer!" Gloria heard Stephanie chuckle as she made her way into one of the rooms and closed the door. She spent a while down in the kitchen area, pacing like a caged tigress, thinking about everything that had happened so far: her father's death, the upcoming funeral, the bar, the will, the house, the past— it was very overwhelming for her. She only stopped pacing when Matthew came back into the house.

"I don't know Ma." Matthew was closing the kitchen door and sounding out of breath. "I went to the house like you asked me to. I heard people inside and the lights were on, but no one came to the door or even acknowledged the fact that I was ringing the door and knocking, too, just in case the doorbell didn't work."

"Oh how rude!" she said angrily. "They probably don't know that you came from the Bunker house, that's all," she assured Matthew. "If they were Daddy's friends, like Stephanie said they were, we have to let them know what happened to him."

You know what, Ma? I'll slip the information into their mailbox plus, being that I am pretty bored, I'll go and clean up the back. Like you said, they might be friends of Grampa's. Once they know who I am, they shouldn't be mad that I'm in their backyard."

"That would be nice, Matthew," she replied as she rubbed his arm. "I'm going to head upstairs to lie down for a spell. I'm tired and my head is spinning like a top on crack!" Gloria made her way out the kitchen, leaving Matthew laughing.

A few minutes later, Matthew was heading out again to start working on the yard.

"Head first to the front of the house and put the funeral information into the mailbox," he thought. As he made a way towards the front, he noticed that there was a dark blue SUV parked in front of the house.

"I wonder if that SUV belongs to anyone inside of the house." When he walked up the porch to the house, he could still hear noise coming from inside. He decided to try knocking on the front door again. He did, but again, no one opened the door.

"What the hell is wrong with these people!" he said as he looked at the house and sucked his teeth. He then decided just to put the info into the mailbox then go to the back. As he headed past the side of that house, he could clearly hear a television on. As he passed more of the windows, he heard a stereo on, plus he saw lights coming from inside of the house. The windows were above his head and he did not want to be rude and peep inside. If these people didn't feel like opening the door, it was a free country. They had every right not to have to answer if they didn't want to. Once Matthew made his way all the way in the back, he was really able to see how junky and messy it really was. It looked like no one had taken care of the yard in a very long time, but when he turned around to face the back of the house, the windows were nice and clean and there were nice curtains hanging in the windows. As he looked back at the yard, he didn't know where to start. He had a broom with him, along with gloves, a dust pan, and a box of garbage bags. He also had a weed whacker and a rake to rake all of the leaves and garbage into the garbage bag. The first thing that he did was attack the weeds with the weed whacker. He used it all the way to the back fence near a big tree that was on the property. Matthew was able to see some carvings in the tree and went to inspect it more closely. As he rubbed his gloved hand over the carved bark, he noticed that there were initials which read, 'M.S. and G.B. 4-ever' He chuckled a few times as he shook his head

The Life and Times of Gloria Bunker

and smirked. "Ma and Mike wrote this back in the day: Forever? I don't think so."

When Matthew was finished examining the tree, he went to get the rake, which was leaning up against the house. He was still able to hear some kind of action going on in the house. He wasn't concerned with that anymore. He was determined to get the yard completed. He began raking the weeds into a pile, then he got a garbage bag and began shoveling them into the bag. While he was bent over, he had a strange feeling that someone was staring at him. He turned and stood up, then stared at the back windows. To his surprise, it looked like he just missed someone staring at him because the person had just walked away from the window. He knew this because the curtain on the first floor was still moving and slowing down back into position. He started to hear doors close and it sounded like the person was making their way out of the house. Maybe if he hurried over to the side of the house, he could see who was coming out.

As he began walking away from the fence and heading toward the front of the house, unexpectedly, something jumped or fell onto his back, causing him to gasp and jump from being startled. Whatever it was, because he didn't know yet, definitely was alive, but by the time he got started swinging at it to get it off his back, it had already fallen into the soft pile of weeds nearby. His heart was beating out of his ripped-up t-shirt that he purposely wore to do the yard work in. When he turned around to see what it was that was on his back, he instantly calmed down. He saw that it was a bird's nest and what he thought was sharp claws was nothing but the nest. It had fallen perfectly atop the weeds and he saw that there were babies in the nest that were now chirping loudly. None of them were hurt.

"These little suckers fell out of the tree my mom and Mike carved their initials in. How ironic and very weird," he thought as he began shaking his head back and forth smiling. He looked up and saw a huge long branch hanging over his head. He even saw the spot where the nest had been nestled in because some of it was still there. "It looks like your home just needs to be pressed back into place, that's all." He was happy that he had the rubber gloves on. He didn't want to leave his scent on the nest. He had heard through old wives' tales that if a human picks up a baby chick or a nest, the mother would no longer want them because it had a human scent to them and they couldn't tell if the chick or nest was theirs.

Matthew picked up the nest carefully, then climbed up the thick tree and shimmied across to the nest area.

Once Matthew reached the top, he carefully took the bird's nest and pressed it securely between two branches. Once satisfied that his job was completed and the nest was tightly in place, he slowly and carefully backed away from the nest. Instead of climbing down, he suspended himself by his hands with his feet dangling below him; looking like he was on his pull-up bar back at school. He then just jumped off into the pile of weeds, purposely falling on his behind, laughing at the top of his lungs.

"Dad woulda been proud, Matt, ole boy," he said to himself proudly.

Matthew went back to picking up the weeds and putting them in the garbage bag, then he remembered what he was about to do before the nest incident had happened. He stopped what he was doing and quickly rushed down the side of the house, heading towards the front. Once he reached the front, he noticed that the SUV that had been in front of the house was no longer there, but he was still hearing noises and voices coming from inside of the house. He went up the porch to check the mailbox to see if the information about the funeral was still there, but when he went to look, to his surprise, the mailbox was now empty. Someone had taken the funeral information.

"I knew that there was someone inside of that house, and they were probably staring at me through the back window."

Matthew was about to go off of the porch so he could head back to the back yard to finish what he had started, but he saw something stuck to the door that caught his attention. It was a white envelope that wasn't there before, when he put the funeral information in the mailbox. He was certain, because when he examined the words that were written on the envelope, he noticed that it was for him. The front of the envelope said, 'For white haired boy cleaning yard.' Matthew took the envelope off the door, then opened it curiously. To his surprise, there were two twenty dollar bills inside. No note, only the money. Matthew smiled happily as he folded the envelope quickly then put it into his deepest pocket. He didn't care now if anyone opened the door. He was rich! He headed back to the yard and quickly cleaned it up. He had really done a good job. He was so happy that as he was bringing the full garbage bags towards the front of the house on the curb, he decided to clean the front yard.

Later on, while the ladies were still up in their rooms, Zoe came back, and Matthew couldn't wait to tell her what had happened while she was gone. He told her everything from 'A' to 'Z'. Even though she liked the part about the money, which he gave her half of, she liked the part about the birds nest, too. Now that Zoe was back, she would help Matthew mind the door and phone, which had been ringing with people giving their sympathies and condolences. Still, the flowers and cards continued to come.

Gloria and Stephanie soon emerged out of their rooms, almost at the same time, and headed downstairs. They both looked a little more rested than they had much earlier. Once the living room came alive with a lot of chatter because the two women were commenting over more flowers and cards, Matthew zoomed up the basement steps taking two at a time, wanting to tell them the story about what had happened earlier at the house next door.

"I thought that you guys would never come out of your rooms!" he said while breathing hard. "I wanted to knock on your doors to give you the news but decided to suffer till you both came out." Once they both gave Matthew their attention, just as he had with his sister earlier, he told his exciting story, but with more dramatic flair this time. Gloria and Stephanie listened intently and every now and then added a little "What?" or "Wow!" They also did a few "Really!" and the ever so famous, "I can't believe it!"

Stephanie stood up from the couch and peeped out the window, so she could see what the back yard looked like. When she finished, she called Gloria over to look, too.

"Wow kiddo, it is much better than before. You did a real professional looking job." She was nodding her head proudly at him.

"Go and check the back. It was worse than you thought," he added.

The two headed for the kitchen, then opened the back door and peered over the fence to get a real good look, and both nodded with a smile.

"Mattster, you really did do a fine job," Stephanie said sincerely.

"Yeah, it was a form of therapy for me. It helped me take my mind off Grampa and stuff." His voice had gotten low and solemn. "Oh well," his voice was now picking up again. "I'm going back downstairs. I've been working on what I was going to say at the funeral." With that, he zoomed out of the kitchen and went back downstairs.

Gloria and Stephanie both looked at one another sadly. They both had sympathy for Matthew. They were too busy thinking about their pain and had forgotten that the twins would be suffering, too.

"Gloria, how did they handle it when you told them that Uncle Archie had died?" Stephanie asked. Gloria took a deep breath then exhaled.

"To be honest with you, they were more concerned for me. Of course, you know that Zoe zoomed into my arms and cried. She shows her emotions more. She kept saying, 'Ma, it's gonna be ok. Grampa is gonna be ok. He's in a better place now.' She had her head on my chest and her arms were around my shoulders, which she was patting. Matthew, on the other hand, was much more reserved with his emotions. He teared up but he was also concerned over how I was. He actually looked defenseless because he wanted to protect me but didn't know how. After a while, he just sat next to me, patting me on my leg, trying to reassure me that everything was going to be just fine. They've been pretty much quiet since they found out, but they also have tried to continue on despite the circumstance. Yesterday when we were still home, I walked past their room and the door was closed. I heard them both talking and crying, even Matthew. But Matthew would never let himself loose like that in front of me. He would do it with Zoe, though. They love each other so much. Their happiness, their sadness, and as you heard, money—they share everything with each other. I guess because they have each other, they are handling it just fine. Isn't it funny how even though they're twins, they are alike in so many ways and yet in others, like showing emotion in public, so different. Zoe wants attention and comfort while Matthew decides he wants to clean the neighbor's backyard!" The two both chuckled over that.

"But Gloria, don't you think that that is kinda weird about what Matthew said about the house next door?"

"I sure do. I wonder why they are so secretive in that house."

"It is also kind of creepy…scary…Do you think that they are doing illegal stuff over there? Lord, Gloria. We are living next to a crack house!" Stephanie's eyes became wide with fear, causing Gloria to laugh over her paranoia.

"Relax, Stephanie. I doubt that my father would've had friends who were living in a crack house or even deal with crack or any other type of drug." Gloria was trying to calm Stephanie down. It was working.

"Oh yeah that's true!" She was nodding her head and smiling in relief.

CHAPTER FIVE:
Wicked Mother-in-Law

Gloria and Stephanie continued talking about the next door neighbors when the phone began to ring. Stephanie was closer to the phone so she reached up and got it off the wall. "Hello, Bunker residence. Well, yes she is. Hold on for a moment." Stephanie put her hand over the receiver. She shrugged her shoulders then looked at Gloria. "It's a woman. She asked to speak to you. I don't have a slightest idea who it is." Stephanie then passed the phone to Gloria, who was wondering who was on the other end.

"Hello?" she said in a friendly manner, looking curious, wondering who could be on the phone. Once Gloria found out who the voice belonged to, she rolled her eyes in annoyance, then slapped her forehead. Stephanie looked at her with concern, then Gloria mouthed the words 'mother-in-law' to Stephanie. When Stephanie saw Gloria's little mime then saw her mouth those horrible words, she also rolled her eyes, stood up quickly, then held up both hands in surrender and headed out of the kitchen, leaving Gloria to talk to a woman that she really had no feelings for whatsoever, and most likely the feelings were mutual.

Ms. Agnes Sinclair Shaw, age 65, was the mother of Gloria's dead husband, Ray, and the grandmother of Zoe and Matthew. She never liked Gloria, even before Gloria and Ray were even married, and she had no problem letting Gloria know how she felt about her. No matter how nice Gloria had been to her, she found nothing but fault in her. "No one is good enough for my baby," she would say of Raymond, and Raymond was a grown man when she had said this. She probably had been saying these words to him his whole life. He never paid her any mind about it and would constantly get into arguments over how she would treat his ex-girlfriends and Gloria, but she never listened. This was who she was and she wasn't going to change, and she still hadn't, even though Ray had been dead for all these years. She was and always would be an old, bitter, manipulative, selfish, thoughtless, self-centered, hateful, mean-spirited fuddy duddy, to Gloria. And these were her good qualities.

Gloria also thought that Agnes was very melodramatic, very theatrical, and it drove her crazy. Gloria hated everything about this old, tired and miserable person, and she hated talking to her on the phone. It would always make her throat feel so tight that it would be hard to breathe and she would become cold all over her body. Gloria had to always tighten her fists till they turned paper white, and she would grit her teeth. Gloria knew that there was going to be a fight every time she spoke to her. Gloria put a feigned smile on her face, trying to psyche herself up to at least be cordial on the phone, but she knew that it was not going to last too long. "Hello Agnes, how are you?" but she was thinking in her head, "Like I really care." Her mouth was curling up at the corners in disgust.

"I guess that you were too good to give me a call when you got in, like you had promised, huh, Gloria." Agnes spat hard and rudely on the other end of the phone.

"I told you, Gloria that it is not worth even trying to be nice to this ole bat!" she said to herself. "Listen here, Ag-nes...!" Gloria spat back her name with utter disdain. "I had other things on my mind that were much more important to worry about than calling you. I don't have to call you the minute I walk through the door." Gloria shot back just as bitterly as Agnes. "I was going to give you a call as soon as I was able. I didn't forget." But in actuality, she really did forget.

"Well anyway, I decided out of the goodness of my heart to call. I have to make sure that SOMEONE is looking out for my grandchildren's welfare.

Gloria didn't like the way that Agnes had said, 'someone,' emphasizing it very strongly. Gloria knew what she meant, too. She was always trying to make Gloria feel like she didn't know how to raise her children. Gloria was starting to feel the blood in her veins boil. She didn't need this right now. Gloria really didn't have to deal with it. She could just hang up on her. That would really get her and shut her up, but no. Agnes knew the all right buttons to push, causing Gloria to stoop down to her level.

"What do you mean by that comment, Ag-nessss?" Are you trying to say that I am not looking out for my children's welfare?" Gloria was following the bait that Agnes had tossed her way. "You know, I've been doing quite well raising the two on my own and they've turned out to be smart, well mannered, respectable teens. As a matter of fact, all my children are doing quite well."

"Well, you didn't do it on your own, dear. My son's insurance policy had a lot to do with it." Whenever Agnes couldn't win an argument against

Gloria, which was 100% of the time, she would always mention the insurance policy that Ray had gotten when he and Gloria got married.

"First of all, the insurance policy that you always like to bring up is for the twins' college. The rest of the money from the policy comes out to be about 250.00 per month, which I have been spreading out over a period of time till the twins reach legal age. My children have everything that they need and most of the things that they want because of me. That's why they like to stay in the house or close by. I know who all their friends are because they bring them to the house instead of them going to their friends' houses, plus I know where they are at all times because they tell me, so I don't appreciate what you are trying to imply." Gloria was becoming very defensive.

"All I am saying, Gloria, is that New York City is, is, so, so unsafe. I mean, l-l-look, at what happened at the World Trade Center! You don't know who you could be sitting next to on an airplane, but nooo, there you go, year after year, sometimes three or four times in one year, sending the twins to NYC on an airplane unaccompanied!" Her voice was becoming louder and Gloria could tell that Agnes was becoming excited because her pitch was becoming higher and squeaky.

"Agnes, the twins loved their grandfather and they love the rest of their family here, and vice versa. Being that the family works, they cannot come to Cali to see them, and because I work, I cannot get to go to NY all of the time, so it is good for them to see their family members. Airport security is much safer than then. I am not going to keep them shut up in the house like two hermits, keeping them away from the outside world. And by the way, the hijacking didn't happen in NY. They only crashed the plane in NY. NY is just as safe as any other city. There are good areas and they know where those are, and then there are bad areas, and thank God, they know where those are too. My children stay away from the bad areas. I taught them the difference between right and wrong."

"Well, well, you might've taught them right from wrong but you didn't teach all those other sickies and lunatics and gang members and hoodlums the same," Agnes spat back, sounding like she was looking for an altercation with her. "Ever since those blacks started their jungle music—what do they call it, hippidy hop? The city just ain't the same!"

Gloria was feeling so dizzy, talking to this narrow-minded ditz that she had to go and sit down. She couldn't believe the nonsense that was spewing out of Agnes's mouth.

"Those city blacks strut around with their pants hanging down, showing their Calvin Kleins, wearing sneakers that they don't even tie up, gigantic gold chains around their necks; they even wear diamond studs in their ears. You cannot tell the difference between the girls or the boys with their hair braided like that. It is just totally unsafe!"

"So, let me get this straight, Agnes. You are saying that the city isn't safe because of blacks and hip hop music and because of the way that they dress and style their hair?" Gloria's anger was subsiding as she started to realize that this woman really wasn't worth her getting her blood pressure up. She had so many other things to worry about. She actually started feeling silly for allowing Agnes to lure her into her trap, but that didn't stop her from putting her in her place.

"Not just them. What about the Italians and the mafia? Don't let me start talking about that!" Agnes added angrily. Gloria really didn't want her talking at all.

"Listen here, Agnes, the mafia has been around long before the Godfather, and before blacks created hip hop music in the city. And for your information, Agnes, white kids are into the hip hop style and culture just as much as blacks. As a matter of fact, your *grandson*," she emphasized strongly, "is into hip hop music and he wears his pants baggy, too." Gloria knew that this would drive Agnes more over the edge than she was already. "So if 'hippidy hop' as you say, bothers you so much, you need to lock yourself away in that depressing place of yours and throw away the key, because gangster rap music was created in California." Gloria said these words ever so sweetly and slowly, so Agnes could digest everything that she was feeding her.

"I knew it! I knew it!" Agnes sounded like she was about to blow a gasket. "You let NYC destroy my grandchildren's young minds! Plus leaving them alone so much and allowing them to watch those MTV and BET shows glorifying all the negativity. I'm surprised that Zoe isn't pregnant and Matthew in jail. NY is a melting pot of nothing but low lives, low class hustlers, poor white trash and darkies, and, and, those Latinos! I forgot about them! How can I forget about them wetbacks?" Agnes was talking a mile a minute and Gloria envisioned drool coming down her mouth which made her laugh, covering her mouth.

"You forgot the Asians." Gloria began egging her on just to see how long Agnes was going to fall for it.

"Oooh, the Asians! You can't trust them. They never forgave us over the war. You mark my words; there's a reason why there's an Asian restaurant on almost every block!"

"And what would that reason be, pray tell?" she said jokingly, but Agnes didn't catch on.

"Well, well, I don't know right now." Agnes was stumbling over her words causing Gloria to laugh as she covered her mouth so Agnes couldn't hear. "But mark my words, one day they are going to avenge the deaths of their forefathers. I see it all the time on television." Then her voice got low, like she wanted to say a secret and didn't want everyone to hear. "You know that they bring that opium drug over from their country?" Gloria was ready to burst at the seams from laughter, but she was trying to retain her composure.

"Everything that you've said is happening all over America; as a matter of fact, all over the world, not just NYC. I am originally a New Yorker, born and raised, and I feel 100% safe sending the kids here alone and I feel safe walking up and down the street with them," she said firmly. Agnes hesitated a few seconds trying to think of what to say.

"Well Gloria, I guess if the city has all these negative aspects about it, you are definitely a New Yorker." Now she was the one who was talking snail-slow. Gloria felt like it was time to put the nail through Agnes's coffin.

"Well Agnes, if that's true, then the same holds for you. You are originally from Mudlick, Kentucky, which makes you 100% a mud licker. Like you said, we are where we come from." Gloria could tell that with that comment, she really got Agnes's goat.

"Well, you look here, Gloria...!" Agnes replied, trying to get the last word, but Gloria wasn't going to allow that to happen, so she just talked over her.

"Agnes, as usual, it was hell talking to you. I gotta go. I'll go get the twins and let them know that you are on drugs—oops! I meant to say the line." Gloria quipped. With that, she put the phone down on the table hard so that the sound would have hurt Agnes's ear, then headed through the kitchen door towards the basement to let the twins know that their grandmother was on the phone.

Gloria looked at Stephanie, who was sitting on the couch reading some of the cards that were with the flowers. Stephanie then looked up and caught Gloria's stare and smiled. "Oh, I see that you've survived, huh?"

"Barely." Gloria pretended to wipe sweat off of her forehead, as if she had just run a marathon.

"That conversation was so difficult that I would've preferred having my hand slammed in a car door with a sumo wrestler leaning up against the door frame!"

Stephanie laughed at the remark, while Gloria went to the basement door. She opened it up and was hit by the sound of loud music. "Hey guys, your grandmother is on the phone. She..." But before she had a chance to finish her sentence, someone turned off the stereo, then she heard heavy sounds of footsteps running towards the steps.

"Grandma!" they shouted in unison as they began zooming up the steps. Gloria stepped out of the way because if she didn't, she would've gotten crushed in the stampede. She watched them as they smiled from ear to ear, eyes wide and breathing hard as they made their way out of the basement, then through the kitchen door. Gloria knew that one thing about the twins was that they loved their grandmother. In their eyes, she could do no wrong, even though she didn't get along with her.

Gloria closed the basement door then looked at Stephanie as she shook her head.

"Oooh that woman!" Gloria exclaimed in a loud growl as she headed towards the big chair. "If I only had a penny for every time that old witch got on my nerves, I would have more money than Bill Gates! She has gone beyond my nerves. She has even gone beyond my reserved nerve!"

"I just don't know how you do it, Gloria. That woman is really in a class all her own." Stephanie was putting down the card that she was reading.

"Tell me where the school is so I can burn it down! She is just plain awful! Bad enough I had to deal with her when Ray was alive. I thought maybe it would've gotten a little better after he passed away, but nooo! She's just been going full steam ahead!" Gloria was leaning back in the chair while putting her feet up on the foot rest in front of her. "She made me so tired that I feel like I have just done the Indy 500 on foot!"

"I've only met her once but I've talked to her on the phone it seems like a painful million times, and that voice! That voice! I'm surprised that I didn't recognize it instantly."

"Being that she is so theatrical, she probably disguised her voice, knowing her. She'll do anything to have her way. It is either her way or no way. If she cannot have her way, she is just more evil than usual, pure 100% evil. Bad enough she was like that with Ray, now she is trying to do that with the twins."

"Now..?" Stephanie perked up. "Gloria, she started as soon as Ray died."

"That ole biddy doesn't have anyone else in her life but the twins. Wouldn't you think that she would try to be civil with me for their sake? That's why I don't let them go over and see her. The only way that they will get to see her is if she is civil to me, so until then, I'm not permitting anyone into my house who does not respect me."

"You are right, Gloria. I don't blame you, not one bit."

"That woman, and I do use that word loosely, has caused me nothing but unnecessary stress, and I mean from the first time that I met her. Raymond had already told me about her even before I met her, but I never thought that anyone could be as bad as he had said. Boy, was I mistaken!"

For some unknown reason, she unconsciously started rubbing her wedding finger even though she hadn't worn a ring on that finger since Ray died.

"You know, Stephanie, Agnes had Raymond when she was only fifteen years old...pregnant at the age of fourteen. I guess in good ole Mudlick, Kentucky, she must not have had a television set. She had to find some way to stay busy," Gloria said with a fake and exaggerated southern accent.

"Oh Glory Gloria, that's terrible!" Stephanie was shocked by Gloria's remarks.

"I'm sorry, Stephanie. She just brings out the worst in me. Well, anyway, Ray said that the small family that she had kicked her out, leaving her and him to fend for themselves. He was all that she had and she loved him very much. She has had a hard life doing menial work and when that didn't work, welfare soon followed. I guess that would make a person bitter, but she loved her Ray Ray. That is what he told me that she called him when he was a baby."

"Ray Ray. How cute," Stephanie responded.

"Even though she was his mother, the age difference was so very close—a baby raising a baby. It was as if she was his girlfriend or something. She kept girlfriends from his grasp because she was so very jealous. It was as if she was trying to keep him for herself. Not in a sexual way, of course, but more like a security blanket. I guess that he felt like she felt that if he had left her, she would be left with nothing. She had sacrificed her life for him and he should do the same for her. When he started to become rebellious, that was when she started showing real jealousy. She wanted to keep him in the house, locked away. She didn't want him to have friends over. She never gave him a birthday party, and she didn't want him to go out with friends. Not even to a movie, but he did anyway. It bothered him for a long time but when he realized that she wasn't going to change and that she would always see him as a little child, little Ray Ray, he was just going to ignore her actions and go on with his life, even though she tried to convince him that her life would end without him. He tried to explain this to his friends and eventually girlfriends, hoping that they would understand. Agnes has done some real cruel things to Ray's girlfriends. Ray told me. He had laughed at it later, but at the time he found out he was very angry with her. He said that she had thrown grape juice on girlfriends' clothes, didn't give him important messages, made up lies about the girlfriends—really crazy stuff like that." While Gloria was talking, Stephanie looked flabbergasted as she shook her head.

"I remember when we were first seeing each other and he invited me over to the house—well, when I got there, this young woman who could have passed for his sister told me that Ray was upstairs in his bedroom with his girlfriend. I didn't know that the woman wasn't his sister. It was Agnes, of course. She was lying....of course. But I didn't know of her evil streak then. I believed what she said and left angrily. I found out all about her when Raymond came to my house later that night, after he found out what his mother had done."

"Oh, that is so cruel. Not just that she did that to you, but that she would do that to Ray."

"Not to her. She thinks that she is a wonderful person and mother. She thinks that she was only protecting him and looking out for his best interests."

"If I had a mother like that, I would rather have been adopted."

"Girl, I know what you mean. I don't know how my Raymond was able to deal with that woman." After Gloria made this comment, she began thinking to herself, then she chuckled. "Stephanie, I thought that Daddy was a trip, but this chick is an adventure."

"Hey, Gloria, isn't it weird that Uncle Archie really liked Raymond and how Agnes didn't and doesn't like you?"

"That's very weird. Daddy was very overprotective of me, but Agnes just went overboard! She needed a life and needs a life now instead of trying to live hers through other people." They both went quiet for a few seconds as they thought, then they both looked at each other as if they both thought of the same thing and couldn't wait to say it.

"Hey! Do you remember when..." Then they both started laughing after they said this in unison. "Stephanie, you must have smelled my thoughts!"

"I know exactly what you are getting ready to say. Do I remember when Uncle Archie met Agnes...Right?"

"Oooh yeah!" Gloria laughed and slapped both knees. "And when you met her, too."

"That's right!" Stephanie nodded so rapidly that her head looked loose from the neck up. "Oh, I didn't like her. I didn't like her at all, the way that she looked at me. She kept saying that I secretly was your illegitimate daughter from another relationship and that you made me live with Uncle Archie so no one would know that you really were nothing but a Jezebel, a whore, a slut..."

"Oh, boy, I remember. She almost made you cry."

"She sure did and she wasn't ashamed about it. At that time, I was so young. I had never had an adult insult me like that before. I just wanted to kill her. But I remember that Ray was just so sweet to me, that he took me into the kitchen and gave me ice cream and cake and had a long talk with me about her. It calmed me down a whole lot."

"I had never seen my dad so mad in his life. At a man, yes, but Daddy was actually so mad with Agnes that I thought he was going to hit her." Gloria started to make angry facial expressions as she spoke. "Hey, Steph, I remember Daddy saying to me, 'Gloria, I thought the devil was inside that little girl from the *Exorcist*, but oooh nooo! It jumped out of her and went into the wrinkles of that trifling bitch over there!'" Gloria was so animated with her reenactment of her father that it made Stephanie laugh in remembrance.

"Agnes made the whole visit miserable, and believe me, I am sure that she had done this on purpose. No one wanted to be around her and she and Uncle Archie kept getting into it—and what about poor Raymond? He was red from the time that we walked through the door till we left. The redness was not from the California sun. He was so embarrassed."

"Yeah, he was. The only thing that he kept saying was, 'I'm sorry. I'm so very sorry.' I felt badly for him. He loved me and he loved his mother. He was so confused, and that's what she wanted. Someplace down under that thick skull of hers, she had actually thought that Raymond would choose her over me." Gloria then smiled widely. "But she thought wrong. Boy, did she think wrong."

"Yeah, Gloria, I guess that Raymond turned into Popeye that night. She had taken him to the limit and it was all he could stands and he couldn't stands no more! As a matter of fact, that was the first time I ever saw a son send his own mother to her room! That scene was priceless!"

"Uh-ha. She kept acting up, being so theatrical, ranting and raving about something or other and…"

"It was about the seating arrangements at the table," Stephanie interrupted.

Gloria then snapped her finger in remembrance. "That's right! It was the seating arrangements. I remember now. She was sitting at one end of the table and Raymond was sitting at the other end. I was sitting next to Joey and I was next to Ray. Daddy and you sat on the opposite side from us, with Daddy next to Ray."

"Yeah," Stephanie said coldly. "Y'all had to leave me and Joey to sit next to the wicked witch of the south. Oh, by the way, I forgot to tell you. Thanks a lot!" Stephanie was playfully cutting her eyes at Gloria.

"But it was funny, though, because you moved so close to Daddy that I thought that you eventually were going to be sitting on his lap!"

"Well, Joey was following my lead too. For a minute there, I had forgotten that you were Gloria. I thought that you were Santa Claus because Joey looked like he was about to sit on your lap and give you his Christmas list."

"Put it this way: that night, everyone felt the tension and it could have been cut with a knife." Gloria added.

"I think that she was in hog heaven, like a pig wallowing in its own feces."

"Which one was Agnes, Stephanie, the pig or the feces?" She said jokingly, causing Stephanie to bulge out her eyes in shock while she laughed. "In all seriousness though, he had prepared a beautiful meal. It was like Thanksgiving."

"That's true. Roasted chicken, glazed ham, sweet corn, mixed vegetables, broccoli, yams and buttermilk biscuits. Only thing that was missing was the turkey. The fruit punch with the fruit cocktail inside was a wonderful touch, too."

"Yeah, it was a prize inside of a prize. What kid doesn't like fruit punch? But you forgot about…"

"Ooh, I didn't forget. My roast beef."

"That's right. Your roast beef," Stephanie echoed.

"I thought that it would be nice to bring something as a gift. Everyone thought it was a nice idea. Ray loved it. But I should've known. Anything that Raymond liked, Agnes was going to hate, from girlfriends to food. You should've seen her face when I presented it to Raymond. When she saw it, she was like, 'What..the..hell..is..tthhaatt??!!' Like it was a dead rat or something. I felt my heart drop right then and there; but Daddy behaved great. Well, considering the circumstances."

"I must agree."

"I remember that Daddy said, 'Don't pay her no mind, little girl. She's just use to catching her own prey with her fake wooden dentures.' When Daddy said that, I thought that I was going to burst out laughing at the table."

"She was so rude to Uncle Archie at the table, though, but didn't he get her every time she tried to throw a zinger at him?"

Gloria laughed and nodded. "Yes he sure did. I remember when Agnes said, 'Hey, Mr. Bunkgunk,' knowing that his last name was Bunker. 'I hope there is enough food at the table for you. The way your buttons are struggling to hold in that big gut of yours, it doesn't look like you shied away from too many meals.' I quickly looked towards Ray's face and he had lowered it, biting his tongue, then shaking his head in displeasure."

"But Uncle Archie was quick. He said, 'Well, let's just find out, Rosemary's baby, by passing me the roast beef, if your pale bony old-looking arthritis curling fingers could manage a task like that.' Oh Gloria, when he said that without missing a beat, I thought that I was going to spit the fruit punch across the table. I wanted to laugh so badly. And the funniest thing about it was he made her look at her fingers to see if they really did look like the way he had said. Oh, Gloria! It was priceless; just priceless!" Stephanie leaned back on the couch and laughed so hard that she began hugging her stomach while she lifted her feet off the floor. She even had tears in her eyes. Gloria looked at Stephanie, which made her start laughing also. After Gloria and Stephanie were able to catch their breath, they continued talking, trying to control their laughter.

"I liked it when she noticed that all of us were hovering around Ray as we ate and that there was a huge gap between us and her. She wasn't getting any attention and she definitely didn't like that."

"Yeah, I remember that. Everyone was eating and enjoying our conversations, but Mrs. Attention-stealer was feeling left out, so she decided to get up. We were all laughing at something Raymond had said, then out of the blue, she said, 'This roast beef is rubbery and it is too salty!' The expression on her face was one that a small infant would make when they don't like the taste of something."

"You know, Stephanie, Ray had put his hand on my leg under the table. He knew what his mother was trying to do. He just wanted me to not pay her any mind. But that didn't stop him from saying something to her. He said that the roast beef actually tasted delicious and that he was about to go for his third helping. Oh, how I loved him so." Gloria smiled like a little girl and fluttered her eyelids.

"Uncle Archie was the best, though." Stephanie felt a laughing attack about to start all over again. "He said something like, 'It's all right there, little girl. You can't blame her for feeling the way that she does. You know that reptiles have to stay away from salt. Salt does something to their skin. It makes their skin saggy and blotchy and it causes the flesh to break out in boils and something that looks like hideous painful puss bumps.' Then he went quiet. After that, he looked at Agnes and said, 'You might as well eat up, Toots, because it's definitely too late for you.' Lord, Gloria! I don't know how he was able to be so funny without bursting out laughing!" hollered Stephanie.

"He was a riot, wasn't he?" Gloria had to agree. "But Agnes sure didn't think so. The look on her face was of pure disdain and outrage. Boy, do I wish that I had brought a camera with me."

"I remember her standing up from the table, being very dramatic as she said, 'Now you see here, Mr. Bunkwipe...' but Uncle Archie cut her off quickly by saying, 'See where? I really don't want to see any more of ya. What I already see is hurting me enough!' Needless to say, Agnes was totally speechless and very insulted."

"She said, 'Raymond, are you going to allow this-this-this fat, balding, New York City sleazebag to come in here and insult your loving mother like this?' She had pointed her long, bony finger toward Uncle Archie accusingly, causing Uncle Archie to rub it in by lifting up his glass as if he was about to make a toast."

"My poor baby was trying to be host and mediator at the same time. He knew that she had started it and that's what he told her. He said, 'Now look, Ma. Fair is fair. You started it. If you can't take it, don't dish it out.

Now please sit back down and let's finish this wonderful meal. You are frightening the children.' He was so nice and respectful, the way he talked to her despite the way she was acting."

"Yeah, but she wasn't nice and respectful the way that she talked to him or us. She was downright crude, rude and obnoxious. She did sit down but that mouth kept going. Remember how she sounded like she was about to erupt? She was like, 'Why should I care about these-these-these New York City sewer rats?' Oh, Stephanie, when she said that about you and Joey, I felt these little hot pricks go up my back, then behind my neck. I was boiling with rage. I was about to go O.J. on her. Thank God Ray felt my anger.

He was actually angry himself. Don't let me tell you about your Uncle Archie. He was not a happy camper. He didn't care what she had said about him, but you and Joey were off limits. That was when, like you said, the Popeye in him took over."

"Oh, Gloria, I remember like it was yesterday. By the way, Joey and I were very offended by the rude remark. She couldn't deal with the punches thrown by an adult. She had to pick on the little kids, because she knew we weren't going to say anything. But Ray was to the rescue. First he said it real low with his head down. I think that he was trying to control his temper. He said, 'Mom, go to your room.' I couldn't believe what I was hearing and apparently neither did Agnes. After we all looked at one another in shock, including Agnes, she said, 'What did you say?' in total disbelief, then he said it again louder but definitely more forceful, 'Go..to..your..room!' Every time Agnes tried to say something, he quickly interrupted, but when he said, 'Now!' I have to admit that I jumped in my seat. That was all she wrote when he said that. Joey and I looked at each other and smiled even though we had our heads slightly down. We were very uncomfortable. We had never experienced anything like that before."

"He knew it was uncomfortable for you, too. That's why it bothered him enough to tell his own mother to leave the table. I was sitting next to him and I saw tears well up in his eyes. Agnes just stood there in utter shock and humiliation as she glanced around the table in total fury. But then she did something that I had never seen an adult do. She stormed away from the table stomping her feet and talking—no-no—mumbling under her breath, 'Why should I have to be the one to go to my room?' She was saying other things but I couldn't make it out as she stomped her way up the stairs, then to her room where she slammed the door shut. She acted just like a little child who didn't get her way."

"No-no, Gloria. She acted like a spoiled brat having a temper tantrum."

Stephanie and Gloria got very quiet for a few seconds, then Gloria spoke. "But, Stephanie, you gotta admit that it was hilarious the way that she stomped away from the table!" Once again, like school-aged girls, they burst into hyena laughing. Stephanie even stood up and started imitating the way Agnes stomped away. They were both having a good laugh at Agnes's expense. While that was going on, the twins came out of the kitchen and then stared at Stephanie with a smile, a curious smile. Zoe looked at Stephanie from head to toe.

"What on heaven's green earth are you doing, Stephanie?" Zoe was now plopping herself into Edith's chair. Matthew walked behind Gloria and started massaging her neck. Gloria saw no reason to tell him to stop. Stephanie was trying to think of a quick lie, because they had caught her off guard. She really didn't know what to say, so she said the first thing that came to her head. "I uh, was just, uh, well, what I mean is that, hmm, it was this, ah, hey! I thought you guys were speaking to your grandmother." After Stephanie said this, Gloria thought that her response was great quick thinking.

"Yeah, we were, but we couldn't talk long because it was long distance. She said that Mom kept her on the phone hogging it up, so there would be less time for us to talk." Zoe replied then she looked over to Gloria. "Come on, Ma. When grandma calls, you have to be fair and share her, okay? You know that we love to talk to her." Gloria leaned over towards Zoe, then patted her on her hands and looked right in her big, doll-sized eyes with all seriousness.

"Honey, I don't wanna share anything that concerns your grandmother. I would rather share the mange than to share anything concerning your grandma."

"Oh my!" Zoe exclaimed, laughing, as she got out of the chair, then she and Matthew headed back down to the basement.

CHAPTER SIX:
Meeting Some Dear Old Friends

Once the twins were gone, Gloria and Stephanie continued in light conversation. After that, Stephanie went back reading cards. Gloria headed into the kitchen to make some important calls. When she was done, she headed back into the living room where Stephanie was. Stephanie looked up at her from the couch as she approached.

"You wanna watch some TV? *General Hospital* is about to come on."

Gloria didn't feel like watching any TV. She was rested, she'd made all of her important calls, she wasn't hungry and she was tired of crying. She knew what she would do.

"Nah, Stephanie. I don't feel like seeing other people cry on a soap. I'm going outside to get some fresh air."

"You're going to sit on the porch?" she asked, getting up. "I'll sit out there with ya if you want."

"No. I am going down to the bar. The neighborhood has laid flowers, cards and candles up against the place. I also just wanna see how the neighborhood has changed. Why don't you come along with me?"

"I would love to, believe me I would, but I've been waiting for that knucklehead agent of mine to get back in contact with me. I've been waiting since earlier and he still hasn't called." Stephanie sat back down on the couch but looked towards the TV, contemplating if she should turn it on to watch *General Hospital*. She shrugged her shoulders, then got up and turned the tube on. While she was doing that, Gloria had walked over to the basement and yelled downstairs to see if the twins wanted to go walking with her, but they declined. She was on her own. Gloria started to head up the stairs towards the bedroom to get her purse and things. While in the room, she checked herself out in the mirror, making sure she looked fine.

"No runny eyeliner from crying", she said to herself as she ran her fingers over her eyes. "Check." Then she began fixing her hair, making sure that it didn't look frizzy or disheveled. "Hair looks to be in place." While Gloria was doing all of her checkpoints, she had heard the doorbell ring downstairs. A few seconds later, she started to hear some talking after the door was opened then closed.

"Well, whoever it is, Stephanie let them come in. It must be someone that I know," she muttered to herself. She tried to make out the sound of the voice but couldn't because the person was talking low, but Gloria could tell that it was a female's voice. Gloria continued fixing herself up, then picked up her purse and started out of the bedroom. She headed downstairs where the voices were becoming more loud and clear. Once Gloria reached the bottom step, she noticed that the woman had her back to her and hadn't heard her come down the steps. She was too busy talking to Stephanie, who was away from Gloria but was able to see her when she came down the steps.

As Stephanie glanced toward Gloria, the woman turned around so she could see her. When Gloria saw who it was, she opened her eyes very wide, showing her total approval. Her mouth dropped in total surprise, and then she screamed for joy. The woman did exactly the same. Standing in front of Gloria was a woman about Stephanie's height, about Gloria's age, full figured and vivacious. She had a natural tanned complexion, big black Spanish eyes with curly full neck-length hair, and she had her hands out to hug Gloria and simultaneously Gloria did the same. Gloria knew who this woman was. Her name was Teresa Betancourt.

Teresa Betancourt was the Spanish tenant who had moved into Gloria's room when Gloria and Mike moved next door. Gloria and Teresa embraced each other tightly as they both started crying tears of joy and they both began talking all at once, the way Zoe and her three girlfriends had talked just a few hours earlier. When they finally released their very long embrace, they extended each other at arm's length so they could really get a good look at each other, and in unison, after checking each other out from head to toe, still smiling, they both said in unison, "You're fat!" Then they both burst out laughing. Stephanie joined in with the laughter, also.

"Oh, Gloria, you are still just as beautiful and youthful looking as you were when I last saw you!" Teresa was wiping the tears away from her soaked eyes.

"Oh, thank you so much, Teresa, and you look beautiful too!" Gloria was now leading Teresa toward the living room for her to sit down. "Please, Teresa, have a seat. Sit in Daddy's chair." Stephanie turned off the television then sat back on the couch. Gloria sat in Edith's chair.

"Wow! I am actually going to be sitting in Mr. Bunkers's chair!" she said in shock. "That truly is an honor!" They all chuckled at her comment, then her face went serious and solemn. "Oh, Gloria, like I was saying to Stephanie,

I am so sorry to hear about Mr. Bunkers. I really did love him. I'm going to miss him." After she said this, Gloria reached across the chair and patted Teresa on her hands.

"Thank you so much. That's very sweet of you to say. He loved you, too. He would always say to me, 'Hey, little girl, I wonder how that little wisecrackin' hot tamale is doing. You know the one. The one who told me to chut up?"

Teresa started telling them stories about Archie, making them laugh. Teresa then started wiggling her butt in the chair as she remarked, "No wonder Mr. Bunkers never liked people sitting in his chair. This chair is very comfortable! I'm much wider than back then and my tush has spread out into all the right spots in the chair!" She threw her hands up, wiggled then stretched. "I feel like the queen of England!" The three were having a good time talking about Archie when Gloria asked her how she found out about Archie passing away.

"Gloria, everyone knows. Mi Novio, Hector, told me. He found out from another bus driver like him, someone who did the bus route over here. Apparently during his lunch break, he wanted to eat at the bar and saw a sign in the window. Yep Gloria, everyone knows. Archie Bunker's place is very popular." Gloria noticed that Teresa still referred to her father as Mr. Bunkers instead of just Bunker.

"I had to come by and show my respects. You guys are very important in the chapters of my life. Even though I haven't seen you in years doesn't mean I don't think about you all." Gloria understood exactly what she was talking about. There were so many times that she thought about Chris, even though she hadn't seen him in decades.

"When was the last time we saw each other? Do you remember?"

"I sure do, Gloria. It was when I came for your mother's funeral." Her voice had gone almost low as a whisper and just as soft. "What an angel she was, Mrs. Bunker, just an angel." Teresa was nodding her head as she looked like she was about to cry, but she tried to control herself. "Now I am going to be there for your father's. At least now they are back together again." Gloria nodded in agreement. "You know, I wanted to call you to give my condolences but I don't have a phone. I..." But before Teresa was able to finish her sentence, Gloria and Stephanie both sighed sadly.

"Oh I'm sorry that you aren't doing well." Gloria replied, but she responded quickly.

"Oh no guys, as a matter of fact, it is just the opposite. See, all our stuff is packed up and sitting in our hallway. We are moving. We were supposed to have been out by now but the landlord at the new place is giving us a wrap around."

Stephanie looked confused, then realized what she actually meant to say. "You mean 'run around,' Teresa."

"That too!" she replied. "He had told us that the place would be ready by the first and today is the fourth and the place still isn't ready. So the phone company had turned off the line in our place then transferred it over to the new one. I do have your number in my phonebook but like I said, everything is packed. I even tried to call from the payphones in the street but they were all broken, so I decided just to come and take my chances to see if you were home, and I am sure glad that I did."

Teresa was now smiling again as she looked at both the women fondly. "So Gloria, how is Joey and did you and Mike ever get back together again?" Teresa was all ears. Gloria took a deep breath and then started telling Teresa about everything, from the time of her mother's funeral all the way up to the present. Teresa was blown away by Gloria's life but was happy and excited to know that she had twin teens and she couldn't wait to see them. Gloria called them up from the basement and proudly introduced them to Teresa. They smiled and greeted her respectfully, which Teresa liked, and she complimented them on their manners and looks. They smiled modestly and talked to her for a few minutes then excused themselves and went back downstairs in the basement.

When the twins left, Teresa shook her head with pure joy. "Oh, Gloria, you should be so very proud. You have some heartbreakers right there."

"Well, what about you, Teresa? How has your life turned out since I last saw you?" Now Gloria and Stephanie were all ears.

"Well, I moved to Flushing after moving around from different places. Being a nurse had brought me to many different hospitals and nursing homes. I had a very close patient that I had been taking care of who had died of old age in my care. It affected me pretty badly and I had decided that I didn't want to deal with sadness and unhappiness anymore. I needed to get into another line of business, so I went from being a nurse to working in a bakery. I started working there at the bottom, just doing the register. I was happy and at peace. I lucked out because the owner liked me and started me out learning how to do everything else in the place, from making donuts and bagels to cookies and cakes. It blew the owner's mind that I picked up so quickly. I never told him that I had actually already had experience. Your mother had taught me how to do the stuff when I was living here. Well, as you can see," she said as she glanced over her body, "that's when I started getting more full figured." She chuckled. "The owner was really happy with my work. He liked me a lot. Speaking of liking me a lot, there was somebody else at the time who liked me a lot, too, but in a different way. He was tall, dark, and handsome with an excellent body which smelled like cologne." Gloria could see that Teresa looked like she was becoming high as she remembered back. "Every morning, he would come into the shop and order the same thing: an everything bagel, dark, with butter on both sides and a regular cup of coffee. He had a thick Latin accent which made me think of home. Hell, Gloria, it also made me want to melt every time I heard him. I got to admit that for awhile he flirted with me but I played hard to get. After awhile, I put away that childish behavior and just said, "Look, do you wanna take me out or what? I ain't getting any younger!" Teresa was imitating herself and how she was back then by putting her hands on her hips and wiggling them. Stephanie laughed as Teresa put on her show. Stephanie never had the pleasure of knowing Teresa back then, but she liked her personality. Teresa remembered meeting Stephanie but Stephanie was so young when Edith had passed away, plus on that day, Stephanie had met so many people that all the faces were a blur. "From that day on, we have been together ever since. Hector, mi novio, has given me three beautiful daughters. My oldest hija, Izabel, she is 20, Carlotta is 19 and my youngest, Yazmin, is 16, and all three are good kids like yours. Izabel goes to Baruch in Manhattan. She wants to be in Management. Carlotta is out of school. She did get accepted to go to college but hasn't decided what she wants to do. She is an excellent dancer and singer, too." This caught Stephanie's attention.

"Oh?" Stephanie replied as she opened her eyes wide, perking up a tad.

"Yeah, she's been in some music videos as a background dancer. She was a dancer; not like those hoochie mommas that you all see on BET or MTV. I only allowed her to be in videos if they were done with her clothes on, and it had to be real dancing. No shaking her tail feathers." When Teresa said this, she started shaking her body, causing the two to chuckle. "Nothing major, though, but she only does those videos for fun."

"And her singing?" Stephanie asked. She and the young girl had a lot in common.

"Nothing yet, she's hoping for something, but like I said, it's all for fun now."

"And Yazmin?"

"Oh, Yazmin," she said so very proudly. "She is a straight A student in school. She's a beautiful little brainiac. She is always studying. She can speak four languages fluently. I don't know where she inherited that from. I can barely speak one! Anyway," she chuckled, "all my girls can speak at least two, and that's more than I can."

"Well, they sound like a wonderful family, don't they, Gloria?"

"Oh, most definitely. Once you get all set up in your new place, we will have you over for dinner." Stephanie looked at Gloria strangely when she said this. "Let's try not to lose contact with each other this time." Stephanie quickly interrupted Gloria before she said anything else.

"Ah, Gloria, you are forgetting something. You aren't staying. You are going back to California." Gloria was stunned, then came back to reality.

"Oh yeah, that's right." She laughed embarrassedly. "I'm sorry, Teresa. I just got so caught up in the moment, seeing you. I forgot that I didn't live here anymore."

"So why don't you just move back, then?" Teresa asked, as if it wouldn't be a problem.

"Oh, Teresa, I have my job there, and Joey is there, plus it's the beginning of September. School just started. I would hate to take them out of school now and relocate."

"I don't know, Gloria. All that stuff sounds easy to do. It would be no big deal for you to move back home. Plus, what is going happen to the bar?"

"I don't know anything right now, Teresa. I am just taking one task at a time."

"I understand, Gloria. Everything must be very confusing for you right now."

"You don't know the half of it," she replied. Stephanie saw that the conversation was on the verge of getting sad again, so she quickly tried to change the subject.

"So, Teresa, why have you decided now to move after being in your location for so long?" When Stephanie said this, Teresa turned from Gloria and was now facing her.

"Well, Stephanie, we just outgrew it. We will still be living in Flushing, though. We're moving over by Main Street but up Northern Blvd. We'll be near Flushing High, the YMCA and Town Hall. You must know the area."

"Yeah, I sure do."

"Well anyway, the apartment where we live at now has completely been going down the chute and…"

"You mean down the tubes?" Stephanie interrupted as she smiled.

"No-no! I mean down the chute, the garbage chute!" Gloria and Stephanie laughed at the remark. "Actually, I should have said down the toilet! Any of those three phrases would have been correct. It was an old building when I moved in there with mi novio, Hector. He said proudly at the time that it had been converted into a co-op…Psshh!" she exclaimed, waving off what Hector had said. "That place was no co-op. It was more of a flip flop if you asked me!" Teresa began rolling her eyes.

"You mean, flop house, don't you, Teresa?"

"That too!" Teresa continued. "Actually we had been looking for a nice place for a while, ever since the landlord at our place stopped making repairs, then the security became almost nonexistent. The neighborhood itself is nice, though. I hate to leave it. With the kind of money that we are paying, we thought that we could find something better. I have three young women living with me. I have to know that they are going to be safe, plus the place is just too small, with only two bedrooms. That's four women and one man using only one small bathroom. It is not a pretty sight. My apartment in the morning looks like Grand Central Station! So, making a long story longer, we began seeing places and filling out applications, but nothing till we saw this beautiful building being put up. Fourteen stories high, with an inside underground pool with 24 hour security and cameras on each floor."

"Wow, Teresa, that sounds wonderful! Have you seen the completion yet?"

"No, not yet, but we did see the model. Our apartment is on the second floor with a terrace. It has three huge bedrooms, and the main bedroom has its own bathroom. The living room is huge and so is the kitchen. I'm a big woman. I need a big kitchen."

"So what seems to be the holdup?"

"Well, the people at the new building office said everything is not quite ready yet. Not all the wall to wall carpet had been laid out yet. Some of the wiring is not done, and the electricity and plumbing is not all in yet. They said that everything should be done by the weekend. If not, maybe just one more week."

"Well, that's good. Thank God they haven't turned off the electricity in the place where you are living now."

"That's true, but we had to pay another month's rent there. We had told the landlord that we would be out by now. He had given the apartment to someone else, but we are still in it. That family has probably packed up and is ready to move just like us."

"Well, come next week, you'll be in a brand new building with wall to wall carpet and an underground pool."

"Yeah, I know. I am really excited about it. It's near public transportation so the kids could get to and fro without doing a lot of walking, it's on mi novio Hector's bus route and last but not least, it's near Main Street where all the stores are."

"When was the last time you went by the building to check it out?"

"Actually, I have only gone once, but Hector, has gone by a couple of times."

"Has anybody moved into the building or is it just your floor that hasn't been done?"

"Well, I don't know because Hector said that when he went there, the rental office was closed and the lobby was locked. He said that he looked through the glass doors and it looked like it had been completed but he said when he stood in front of the building and looked up, it didn't look like anyone had moved in yet. But the landscaping was all done and the windows and terraces were all completed and clean. That's good because we've paid a lot for perfection," Teresa said proudly.

"Are you going to be paying the same amount there that you are paying where you are now?"

"Exactly the same amount, plus we get an extra huge bedroom, an extra bathroom and terrace, plus everything is new, new, new and brand new. Only thing was that they asked for two months rent in advance and two months security, not to mention, we had to put a binder on it immediately so no one else would get it. They also asked for an application fee. It's a lot of money but it's worth it."

"That sure does sound like a lot of money." For some reason, Gloria did not feel comfortable about this apartment deal. She shot a look toward Stephanie, who caught her look. Gloria had a feeling that Stephanie felt the same way that she was feeling, but Gloria wasn't going to tell that to Teresa.

The three continued talking for awhile, and Jerry still hadn't called Stephanie. She excused herself and headed into the kitchen to talk privately. While she was gone, Gloria and Teresa continued talking till Gloria asked Teresa if she would like to walk with her to the bar and she said yes. Before she left, she went to the basement and yelled down to the twins that she and Teresa were heading to the bar. She did the same to Stephanie, too. Once that was all done, Gloria and Teresa left out the house and headed to the bar.

CHAPTER SEVEN:
Gloria's Off to See the Bar

As they both headed down the blocks, they pointed to where one-family houses used to be and who used to live there. Now in those lots stood tall apartment buildings with terraces. No front yards with little kids playing in them; just concrete sidewalks leading you toward two glass doors which led into lobbies with elevators. Mostly all the new apartment buildings or co-ops had that light colored brick look on the outside or had that fancy stone design to it. They also commented about the stores that were still in the neighborhood and businesses that had long gone. They passed by one block that used to have three bars. One of them was at the corner; the other two were separated by two stores in the middle. The corner bar was still there but the owners were Chinese and only Chinese patrons went there. Even the awning was written in Chinese, which wasn't very welcoming to an American. It kind of told the neighborhood what kind of clientele they wanted inside. The other two bars were long gone. The one on the right side used to be where all the Irish patrons went to drink and be rowdy. Now it was a Korean dry cleaning store. The other bar on the left side was where the so-called Americans went. It was now a Chinese herbs and spices shop. The two stores in the middle used to be a Jewish sewing shop. They were now a Chinese grocery store that sold all American products. On the opposite corner used to be a luncheonette run by Americans. It was now a video rental store with American and Asian tapes. Gone were the pizza shops and hamburger and ice cream joints. In all their places were Chinese restaurants, herbal shops, flower shops and nail salons. If the old timers in the neighborhood wanted to go shopping for American food, they would have to walk over to Northern Blvd. or walk the opposite way toward Roosevelt Avenue for McDonalds, Burger King, Pizza Hut or Dominoes, or even one of the big American supermarkets. They definitely commented on how the neighborhood had changed.

As they finally made their way to the block of the bar, Gloria could see from afar that people were stopping in front of the place and reading the sign that was posted on the gate. Some walked away shaking their head, not believing that Archie was actually gone, while others were writing down the information about the funeral that was on the sign. It really touched Gloria's heart that people cared for her father.

Gloria didn't rush to get to the bar. She took her time, probably on purpose. She continued admiring all the new businesses that were on the block, but deep down inside, there was a reluctance to get to the restaurant. A little while earlier, she couldn't wait to get out the house to get there. Now that she was almost there, what could be the problem? Maybe her opening up the door and not seeing him there would convince her that he was really gone? Gloria started to think back from the time he took over the place from Kelsey, who had it for years before him. If he had ever missed a day of work, she couldn't remember. She doubted if Archie ever didn't show up or at least had the place closed. He spent more time at the restaurant than he did at home. Whenever she called from California to speak to him to see how he was doing, she would call the restaurant first. He had loved working there. He himself was Archie Bunker's Place. Yes, people did come to drink and eat and have a good time at the restaurant, but like everyone said, her daddy Archie was a unique character. Regardless if the food was excellent and the drinks were filled till overflowing, people wanted to know about this person the bar was named after. Now the gate over the door was down, closed and locked, holding in memories of her father, who she would never see again on the earth.

Gloria and Teresa were now walking past the shop that shared the alleyway with her father's place, but Teresa was the first one to suddenly stop. They both had smelled burnt wood at the corner of the block, but neither paid any attention to it till now. Teresa spotted it first. The shop that they were standing in front of had caught on fire a while back. They instantly knew that because the charred smell wasn't very strong but was lingering in the air. The gate was down over the entrance just like Archie's place, but the gate had big holes in it where a person could look inside. When Teresa stopped, Gloria stopped too and was able to see inside.

"Oh my God!" she gasped. "I wonder what happened here!" Gloria was now stepping close just like Teresa and was looking all around inside from where she was standing. "I wonder what kind of shop this used to be." The structural damage wasn't bad but everything inside was all charred black and destroyed. Broken glass, chairs, a counter, signs on the walls and lights were all destroyed. "This place has been so many different things that I can't even remember."

While the two talked as they looked through the gate like little kids who sneaked into the circus looking at one of the circus performers in their trailer, they didn't realize that someone was approaching from behind.

"That was terrible about that fire there," a sweet, weak female's voice said nonchalantly.

Gloria and Teresa turned around and saw a tiny black woman who looked to weigh no more than about ninety pounds with salt and pepper hair pushed back tightly into a neat bun talking to them but not really looking at them, though. She was looking at the building that the two women were looking at also. She was at least seventy-five years old but her skin looked smooth as a baby's bottom. She had thick glasses over her face, making it very hard for the two women to describe her eyes. She had a little pug nose that the glasses sat on, and a very thin mouth that quivered when she talked. She also was dressed very nicely. She reminded Teresa of a librarian. She had a white sweater on over a grey blouse and a long black skirt that came down to her knees. Her pocketbook matched her blouse. As she looked up toward the top floor of the burnt-out building, she squinted and her mouth showed her top teeth and deep dimples on the side of her face. "It's amazing how the other buildings didn't catch fire because of the blaze. The fire department must have been here in no time. I don't know if anyone was injured in the blaze. God, I hope not. It was electrical, you know; well, that's what I had heard."

Gloria and Teresa both looked at each other in confusion.

"I beg your pardon?" Gloria responded.

"Electrical. The fire had something to do with bad old electrical wiring. That's what we heard." Gloria and Teresa were now nodding in understanding.

"Excuse me, ma'am, but what did this place used to be?" Teresa asked.

"How far do you want me to go back?" She said jokingly then started laughing weakly, actually sounding like someone who had continued hiccups. Before Teresa could respond, the woman continued talking. "I remember that it used to be one of those shops that made horse shoes. The horses would wait in this here alleyway while the guy made the shoes." The old woman pointed to the alleyway as Gloria and Teresa glanced in that direction. "After that closed down due to the fact that people were able to buy cars, it became a hardware store. It was a hardware for-for ages, my, my, my." She shook her head and blinked her eyes as she remembered back. Gloria and Teresa tried to interrupt her but when it proved useless, they just listened patiently. "After the hardware store relocated, it became a stationery store, a malt shop, an automat, a tailor, a barber shop, a beauty salon, a novelty store..." When the old woman said that, Gloria perked up a tad and her eyes lit up like a candle.

"I remember that!" she said excitedly. "I haven't thought about that novelty shop in ages. This place sure was a novelty store." Gloria began nodding as she smiled. "I was just a little girl then when it was a novelty store. During Halloween, this place was where we all came to buy our costumes. It was quite popular. I remember one year, my boyfriend Chris and I were about eight years old. I wanted to be a witch and he wanted to be Dracula. He bought his fangs here; the makeup and cape too. The owners had given me stuff for my hair to make it look old and gray, false teeth and makeup plus the black outfit along with the fake crooked bumpy nose. This place was just excellent!"

"Yes, it was," the woman said in agreement as she nodded with a slight smile.

"It seems like you've been here for a very long time," Teresa replied.

"Yes, I sure have," she said proudly. "I've lived here my whole life."

"What else used to be here?" Teresa's interest had perked up. They were both still waiting with much excitement to hear what the store was before it had burned down.

The old woman began rubbing her tiny chin, then tilted her head to the side as she began trying to remember the other shops after the novelty store.

"Well, after the novelty shop, it was a gadget shop, camera shop, a check cashing place…"

Gloria was nodding in agreement as the old woman continued talking. The last shop that Gloria remembered was the check cashing place. "It then sat vacant for awhile. I had asked myself what else is there in the world that could go into this spot? By then, the neighborhood had changed a lot. What could go here that the neighborhood would like? It became a record shop, one of those urban record shops that the young kids liked, like rap music, reggae, heavy metal—that sort of stuff. Not to my liking, of course. I'm an Ella, Duke and Dizzy type of gal, I must say," she commented proudly. This caused Gloria and Teresa to look at each other and smile. "They also sold those t-shirts with musician's name and face on them. It was here for a long time till that big music mega store opened down the street. It then became a pet shop that sold birds, hamsters and fish. Then last but not least, an Internet café. That's how the fire started, I bet." She was now nodding her head. "All those computers and wiring and such. That old wiring just couldn't handle it all. They had about one hundred computers inside, too. They must have been making good money because every time I walked past the building, the place was always packed with people using the computers plus people waiting to use them. I never went inside, though. I just looked through the window. An old woman like me has no need to use the Internet or a computer. Everything that I need to know is right up in here." She was now pointing to the top of her head.

"You most definitely have a good memory," Teresa remarked.

"Well, yes and no. Sometimes these places go out of business so quickly that I forget where they were. I have to think for a long time but eventually I remember." She then looked towards Archie's place. "He just passed away yesterday." She sucked her teeth then shook her head back and forth.

"Did you know him?" Gloria asked. She wanted to hear what the woman had to say about him before she told her that she was his daughter.

"Did I know him? Everybody knew Archie Bunker!" She was acting surprised that Gloria would even ask a question like that. "He was quite a unique character. He definitely was one in a trillion." These were the same words Gloria had been hearing all day. "I remember one time that I had gone in there. I guess that it was maybe ten years ago. I went in and sat on the stool instead of sitting at a table or a booth, and then a few seconds later a black young lady came and took my order. After that, Archie came over to me and leaned across the counter and said in a low, almost a whisper, 'You know, ma'am, you don't have to do a Woolworth's sit-in in here. We serve you people. Hell, we serve everybody.' He looked at me very seriously. At first, I didn't know what he meant by the comment, then I got highly offended. I then looked around and noticed that I was the only black in the place. I turned and looked back at him, frozen at first, then we both burst into laughter." She had a big smile on her face as she continued looking at the place. "See, not everyone understood him. That's why he was such a character. I think that he would say crude, rude and obnoxious things just to see people's reaction. People love to hate him, but like in a fun way, you know?"

Gloria and Teresa both looked at each other and nodded rapidly with smiling faces.

"Oh believe us, we definitely know," Gloria replied. "Try growing up with him," she added, while looking at Teresa for support.

"Yeah, try living with him for a year!" Teresa was leaning on Gloria as she laughed. The old woman looked at the two with confused eyes.

"I beg your pardon?"

"We understand what you are saying because I am his daughter Gloria and this here is Teresa. She rented a room in the house many years back.. She's also a family friend."

"Oh," she said in relief. "Thank God I didn't say anything bad!"

"We wouldn't have been surprised if you had. Daddy was known to have ticked off a lot of people including me and friends because of his views. But those who knew him got over it quickly. When God created Daddy, he broke the mold."

"On purpose!" Teresa added quickly.

"Well then, I do want to give my condolences to you and your family."

"Oh, thank you so much, aaah..." Gloria was waiting for her to give her name.

"Oh, I'm sorry. My name is Irene. That's Ms. Irene. My last name is Parker."

"Well, it's so very nice to meet you, Ms. Parker." Gloria and Teresa extended their hands for her to shake them.

"Please call me Irene." She accepted the hand gesture and shook both gently.

"So, are you going to be running the place now that your father has gone home to glory?" Irene asked seriously.

"Oh, I don't think so, Irene. I am going to head back home to California."

"Oh, that is such a pity. There is no other place like this place in the community. What are you going to do about it? I mean, are you going to keep it going?"

"Oh, Irene, I don't know anything right now. I'm just taking it one day at a time." Gloria started to feel like a broken record saying the same thing over and over again.

"Well, whatever you decide, I wish you blessings. I know that this is a confusing time for you and your family, but everything will work out just fine." "Oh, Irene, thank you so much for your kind words."

"Well, I think that I better get going. I've held up enough of your time. Nowadays, youngsters like yourselves..." When she said this, Gloria and Teresa looked at each other then smiled bashfully. "Usually don't have time for an old lady like me. They think that all we old people do is yap yap yap about nothing." Irene then chuckled a tad.

"Not at all, Irene. It was a pleasure, really it was."

"Yes, I agree too, Irene. It really was an eye popper." When Teresa said this, Irene looked at her with confusion then she looked at Gloria. Gloria decided to intervene and help Teresa out.

"She meant to say that the history of the building was an eye opener."

"Oh, okay. Now I understand." Irene relaxed her shoulders and smiled in relief.

After they finished with their goodbyes, they began walking away. Teresa then noticed that Irene had suddenly stopped. She began peering around, looking a tad disoriented. With concern, Teresa nudged Gloria so she could see Irene's actions, causing her to become concerned also.

"Let's go back and see if there is a problem. I would hate to leave her out here in a confused state of mind." Teresa nodded in agreement.

The two walked back over to Irene and asked her if everything was fine.

"Well, I am just a tad confused here. Ever since they've been working on the sewer pipes in the street, they keep changing where we normally catch the buses. I was actually walking towards the old bus route when I just realized that it's not there anymore."

"Bus routes? Well, bus routes are my specialty." Teresa said proudly. "Now, which bus are you looking for?" she asked as the woman took hold of her and the two began walking away. Gloria didn't hear what bus number the woman said because the two had started walking. Teresa turned around toward Gloria and told her that she would be back in a few minutes, after she showed Ms. Irene where the rerouted bus stop was. Gloria nodded and turned back around and started walking toward her father's place. She walked past the alleyway, peered down it, and then stood in front of the closed gate.

There, she stood facing her father's restaurant. While standing a few steps back from the candles that were lit and the cards with teddy bears next to them, she noticed that someone even left a six-pack of beer. Gloria chuckled and shook her head back and forth. She then looked straight at the sign that was hanging on the gate and it was exactly eye level to her. It read, 'CLOSED TILL FURTHER NOTICE' at the top, then underneath it said, 'ARCHIE BUNKER DIED SEPTEMBER THIRD.' Underneath that it read, 'YOU WILL BE MISSED' and underneath that it read, 'CHEERS!' Gloria started thinking that the person who wrote the sign that was hanging on the gate probably was the one who left the six-pack. Underneath that paragraph, it had the information where the funeral would be, and the day. For some reason, Gloria had the urge just to run her finger across the sign. As she did this, she began to get teary eyed.

"Well, now you know for sure that your daddy is gone," she said to herself. "It's right here in bold writing." The finger that she used to run across the writing on the notice was also used to wipe the tears from her eye. She stood there for a while just staring at the sign almost hypnotized. After she finally snapped out the trance, she picked up one of the cards that was in front of the restaurant and began to read it. She commented that thank God it wasn't a windy day or all of the cards would have been blown all over the place. She opened up her purse and started putting the cards inside. She bent back down and picked up another card to read, but as she came to an upright position, she noticed that there was a huge shadow being cast off the sidewalk and part of the building, totally engulfing hers. Gloria then felt hot breath on the back of her head and neck. After that, she felt a heavy, hot hand on her shoulder, a very heavy hand, and the only thing Gloria was able to see was the hand, which definitely was a man's huge white hand with hairy knuckles. It had tattoos on the fingers and the hand was inside a leather glove. Gloria was even able to smell the leather. The first thing that she wanted to do was scream but the sound got caught in her throat. Her next thought was to take her foot and do a donkey kick right into the man's private area but instead she remained cool and calm and very ladylike, saying, 'Whoever you are, if you don't take your fifty pound ham hock of a foot off of me, I am going to pick up one of these candles here and throw the hot wax right into your face!"

Gloria's voice rose as she spoke, sounding just like a typical seasoned New Yorker. Needless to say, the hand came off quickly and Gloria heard a hearty sound of deep, husky laughter.

"Still just as tough as ever!" she heard the voice say.

Gloria turned around to face a 6"1, 350 pound wall of a man, 40, who was solid muscle, which Gloria was able to see because his chest bulged out like football chest pads, and his arms were huge like the Hulk's. Gloria was looking up at a machine that was twice the size of her. She also noticed that he had jeans on; tight, that showed that he had leg muscles underneath and he had on heavy black thick boots. The top of his head was in a Mohawk style. He had earrings in his ears and one in his nose, pierced and hanging down on the side. He also had a goatee around his full lips, which were now open, showing teeth; some gold, some missing, while he laughed.

"Gloria!" he shouted between laughs.

"It can talk!" she replied as she continued looking at him. "And it knows me!"

"Of course I know you! How can I forget the first woman to ever beat me in arm wrestling?" His bright green eyes stared into hers, blinking as happy tears filled them. His face revealed a lot of emotion, happily surprised at seeing her there, full of excitement and delight at her sight.

"Iggy!" Gloria shouted as she smiled widely. Gloria jumped into his arms as he picked her up and started spinning her around. When he stopped, Gloria had tears of joy on her face. She couldn't help but look at him from top to bottom as she shook her head in total disbelief. "Little skinny Iggy Van Horn! Oh my gosh! Boy, have you grown!" Gloria had her hands out to him as if she was going to introduce him. "Look at you. You are absolutely gigantic! Oh, Iggy, you look fan-tab-u-lous!"

"Oh, forget about me. You still are just as beautiful as ever. How is my number one favorite babysitter doing?" When he said this, Gloria quickly glanced at the sign on the gate, then down at the candles, cards and teddies leaning up against the building.

"Oh, Iggy, I could be better, believe me."

Iggy stopped smiling for a few seconds then replied, his voice very low and somber, "Oh, yeah, Gloria. I'm so sorry to hear about Archie. I didn't mean to be so boisterous. I was just so happy to see you, that's all. I didn't mean any disrespect." He dropped his head down guiltily, as if he was caught taking cookies out of the cookie jar. He even poked out his lips like a little child.

"Oh nonsense Iggy, there was no disrespect done. I'm just as happy to see you, too. Despite your muscular behemoth size, you are still very sensitive and caring. You haven't lost that quality about yourself." When she said that, Iggy just blushed. He was now smiling again the way that she liked.

Gloria noticed that he looked like a big kid when he smiled. His cheeks went all the way up to the lower part of his eyes, causing little creases. "My gosh Iggy, I haven't seen you since forever!" Gloria began checking him out from the top of his spiked hair down to his huge leather boots.

"Yeah, it's been a long time. Hey, how are little Joey and Mike?"

"Oh Iggy, I guess we really haven't seen each other for a while." Gloria started chuckling over that. "How much time do you have?"

"Don't worry. I have enough time. I'm on my lunch break. It's a late break though, but it's ok."

"Hey, come on inside and we'll talk. You can raid the kitchen, like you did when I had babysat you." Gloria said excitedly.

"Just like old times. You got yourself a deal."

Gloria dug down into her purse then took out the keys to open up the gate. Once she got them out, Iggy volunteered to do the locks for her. While this was going on, they were still casually talking. Once the gate went up, Iggy started picking up the cards and the teddy bears. Gloria picked up the six pack. They would have to make another trip once again to pick up the candles. Iggy had the teddy bears and cards in one hand, and with the other hand he was unlocking the front door with the key.

Gloria had to go in first to turn off the alarm. Once she turned it off, she put her stuff on the counter. Once Iggy came in behind Gloria, he did the same. At first, Gloria didn't have time to notice it, but after the candles were brought in, she was able to smell wood floor polish, Windex and beer from days long gone. Iggy commented that he should lower the gate at least halfway. That way, people passing by wouldn't think that the place was open, plus, they would still be able to see the sign giving the information about Archie's passing. Gloria thought that that was a good idea.

As Iggy headed to the front, he ran into Teresa. At first, they didn't recognize each other, but once they got a good look at each other, they greeted each other affectionately. Neither woman had seen Iggy in ages. As Teresa came in, Iggy closed the gate halfway. Once the gate came half down, the place became dark. Gloria hadn't yet turned on the lights. Once she did, she looked around the whole place and got a feeling of pure emptiness, even though the place had everything in it: the kitchen to her corner right, the counter in the middle right, booths in the corner right all across the wall to the left side corner, and to the left side and part of the middle were the tables and chairs. The jukebox and the small piano were lined up against the left wall.

The walls were red brick, and hanging from these walls in frames were photos of famous people that had come into the establishment. Some of the pictures had been there since the place used to belong to Kelsey. The booths were wood but the cushions were red. Tables were all wood, and the chairs were like the booths. So were the stools. Behind the counter was the display of all the liquor in front of a huge mirror that stretched the distance of the counter. By the front door to the side were the bathrooms. Overhead, down the middle ceiling, were ceiling fans with lights in them. Over each booth were light fixtures hanging down, and over the tables and chairs on the left wall hung the same. The bar counter area had track lights overhead. The floor was wood.

At the present time, all the chairs were on top of the tables and the stools were on top of the counter. She walked randomly to a table in the middle of the room and took a chair down. Teresa and Iggy followed right behind her, but before they sat down, Gloria told them both that they could go into the kitchen and raid the fridge. Iggy was gone almost before she even finished her sentence. Teresa, on the other hand, went behind the counter and plugged in the coffee machine. A few minutes later, everyone was back at the table talking, eating and drinking. Iggy had made himself a huge chicken sandwich with mayo, cheese, lettuce and tomatoes with a soda. When Iggy drank a soda, it wasn't from a glass. He brought back to the table a huge pitcher usually used for a table of four.

Teresa had a cup of coffee and a gooey microwave Danish. She also brought Gloria a cup of coffee which she was sipping on as Teresa told Iggy about her life since she had moved from Hauser Street, keeping Iggy very interested.

"Wow." Iggy put down his huge sandwich, which he had left finger prints in the bread, and wiped his mouth with a napkin. "Teresa is living with her long-time beau along with her three beautiful daughters and Gloria is no longer a Stivic. She took back her maiden name, became a Bunker again, remarried, and had twins of all things!" Iggy began to chuckle. "Then she became a widow and now she is Gloria Bunker Shaw. You ladies have led very interesting and busy lives."

"So what about you, Iggy?" Teresa asked as she bit into her pastry. "Do you still love iguanas?"

"Oh, Teresa, how could you even ask such a question like that? I have seven now, one for each day of the week."

"What are their names, Monday, Tuesday, Wednesday, Thursday, Friday, Saturday and Sunday?" Gloria asked jokingly, but Iggy looked at her seriously.

"Yepper." Iggy then picked up half of the sandwich and took a huge bite, almost devouring it. He left a tiny piece hidden between his huge fingers.

"Are you serious?" Gloria was surprised, but Iggy nodded, then he grunted a yes as he chewed.

"No girlfriend or wife, Iggy?" Gloria asked.

"Any kids?" Teresa asked. Iggy finished chewing and was now licking his huge fingers where the mayo had squirted out.

"The answers are not right now, hell to the no, and yes, seven. Their names are Monday, Tuesday, Wednesday, Thursday, Friday, Saturday and Sunday." When Iggy said this, the two women looked at each other with surprise.

"Iggy, I don't understand why a handsome, huge, muscle-bound guy like yourself doesn't have a wife, girlfriend or human children." Gloria continued sipping on her coffee.

"Yeah, Iggy," Teresa interjected. "You would be a catch for any woman."

"Well thank you so much for the kind words, but let me explain. I've just gotten out of a relationship. We were going together for a while. She was rich, successful, beautiful, intelligent—everything that I wanted in a woman—but she didn't like to be seen with me in public. For a long time, I didn't notice this. My friends would always say things and try to talk to me to open up my eyes, but I just shook their comments off like water on a duck, but you notice things once the relationship was over. She loved being around my friends and she loved being with me as long as her friends, family and business peers didn't see me. Basically, she wanted a suit-and-tie or preppy, GQ-type of guy, greased haircut, low behind-the-ear type of guy. As you ladies can see, I am definitely not that. I know that we were total opposites but she got along fine with everyone I knew. She was comfy in my world as long as her friends, family and peers weren't around. She just didn't want me in her world where they would be able to see me." While Iggy was saying this, Teresa and Gloria began shaking their heads. "Look, I am me, Iggy. I am not going to change myself for anyone. I am who I am and bunk whoever don't like it." Iggy then banged his hand on the table causing everything to shake and shift a tad, but that didn't faze the two women.

"Aye, aye!" Teresa yelled as she held up her pastry then took a bite from it.

"You mean 'here here' Teresa!" Gloria corrected then laughed.

"And that too!" Teresa took another bite from the pastry, smiling widely.

"So when did this Iggy-look right here come about?" Gloria pointed to him from head to toe as if she was modeling him.

Iggy was now on his second half of the sandwich, which he was gripping as if it was about to run away from him. Once again, he took a huge bite, swallowed then washed it down with some soda. When he finished doing that, he slapped both hands together then placed them on his muscular thighs.

"You used to be so skinny."

"Yeah, when did you get so ignited?" Teresa took her hands and started raising them as if she was holding an invisible balloon that was being filled up with air.

"You mean, 'inflated' Teresa." Iggy leaned toward Gloria as he continued looking at Teresa with a smile. "I still see that Teresa hasn't mastered the English language." Gloria just nodded and smiled.

Teresa playfully leaned toward him and hit him on his mega shoulder.

"Well, let's start from the beginning." His hands were back on his massive thighs again as he occasionally turned to both women. "Yes, it is true. As we all know, I was a walking, talking bone, a human number one, an uncooked French fry, a Q-tip and the dreaded pencil. I was so skinny that I could have used a Cheerio as a hula-hoop. I was so skinny that when I washed up in the tub, my mother had to make sure that she covered the drain so I wouldn't get sucked down the hole." While he was teasing himself, he chuckled, causing the two women to chuckle along with him as they remembered. "What made the matter even worse was that I was also so little! My teacher would mark me absent…and I sat in front of the class! When I use to play tag with my friends, I would never get caught because my secret was to hide behind a baseball bat. But on days that it had rained, I never got wet because I used to run between the raindrops."

"Oh, stop it Iggy. You are such an exaggerator." Gloria slapped him on his shoulder.

"You are such a full deck." Teresa exclaimed.

"A card, Teresa. He is such a card." Gloria corrected.

"Look at the size of him, Gloria. He is definitely a full deck!" Teresa then corrected Gloria.

"In all seriousness, though, I would eat like a pig as y'all know, but I just couldn't gain anything."

"Yep, we could vouch for that. You sure did eat!"

"Well, the eating started catching up to me in a good way once I hit about 16 years old. I grew ten inches in like five months. By the end of the year, I started bulking up. That was great, but the bad news was that I had become real popular and people wanted my attention; especially girls, so I began lifting more, then got involved with steroids. After steroids came drugs on a regular basis. I started cutting school till eventually I dropped out. No one in the neighborhood knew that I was into the drugs because I would hang out cross-town, but my family knew. Needless to say, they were hurt. I was totally out of control. I was hanging out with the wrong type of people, being rowdy and fighting all the time. It was horrible. I got involved with crack cocaine, alcohol, Ecstasy, Oxycodone, on and on and on. I wasn't doing it to escape an abusive home or because I was poor or because my family had never showed me any attention. If I told you that, you would automatically know that I was lying. My family is the salt of the earth. I did it because I just wanted to even though I knew that it was hurting people that I cared for."

Gloria and Teresa looked frozen; the looks on their face showed that they couldn't believe what they were hearing. "Eventually, I started stealing from the very ones that I cared for. Remember, I was still young and didn't have a job. When that stopped working, I started selling it so I could have money to buy it. It was just horrible. This went on for a long time. I just got heavier and heavier into the drug game, using and selling, using and selling, not to mention that by this time, I was lifting close to five hundred pounds. I had bulked up to 280 pounds by then. I was into a lot of illegal businesses. A guy my size was needed in these kinds of businesses. I was wanted everywhere. I had a lot of money but I also had a lot of problems. Years went by and I just got deeper and deeper into the mess, until finally I got saved from drowning."

"What happened, Iggy?" Teresa asked anxiously as Gloria remained glued to the story.

"I got arrested." Iggy took a quick big bite of his sandwich, leaving crumbs, and then he took a quick swallow of soda. He then used the back of his hand to wipe his mouth clean.

"Yep," he said nodding his head. "Uncle Sam sent me to the big house for seven years."

"Wow, Iggy. Seven years! I had no idea." Gloria was shaking her head.

"Nobody knew, Gloria, not even my family. Before I got arrested, I hardly ever was home. Anyhoo, I would stay away for months, days and even weeks at a time. For a while, I would just call the family from the Federal prison but I never told them where I was. I told them that I was living in Fort Dixx, New York. I just never told them that it was a federal prison. They never asked to come see me because they figured that I was still using or selling drugs. They didn't want any part of that. It was lonely, very lonely. There I was, 20 years old, doing seven years. Those were supposed to have been the best times of my life, but I know, all the stuff that I was doing up in the streets, I would have been dead or would have killed someone. While in prison for all those years, I reanalyzed my life over and over again and I just felt disgusted. I started seeing what drugs had done to the guys in the joint and I didn't want to turn out to be like that, so over those next seven years, I became a new person. I changed my whole life around. I became a model inmate, came out of prison a model citizen and family member. Of course, I eventually told the family. Though furious with me for not telling them, they were very proud of me that I was able to work it out and handle the consequences on my own. That was 13 years ago. Now, I have my GED, I've taken college courses, I know the computer, which I learned in the joint, I go to the schools and talk about the dangers of drugs, my body is drug free, I volunteer down at the Jefferson-Willis Memorial Help Center, and I support myself and my seven children by doing carpentry work. I've been doing it for 13 years now."

"You are the second person that I have spoken to today that is in the carpentry business, you and Chris. By any chance, do you remember Chris? Chris Barlow?"

"I sure do. He used to be your boyfriend for centuries." Iggy was nodding his head. "I think that you also need to know, Gloria, that Chris is my boss." When Iggy said this, he could've knocked Gloria over with a feather.

"Are you serious?" Gloria asked with her eyes wide.

"I sure am. I am serious as marriage. He hired me on the spot when he saw me. He was like my idol when I was a kid. I always looked up to him and I still do. He has taught me everything that I know. I remember as a kid when you used to babysit me and he would come over to see you. He would give me a dollar. A dollar was a lot back then, so to me, a dollar was like a million dollars. He would say to me, 'Here you go, Iggy. Buy yourself and your iguanas some real food.' Now, every week, he gives me a big check. Do you know that for the past 13 years, whenever he pays me, he says those same words? It never fails." He said fondly, "Yep. That Chris there, he's one of the good ones." Iggy was now nodding his head.

"Yeah, he is, Iggy. He is one of the good ones."

"So, now that you are moving back and stuff, and you and Chris are both single, maybe..."

"Oh, hold it, Iggy, before you say what you are going to say." Gloria threw up her hands, "Unfortunately, Iggy, I won't be moving back. I'm only staying to take care of Daddy's things. I'm probably going to sell the house and right now, I don't know about the restaurant. I'm just taking it one course at a time. Everything has happened so fast that I haven't had time to think much about anything else."

"I know Gloria, and believe me, I feel your pain. I'm sure that Teresa can vouch for me on that. We all knew him on a personal basis. You know that I am here for ya and if you need anything, just ask. You know that I would do anything for you."

"And that goes ditzo for me too," Teresa added.

"You mean, 'ditto' Teresa." Iggy was rolling his eyes and shaking his head. Again, Teresa playfully gave him a good sock in his arm, which barely budged the leather sleeve, but Iggy laughed anyway.

The three continued talking, with Gloria getting up and refilling Teresa's cup and her cup with coffee, then she got another pitcher of drink for Iggy who gladly accepted it with a nod and a smile. A little while later while Iggy was into one of his jolly laughs, the three started hearing noises coming from the front door. Someone was using keys to come into the restaurant. Gloria was facing the door curiously, which caused Iggy and Teresa to turn in that direction to see who was trying to come inside. The person pushed at the door again to see if it was locked, then used the keys that were jiggling to open up the door and came inside towards them.

Gloria was looking at a beautiful black woman, medium build and a beautiful shape, a little bit taller than her, about Teresa's height, 40, shoulder-length curly hair, big Diana Ross eyes, mousy nose and full lips. She was wearing a one-piece, body hugging dress which came down to her athletic looking thighs. The dress was flowered and it complimented her bust and her butt, ,also showing a tiny waist. She also was wearing a pair of black shoes. In her hands, she had the keys making the clinging sound, her pocket book and a shopping bag which she was now putting on top of the bar counter. She saw Gloria and she had her now-empty hands outstretched to greet her.

"I was just walking through the neighborhood and decided to walk past, not expecting to see anyone inside, but when I did, I decided to come on in. Hello Gloria. Oh, I am so sorry to hear about what happened to Archie." She said this all in one long breath.

Gloria was familiar with this person. Her name was Faye and she was Archie's assistant manager. She came to Gloria so quickly to hug her that she didn't have time to stand up, but she did accept the hug in the chair and hugged her back.

"Oh thanks Faye, how ya doing? I appreciate your kind words." Gloria patted Faye's back while she hugged her. While this was going on, Iggy was looking at Faye and made a wise remark.

"Oh, look! If it isn't the black Martha Stewart!" he said as if he was introducing her like Ed McMahon used to do with Johnny Carson.

When Gloria and Faye finally released their embrace, Faye turned towards Iggy and put her hands on her tiny waist, then gave him some attitude by moving her head around her neck and rolling her eyes.

"First of all, why do I have to be the BLACK Martha Stewart, huh? Why can't she be the WHITE Faye Grant?" Then she stopped rolling the head at Iggy then smiled towards Teresa and extended her hand. "Hello, my name is Faye. I'm the head chef here."

"My name is Teresa. Teresa Betancourt. I am an old friend of the family. Mucho gusto a conocerte." Teresa shook Faye's hand with a smile.

"Egualmente, Teresa," Faye responded.

"Oh, you speak Spanish, Faye?" Gloria asked with a surprise.

"Hey, working in here for over ten years, you learn to speak a little bit of everything."

"Hey, who told you that you were a chef?" Iggy was looking at Faye with surprise. "I thought Archie had you back there making weapons of mass destruction and explosives!"

"Oh yeah, Iggy?" she said quickly then patted his big girth. "Only thing that's exploding around here is that big belly underneath your Hells Angel

The Life and Times of Gloria Bunker

T-shirt, Mr. I-eat-here-about-five-times-a-day." When Faye said this, Gloria and Teresa burst into laughter.

After Gloria calmed down from laughing so hard, she turned to Teresa. "Despite what this woman said about being head chef, she refuses to admit or at least tell anybody that she pretty much runs this place. Faye is really Archie's assistant manager, but she prefers to do the cooking. She also hostesses sometimes, does the bar, cashiers, buses tables even though she doesn't have to. Daddy wouldn't trust anyone to run the place, let alone have the keys if it's not Faye."

"Faye, if you weren't needed by society, I would marry you and make you a Van Horn and keep you at home all to myself." Iggy was looking at her impishly.

"If you married me and made me a Van Horn, I would put you in a home because after the honeymoon, you would be immobile for the rest of your life!" Quick as a snap of her finger, she replied, then she winked her eye seductively at him, causing him to throw his hands up in surrender as he began to blush.

"Whoa there, Faye! On that note, I think that I better get going. Really, I would love to hang around here all day but..."

"There's a beam above your head." Faye reminded him as she interrupted him.

"As I was saying..." Iggy playfully cut his eyes at her. "But I have to get back to work. I'm doing some electric and plumbing work at a soon-to-be noodle shop around the corner, and then I got to lay up some sheetrock and stuff." Iggy was now getting up from his chair.

"Hey, Faye, why don't you go and help yourself to some coffee over by the bar or go into the kitchen and fix you something to eat." Gloria offered to Faye, who nodded then started to head towards the kitchen. Gloria stood up and gave Iggy a huge hug.

"Oh, Iggy, I'm so glad that you came by. Despite the circumstances, today has been one great surprise after another. It's so great to see you again." Iggy dug into his pocket and pulled out a card and handed it to her.

"If you need me for anything, you better call me. Don't lose it. Even if you do, I am in the book, okay?" He was now turning to Teresa, who also was standing up. She got a huge hug and kiss from Iggy. "You take care too, Teresa. I'll see all of ya's tomorrow." Iggy picked up his plate and glass and started towards the door, but Faye stopped him and said goodbye. She then told him that she would take the plate and glass, which he gladly gave to her. He then said goodbye to her and turned the key in the door and left.

Gloria was right behind him to lock the door. A few minutes later, all three women were at the table with fresh cups of coffee, but this time, Gloria was eating a microwave pastry, Teresa was on her second and Faye was eating a ham and cheese sub with mustard, lettuce and tomatoes. They were having a conversation about Iggy and how he had turned his life around. Every now and then Faye would say something smart or sassy to make the two women laugh. Gloria had to comment to Teresa.

"She is always like this, Teresa. She never lets up! She can put a customer in their place with just a look or a snide comment. Sometimes once she is on a roll, there is no stopping her. Yes, it is true that people come from everywhere to see or have a conversation with Daddy, but many customers, male and female, come just to sample her amazing Cajun, down home, Jamaican, Spanish, American..."

"Oh?" Teresa turned and looked at Faye who just listened, looking modest.

"Tanduri," Gloria turned and looked at Faye. "Did I miss anything?"
"You forgot, Philippine, Shechuenese, Vietnamese and Chinese...and, oh yeah, Italian." After she said that, she took a bite out of her sandwich, then she swallowed. "But who is counting?" She winked her eye at Teresa, and then went back eating her sandwich.

"That is absolutely amazing, Faye. How did you learn all those dishes?"

"I did at lot of reading as a child and I learned my way around a kitchen at a very young age. I always loved making different dishes, and my family never complained. As my curiosity grew, so did my repertoire of ethnic recipes. I mastered almost everything. I just don't get into those recipes that involve stuffed monkey brains, snake, seal and animals like that."

"Thank God for that."

"I remember when I first came in here many moons ago. A few days before, I had quit my previous job because of sexual harassment by the owner. It wouldn't stop. No matter how many times that I told the owner that I wasn't interested, it went into one ear and out the other."

"You should've castrated him. Take the two balls, let it hang then just slice!" Teresa remarked angrily.

"Oh, I would have done that, but the owner was a female." When Faye said this, Teresa opened her eyes wide.

"A dios mio!" Teresa acted as if she was in church and her pastor used profanity.

"So you could understand that I was very apprehensive about requesting a job. I was at the other job for such a long time. I really hated to start all over again at a new place, but I had a bad habit. I had to eat. So I had to find something. Well, anyway, I remember that when I walked in, it was packed. The bar stools all had butts in them, just like the booths and the tables up against the wall and in the middle. Busboys were cleaning off tables before the next group of customers came in to sit down. Somebody definitely made a profit that day. As I went in, I didn't know who Archie was and I didn't know about his, a-hum, reputation…"

Gloria and Teresa smiled because they knew what she meant. "He was having a heated discussion with one of the patrons. I believe that it had something to do with the public school system or other. I waited patiently till he was done, which seemed like it would never come. That was when I approached him. His first response once I got his attention was to look at me angrily. He then pointed his finger at me accusingly and said, '…and you…' I was thinking, oh my God! What have I gotten myself into! He then said, 'Diana Ross! That wasn't nice there, what you did to that gal in the Supremes. You gals were my favorite colored, oops, Negro, oops, black groups of all time.' He looked at me totally seriously. I said to myself, 'I know that this man doesn't really think that I am Diana Ross!' When everyone at the bar laughed, that was when I knew that he was joking. I didn't know if I should be insulted, amused or what, but I know that I was speechless for a few seconds. I only snapped out of it when he asked how could he help me. I said to him that I was inquiring about the help wanted sign in the window. That was when he told me that he was looking for a cook, but he said, 'Hey there, miss, I think that you are in the wrong place. Roscoe's chicken and waffles is in another state.' I blinked in confusion, not knowing what to say, but when I saw everyone laugh again, I knew that I was being made the butt of his jokes. Before I was able to respond, he wanted me to prepare a meal so he took me back into the kitchen then he said, 'Surprise me.' Then he left. In the kitchen, there was already someone cooking and she looked like she was about to pull out her hair. She didn't speak to me. She just nodded. I did the same. Well, I started to think of a dish to make that wasn't on his menu, so I prepared smothered chicken in homemade mushroom gravy. When I was done, I brought it out to him. The place was still packed. He looked at my dish and said, 'What is that?!' as he pointed at it angrily. I said that it was smothered chicken in homemade mushroom gravy. Do you know what his response was? He said, 'You're a cheater! All black people know how to make chicken dishes! You probably knew how to make that before you knew how to walk.' Someone at the counter grabbed the plate from Archie and stared at it as he licked his lips and said, 'Hell, Arch. If you ain't gonna eat it, I will." Archie then said, 'Why don't you hop on a uptown train and go to Harlem. I heard that Sylvia's is hiring. It's down the block from the Adam Clayton Powell building.' Girls, he was still making fun of me. I had the mind to go and get my things and leave, but that would've been easy. Maybe he thought that I was going to leave, but I turned back around and started preparing another meal. I didn't know what to make. He didn't have a lot of seasoning for me to really do something extravagant so I had to improvise. First I made a sauce using ginger juice, vinegar, sherry and a little bit of tomato ketchup. After I heated it up in a pan, I added lime juice, butter and some tomato water. After that was done, I poured it over some fish that was being cooked while the sauce was simmering. I then presented it to Archie along with coconut jasmine rice. The smell had lit the whole restaurant up, so by the time I had come out, everyone was already commenting. Archie took a whiff of it, tasted it, and child! I thought that Archie's racist head was going to start spinning like a top! The way Archie's eyes went into the back of his head, I thought that I was going to see two jackpot signs in their place. He smiled at me, then he nodded and said, 'Chaka Kahn, you definitely surprised me." The same guy who grabbed the smothered chicken plate from Archie earlier was now reaching for the plate again and said, 'If you ain't gonna eat it..." but Archie cut him off and pulled away from him and said, 'Back off, Heb! You people always got your hands out for things that don't belong to ya!' I was shocked, but the man just laughed. He wasn't offended at all! It was almost as if he liked the insult! That was when I realized that this guy here by the name of Archie Bunker was a very comical jokester and quite harmless as long as you didn't take him seriously. He looked at these customers as his audience and he was the star. He definitely was a rare character. Well to finish off the story, after he ate the food, he hired me on the spot. A few hours later, when it was slowing down some, I felt a hand on my shoulder and it was Archie. He leaned close to me as he whispered in a very low voice and said, 'Oprah, the minute that I saw you, you had the job.' I turned and faced him and asked why he made me do the cooking if I had the job, then he said, 'I like to keep people on their toes and see how they are under pressure.' Then he hesitated a minute and said, 'Plus, with those looks and that sassiness about yourself, you are going to make us a lot of money. I'm tired of the Jews always exploiting you people with all them there blaxploitation movies and stuff. I want a piece of the action there.' Then he turned and walked away. I fell out laughing when he said that!" Faye began laughing again as she thought about it. "After a while, every time he made a snide or racist remark, I was on him like flies on garbage! Oh, I am going to miss him. I'm gonna miss him a lot." She was nodding her head as she smiled, but before she took another bite from her food, she wiped a tear from her eye.

"Oh, Faye, that was a nice story."

"I remember this. Daddy did his four-time-a-week call down to Cali checking on me, still trying to get me to move back to NY. He'd told me that he'd hired you. He said, 'Little girl, I got a winner here. I hired a black beauty!' I got on his case when he said this. I said something to the fact that you are human, not some sort of horse, and he said, "Oh, stifle there, little girl. Those people like when you call them that. Don't they always say that black is beautiful?"

Gloria sure knew how to imitate her father better than anyone. She even threw in the woopty do that would get everyone laughing. Since it was exaggerated for comical purposes, it was funnier to watch.

Gloria kept the conversation going while Faye was able to eat her food and Teresa was able to finish her coffee. She was telling them the plans for the funeral and how she wished that she knew how people would handle it at the funeral home.

Once Faye finished eating her sandwich and finished drinking, she cleared off the table. When she came back and sat down, she put her elbow on the table then put her chin on top of her folded fist and looked at Gloria with all seriousness.

"Now that we all got our stomachs full and our lips nice and moist from drinking, what are you going to do about the bar, and when do you plan on moving back?"

The first thing that went through Gloria's mind was, "Here I go again; the same speech, the same record." Then she realized that she was going to have to keep saying it till she left. She was just about to answer Faye's question when Teresa intervened.

"Oh, Faye, I am so sorry to tell you this, but Gloria has decided that she is not going to be moving back here. Can you believe that?!"

Faye first looked at Teresa with surprise, then she looked at Gloria the same way. "You're kidding, Gloria. Please tell me that you are kidding." Faye took her head off her hand and took her elbow off the table. She was sitting straight up in her chair and looking at Gloria like she just told her that she really was a man. She couldn't believe what she was hearing.

"Gloria, your father would always tell me that he never understood why you stayed in California. His dream was that you and the kids would move back to NY to be near him, especially after your husband had died. To be honest with you, Gloria, he told me after I started working here that he had fixed the basement up, hoping that you would get the hint to move back, but he said that you didn't."

Now Gloria was the one who was looking at Faye as if she had said that she was a man. Gloria had no idea that her father had thought these things.

"Did Daddy really say that?" When she asked this question, Faye nodded with all seriousness.

"Gloria, he was always thinking about you. He knew that you weren't having an easy time raising three children out there with no family near you. Gloria, that's why he would call you so much, plus he was getting older. He wanted to spend more time with you and his grandchildren. Stephanie had moved away, so he had that big empty house with no one to fight with. That is why he spent so much time here at the bar." Gloria was stunned. She had never heard this about her dad before.

"Gloria, he and I spent a lot of time together and all he ever talked about were you and his grands, and when they came to see him for those holidays, I never heard so many woopty-dos in my life!" Faye leaned back in the chair and clapped her hands as she smiled.

Gloria had chills all over her body and she started blinking rapidly because she felt like the floodgates were about to overflow. Her mouth became dry and at first, she didn't know what to say. She had no idea that her father was lonely. She had never thought about him living in the house all by his lonesome and she never offered for him to move to California.

"How come I never did that?" she thought to herself. He wouldn't have done it anyway, but she still should have asked him. Life hadn't been easy on her once she left NY. It had always been a struggle, especially right after Ray died. She tried to budget herself on his insurance policy, but she calculated that if she budgeted right till the twins were eighteen years of age, the money would come down to about five hundred dollars a month. Not much to live off of for a woman with three young children, two of them still in diapers. Why didn't she just go back home? Maybe because deep down inside, she wanted to see if she could do it on her own. But couldn't she have shown her independence in NY. Why California? Once she and Mike got divorced, there was no need to stay and once Ray died, there was no reason to stay. She still didn't understand why she wanted to go back to California instead of moving back to NY now.

"Joey!"

Gloria didn't want to leave Joey in California if she decided to move back to NY. But Joey was a grown man and he was living on his own, plus he had a job. He would not want to go back to NY to live. But why was she so concerned for Joey? Joey was a man. He could make it without her. He could make it on his own. Not once since he had moved out had he ever asked for anything. Could it be that the twins needed to be near their brother? They loved him, but was she using that as an excuse too. The twins loved their grandfather, too, and she made sure that he seen them at least four times a year. No reason why they couldn't do that with Joey, or Joey could come and visit them during school breaks and summer. If she moved back to NY she could even do real estate in NY.

All these thoughts were twirling around in her confused mind, and she didn't know what to do.

Once Faye finished telling Gloria how her father felt, Gloria began to stumble over her words.

"I-I-I don't know what to say, Faye. I am absolutely blown away by what you've just told me. I just pray that whatever decision I make, it will be the right one, but if I close down the bar, would you be okay? I mean financially?" Gloria had a huge look of concern on her face as Faye stared at her, then waved her off.

"Who me? Girl, I'll be just fine. The owner of Bennet's over in College Point always is trying to steal me away. So are a few other places, like Nedra's on Jamaica Avenue, and Roosevelt's, not too far from here, but I am totally loyal here, right to the very end. Don't worry about me, Gloria…But…" Faye did hesitate before finishing her sentence.

"What is it, Faye??!! Just say it." Gloria's coercion caused Faye just to spit it out..

"Okay, Gloria. Look, you and I hit it off immediately, from the moment we met, and we've even talked personally to one another about certain things going on in our lives. We've laughed, cried, yelled and joked with one another…" Gloria was nodding in agreement as Faye talked. "We've been to each other's house and we've even hung out occasionally, so I think that I can speak freely and say that in my opinion, you really should come back to New York, and this is the reason that I say this: Sometimes we cannot see ourselves the way other people do. We might say something but our body movements say something totally contrary. The twins don't care where they live as long as it is with you, but in your case, I saw how you were when it was time for you to head back to Cali when you came for a visit. You started to suck your teeth, roll your eyes, drop your shoulders— girl, you looked like you were lugging a safe full of heavy weights on your back. You never rushed to the airport. You dragged yourself there. I've seen this in you and definitely your dad saw this. Gloria, I know that you have a lot on you right now and I really feel badly for that, but just think about what I said."

"Oh, Faye, thank you so much for your words and thank you for the advice. You are right. I do have a lot to think about." Gloria's mind wandered away for a few seconds then when she came back to where she was, her mind snapped back in remembrance.

"You know something, ladies? I forgot that I don't have anything to wear for the funeral. I really don't know what your plans were for today but how would you two like to go shopping with me to buy something?"

When Gloria said this, both ladies looked at each other then nodded. "Sure Gloria, of course," they said in unison.

"Not today, though, because it is getting late and I have to get ready and meet someone tonight at the house, plus Zoe has to come along, too. Matthew, I don't have to worry about. He already has a black suit, so how does tomorrow sound? We will meet right here, same time?"

"Sounds good to me, Gloria."

"Ditzo, no ah, ah, ditto for me, also." Teresa added as she corrected herself as they chuckled.

The three continued chatting like hens till it was getting late, but while they talked, Gloria was noticing that Teresa and Faye were really hitting it off well. They were laughing and slapping each other on the leg as they made their point, just as if they had known each other for a very long time. Gloria liked that because she had known both women for a very long time and she could honestly say that both of the women were good people with caring hearts.

Gloria eventually started standing up and stretching, bending from side to side.

"Well, ladies, I could talk all night and believe me, I really want to, but I have to see someone tonight about the house." The two women looked at her cautiously.

"Relax, relax! I am not going to make a decision tonight on the house. I'm just going to hear the offer and take it from there, that's all. We'll discuss it tomorrow when we meet back here. I will let you know how things went."

Teresa and Faye stood up and Faye headed toward the counter to get her things, with Gloria and Teresa right behind her. As Gloria gathered up her things, Faye offered to drive both women home, Gloria first, then Teresa. They both gladly accepted the offer. Once Faye gathered up her things, Gloria told the two that she would lock up, so Faye and Teresa both walked out and waited for her to come out. Gloria put the cards that were on the counter in her purse. She left the candles and six pack but she took the teddy bear. She then turned and faced the whole bar, stared at it, took a deep breath and exhaled. She then turned the main switch to turn off the lights. She set the alarm and headed out the door. In all the years Archie had run the bar, she had never been in it without him there, and this was the first time that she had closed up.

CHAPTER EIGHT:
A Billionaire, Mexico, and More—Oh My!

Once Gloria reached the house, she was greeted by more flowers and cards.

Stephanie was sitting in the living room watching television, but she had moved from the couch to Archie's chair and had her feet up on the foot rest wiggling her bare toes.

"So, how was your walk?" She lifted her head over her shoulder as Gloria made her way to the couch, where she lay across it on her back.

"Stephanie, it was wonderful. Iggy and Faye stopped by. We all had a good time despite the circumstances. Faye and Teresa had never met but they got along like they were friends forever."

"Well, like ten minutes after I got off the phone with the absentminded professor, the phone and doorbell were in competition for our attention." She waved her hands over the flowers and cards as if she was modeling them.

Flowers covered every table, the top of the television, near the phone and the big ones on the floor covered almost every inch of the living room and dining room.

"So, who called while I was out?" Gloria asked Stephanie.

"Joey called and..." When Gloria heard that, she turned and looked at Stephanie anxiously.

"Joey called! What did he say? Is he ok?" Stephanie was surprised by her reaction.

"He's fine but he is very busy. He said to tell you that he wouldn't be able to make it out here today. It's the beginning of the school year for him and the administrator is having a hard time getting Joey's class covered while he will be gone, so he will be leaving tomorrow evening after school is out. He said to tell you to call him later tonight if you want."

"Thank God the funeral is Saturday. There's no school then." Stephanie just nodded

"Mike called too. They are here and they are staying at the LaGuardia Sheraton. He said to tell you that they will be by tomorrow to see us."

"Well, that will be good." Again, Gloria nodded. "So, where are the twins?"

"They are still downstairs in the basement apartment. They must really be planning something nice for Uncle Archie's funeral. When I was putting that big plant near the basement door, I heard Matthew reading something that he had written and then I heard Zoe tell him that what he had written didn't sound right. He started throwing ideas towards her, then she said that she liked it, so he wrote it on paper and said it over again, using the line that Zoe liked."

"I'm sure that whatever they do, it will be very moving and special. They really loved Daddy."

"This is true." Stephanie added as she nodded in agreement. "And you know something, Stephanie? Daddy really loved them too. You know how much? Well let me tell you what Faye told me down at the bar..." Gloria was now sitting up on the couch as she began telling Stephanie everything that Faye had told her earlier.

"Oh, Gloria, that is so touching. Uncle Archie was really a special man."

"Stephanie, not only that. He also was a special father. He was always thinking about me and I was unaware of how much." Gloria looked up and raised one hand. "Oh Daddy, please forgive me of my blindness."

"So, does this mean that the Bunker Shaws will be returning after all?" Stephanie was now sitting sideways in Archie's chair, anxiously waiting to hear her answer.

Gloria just looked at Stephanie, lifted her shoulders up some then started laughing, not giving Stephanie an answer and causing her to wonder.

Later that same evening, while Stephanie was preparing a big dinner of roasted chicken quarters, vegetables and brown rice, applesauce and biscuits with the leftover potato salad from earlier, Gloria had dozed off watching 'Access Hollywood,' and the twins were still downstairs in the basement. The whole house filled with the aroma of Stephanie's food. Stephanie was on her way out of the kitchen, saying in a loud voice that dinner would be ready in about ten minutes. She didn't have to open the basement door for the twins to hear her. They showed that they heard her by yelling back in unison, "Okay."

Gloria, on the other hand, jumped out of her deep sleep, looking dazed and disoriented. When Stephanie saw Gloria's reaction, she quickly apologized.

"Oh, Gloria, I am so sorry. I didn't know that you had fallen asleep. My bad."

Gloria began blinking rapidly to get her bearings, then she rubbed her neck and twisted her head from side to side. "It is okay, Stephanie. I had to get up anyway. I have to call Mr. Kindred to let him know…" But before Gloria had a chance to finish her sentence, she was interrupted by a commotion in front of the house. Someone was hitting their car horn to the sound of 'la cucaracha.'

"Do you hear that, Stephanie?" she asked as they both went to look out of the window to see who was being so rude and obnoxious. Gloria was closer to the window because the couch was in front of it. Within seconds, Stephanie was right next to her.

As Gloria and Stephanie looked out the window, they stared in awe with their eyes wide and mouths nearly dropping to the floor at a white, shiny Lincoln stretch limousine with gold designs all around it. They couldn't see inside the limo's windows because they were very dark tinted. No one had gotten out of the limo yet, but Gloria noticed that whoever was inside was getting a lot of attention from people who were walking up and down the block because everyone had stopped and was staring. Some were even pointing.

"Gloria-Who-Could-that-Be-Inside-There?" she asked excitedly as she emphasized each word.

"Maybe they live in the house next door or are visiting the people in the house next door. Whoever they are, Stephanie, do you think they are on welfare?" Stephanie looked at Gloria like she was crazy, then they both started laughing.

The limousine just sat in front of the house for about two minutes. The twins came out of the basement with excited expressions on their face, as if they had won a free pass to Willy Wonka's chocolate factory.

"Hey you guys! Do y'all see that huge stretch in front of our house?!" While Stephanie was asking, Zoe skipped over to the window quickly, like a giddy schoolgirl, and stood next to the two.

"Actually, the limousine starts at our house but ends at the house next door," Gloria added quickly as she continued staring in awe.

"Yeah, we saw from the basement when it pulled up, but we didn't get a good look at it because we could only see the tires," Matthew added as he made his way closer to the couch and window.

The next thing that everyone knew, the chauffeur was making his way out of the driver's side. The uniformed chauffeur's outfit was the same color as the limo and had the same design. So did the cap. He was black, six feet two inches tall, and he looked like a model from one of the GQ magazines. He was making his way around to the rear door to let out whoever was seated there. Once he got to the curb, he straightened up his uniform then opened the car door with his white-gloved hand. Gloria noticed that there were only three people in the rear, and the first one was getting out. It was a man, a middle-aged white male, very thin and about five feet four inches tall. His hair was straight but spiked high up in the air like Don King, and the hair was auburn. He was wearing black thin-framed glasses, making his eyes look Chinese. He was clean-shaven and had cheekbones so accentuated that they looked like he was wearing blush to bring them out more, and he had pencil-thin sideburns. He was wearing a very bright and light shirt, opened with a white t-shirt showing tucked-inside bright red, baggy pants. He was wearing black casual shoes with no socks and he was being helped out of the limo. Once out of the limo, he stood to the side, making space for the next person to get out. The thin man looked up and down the block and across the street as he squinted. He had a serious, disdainful expression on his face.

"That man looks like a flaming faa..." laughed Zoe as she pointed, but Gloria quickly cut her off.

"Don't say it, Zoe. That's not nice." When Gloria finished, it got quiet for a few moments but as they continued staring at the thin man, all four started laughing at his behavior.

The four continued staring out the window, waiting to see who would be the next person coming out of the limo. As they stared and guessed, the chauffeur extended his white-gloved hand again and helped the next person out of the limo. It was an older man, in his fifties. As he was exiting, he nodded his head to the chauffeur and smiled. The chauffeur did the same. His face was round and was thinning slightly on the top. His part was very close to his left ear and had long pieces of hair combed all the way over close to the right ear. His face was very pleasant, with thin-framed glasses that made him look very business-like. Being that he was clean-shaven, Zoe noticed that he had liver spots on his face and commented about it, keeping the family in stitches. The man was wearing a baby-blue business suit and a white shirt with a red tie with a black and grey design going through it. He also was wearing very expensive black shoes with blue socks. He was also carrying an attaché case which he was gripping tightly with both hands. He also looked up and down the street then toward the Bunker house and the house next to it. This caused the family to duck and chuckle like little children who didn't want to get caught by the teacher doing something wrong. He stood on the other side of the limo door opposite the thin man as he waited for the next and last person to exit.

The last person to come out of the rear of the limo was an older man, very distinguished. He might have been about 55-60 years of age but he had a full head of bleached blonde hair that was shoulder length in the back. He was tall, six feet three inches, and was in excellent physical condition. He had some wrinkles around the eyes but they didn't make him look tired or old. He did have a few wrinkles on his forehead. He had a deep bronze tan that complemented the white hair well. He was wearing an expensive gray Italian suit matching his gray shoes. When he smiled as he came out the limo, his teeth sparkled just like the tons of jewelry on his hand, ears and neck. He also looked up and down the block and nodded with approval for some reason. Whatever he was looking at, Gloria could tell that he was quite happy and satisfied with it. She also noticed that people on the street were pointing and smiling and whispering to one another as they nodded and smiled too. Some even waved toward him, and he waved back happily. She could tell that this man loved to be the center of attention.

"Matthew, that's not his natural color, right?" Zoe still joked as her eyes bulged in fascination.

"Zoe, you are bad!" exclaimed Stephanie as she playfully hit her on her arm.

"No, he definitely dyes it. I should know!" Matthew said, then started rubbing his hair with his hands.

"You know, you two. There's no curing you." Gloria shook her head as she laughed.

"Oh my God, Gloria, his teeth are brighter than the Osmonds'" Stephanie joked as Gloria nodded.

"Yeah girl, that one with the long white hair is gorgeous! He looks like a movie star!" added Gloria, who was checking him out from head to expensive shoes.

Everyone on the street continued staring at the men who had just gotten out of the limo, wondering where they were going. Gloria and the crew were wondering the same thing.

While standing in front of the limo, the one with the long white hair straightened his suit, shirt and tie, made sure that his jewelry was looking fine, rubbed his finger across his top teeth then sprayed breath freshener into his mouth. After licking his lips a few times, he also began looking up and down the block on both sides of the street, then straight ahead toward the Bunker house.

"I wonder who he is," Zoe said.

"Is he somebody famous?" Matthew asked

"I don't know, but I wouldn't mind being his leading lady," Stephanie replied impishly as she did the 'Groucho' with her eyebrows.

The chauffeur made his way back around to the driver's seat as the three men stood out in front of the house talking. The four had no idea where the three were going, till the shorter of them started making his way up Gloria's porch, along with the man holding the attaché case.

"They're coming up here!" shouted Zoe excitedly.

"Hurry, hurry everyone!" shouted Gloria. "Go sit down and act natural!" Gloria waved her head for them to go. Everyone began scurrying away to find somewhere to sit, laughing gaily in the process. A few seconds later, the doorbell rang and everyone stared at each other, acting like they didn't know what to do.

"Who is going to answer the door?" Stephanie asked from her spot at the other end of the couch from Gloria. Matthew sat in Edith's old chair as Zoe sat in Archie's.

"Go for it, Zoe!" Matthew said as he nudged her excitedly. Zoe squealed with happiness, as if she was about to meet a movie star. She jumped up and quickly ran to the door and started spinning around in circles nervously as she smiled.

"What do I do, what do I do?" she kept asking over and over as she laughed.

"Open the door!" shouted Matthew from his spot.

"Zoe, calm down. They probably can see you from the glass on the door." Gloria scolded, which caused Zoe to instantly stop, get her composure and wipe the sweat from her palms. Zoe took a deep breath then casually and nonchalantly opened up the door.

"Hello. How can I help you?" she asked, acting unconcerned about the visit.

"Good evening. Is it possible that I could speak with Ms. Gloria Bunker Shaw?" the man with the attaché case asked, very businesslike. When he asked this, everyone looked at Gloria, who was looking very surprised. Gloria began to stand up slowly and start walking towards the door.

"My name is Daniel Kindred." He extended his hand with a smile then shook hers, but before he had an opportunity to finish his sentence, Gloria interrupted.

"Well, I'm Gloria Bunker Shaw, nice to meet you." Gloria smiled warmly as he shook her hand. Mr. Kindred then faced toward the thin man standing next to him then introduced him to her.

"This gentleman here is Miles O'Shea. He is my assistant." O'Shea was sashaying like he was a runway model. Gloria noticed but didn't comment, although she wanted to laugh.

Gloria extended her hand to O'Shea, who shook it very femininely and limply. "Please come in."

As Kindred and O'Shea walked into the house, they nodded towards everyone courteously and said, "How do you do?" O'Shea never once smiled. He reminded Gloria of a gay version of one of the men in 'Dragnet', even though he wasn't a cop.

Mr. Kindred began looking around the house as if he was an inspector checking out the flowers.

The Life and Times of Gloria Bunker

"Such beautiful flowers." He commented ever so sadly. "Such a pity that such beauty is given on such sad occasions." He sucked his teeth then shook his head. He then extended his hand again to Gloria. "Once again, Ms. Bunker Shaw, I do wanna give my condolences to you." Then he looked at the rest of the family. "And your family for your loss." He took hold of her hand gently again and shook it once.

"Thank you so much again, Mr. Kindred. Won't you two please come and have a seat?" Gloria asked very graciously.

"Thank you," he said, not moving yet. "But I didn't come alone. I know that we were going to meet today and that you were going to call, but we were in the neighborhood. We wanted to make sure that we weren't disturbing you and your lovely family."

"Oh no, no, Mr. Kindred, it's no problem. You're not disturbing us. We're just getting ready to…" Gloria then looked at Stephanie, who waved her off concerning dinner. "We're just sitting around watching television. As a matter of fact, I was going to call you. I'm glad that you came."

"Well, I'll let Mr. Hanley know that it is okay for him to come in." Immediately O'Shea turned around and headed back towards the door where Zoe was and headed down towards the man. They talked for a few seconds, then O'Shea opened up the back door of the limo and took out a big flower pot. He headed back up the porch but permitted the distinguished man to come in first. He walked into the house slowly and he had his hands extended as if he entered a room to the sound of applause and he had a smile wider and longer than the Great Wall of China.

"Allow me to introduce myself," he exclaimed very confidently. "My name is Rupert H. Hanley. The H is for, 'how is everybody doing?'" He chuckled twice. Gloria could instantly tell that when Hanley walked into a room, he commanded attention. He definitely was the star of the show. As Gloria watched him as he came in, she was thinking that he was much better looking up close. She also noticed that he had a good air about himself. A person just couldn't be mad around him. As Gloria looked at her family, she was able to see that the family was highly impressed by what they were witnessing.

Once Mr. O'Shea made his way back in, Zoe closed the door, then O'Shea stood at attention near the stairs, still holding the flowers, while Hanley talked.

"I am looking for Ms. Gloria Bunker Shaw," he stated, as he looked at Stephanie and Gloria.

"That would be me." Gloria was now walking towards him, but he stopped her.

"Ms. Bunker Shaw, during this grievous occasion, you don't come to me, no sir. I come to you," he said very humbly, then walked over to her and extended his hand. When Gloria took hold of it, he shook her hand firmly but in a nice and kind manner. For some strange reason, Gloria felt like she was going to melt. "I am so truly sorry for the loss of your father. I extend my greatest sympathy," he said very humbly. Gloria was very touched and very attracted to him.

"Thank you, Mr. Hanley."

Without looking towards O'Shea, he kept his eyes on Gloria then snapped his fingers. O'Shea zoomed from where he was standing and was at Hanley's side.

"I stopped at a florist and I told him to give me something that celebrated life, so he gave me these. I hope you like them." Hanley said as O'Shea gave them to her.

"Oh thank you so very much, Mr. Hanley. They are so very beautiful." Gloria smelled them, then put them down near Edith's chair. "Please, allow me to introduce my family," she said proudly.

When Gloria began introducing everyone, Hanley went around the room shaking everyone's hand politely. Zoe was the last one, and she couldn't hold back her excitement. Her face was crimson red and she laughed bashfully and ran past Mr. Kindred, then right by Matthew.

"So now that we have the formalities out of the way and I've been introduced to a very beautiful family, let me tell you who Rupert H. Hanley is. I am the owner of Maximum properties. The most! Rapidly growing! Real Estate powerhouses! In all! Of! America!" he sounded as if he was talking in front of a stadium of people.

"Sixty locations nationwide, and all of them are owned by moi," he added in a conceited, joking manner, then pointed to himself as he stuck out his huge, muscular chest.

"I'm growing like Starbucks!" He began to slowly turn around in circles.

"I've heard of you before. You are listed in Fortune 500!" Matthew replied quickly and excitedly.

"Not only are you a handsome young man, you are also very smart." Hanley walked over to Matthew and squeezed and shook his cheek, then rubbed his hair as if he was a little boy. Gloria could see that Matthew didn't like it and it made Gloria want to laugh, but she controlled it.

"Yep, yep and yep," Hanley responded while reveling in his own glory. "I made the list, but you know who didn't? I'll tell ya: Trump. Trump didn't make it. I make Trump look like a value meal, while I am supersized!" Hanley did a little dance in the room as if he was getting the Holy Ghost, shuffling around deep in his bones.

Gloria and the family were enjoying him immensely. Gloria could tell by the smiles on their faces; even Matthew had forgotten about the 'patting of the head' incident. They really liked his style and his charisma, and Gloria had to admit that she was feeling the spirit like he was. She wasn't quite sure how everyone was feeling towards O'Shea because he had been forgotten about. Both the men were still standing, but O'Shea went to stand by the door as if he was a guard at Buckingham Palace; Kindred was by the stairs, while Hanley on the other hand had all eyes on him and his eyes were totally fixed on Gloria. He just wouldn't stop smiling as he stood near her. Gloria was feeling flattered, and she was hoping that she wasn't blushing.

"Well, Mr. Hanley…"

"Please call me Rupert, if you don't mind," he asked as he touched her hand ever so friendly.

"Okay Mr., ah, Rupert. What brings a busy famous and important man like yourself to Hauser Street?" Gloria was really feeling flushed.

"Well, that is a very good question, my fair lady. I flew in today unexpectedly to check and see how my NY office, well, one of my NY offices, I might add, was doing. I like to keep them on their toes, you know." He then looked at Kindred quickly. "Isn't that right, Kindred?" Kindred gave him a smile and a nod.

"Yes sir, that is correct."

"Well, while we were having our little meeting, I found out about your loss. Other companies could care less about every aspect of a potential client. That is what sets us apart from all those other no-need-to-mention real estate companies. We don't want to be just the best. We want to be the most concerned and caring entities in America and eventually, worldwide. As soon as I found out what happened, that's when I asked my good man here, Mr. Kindred, how maybe I could put a little crack of a smile on that family's face. That's when the idea of the flowers came into plan. I was just going to send them via messenger, but when he had said that he had an appointment to see you, well, that's when I decided to come personally."

He looked at Gloria from head to toe. "And I am so glad I decided to come in person."

Gloria was about to tip over from all of the flattery, and she wouldn't have minded the injury. She quickly eyed the twins and gave them a look to allow company to sit. Eventually the twins got the hint and got up and went towards the dining room table. Gloria then motioned to the two chairs and the couch with her hands.

"Well gentlemen, won't you please come and have a seat?" Gloria noticed that Kindred and O'Shea weren't going to move till Hanley had initiated it. They kept their eyes on him to see what he was going to do, but he just stood where he was and began sniffing around the room.

"What is that wonderful aroma that I smell?" Hanley was pleased by the aroma. Everyone was able to tell by the huge smile on his face.

"Oh, that is dinner, Mr. Han, ah, Rupert. We were just getting ready to sit down to eat."

"So we have come at a very bad time." He eyed Kindred angrily.

"Oh, no, please, it is okay!" Gloria began defending Kindred, who looked very relieved. "I told him that you weren't disturbing us. He had no idea about supper, plus the twins and Stephanie were going to eat now. I can eat after we talk, or you are more than welcome to join us. We have more than enough."

"I have a better idea. Why don't you come and join me for dinner?" When he asked this, Gloria looked towards the twins, who were sitting at the dining room table, then at Stephanie, who was still on the couch. She didn't know what to do. The family looked at her excitedly.

Hanley saw her apprehension. "Oh, come on. It will be great." He was trying to convince her.

"Oh, I really don't know, Ru..." Gloria was trying to make excuses but Hanley was going to be persistent. He kept cutting her off.

"It is a beautiful night to go out, dine and do business. Why don't you come and enjoy it? That is what nights like these are for, to enjoy. People don't take advantage of their surroundings. They want to stay bored and depressed and never want to do anything to get out of that rut. That goes for the rich as well as the poor. Live life! Take advantage of things! Go for it! That's my motto. Get out of your comfort zone." He grabbed her hands, then pushed and pulled them like they were doing the Twist.

"Oh, that is not it, Rupert. It is just that Stephanie made this big meal and..."

"Oh, I'm sure that, ah, Stacey, er, ah, Sherrie, er, ah..." he began to snap his finger at Stephanie as he continued looking at Gloria. He couldn't remember her name.

"My name is Stepha..."

"That's right. That's what it is. How could I have forgotten? I'm sure that she wouldn't mind."

"Go for it, Gloria. I don't mind. Go and enjoy yourself. You deserve it. And don't worry about the food. I'm sure that Matthew will be able to dispose of it pretty well with no problem."

"See, there you go!" Hanley said as he clapped his hands together one time. "We'll have a wonderful time if you say yes.

"Hey, Ma there's nothing holding you back."

"Yeah Ma, when are you going to have a chance to chill out in a custom made stretch limo like that...plus with a man in fortune 500?!"

"Now, how are you going to top that!?" Rupert added, with his hands pointed towards the twins.

"Well, well, I don't have anything special to wear." Gloria was about to break and he knew it, but she was still making excuses.

"Look, put on anything. Don't worry about being too fancy. We are just going to dine, not to the Oscars." Gloria hesitated as she thought about it, and then made her decision.

"Well, since everyone is in agreement for me to go...Rupert, I would love to."

When she finally said yes, it was as if she hit the home run to win the baseball game, because everyone except O'Shea jumped up and started to cheer.

"Great!" Hanley exclaimed triumphantly. "We'll meet you in the limousine. Take all the time you need. The night isn't going anywhere, but you and I will."

He finally took his eyes off of Gloria and headed towards the front door. "It was truly a pleasure meeting each and every one of you." He then turned to Kindred and whispered, "Shake everyone's hand for me." He then snapped his finger towards O'Shea, who quickly opened the door to let him out. O'Shea then turned to the family and nodded his goodbyes and walked out behind Hanley quickly.

Kindred started shaking everyone's hand again, starting with the twins and working his way towards Stephanie, then apologized again for their loss before he, too, was out the door.

Stephanie was the one who jumped up quickly and locked the door, then she and the twins began screaming joyfully and ran over to Gloria excitedly and started congratulating her.

"Did you see the way he was looking at you, Ma?! He likes you!" The twins exclaimed excitedly.

"Gloria, you are absolutely glowing! You sure know how to play hard to get! Shoot, I was at the point that if you didn't go, I was going to go in your place,." Stephanie joked.

"Oh Ma, I can't wait to tell the girls that my mom went out with a billionaire!"

They surrounded around her like she was that ugly duckling girl at school who was just invited to the prom by the most popular and handsome boy in school.

"Girl, not only is he a billionaire; he is also fine as can be," commented Stephanie.

"He is fine, isn't he?" Gloria exclaimed. "Out of all the houses in God's USA, he had to come into mine." Gloria hesitated for a quick minute then looked up to heaven. "Thank you, God."

Once they finished patting Gloria on her back, Gloria zoomed up the stairs nervously as she thought about what she was going to wear. Before she attacked the suitcases, she went into the bathroom and prepared herself a hot shower.

"You can't rush a woman going out on her first date in ages," she said to herself. She didn't take too long in the shower, the way that she wanted. All the time that she was washing up, she kept thinking how all these positive things were happening to her. She was just totally blown away by it all. When she got out of the shower, she dried herself then she added the lotion.

After she attended to her body, she freshly did her makeup, which for her always came out perfectly after a nice shower. Her hair was wrapped under a shower cap and she would attend to that area last. She then wrapped herself up in her body towel and headed toward the bedroom to finish the job.

Once Gloria closed the door of the bedroom, that's when she totally started panicking.

"Skirt, dress or pants?" She questioned herself over and over out loud but in a low tone as confusion was written across her face. She began throwing all of her clothes around, trying to decide what to wear. "Oh, and shoes, shoes. Oh, God such pressure! Guys don't have the same problem that we have to endure. The only thing that they have to do is spit, shower and shave and they are done, but noooooo. You had to make me a woman." Gloria realized what she had said then changed her attitude quickly. "Oh, Lord. I am so sorry about that last comment that I made. I love being a woman. I wouldn't change it for the world."

Gloria started pacing back and forth as she looked at herself in the huge mirror and continued talking to herself.

"Ok, Gloria. You are a billionaire and you invited a woman to go out to dinner. What would you want to see her wearing?" Gloria calmed down and walked back over to the clothes that were sprawled all over the bed. She had one finger tapping her closed, puckered mouth and she was tapping her left foot. "Well, whatever she had on, it would have to complement me also. I would want eyes on me, but I would want all eyes to be on the woman I came in with." She continued talking to herself then grabbed an outfit off the bed. "Well, this is gonna have to do. I told him that I didn't have anything to wear. This just will have to do."

Twenty minutes later, Gloria was making her way down the steps. Stephanie and the twins were already at the table but were facing the steps once they heard the bedroom door open from upstairs. When she reached the bottom stairs, Gloria walked slowly towards them as she smiled widely and bashfully, like a high schooler getting ready to go to her prom. Gloria noticed that the family's mouth dropped into their plates as they stared intensely at her.

"So," Gloria said, as she turned around. "Do I look at least halfway decent? I told him that I didn't have anything de..." Gloria didn't finish her sentence because the family interrupted her.

"Oh, My, God, Ma, you look absolutely breathtaking." Zoe got up from the table and headed towards her to see her more closely.

"Ma, you look stunning." Matthew followed his sister's lead as he smiled widely and nodded.

Stephanie was looking like a proud mother as she stood up with her hands folded near her mouth, looking like she was about to cry tears of joy.

"My my my, Gloria. You still know how to work it. I hope that Mr. Hanley has a pair of boxing gloves in the limo because he's gonna have to fight off all the men!" She was now walking towards Gloria, checking her out from head to toe.

Gloria was wearing a long, dark blue dress that stopped a few inches past the kneecap. The dress enhanced her beauty and complemented what God had given her. It was sleeveless and came down to a V shape in the front, showing her bust line. There was another piece to the dress. It was long sleeved but it only covered her breast area, with a white button in the middle and it didn't cover the bust line. For jewelry, she wore a gold chain necklace with matching earrings and a bracelet, and she had on open-toed black high heeled shoes. The pocketbook she was carrying was small and the same color as the dress and shoes, blue but outlined in black, and she had her blond curly hair flowing past her shoulders. She might not have been rich but she definitely was wearing a million dollar Cheshire cat smile.

"So guys, do you think that I did too much?" she asked as she exhaled.

"Gloria, why are you so worried? He should be the one worried." The twins nodded in agreement with Stephanie's comment.

"Look, just relax, eat, talk business and have a good time. This is once in a lifetime."

"Ok, ok, ok," she said psyching herself up. "I don't know why I am so nervous. Ok, ok, let me get going. I think that I've made them wait long enough."

Gloria started heading towards the door but the phone rang right as she was walking by it. By instinct, she picked it up.

"Hello, Bunker residence." She was frowning for picking up the phone, but her voice was kind and cordial.

"Hello Gloria. It's me, Chris..." When Gloria heard his voice, her heart relaxed as she imagined seeing his face as he talked to her, then all of a sudden she felt guilty.

She really was happy to hear his voice, but it was just bad timing. She would be willing to talk to him all night if she didn't have this dinner invitation.

"Hello, Chris. How are you?" Gloria began looking at the phone with a smile then began looking toward the front door, not knowing which one was more important.

"Oh, I'm fine. I just came in from work a while ago, took a nice long shower and now I am just watching the TV stare back at me," he said as he chuckled. "I am just calling to see if maybe if you are not busy, you could take me up on my offer for something to eat. I know it's late but..."

"Oh, that is so sweet of you, Chris, but I've unexpected plans for tonight. I'll give you a call tomorrow. Maybe we could do something then, okay?"

"Sure. That is not a problem. I'll talk to you then. You have a good night."

"I will, Chris, and you do the same. Bye for now." Gloria put the phone down then began to look sad. Stephanie picked up on it and looked at her with concern.

"What's wrong, Cousin Gloria?"

"That was Chris on the phone. He wanted to see me tonight, but I had to tell him no. I told him that maybe tomorrow we could get together."

"So, that was nice. Why do you look so down, then?" She was looking at her in a puzzled way.

"Well, it is just bringing back memories of when I used to make excuses to Chris when I didn't want to tell him that I really wanted to go out with Mike."

As Gloria made her way out the house and on her way down the porch, the chauffeur quickly jumped out of the driver's side of the limo and went to open up the rear door for her. When he did, Hanley stepped out and put on his huge smile.

As she was approaching, he met up her and extended his hand for her to take it, then he looked at her from head to toe.

"Ms. Bunker Shaw, you look totally radiant." His voice was almost hypnotic.

"Please Rupert, call me Gloria," Gloria asked bashfully as she blushed like a little girl.

"Then Gloria it shall be," he responded as he nodded his head, then led her to the limo and helped her inside. He got in after her and the chauffeur closed the door.

Gloria had been in just a few limos in her lifetime, but nothing compared to the one she was sitting in. It was absolutely huge to her. The limousine was white all over, with gold trimming all around it. Just like a living room, there was a leather sofa and love seat. The long sofa was on the opposite side of the doors. The other sofa was at the back facing the front. Built into the sides of the sofas were stereo speakers. On both sides of the sofas were end tables, which held a telephone, fax machine, computer with keypad and a printer. All could be pushed down into the end tables and hidden. Also built in one of the end tables was a CD player. The windows all around the back of the limo had white blinds with the gold decorations around them. Above their heads were little lights that went all around the top and sides of the rear. Some were at the bottom. In the middle of the ceiling was an octagon shaped bright light and in front of that was a projector for the VCR/DVD/Blu-ray, which could be hidden in the ceiling. The screen was the glass partition separating the front two seats from the rear. The screen was not visible at the present time, but with a touch of a remote, it would appear over the glass. Under the glass partition were two leather chairs which at the present time were folded up and hidden. They were movable on a track and could go from one side of the rear all the way to the back and could swivel and lock into place. Also built inside the sliding limo doors were the bar area, and there even was a fridge. The floor was carpeted, white with gold designs, and so was the ceiling.

Once Gloria got inside, she sat on the long sofa opposite the door. She noticed that Mr. Kindred and O'Shea were sitting in the back, which seemed so far away. She thought that she would have to scream or make a phone call for them to hear her voice. She nodded towards them with a smile as she made herself comfortable, which was quite easy because of the cushions.

"Ms. Bunker Shaw, my, you look quite stunning," Kindred remarked with a smile. O'Shea had his hand under his chin and was tapping his cheek with his long finger as he scoped her up and down.

"Yesss," he agreed holding the word extra long. "Quite quite stunning and beautiful, I might add. That color really brings out your complexion, and with you hair? Just simply goddess-like." Gloria was shocked to see O'Shea smile. Now she knew how to get O'Shea to talk and smile. All she had to do was just talk about fashion.

"Why thank you so much for those compliments, you fine gentlemen," she responded just as Hanley was coming in to sit next to her. He unbuttoned his suit jacket and sat to her right as she sat in the left corner of the sofa, closer to the partition. He was making himself comfortable as he began to face her sideways with his back slightly to Kindred and O'Shea.

"Look at this, gentlemen," he commanded boisterously as he took his hand and motioned towards Gloria from top to bottom. "For a woman who had nothing to wear, she sure looks ready to walk arm and arm with me down the velvet rope!" Gloria thought that he sounded like a preacher when he talked. He was exciting, fascinating, intriguing, pompous, arrogant, conceited and she loved every bit of it. She couldn't remember the last time she had someone fuss over her or showed her this much attention.

Chris.

After he made the comment about the way she looked, the chauffeur had already made his way back to the front and had begun to drive away. She blushed again over the little effort it took to entrance Hanley as quickly as a flute entrances a cobra.

"So," she said as she looked around the limo. "Where to?" Without looking towards O'Shea, Hanley snapped his finger, and like an obedient trained animal, O'Shea hit the CD player and instantly Janet Jackson was singing seductively out of the speakers.

"Well, I thought that we would first stop at the White Castle down on Northern Blvd. near Junction Blvd. for appetizers, then..." he said jokingly, and Gloria slapped him on his leg, which really surprised her. She had just met him and she was acting as if she had known him for years.

"Seriously!" she responded as she smiled.

"Do you like spicy food...hot foods?" he asked seriously. "Yes, I do."

"I know a perfect place to dine. I think that you would really like it. Do you mind if I keep it as a surprise?"

"Oh, not at all. I'm sure wherever it is, I'll like it."

Ten minutes later, the chauffeur dropped Kindred off at the office, where his car was waiting for him. He handed the attaché case to O'Shea and left. Twenty minutes after that, the chauffeur dropped off O'Shea at his hotel. Ten minutes after that, Gloria noticed that the limo was heading towards a private air strip near Flushing Airport.

"Rupert, why are we heading towards the private air strip? There aren't any restaurants there; well, not that I know of unless it is hidden." Gloria was looking at him totally confused, and this only seemed to turn Rupert on.

"Well Gloria, I told you that I knew a perfect place to dine," he said very innocently with just a hint of sneakiness. "You said that I could keep it as a surprise."

"Well, maybe you could keep the restaurant as a surprise, but you could at least tell me where the restaurant is."

"Oh, that's not a problem. The restaurant is in Florida," he said very nonchalantly, with a smile on his face.

"Florida!" Gloria shouted, and the chauffeur and Hanley chuckled. Gloria turned to look at the chauffeur then turned and looked back at Hanley with surprise. Gloria's heart was racing. She didn't know how to feel. She was speechless.

"Whoa, wait a minute, Rupert. We can't go and just fly off to Florida!" Gloria panicked.

"Well, do you know another way of getting there quickly? A car and a boat are just not fast enough," Rupert joked with a smile, but Gloria wasn't smiling.

"I'm serious, Rupert!" snapped Gloria.

"Well, what's the problem? Gloria, look. By plane, Florida is only a few hours from here. Some people travel to work two hours one way, two hours back, but they travel by car or public transportation, and they are staying within the city. What's the big deal if we fly to another state within the same time span?"

"Well, well, well, I just flew in from Cali today." Gloria was making up excuses again.

"Gloria, this morning, I was in Puerto Rico, then I flew to Dominican Republic, I then flew to Miami, then to here. What's the problem? Some people travel in cramped spaces. I travel in luxury, and I want you to have the experience that I have every day of my life. Won't you please share that with me?"

Gloria noticed something different about his tone now. He wasn't being boisterous or flamboyant. She noticed that he was being very serious and he didn't sound like he wanted to discuss any kind of business. She also noticed O'Shea had left with the attaché case that probably held documents concerning the house. Gloria finally realized that she was strictly on a date.

"Mr., ah, Rupert, why are you doing this?" When Gloria asked this question Hanley first smiled then faced her with all seriousness in his face.

"It's just because I like you." This comment really touched her heart, making her speechless.

"Rupert, you don't even know if I am married or have a boyfriend." When Gloria said this, it only caused Rupert to chuckle, causing Gloria to feel a tad embarrassed.

"It would surprise you what I know, Gloria. I know that you don't have a husband because you are not wearing a wedding ring. You can't tell me that you took it off, because you said that you arrived here from California. There are no tan lines on them pretty little fingers."

Rupert then took hold of Gloria's hand gently. "And I know that if you did have a boyfriend, the way that you look, and I am not just talking about your beautiful outfit, he would have been right by your side, never letting you out of his sight."

Gloria felt like she was about to faint. There is an old saying, "If looks could kill…," but in Gloria's case, if words could kill, she would have been dead by now and Hanley would have been charged for her murder. Gloria remembered that in the 70s, Roberta Flack had a number one song called, 'Killing me softly,' and Roberta made it sound like she was being killed ever so painlessly, easily and passionately. That didn't compare to the way that Gloria was feeling at that moment.

"Rupert, you are right. I am not married and I am not dating. There is no boyfriend, but I'll tell you one thing that that I am, and that is flattered. If you treat people like this that you like, I would hate to see how you treat people that you don't like."

"Oh, you wouldn't want to know, and anyway, I like you differently than I like the average person. You are a female, a beautiful female. Anything and everything that is beautiful needs to be handled and treated much differently. You just can't treat it any old way. Gloria, I am a good judge of character.

When I like something, I go out and try to get what I want. I didn't become a rich and successful man by being timid. I say and tell it like it is."

Gloria noticed that Rupert still hadn't let go of her hand, and she wasn't pulling away.

"So, what you are saying is that you acquire females that you like the way that you acquire property?" Gloria asked this jokingly and a tad sarcastically.

"Yes and no," Rupert responded quickly and seriously. "Liking a female and liking a piece of property have some things in common and some not. A piece of property that I like will never like me back, no matter what I do to or for it. A female is different. Given a chance, a female could have feelings for me, also. That is just an example. I won't list and compare right now because we have a plane to catch to Florida. Are you game?" he stared at her as he waited to hear her answer.

"Oh sure, why not?!" she said as she rolled her eyes and smiled.

Just as Gloria gave her answer, the limo had pulled up to a private airplane. Gloria could see that it was not just a private airplane. It was a jet airplane, one of the newest lines on the market. She frowned slightly, which caught Hanley's eyes and he became concerned.

"Is there a problem, Gloria?"

"No one has ever done anything like this for me in my whole life. The fanciest place that my first husband took me was a celebrity filled charity/fundraiser held at the Waldorf Astoria in Manhattan to save the whales. My second husband, may he rest in peace, took me to a fancy villa in Beverly Hills, where we got married. It was nice and fully paid for by the California Veterinarians' Society. But neither compares to what I see before me," she said as she looked up toward the private jet, which had just started warming up for takeoff. "Rupert you have to understand. It is just that this is so extravagant! So expensive! I just feel so guilty. So…"

As Gloria was speaking, Rupert quickly cut her off. "I hope the word that you are looking for is 'special,' because that is the way that I want you to feel. Just let me drive. Just sit back and enjoy the ride." Rupert then leaned closer to her, to the point that she was able to smell his expensive cologne and breath mint. She had to admit that he smelled good.

"Gloria, there are places where we work, shop, and visit on a daily basis in our neighborhoods, and then there are the places where we can live our lives to the fullest, extraordinary places to revive the spirit, even if it is for just one day or a few hours. Allow me to let you experience it. I guarantee that you will not return home disappointed."

Gloria had to admit that she was a tad reluctant but she was fascinated about this new experience.

Once Gloria made her way out of the limo and onto the jet, she was greeted by the pilot and the airplane staff. They greeted her with smiles and nods, as they did the same for Hanley, who had his hand on Gloria's back, guiding her in.

Once the airplane door closed, Hanley was once again Mr. Showman, joking and being pompous with the pilot and staff. They laughed as they enjoyed his behavior. As she walked farther in, she was having a hard time trying not to show how astonished she was.

"Oh my gosh, Rupert!" she exclaimed as she looked around in awe. "It is a flying yacht!!"

Rupert laughed arrogantly in his pompous conceited manner, which she thought was all for show.

"It's another one of my babies." Then he raised his hands in the air and spun slowly. "Gloria, you are about to hit the skies with the jet flying! Limousine ridin'! Mega travelling! Mover and shaker! Architect of wealth-And-style…Rupert H. Hanley!"

"There he goes!" she thought to herself as she shook her head slowly and smirked. "He is preaching to the congregation again."

"Allow me to show you around before we take off, hmm?"

The jet had a movie lounge with a pop-up plasma screen and movie theater seating. It also had a television lounge, huge bedroom with a sofa, desk, and a mirror hiding another plasma television plus enough room to walk around. There was a dining room which seated eight with a pantry and buffet, service counter, and there was a salon which was spacious enough to have a cocktail party.

"Gloria, Forbes doesn't even have one of these." Rupert boasted as he stuck out his chest proudly. "Once we hit the friendly skies, you will never even know that you are on an airplane. You will think that you are in someone's apartment. It's just that smooth." Rupert was feeling very proud showing off his plane as the stewardess approached to tell them to get ready for take off.

Once in the air, they went to the movie room where there were stacks of brand new movie releases to watch. Once they got comfortable, the stewardess came with drinks and a light meal. Hanley allowed Gloria to pick the movie to watch, then they sat in the reclining movie theater chairs, laughed and lightly chatted and ate. Gloria was really enjoying Hanley's company.

Hanley had been a total gentleman since the moment she met him. She didn't know that men like this still existed—manly but still gentlemanly with class, style finesse…

Chris.

By the time the movie credits were ending, the stewardess was back to tell the bubbly two that it was time to preparing for landing. Gloria was having such a great time that she had forgotten where she was and where she was going.

Once they landed and made their way out, Hanley surprised her again by instead of getting into a limousine to take them to the restaurant, making their way to a private helicopter.

"Rupert, why didn't we just take a taxi or limo to the restaurant? You didn't need to do this."

"Well, to be honest with you, I wanted you to see another one of my babies, plus it would take too long to get there by highway. I still wanna have you home at a decent time, plus..." he began to stall, knowing it would spark her curiosity.

"Plus what, Rupert?" She knew he was about to say something that was going to surprise her, so she braced herself.

"Plus we couldn't take the jet because they haven't made a jet yet that could land on roofs." Hanley started laughing.

"Land on roofs!" she said in shock, only making Hanley laugh more. Gloria decided to just be quiet and expect the unexpected.

Fifteen minutes later, they were landing on top of Hanley's forty story resort, feet away from a private, secluded, sandy beach. Gloria was simply blown away.

"Rupert, I am never going to forget this night. Not ever!" she exclaimed as they walked toward the penthouse.

"I hope you don't, Gloria, because everything that I do is memorable." Then he turned into Mr. Preacher man raising the dead. "Memorable! Exciting! Unbelievable! Unique! And exceptional! Do you know why, Gloria? Because I am..."

Gloria decided to join in with him playfully. "Rupert H. Hanley!" Then they both started laughing.

"You forgot one thing, Gloria," he said, looking at her seriously for a moment. "The H. stands for 'how sweet it is to be Rupert H. Hanley!'" Then he did a quick little Holy Ghost jig. Gloria just shook her head again at him as she smiled.

Once inside his huge 4000 square foot ocean-front view penthouse, he began to show her around. The penthouse had three huge bedrooms, a media room and a large open area with a sitting room, living room and dining room, which overlooked the pool and Jacuzzi. The two and a half bathrooms were the size of her living room in California and the kitchen was the size of the kitchen at Archie's bar. Inside were vein-cut travertine floors, St. Laurent marble countertops, Viking appliances and a state–of–the-art home automation system that controlled everything from the lighting to the HVAC, all from a single remote. Hanley's style in furniture and fixtures was a mix of vintage sixties and seventies, along with some contemporary items.

Gloria was very impressed by his style and elegance and taste.

"Gloria, everyone who walks in says it's one of the sexiest spots they have ever seen," he proclaimed very modestly.

"The view from the swimming pool at night is really unbelievable. Rupert, you can see all of Miami lit up. Oh, Rupert, you gotta appreciate a place like this!"

"Oh, I do, Gloria. Every time that God allows me to wake up in the morning, I thank him so much. If it wasn't for him, I would be I don't know where. I appreciate everything that God has given me, this place and my ten other places." Rupert was smiling widely. "But not all are penthouses. Some are on their own island, some are in different cities and some are in different countries. Unfortunately, I don't get to stay in them much because I am always travelling, like I told you earlier…But I do try to enjoy them when I am here." Hanley then began to rub his stomach in a comedic manner.

"My stomach and mouth are telling that they are ready to get their chow on. Are you ready to eat?" Gloria nodded her head as Hanley led her to the private elevator.

"So, where is this restaurant where we will be chowing down?"

"It's on the main floor. It's a five star restaurant and it is the rave in all of Florida. It's always featured in all the top magazines. The food will actually melt in your mouth. You won't even have to chew." Rupert sounded as if he was doing a commercial for the restaurant.

As they made their way on to the elevator, Hanley started telling her about the history of the building and how many rooms, spas, pools, Jacuzzis and restaurants it had.

Once they reached the main floor and stepped off of the elevator, as Gloria looked around, it reminded her of Grand Central Station. It was packed with people going to and fro quickly. There was lively music coming from everywhere and everyone looked to be enjoying themselves.

Gloria and Rupert made their way into a packed restaurant, where a million different aromas hit their noses, and they all smelled mouth-watering. Once the host saw Hanley and Gloria—which was as soon as they walked in—he led them to the best table, which had already been reserved for them ahead of time. Hanley gentlemanly led Gloria to her seat and pulled out her chair for her to sit ,then he sat across from her at the comfortably sized table.

'Spamerica' was the name of this hot spot. Gloria saw it written over the top of the entrance and on a brick wall, all in bright colored neon lights that flashed on and off. The place was fast-paced and exciting to Gloria. It had a mixture of patrons from young urbanites to yuppies and preppies and the rich. Everyone was having conversations that mixed in with everyone else's to produce a sound frequently punctuated with laughter. Besides the mouth-watering aromas of foods and pastries, Gloria was able to smell expensive perfumes and colognes and one smell that reminded her of the bar…alcohol.

The place had a live hip band that had the people on the dance floor, which was huge. There had to be about six hundred people in there mingling, dancing and eating, not counting the people who lined the wall waiting to get in.

Even though the place was packed with people having a good time, Hanley was still able to talk to Gloria without raising his voice.

"So, how do you like the place?" he asked as the table was soon bombarded with the staff bringing them bottles of champagne, wine, menus, bread and other light snacks before the main meal arrived.

"I like it a lot!" she replied happily, which made Rupert smile confidently. "The place is very alive!" Gloria didn't realize that she was bopping her body to the music. He could see that she was content.

"I wonder what 'Spamerica' means," she said in conversation, not really expecting an answer, but Rupert surprised her.

"Oh that's easy," Rupert responded with surety. "Spamerica means that the food is of a Spanish and American cuisine. That's all. One thing about Miami is that there are a lot of Latinos here and they know how to party and cook!"

Rupert began to tell Gloria the history of the restaurant and how it got the name. Gloria was impressed by his quick response and was curious to know how he knew so much.

"So, Einstein, how do you know so much about this restaurant? Do you eat here a lot or do you know the owners or something?" Gloria began laughing lightly. A few seconds later, Rupert started laughing, too.

"As a matter of fact, Gloria, I do eat here a lot and I do know the owner. I know him quite well. It is me." When Rupert said this, Gloria looked at him for a few seconds with confusion then looked at the crowd of people in the place and watched the waiters and waitresses run all over the place trying to get everyone's food, then watched the live band then went back staring at a very proud and smiling Rupert. Gloria reached across the table and hit him playfully on his shoulder.

"You stinker! Why didn't you tell me that Spamerica was your restaurant?"

"Are you kidding?" he said seriously. "First of all, Spamerica is just one of the restaurants that I own, not just my favorite, I might add. I have other restaurants in other cities and states, not to mention in other countries. Second, I am not going to tell you that something is mine unless I know that you like it. That's why I kept asking you if you were enjoying the food. I had to make sure that the coast was clear for me to come out of hiding. Well, the coast got clear, so here I am!"

"Well," Gloria responded as she nodded her head and looked around happily and contentedly. "There's nothing to be ashamed of about this place. Everything about this place is wonderful."

"Thank you so much, Gloria. This is another one of my toys, my babies." "And a beautiful baby she is," Gloria added.

Rupert was now accepting a glassful of champagne from the waiter. Once finished with Rupert, the waiter began making his way to fill up Gloria's glass, also. Once done, Hanley lifted his glass towards her. "May I make a toast?" Gloria raised her glass, then nodded with a smile.

"To life and to love: may there be plenty more to do it and have it." Rupert winked at Gloria after toasting. Gloria thought about it for a few seconds, then agreed with Rupert. She smiled and nodded, then lifted her glass to his.

"Yes Rupert; to life and to love." Gloria nodded as they clicked glasses.

Gloria had seen more money, more beauty, more wealth, more riches, more class and charm plus excitement in one evening than she had seen in her entire boring life.

For Gloria, Spamerica lived up to the hype, rave and reputation concerning the glitz, glam and food—especially the food.

Dinner was perfect and so was the atmosphere. They ate flawless shrimp and salad with bread and butter, not to mention the tangy sauce to dip the shrimp into. And that wasn't even the main meal. For dessert, she had an Oreo cookie vanilla meringue pie with an Oreo cookie crust topping. It also had strawberries on top, with just a tad of chocolate sprinkles.

"Very interesting concept and taste!" she exclaimed, looking like a kid in a candy shop.

Throughout the whole meal, they continued discovering things about each other with great, flowing conversation, just as if they were comfortable friends who had known each other for many years. For her main course, Gloria had ordered a spicy roast duck that was so moist and juicy that it was coming off the bone. The broccoli was as thick as tree trunks and seasoned with what tasted like garlic butter. She could have eaten a whole forest of it, and her huge baked potato was filled with real bacon bits and topped with a spicy cheese sauce…hot!

Halfway through the super-delicious meal, Gloria realized that they had not yet discussed the proposal for Rupert to buy the house. She was too busy chatting about her life in California, her job as a real estate agent, her children, parents, music and much more, without once finding herself lost for words; likewise with Hanley.

"You know Rupert, this whole time together, we have not mentioned once about the house."

"Oh, I am sorry." Rupert began to scoop out the inside of his potato. "I thought that you had already given me your answer."

"I beg your pardon?"

"Well, the way that you've been talking, I thought that you didn't want to sell. Was I mistaken? Even I every now and then misinterpret someone."

"Oh, Rupert, I really don't know. Everything is rushing so quickly, like water escaping from a broken levee. I don't know what to do." She had her head down slightly as she shook her head.

"Well, Gloria, Kindred could see you tomorrow and you and he could talk that out, about setting up a time to discuss the house. It's all up to you. No rush, of course."

"Okay. It couldn't hurt. I'm just going to be hearing an offer anyway, right? I'm still going to have to think about it after."

"Oh, of course. There you go. You just might be surprised how much he'll offer now, now that you and I've become acquainted with each other." Rupert was smiling suavely at her.

"Oh, Rupert, I must admit that you definitely are a connoisseur when it comes to flattering and treating a woman." Gloria was redder than the strawberries that were on her dessert.

"Well, Gloria, I have always heard that flattery, especially when it was true would get me everywhere." He laughed lightly.

"But why me, Rupert? You are a worldly man, a travelling man, a man who's been around the rich and famous, not to mention all of the beautiful people. Why would you do all this for me?"

When Gloria made this comment, Rupert's face showed shock and confusion.

"Gloria, don't you think that you are beautiful?" Hanley looked like he had just been slapped. "You've been so busy raising your family on your own and dealing with daily problems, you forgot about that woman in the mirror. You are beautiful, witty, funny and definitely desirable. Any man would be a fool not to see that. You have a natural beauty that comes from the inside and radiates out of you. You are a joy to be around. Gloria, I want you to know that I didn't come to your house thinking that I would have you here with me right now. I came to your house because of what Kindred had told me. I surprised him by saying that my assistant and I would be coming with him to your house. None of this was planned. But when I saw your face, I was immediately drawn to you and I wanted to get to know you. You are something special, Gloria. That's why this is a special occasion, for me if not for you."

Gloria began to fan herself as she became hot all over.

"Whew!" she said jokingly. "Is it hot in here or is it just me from eating all this spicy food!?"

"You being hot has nothing to do with the food. You are just naturally that way." Rupert reached across the table and took hold of her hand. "I don't mind being burned by touching you."

With all of the special attention that Rupert was giving her and all of the wonderful foods that she had eaten that night, not to mention the excitement

The Life and Times of Gloria Bunker

and spontaneity, Gloria deep down inside was hoping that the night wouldn't end.

Once they finished eating and drinking champagne, they were both wishing that they had the power to make the clock go backwards or freeze in time, while the fun and excitement continued.

"Gloria, I wish that I had time to really show you the town. Miami is one of the trendiest, most happening cities in America. They call New York 'The city that never sleeps'—if I had a slogan for Miami, it would be 'Miami the city that never stops partying,' and this is so very true."

"This is my first time in Miami, and even though I've only been inside your beautiful and most luxurious and posh building, I could just imagine what's through your glass doors." Gloria began looking out of the glass doors from her chair and was only able to see bright lights above the city.

"Well, there is always tomorrow." Rupert responded by smiling impishly and doing the Groucho with his eyebrows.

"What do you mean, Rupert?"

"Well, we could do this again tomorrow. It could be a different restaurant if you want. It could be in a different city or state. As a matter of fact, it could be a different country, if you desire."

"Oh, believe me, Rupert, I would love to, believe me I would, but I want you to know that my daddy's funeral is Saturday and I still have a lot to do before then."

"I truly understand. I'm sorry. I almost forgot."

"It's okay, Rupert. I want you to know that this has been wonderful and I would love to spend more time with you, but it would have to be after everything is over concerning my daddy."

"Well, I think that is fair." Rupert kept looking at his watch, while not hiding his disappointment.

"Well, my dear Ms. Gloria, I think that it is time to get you back to New York. It is almost tomorrow and like you said, you have a lot to do."

"Oh Rupert, how I wish that I was dreaming. How I wish that I was still in California and my daddy was at home yelling at the television. Boy! I really don't wanna wake up."

Gloria inhaled then exhaled hard as Rupert got up from the table and made his way to her side to help her out of her chair. He then put a tip on the table and the two headed back towards the private elevator leading to the penthouse. All the while, Gloria couldn't stop talking about how what a wonderful time she had had with him. Not only was she excited, like a child's first time at a carnival or a circus, she was actually making Rupert blush. Rupert loved the childlike qualities about Gloria, and how she talked with such emotion and how she emphasized with her big and beautiful innocent eyes. He had to admit, also, but only to himself, that he hadn't had a wonderful and honest date like this in a very long while. The women that he had fancied clung to him or tried to dominate him, but those relationships only lasted for a very short time. He was beginning to develop blisters on his big toe from kicking women to the curb. He thought that he might have found a woman who was his equal. Maybe not monetarily but equal meaning that they liked and dislike the same thing and shared the same views, hopes and ideas. He thought that maybe he had found her in Gloria.

Five minutes after arriving back at the penthouse, they were back in the air and two and a half hours later, they were at Flushing's private airstrip. Fifteen minutes after that, they were in front of the Bunker house in the stretch limousine. Gloria looked toward the house and noticed that the porch light was the only light on.

"Well once again, I'm glad that you had a good time and that you decided to go out with me. Believe me; I enjoyed it much more than you." Rupert was now digging into his pocket looking for something as she stared curiously. "Before you go, I have something for you." Rupert pulled a small, long box out of his pocket and presented it to a surprised and speechless Gloria. She slowly took it from him as her hand shook nervously. She looked at him, then looked at the box, not believing what he had done for her. When she finally opened it, she couldn't believe her eyes. She had to blink just to make sure she wasn't seeing things.

Gloria was holding in her shaking fingers a Female Oyster Perpetual Date Just watch, which was 18 carat yellow gold with deployable clasp on a leather strap.

"Oh..My..Gosh..Rupert! This is a Rolex watch!" Gloria couldn't take her eyes off it.

Rupert took it from her and put it on her wrist. "Yes, it's a Rolex. So you can always remember the TIME that we shared together."

"Oh my gosh, Rupert, how could I ever forget? Nights like this are supposed to be remembered forever." Gloria didn't know if it was because she was full of champagne or just drunk from excitement, but she had the courage to reach over towards him and give him a hug. She thought that was the least she should do.

"Rupert, I will cherish and remember it forever. You have made me feel like royalty. Like a queen. Who could ask for more?"

"I could," Rupert quickly responded. "But I will be patient," he said in a joking manner. Deep down in his heart, however, he was being very serious. He was surprised that she had a remark ready.

"I'll try not to make you wait too long." When she said that, he was speechless. Hanley then knocked on the glass partition of the limousine and instantly the chauffeur was out of the driver's seat, out of the door and was opening up the rear door to help them out.

"Let me walk you to your door, madam," Rupert said in an old English gentleman accent.

"I wouldn't have it any other way." Gloria responded kindly.

Rupert got out the limousine first, while the chauffeur stood near the door, and then he extended his hand towards her so he could help her out of the rear. Gloria graciously accepted the gesture.

As she got out with the help of Rupert, she greeted the chauffeur, who was surprised to be acknowledged by her. He smiled a set of pearly whites at her and nodded. Even though Rupert was only walking her to her door, he still straightened his clothes just in case, even though it was early morning, he might see someone and they would have the honor and pleasure of seeing him.

Rupert escorted Gloria up to the porch and stood by her as she searched her purse for her keys. Once she found them and took them out, she turned and looked up to him. She really wanted to put her head up against his huge, muscular chest.

Chris.

Instead in a sweet and appreciative voice she uttered. "Once again, Rupert, this whole night was totally remarkable, just simply perfect in every way. I don't think there could have been any other way to top off the evening."

"Well, I'm glad that you've enjoyed it. You were worth it, and it was my pleasure."

Gloria then put the key in the door and opened it. The smell of the flowers, so aromatic and fresh, hit her nose pleasantly. "Thank you for treating me like a woman." She then gave him a kiss and watched his expression.

Rupert put his huge hands on the cheek where she kissed him and smiled widely.

"Whew!" he screamed as he began to rub it. "I'll never wash this side of my face again!"

After he made the comment, Gloria smiled then shook her head and went into the house. Once she was inside and closed the door, she stood near the window with the lights still off, watching Rupert walk off the porch, down the stairs, and back into the limo. She watched as the chauffeur closed the rear door then walked quickly to the driver's side, got into the limo and drove off.

CHAPTER NINE:
Gloria to the Rescue

Once the limo was out of sight, she leaned up against the door then slowly slid down it with a smile. She was partially sitting and lying on the floor, shaking her head back and forth slowly, still not believing what she had done the whole night. Gloria heard an upstairs door open.

"I know that I heard the front door open." Then she saw the upstairs hallway light come on. "I know that I am not going crazy." Stephanie was talking to herself as she began to make her way down the stairs.

Once she got to the bottom of the stairs, she turned on the living room light by flipping the wall switch. She then looked towards the door and saw Gloria half-lying on the floor. This startled and scared Stephanie.

"Aaah, Gloria!" she screamed as she ran towards Gloria to see what the problem was. "Are you hurt? What did that beast do to you?"

While this was going on, Gloria heard a rumble from the basement, then the twins zoomed through the door to see what the commotion was all about. Zoe had a bat in her shaking hands as she hid behind Matthew.

"What's going on? We heard a scream." Then they saw Gloria on the floor then they ran towards her. "Oh my God, Ma, are you all right? What happened?"

Everyone was at her side trying to help her up as she was trying to calm them down.

"Guys, please relax. I am fine. I am just overwhelmed by my night, that's all."

Gloria was still smiling widely. "I've just been to Aurora via chariot and returned via magic carpet. I ran barefooted through the enchanted forest and danced on the moon with Prince Charming." While Gloria was explaining how wonderful her night was, the three just looked at her, then looked at each other in confusion.

The Life and Times of Gloria Bunker

"Is Ma drunk?" Zoe asked with a serious expression on her face.

"I don't know." Matthew responded.

As Matthew began to help his mother up, he started to examine her from head to toe.

"Ma, are you drunk?" After he asked this, Stephanie started to fix Gloria's hair and dress, looking at Gloria confusedly. Gloria began to spin around with her hands in the air like a ballerina with her eyes closed.

"No, no, no. I am not drunk on booze. I am drunk on life! Tonight, I was the belle of the ball. Oh, it was so wonderful. No, no spectacular. The limousine, the private jet..." Gloria had spun all the way to Archie's chair.

"A private jet!" The family shouted in unison as they interrupted her.

"Yes, I did say private jet. And that's not all—a helicopter that landed on top of his resort hotel!"

While Gloria was explaining her special day, Matthew was behind the chair, Stephanie was sitting in Edith's chair and Zoe was on the floor with her head leaning on Gloria's leg, and they were all listening intently with their eyes wide like owls.

"Where did you fly to?" Stephanie asked anxiously as she leaned in closer to hear.

Gloria hesitated to build up their excitement, then sprang it on them, sounding like a game show announcer.

"Miami!"

"Miami!" they all screamed and echoed as Stephanie stood up and started stomping her feet. Matthew started jumping up and down and Zoe started slapping Gloria's leg. They were acting as if their favorite team won the Super Bowl.

"Oh guys, he was so charismatic, funny, charming, exciting, loud, boisterous, wonderful, and full of energy, and he was a total gentleman. He treated me with such style and class. Kids, I loved your daddy, this is no lie, but I never knew that a man could be like, like, like..." Gloria was looking for the right word.

"A total package!" *Chris*.

"Oh, Ma, I'm glad you are so happy. I've never seen you so happy before."

"Yeah Ma. You look so young right now that you and Zoe look like sisters."

"Yeah Gloria. You're glowing, sparkling and shining like that watch on your arm."

Stephanie said casually then she realized what she said and did a double-take at the watch that Gloria had on her wrist.

"Watch? Gloria! Where did you get that expensive timepiece from? I know that you didn't have that on when you left last night." Gloria had her arm stretched out admiring the watch, then she began to show it to the family.

"Do you like it? It's a Rolex. Rupert gave it to me just a few minutes ago."

"Oh, Ma! Look at the size of that!" Matthew took hold of his mother's hand and stared at the watch as if he was in a daze.

"Gloria, that cost a pretty penny. I would have to do a lot of voiceovers and background vocals just to be able to put a down payment on something like that. Even after that, I don't know if I would still be able to afford a lay-away plan!"

"Mommy, that's so romantic." Zoe said softly, looking straight ahead as she laid her head on Gloria's lap. She almost had tears in her eyes. "It's like in those fairy tales. A handsome prince comes and swoops up the damsel and takes her to his castle in the sky. It's just so beautiful."

"It was honey, it really was." Her voice was soothing as she began to stroke Zoe's head.

"Well, I wanna hear all about it later, Ma. Right now, I wanna go back downstairs and get some sleep. I am exhausted."

Matthew turned and headed down into the basement.

"Me too, Gloria, as long as you are okay. That was my main concern. I wanna hear about it also, and don't leave anything out." Stephanie turned and started up the stairs, then turned to her one more time. "Gloria, I'm really glad that you had a good time. You deserve it."

"Thanks Stephanie. See you in the morning." Gloria said as Stephanie continued up the stairs, but suddenly Stephanie stopped at the top of the stairs and looked at her watch.

"Ah, hellooo, Gloria. Have you looked at your brand new Rolex lately? It is morning."

Gloria looked at the Rolex then realized what time it was.

"Oops, oh yeah that's right. Well, in that case, I will see you in a few hours."

Gloria and Zoe were still in the living room, Gloria in the big chair, Zoe on the floor with her head being stroked by Gloria as it lay on her lap.

"So Mommy, it's not too late for me?"

"Is what not too late for you, honey?"

"For me to find that special knight in shining armor."

Gloria laughed then leaned down and gave Zoe a kiss on top of her head.

"You know, honey, I thought it was for me, but Rupert stirred up feelings in me that I thought had been buried over with time. Right now, I can honestly say that I don't think it's ever too late. But why are you worrying about that now? You are still so young. You shouldn't be thinking about that now anyway. You should just worry about being a teenager and how to keep those straight A's coming."

"But Ma, how do you know when it is right? I mean, guys are such jerks in my generation. No Chris's in this generation." Zoe said nonchalantly. The comment shocked Gloria.

"Zoe, what made you say that?"

"Well, I had heard that you and C.B. used to go out with each other. Grampa used to say that you used to call C.B. your knight in shining armor."

"There goes that word again," Gloria thought to herself. "But what would make you bring up his name out of everyone that you know?"

"Well, because you were speaking to him right before you left, plus I had seen him earlier when the girls and I left the house, and Stephanie and Matthew told me that he had come over and that you and he spent some time together, that's all, why? Did I say something wrong?" Zoe had a sound of concern in her voice.

"Oh, of course not, honey. Of course not." Gloria kissed Zoe again on the head.

"I keep forgetting that C.B. has been a part of your life since you were little."

"I heard the same about you. That he's been a part of your life since y'all were little."

"Well, only till I married Mike. Yesterday was the first time that I've spoken to him since then."

"But Ma, can I ask you a question? How did he go from being your knight in shining armor to not seeing him till now?"

"Good question, honey." Gloria said. "It just happens like that sometimes." Gloria left it like that, especially since that Zoe hadn't insisted on more info. She seemed satisfied with that little remark. Zoe brought Chris into her thoughts along with Rupert as she just sat in the chair and slowly and peacefully drifted off into sleep.

Gloria had been so tired that she didn't even have the strength to climb the stairs to her room. She didn't mean to conk out on the chair, but she did. She drifted deep into her thoughts, only to be awakened after what seemed to be maybe five minutes of sleep.

"Someone is knocking at the door," she said to Zoe but she was not in the living room. "She must've gone back downstairs. She probably didn't want to wake me."

Even though Stephanie had turned on the living room light, for some reason to Gloria, the whole room was kind of blurry and foggy. Even the knocking of the door sounded strange, like it was being done in slow motion. She figured because she had just woken up, all her senses weren't functioning correctly yet. For some reason, she didn't jump up to get the door. She tried to get her bearings first.

Eventually the whole living room slowly began to come into focus, but it was no longer blurry, just foggy. She was able to hear the clock ticking on the wall plain as day but for some reason, the knocking still sounded far off and like it was being done in slow motion. She glanced to her left and looked towards the window and saw that it was still dark outside. She slowly got up and stretched and twisted her head from side to side as her neck made little cracking noises. Gloria noticed that there was something around her neck and it wasn't just the necklace she had on earlier. She put her head down to face her neck and chest area, then she noticed that she had diamonds hanging around her neck down towards her bustline. She also noticed that on her wrists were diamond and gold bracelets. She still had the Rolex on, too. The dark blue dress that she was wearing was gone, replaced by a flowing, loose-fitting white gown, but it wasn't a wedding gown. She stared at all these items with confusion.

"Where did all this jewelry and this outfit come from?" Gloria was very puzzled. "Oh, I get it!" She remarked as she smiled and nodded her head. "I must be dreaming. The limousine, the chauffeur, private jet and helicopter—all of that wasn't real. I'm probably still lying on the couch waiting for Stephanie to finish preparing dinner."

The knocking at the door continued in slow motion as Gloria headed around the chair, past the couch and made her way to the door.

"Who is it?" she asked very casually.

"It is Mr. O'Shea," the feminine voice responded on the other side of the door.

Gloria was wondering why O'Shea would be at the door. He had been left at the hotel.

"Oh yeah I forgot. I'm dreaming. This is all just a dream that I have conjured up in my mind."

Gloria opened up the door and saw O'Shea standing there with one hand on his hip and the other hand under his chin as one finger tapped his cheek as he checked her out from head to toe.

"Girl, you look fierce! You are working that gown and the jewelry! You remind me of that girl from the 'I can't believe it's not butter' commercial with Fabio in it. Only difference is that she didn't have all that jewelry on and she was a brunette." O'Shea's face went serious for a moment as he stared at Gloria's scalp and then, uninvited, ran his hand through Gloria's hair slowly. "You are a natural blonde aren't yah, girl?"

"What!" Gloria said as she looked at him like he was crazy. She then shook her head quickly and said to herself, "Gloria, forget it." Then she said to him, "It's late, Mr. O'Shea. We are all sleeping at this present moment. What do you want?" Her voice was a tad cold and abrupt, but O'Shea didn't seem to notice or if he did, he didn't pay it any attention.

"Didn't the limousine drop you off at the hotel? Did you leave something here?"

"Ssshh!" he said sneakily as he put his finger over his puckered lips. Gloria thought that he looked like he had lipstick on.

The Life and Times of Gloria Bunker

O'Shea smiled widely after he removed his finger from his lips then looked both ways.

"I know that it is late," he whispered. "But I want you to come with me. We are going to take the private elevator."

"The private elevator?" Gloria echoed with confusion.

Gloria was wondering what the hell he was talking about. She was about to close the door in his face but she had to remind herself that this was all a dream; that she was actually sleeping in the living room.

"No need to change your gown, Gloria. You look fab-u-lous!" He then snapped his finger. He then held out his arm for her to take it. Reluctantly, she took it then stepped out the front door. Once she did that, the door disappeared and she found herself in Rupert's penthouse hallway walking towards the private elevator.

As she walked with O'Shea leading her, she squeezed his arm and she was able to feel his boniness through his clothes.

"He feels so real, though." She started to wonder if she was really sleeping after all.

"Oow!" he screamed angrily. "Why did you do that? I'm not a roll of toilet paper, you know!" O'Shea then rolled his eyes at her.

Gloria laughed as she began to feel embarrassed. "Oh, I'm sorry, Mr. O'Shea. I guess that I am just excited, that's all."

"Well, let's try to keep your arousal to a minimum, shall we?" Gloria nodded as they now stood in front of the elevator.

"So," she said, "Where are we going? Are we going to see Rupert? Is he waiting for us in the restaurant?" Gloria started firing off questions rapidly.

"Hey, hey, hold the train, conductor," he responded to Gloria. "You'll find out in a minute!" He had his hands up in front of Gloria in surrender as he sucked his teeth and rolled his eyes.

Gloria wanted to laugh again, but decided to show a little patience over her eagerness.

"I wonder what surprise O'Shea has for me," she thought silently as she waited for the elevator.

Finally the elevator came and they both went inside. Once inside, O'Shea pressed the bottom button as the door closed, then the elevator began going down. She felt her stomach churn as it began moving fast. She looked towards O'Shea, who was at her side but he was staring straight ahead out the door like he was a pillar of frozen ice. He was so still, so silent, that it almost felt eerie and creepy.

Finally the elevator made it down to the main floor, which, was packed with people, hustling and bustling in and out of the different restaurants and spas and stores, only this time Gloria noticed that everyone was moving in slow motion. The only ones that were moving at normal speed were O'Shea and herself.

"Wow, Mr. O'Shea, do you notice this? Look at everyone. This is so cool."

As Gloria was being amazed by what she was seeing, Mr. O'Shea pretty much just ignored her as they moved through the crowd.

"Hey, Mr. O'Shea, do you know what this reminds me of? This reminds me of that movie, *The Matrix*! By any chance, did you see that?"

"Oh, yes. *The Matrix*!" O'Shea mimicked arrogantly and rudely as he rolled his eyes and curled his mouth up in the corner like Elvis used to do. Gloria was getting a tad annoyed by his rudeness and was just about to give him a piece of her mind.

"Hey, listen here, O'Shea, let me tell you something..." Gloria had her hand on her hip and the finger was just about to reach O'Shea's face when all of a sudden, O'Shea began acting like a little boy at an amusement park. His eyes became huge and his mouth dropped as if it was the first time that he was told that he was going to see Santa Claus. Ignoring Gloria as she was talking, he interrupted her as he began to speak.

"Oh look. Come on, Gloria! Let's go outside! I wanna show you the private secluded beach!"

Before Gloria had a chance to respond to what he had just requested, O'Shea grabbed her hand and led her out the main lobby doors. While she was being pulled by O'Shea, deep down inside, she wanted to tell O'Shea that he was not the type that she wanted to go to any private secluded beach with, but she decided to bite her tongue.

Even though Gloria would've preferred to have been led by Rupert, she decided just to go along for the ride and see what was going to happen.

Once outside the back of the hotel, she was able to smell the salt from the ocean. Spanish music was being played loudly on the beach, and she saw people dancing erotically and smiling widely in the sand, but just like inside the hotel, everything and everyone were moving slowly.

"Come on, Gloria!" O'Shea asked as he began to skip in the sand like a little child. "Let's take off our shoes and frolic in the sand near the water!"

Once again, before Gloria had a chance to respond, she noticed that O'Shea began spinning and jumping, then he fell in the sand laughing his head off. This was not the O'Shea that she had first met just a few hours before. Gloria just stared at him as she began to laugh.

Gloria watched him as he took off his shoes in the sand and left them as he began to run way ahead of her.

"Come on, Gloria!" He was motioning for her to come on with his boney hands. Gloria was enjoying having the cool air on her face. She also was feeling like a little girl.

"Oh, what the heck?" She said in fun surrender as she took off her shoes in the sand then started after O'Shea, who was now pretty far from her. It was still dark outside but the lights around the hotel allowed Gloria to be able to see the water.

"Hey, wait up, Mr. O'Shea!" Gloria began running after him. "Oh hell! I'll never be able to catch up to him if he doesn't slow down!" she said to herself.

The waves in the ocean were gentle for that time of night and she was able to taste the salt on her tongue as she got closer to the water and ran along the shore. She started speeding up because the sand was now harder under her feet.

"O'Shea!" Gloria yelled again, but he wouldn't stop. He turned around every now and then, said something with a smile on his face, and then faced forward again. Gloria was running very fast but she didn't seem tired or out of breath.

"Hey, O'Shea, what the hell is the matter with you?!" He was starting to tick her off because she thought that he was teasing her. Every time that she ran faster, he would decide to speed up as if he didn't want her to catch him. Gloria wanted to know why he was acting so very strangely. Why did he come to get her then, once they got on the beach, decide to run in front of her?

O'Shea turned to face her again, but this time he began pointing in the direction he was running. He was moving his mouth but she couldn't hear or make out what he was saying. He was just too far away.

"What the heck are you saying?!" she yelled angrily, but O'Shea just ignored her and continued to run faster and farther away.

Gloria began to pick up speed, and when she did, he did too, but she was gaining on him. She also noticed that she was farther from the hotel than she really wanted to be. She could hardly hear the music now and she didn't see anyone in the water, despite the fact that there had been a lot of people on the beach and the current was smooth and calm. Where O'Shea and she were, there weren't even any people. The only thing she saw was huge boulders in the water and to her right, a lot of underdeveloped land. O'Shea started climbing on the top of the boulders. While he was still doing this, he still motioned for her to follow him.

'Doesn't this fool know that I have an 'I don't believe it's not butter,' gown on and that I am a woman?" she yelled out. She was so angry with O'Shea that she wanted just to strangle him. She never stopped running, even when she got to the boulders. She began to climb them.

Gloria's legs began to hurt and her hands hurt from heaving herself up and over the huge dirty boulders. She was getting higher and higher, to the point where she was afraid to look down.

Eventually, she turned and looked down. The hotel was so far away that it barely resembled one. Gloria looked back up and noticed that she was almost at the top. She hadn't climbed that much but when she looked down; it looked like she was hundreds of feet above the water.

Once at the very top, she was able to stand straight up. She looked at her hands and nails, and they were filthy. Even some of her nails had been broken off. She looked at her white gown and it was no longer flowing, and it was no longer white. It was now dirty with perspiration and dirt and it was clinging to her body.

Gloria began to wipe her hands on her gown as she looked around for O'Shea.

"O'Shea, when I find you, I am going to kick your skinny, puny, runty behind!" she expressed angrily with her hands balled up into fists at her side.

"Girl, what's with all the drama?" a voice coming from behind her asked calmly.

The voice shocked her but she quickly turned around and saw O'Shea standing there with one hand on his hip and the other hand up and tilted to the side like he was a human teapot.

"What the hell is the matter with you? Why did you run away like that and leave me? Then of all things, you start climbing up a damn cliff, making me get all dirty and stuff, then you have the gall to ask me about drama?! No, O'Shea, this is not drama. This is about me getting ready to whip your booty. No drama, only horror!"

As Gloria began walking towards Mr. O'Shea angrily and getting ready to knock some sense into his head, Mr. O'Shea quickly threw up his hands in a surrender motion with his eyes bulging out in a panic.

"Calm down, Miss Thang. There ain't nothing wrong with you." He quickly replied, unraveled by her outburst. "Girl, you are still running it." He then snapped his finger again with a smile now forming on his face as he scoped her from head to toe.

"What do you mean there ain't nothing wrong with me?" she asked angrily as she mimicked O'Shea's voice. "How can you say that, you fool? I am filthy!" Gloria then looked down at her gown and noticed that the white gown was gone. She was now wearing a long, strapless red gown with gold trimming and around her shoulder was a matching shawl. Gloria also noticed that she was wearing red open toe shoes and she had an ankle bracelet on…diamond.

"Oh, this definitely has to be that spicy sauce that I had in Rupert's restaurant," she whispered..

O'Shea walked passed her then turned to face her. "Follow me. The show is about to start. We have first row seats!" he said with a lot of enthusiasm.

Gloria looked around and didn't see any building or anything, but she began to follow O'Shea.

"Don't run, O'Shea. I have shoes on," she warned, but he didn't respond.

As the two walked for a while, not talking, Gloria saw something up ahead but she couldn't make it out that well. She was going to ask O'Shea what it was but decided just to keep her mouth shut. She figured that they were going in that direction. She'd find out in a moment.

As Gloria got closer, she spotted two trees, each with a very long, thick branch. Hanging from each branch was one rope. Hanging from the two ropes were two figures, but she couldn't make that part out yet.

Closer and closer she got; she started picking up speed, forgetting that she had shoes on. The two figures became clearer and more in focus, and she was able to see what was going on. Hanging from the two separate trees were people that she knew and cared for.

"Chris! Rupert!" she screamed as she put her hand over her mouth in shock. She couldn't believe what she was seeing.

Chris and Rupert were hanging from the trees, tied by their hands with rope, and they were over something that looked like quicksand. Their feet were tied also and there was tape around their mouths, preventing them from screaming for help. Gloria was able to see the panic in their red and tearing eyes. The only thing she knew was that she had to save them quickly.

"Go and get help, O'Shea!" she ordered strongly, but when she turned to face him, he was sitting in a movie theater chair eating a box of popcorn.

"No, I'm not going to do anything." He had one naked foot on his thigh, wiggling his toe, trying to get the dirt from between them.

"Well, if you aren't going to help them, then I just will have to," she said angrily.

"Well, I hope so," he replied with popcorn in his mouth. "You are the star of the show, you know."

"I am the star of the show?" she repeated. "What do you mean that I am the star of the show?"

Gloria was completely puzzled and confused by what he had just said.

"I mean that you are the star of the show." He reiterated then rolled his eyes, put down his popcorn and sashayed over to her. "Look, girlfriend, let me play the scene out for you, okay. You have two very handsome and dashing men before you that you care about. On this side," he said, pointing towards Chris, "you have a man that you've known your entire life, and he was your boyfriend up to your teenage years. He's everything that you've ever wanted and he has always treated you well. Deep down inside, you know that he was the perfect catch that you let go, but now you have a chance to have him back, plus he still wants you and would do anything for you." Then O'Shea pointed toward the other direction. "Now on this side, you have a man that you've just met that has set your world on fire. He's handsome, funny and witty, exciting, strong mind and body, plus he is rich. He gave you just a small taste of the good life and you liked it. No, no, you loved it! He is also everything that you've ever wanted in a man and he is willing to do anything for you, and if he's willing to do anything for you, that goes for your family, too. You know that you wanted to be intimate with him tonight, am I right, girlfriend?" He then laughed with contempt. He put his hand on her shoulder but she knocked it off of her.

"Screw you, O'Shea!" Gloria responded quickly and angrily. That is none of your business!"

Gloria then began to run towards the two men that she cared about, but O'Shea wasn't done teasing her.

"Hey, Gloria, the one that you save is the one you truly wanna spend the rest of your life with!" he yelled as he began to sit down and eat the popcorn.

When he said this, she instantly stopped, then turned back and looked at him. Gloria's chest was burning like fire as she breathed hard.

"Yep Gloria, that's the catch. They've proven to you that they are willing to do anything for you. It's time for you to do the same."

"No problem, O'Shea." Gloria was the one who was smiling now. She took off her shoes and ripped the full length dress almost in half then she took off the shawl.

"I'm not just going to save one. I'm going to save both!"

Gloria thought that she had outsmarted O'Shea. She continued running to them, and she was just approaching the middle of the two trees and the two holes, which looked to be filled with quicksand, when she heard O'Shea yell towards her again.

"Hey Gloria!" O'Shea sang in a teasing manner. "I forgot to tell you. The first one that you save is the one that you truly wanna spend the rest of your life with!"

This made Gloria instantly stop running. Now Gloria was the one who was standing between two men that she cared about, frozen like a piece of ice, not knowing which one to save first. Her heart was racing and she was sweating profusely.

"Hey Gloria!" O'Shea sang again.

"What the hell do you want, O'Shea?!" Gloria yelled in a very annoyed tone. This only seemed to excite O'Shea even more.

"Do you wanna know why their mouths are taped over?" O'Shea mumbled with popcorn in his mouth. "Because it wouldn't be fair if you are persuaded by their smooth and suave voices....Well, in this case, scared and panicked screaming voices!"

"I don't know what to do!" She yelled back without turning her head towards O'Shea. "I care for them both!"

"Well, you got a real problem, girlfriend, because it's just about to get even more interesting!"

As Gloria continued looking at both men, she started to notice that the branches that the two men hung from were slowly being lowered into the hole of quicksand.

"Hey Gloria, to make matters worse, you don't have much time to decide! You better hurry up! The longer that you wait, the harder it will be to save them!"

"You bastard, O'Shea!" Gloria cried out to him angrily.

O'Shea put his hand on his chest indignantly and looked at Gloria in utter surprise and shock.

"Why are you getting mad at meeeee?!" he cried, almost looking like he was innocent and about to shed a tear. "This is all you, Gloria. I'm just here to see the show, you know. I wanna see how it's going to end, that's all."

"It's- it's too much pressure! I need time to think!"

"If you take too much more time, they are going to die, or you might be able to save one but not the other. Choose, Gloria, choose!" he challenged her teasingly.

"I can't! I can't! I, I, I don't know who is the right choice!" Gloria's voice was cracking and filled with uncertainty.

"Gloria, whatever choice you go with will be the right choice." He saw that Gloria was crying. "Listen, girlfriend. You don't have a lot of time! Just follow your heart!"

"Follow my heart," she repeated as she looked toward Chris and Rupert.

"That's right, girlfriend. Follow your heart," he cried as he looked at her seriously, then he started banging in rhythm on the chair with his hand. Follow your heart, follow your heart, follow your heart, follow your heart."

Gloria kept repeating this over and over in her head until she became dizzy and fell on the ground. She tried to continue looking at the two men, but they were becoming blurry and hazy. Everything around her was becoming blurry and hazy and then eventually dark, but inside her head, she kept hearing those words, 'Follow your heart.' And she kept hearing knocking, but it wasn't in rhythm like before.

Gloria was slowly coming out of the darkness. She wasn't feeling dizzy any longer and she was slowly seeing brightness. She was actually opening her eyes, which were trying to get adjusted to where they were. What was staring back in front of Gloria was a television set.

CHAPTER TEN:
Clothes, Catering, and Chris

When Gloria finally got her bearings, she realized where she was. "I am in my daddy's house in New York," she said to herself. On the floor next to her was Zoe, who had fallen asleep with her head in Gloria's lap. Gloria's hand was still on top of her head.

"Oh, it was all a dream," she thought happily and with much relief. Gloria examined what she had on and what kind of jewelry she wore, and she noticed that she still had on the dress that she had gone out in just a few hours before, plus she still had the special present from Rupert on her wrist—the Rolex.

"It might've just been 'a dream,' but last night wasn't. That was a 'dream come true.'"

Gloria looked around the room and was surprised that she had fallen asleep in the living room in her father's chair.

"Teresa was right," she thought as she nodded. "Daddy's chair really is that comfortable!"

Zoe was stirring in her spot as she also began waking up.

"Good morning, sunshine!" Gloria said as she began rubbing Zoe's head again.

"Morning, Ma." She was now yawning and stretching and loosening up her body.

"I can't believe that we fell asleep in the living room." She was now standing up and touching her toes, still trying to get out all the stiffness.

"Me neither, but you know something..." Before Gloria could finish what she was about to say, someone was knocking at the door. "I knew I heard knocking."

Gloria was just about to get up to get the door, but Zoe was already standing.

"I'll get it, Ma."

Gloria looked out the window from the chair and saw that the light was trying to make its way into the room. She was wondering what time it was but then she remembered that she had that new Rolex on strapped around her wrist. She looked at it and saw that it was nine-thirty in the morning.

As Zoe made her way to the door and opened it, she stood there frozen with her mouth agape. By this time, Stephanie was coming down the stairs, still in the sleeping gear she had on last night, and Matthew was coming out of the basement in his same sleeping gear also.

"Oh...My... gosh... Mommy! Boy, do we have a delivery!"

Gloria figured that it was some flowers or something like that, so she didn't think too much about it. She told Zoe to tell them to bring it in, so Zoe did what her mother told her to do.

"My mother said come on in," Gloria heard Zoe say. So that's what the delivery people did. They came on in, wheeling racks and racks of black clothes on hangers, for females and for males. Gloria jumped up out of the chair and came to the door and saw a truck with deliverymen loading and unloading clothes.

"Oh my God, what is all of this?!" she said in total surprise and shock.

Everyone was in shock as they smiled widely and looked at the clothes. None of them really knew what to do. They were speechless.

"Who is in charge here?" Gloria asked as the deliverymen continued coming into the house, not answering her question. "Are you sure you got the correct address?" She asked to one of the deliverymen who, with the help of his partner, was moving furniture out of the way to make room for the clothes.

"Oh, it's the correct address, Mrs. Bunker Shaw," she heard a voice say from behind.

When Gloria turned around after hearing the familiar voice, there standing by the front door was Miles, with his hands on his hips, supervising the deliverymen as they unloaded the truck.

"This is a gift to your family from Mr. Hanley. He knew that you hadn't bought clothes for you and your family for your unfortunate day tomorrow, so he wanted to surprise you with new clothes." Gloria was surprised to see O'Shea smiling.

"B-b-but we can't take all of these!" Gloria responded as she began looking at all of the racks that were in the living room and the racks that were being carried up the front stairs into the house.

"Oh, of course not, Ms. Bunker Shaw," he said as he rolled his eyes at her impatiently. "Just take everything that you and your family need." He then touched some of the fabrics of the clothes as the deliverymen continued bringing clothes in.

"Oh my God, Gloria!" Stephanie exclaimed as she also began looking at all of the expensive clothes that were being rolled into the house and the ones that were already in the living room. "I can't believe what I am seeing. These dresses and suits are absolutely beautiful and elegant....and expensive!"

"Yes they are, young lady," O'Shea replied. "Whatever you like is yours. There are even shoes to go along with your clothes," he added enthusiastically.

"This is so nice, Mr. O'Shea. How was he able to get all this done so quickly?"

"Oh, that is so very easy." O'Shea responded quickly and proudly. "It is because he is Rupert H. Hanley." He was now motioning for Gloria to come to him, which she did, then he whispered to her, "You know, Ms. Bunker Shaw, he really does care for you. I haven't seen him this happy since the time he won the Acapulco Royal Hanley Resort and Spa in a game of poker." Then he put his hand on his chest and laughed, not like he did in Gloria's dream, but the way a socialite might laugh at a gathering or function. "He wouldn't do any of this if he really wasn't attracted to you. You should really be flattered."

"Oh, believe me, Mr. O'Shea, I am." She smiled at him. "I really am."

O'Shea had his hands folded across his chest as he stood still and moved his head towards Gloria as he talked. They looked like two women gossiping.

"You know, Ms. Bunker Shaw, when he got back to the hotel this morning, he was like a child, sounding like a little boy who just came back from summer camp. I think you are good for him. You two make a wonderful looking couple."

"Well, I appreciate that, Mr. O'Shea."

"Oh, please. Call me Miles," he asked as he lightly hit her on her shoulder. "Miles it is, then. I want you to call me Gloria, then."

"You got a deal....Gloria." Then they both laughed like rich socialites attending a ball.

Once all the clothes were in the house, four staff members, three female and one male, attended to the family privately, as they were about to try on the clothes. Gloria noticed that Miles was still standing by the door, looking preoccupied.

"Please Miles, come on in. Is there a problem?"

"I feel like I'm forgetting something but I can't remember." He sucked his teeth then stamped his foot one time.

"Well, come and sit down and take a load off your mind." Gloria said this in a joking manner, but O'Shea didn't respond to it. "I'll make some coffee. We have just woken up and haven't had a chance to have breakfast and..."

Before Gloria had a chance to finish her sentence, Miles clapped his hands together, as he had just remembered what he had forgotten.

"I got it!" he yelled happily as he looked towards Gloria, then he snapped his finger and waved toward someone to come to him. To Gloria's astonishment, there was a small van behind the truck with the deliverymen inside. There were three people dressed in all white, now unloading the van and bringing in different foods and pastries. Gloria marveled at the sight. They came up the porch with the food quickly as Miles pointed for them to come in and go over by the dining room table, which had been moved up against the wall to make room for all the clothes. As they came in, Gloria commented to Miles, "I could learn to get used to this."

"Well, that's the plan, Gloria. That's the plan." Then he laughed again as both made their way into the house where the family, staff members and the caterers were all a stirring about, going here and there very quickly.

"Hey Ma!" Matthew yelled with overwhelming excitement. "I feel like Prince William and Andrew!" Matthew was being measured from head to toe by the male clothing staff member.

"And, Ma, I feel like one of those models that get to try on clothes before she hits the catwalk!" Zoe added, also grinning like the Cheshire cat.

"Gloria, I don't know what I feel." Stephanie said. She still looked like she was dazed as she shook her head slowly, looking at everything before her.

The two female staff members who were to attend to Stephanie and Zoe were now leading them to the clothes rack to start picking out things to wear. Gloria's female assistant was near her, smiling and waiting for her to start picking out clothes and to finish talking to Miles.

"Go on now Gloria and get some clothes." Miles was nudging her closer to the racks. "Shop till you drop!" He had his hand on her back.

"Go help yourself to the food, Miles. We'll eat after." With that, her mind went towards picking out clothes as Miles headed near the dining room table.

A few minutes had passed by when all of a sudden Gloria gasped then started frowning.

"What's the matter, Gloria? Don't you like the clothes?" Stephanie asked. Miles looked up from the dining room table towards Gloria with a concerned expression on his face.

"That's not it. I had promised to meet Teresa and Faye this afternoon to go shopping. They're making time in their schedules to be with me and here I am already getting clothes."

"Well, call them on the phone and have them come over." Miles interjected; he acted like it wasn't a big dilemma. "There are more than enough clothes, Gloria." Then he rolled his eyes and sipped on his hot coffee that the caterers brought. Gloria looked toward Stephanie, who shrugged her shoulders.

"That's not a bad idea, Gloria."

Gloria thought about it for a few seconds, then agreed that it was a good idea. Gloria excused herself and went into the kitchen to the bulletin board for Faye's number. She called her and invited her over. When Faye heard about the clothes, she was delighted and accepted the invite. Since Teresa didn't have a phone due to the move, Faye said that she would drive out to her house, hoping that she would still be home, and bring her back to the house. With that, she hung up and headed back into the living room.

Gloria was looking at her family as they enjoyed what was happening. They'd never had so much attention in their life. It was written all over their face. That made Gloria happy. She wanted her family happy. They'd been through so much the last few days. She had too, but she was so concerned for them. She was so concerned that even though Joey hadn't arrived yet, she had clothes laid out for him, too. She was happy that she knew his size in clothes and shoes.

All kinds of clothes filled the living room, along with all different kinds of pastries that lined the dining room table. The plants, big and small, were taken into the kitchen so there would be more room for the clothes. There were clothes for the funeral, evening and formal wear, and casual as well as sporty. The family had so many clothes and racks to go through. Once everyone got finished with the racks that were in the living room, the delivery men would haul those out and bring more in.

Gloria was just about to continue looking through the racks when the phone rang again. She figured that it was Faye calling back so she decided to pick up the phone in the kitchen.

Gloria made her way into the kitchen and sat down at the table. "Hello, Bunker residence."

When Gloria realized who was calling, she showed her approval by widening her smile.

"Good morning, Rupert. It is so good to hear your voice again." Gloria's heart was beating fast and her body became warm all over. She closed her eyes as she envisioned his handsome, strong, chiseled face.

"Good morning there, Purdy lady!" he said sounding chipper and like a cowboy.

Gloria chuckled over his imitation. "I figured that with all that traveling you did yesterday, you would still be sleeping, but nooo. You wanna audition for *Hee Haw*!"

Now Rupert was the one who was laughing. "How are you this morning? Did you sleep well?"

"Well, I fell asleep in my clothes, in my daddy's living room chair with my daughter's head in my lap. I was so overwhelmed by my special treatment last night that I didn't have the strength to walk upstairs to my bedroom!" Gloria had one hand on her forehead as she rolled her eyes.

"Oh great, so that means that I accomplished what I had set out to do."

"I should say so. So, what are you trying to do this morning? Trying to top what you did last night? Or should I say, a few hours ago?" Gloria began twisting the coil on the telephone with her fingers as she smiled.

"Aaah!" he said in a sigh. "So that must mean that the clothes and the caterers have arrived, huh?" He was chuckling again.

"You know, Mr. Rupert, you are just filled with surprises."

"Yes I do, do you wanna know why, madam? Well, let me tell you. It is because the 'H' stands for Hocus Pocus!"

Gloria could tell that he was preaching again. She liked when he did that. She could only imagine him skipping and jiving around his room as he talked to her.

"Rupert, you are CRAZY," she exclaimed as she laughed. Rupert's voice became normal and serious and Gloria could tell that he was speaking from his heart.

"Yes, I am crazy, Gloria. I am crazy about you." When he said this, Gloria became speechless and her heart began to flutter.

"Oh, Rupert, I think that I am falling for you." Gloria couldn't help what she just said. It just came out before her brain had a chance to even register it. Now she couldn't take it back......But did she really want to?

"Is that for real or are you jesting with me?" he asked, still being very serious.

"Rupert, after meeting you, I believe that even if you didn't have all this money, you would do whatever you had to, to get what you want, and once you got it, you would treasure it. You are an exciting and amazing human being with all the qualities that I find attractive in a man. Rupert, I am speaking from the heart when I say this: No, I am not jesting."

"Well, you know, madam, you have made my day."

"Well, you know, kind sir, I like you very much."

Gloria continued talking with Rupert for a very long time. By the time she came out of the kitchen, the family had stopped trying on clothes and were taking a breakfast break. Gloria really didn't have a chance before to examine all the pastry dishes and other dishes that the caterers brought in.

"So, who was that on the phone?" Stephanie asked as she ate a jelly donut and drank a cold glass of milk. Gloria walked towards the dining room table to inspect and to fix something to eat.

"That was Rupert," she responded as she began to pour herself some coffee, and blushed

"Did you tell him 'thank you' for all the clothes?" asked Zoe, who was leaning on Matthew as she ate a buttered roll and drank coffee. Matthew was the only one who had a plate stacked with eggs, sausage, bacon, pancakes and syrup with butter.

"Yeah, Ma, not just, 'thank you' for you, but for all of us?"

Gloria barely understood him with his mouth full of food."Yes, guys. I told him, 'thank you' from everyone. He appreciated it."

Besides everything that was on the family's plates, on the dining room table were French toast, tea biscuits, bagels, cake, tea and grapefruit juice. Gloria began to fix her plate. She had French toast with butter and syrup. Before she sat down to eat, she told the staff and even the caterers to eat, too, which the staff did. The caterers politely declined after looking at Miles, who began cutting his eyes at them. Gloria did not notice this because if she had, she would have said something to Miles. The caterers just stood by the table, making sure everything was still neat and hot. Gloria was about to sit down to eat when the doorbell rang.

Stephanie headed towards the door but Zoe stopped her because she was closer. When she answered it, Faye and Teresa came in, looking shocked and amazed, not to mention speechless.

"Oh my God!" Faye exclaimed as she looked around the packed living room. "Look at all the clothes!"

"And the food!" Teresa was eyeing the dining room table with a smile on her face. She playfully licked her lips, causing the three at the table to chuckle.

The twins already knew Faye but didn't know Teresa. They cordially introduced themselves to her. She hugged and kissed them both with such force, as if she had known them ever since they were little and hadn't seen them in years. The twins accepted it graciously as they laughed and blushed modestly.

"Gloria, they are absolutely beautiful!" she exclaimed as her voice cracked.

"Thank you, Teresa" Gloria quickly responded. "Hey you two, come on and eat before you shop." Gloria began to wave the two over toward the table.

Twenty minutes later, after everyone finished eating, they were trying on clothes again just as if they were in a clothing store. Gloria told Teresa that if she knew her family's size, she could pick out clothes for them too. Teresa appreciated the offer and gladly accepted it, but told her that only her daughters would be going with her. Her better half would be working. Gloria had already known that Faye lived alone, so she would just be picking out clothes for herself.

As the last racks came in, everyone still had the energy, vigor and stamina to continue trying on clothes and shoes. Matthew had picked out one suit for the funeral, with black shoes, a shirt and tie. He picked out five pairs of jeans, name-brand shirts and sweaters and Reeboks. Zoe picked out a two-piece black dress, black stockings and shoes, for the funeral and three pairs of jeans and three skirts, five blouses and sweaters, two pairs of regular shoes and sandals plus three pairs of Nikes. Stephanie also picked out a two-piece long black dress with black hat and veil, black stockings and shoes for the funeral, five blouses and five jeans, two regular dresses and two pairs of Nike sneakers. Gloria picked out the same black two-piece outfit that Stephanie, with a different collar. Her collar was rounded. She also chose black stockings and black shoes, five elegant dresses and five casual, five pairs of shoes and two pairs of Reeboks.

Gloria picked out a black suit for Joey for the funeral, seven shirts and ties and six casual suits. She knew that he was a teacher and he had to look good in class. She picked out one black pair of shoes for the funeral and three regular casual pairs plus two pairs of Nikes and one pair of Reeboks. Faye had only picked out two casual dresses but was encouraged to get more, and Teresa picked out one outfit for the funeral for her and her three girls, plus shoes. She was also encouraged to take more. So far, Faye and Teresa hadn't seen anything else they felt comfortable getting. They were happy with what they had so far, but they were still looking.

Fifteen minutes later, the caterers started clearing off the table and were getting ready to leave. Gloria opened the door for them when they walked towards it. All the leftovers were left in the kitchen.

"Oh, thank you so much for the food," she said cordially and with much appreciation.

"They're coming right back, Gloria. They're going back to the van for lunch," said O'Shea who had been supervising the whole operation and doing a quite good job.

"Oh, I understand. They're taking a lunch break. Well, they should." She added, "They have been…"

"No, Gloria, you don't understand," O'Shea said, rolling his eyes. "They are going to bring in lunch. It is lunch time."

Everyone in the living room started laughing as Gloria turned crimson from embarrassment.

"Oh." Then she laughed. "You're right. I didn't know, after all. I didn't think that there would be more food. We just ate." Gloria then started watching the caterers head off the porch and toward the van.

Meanwhile, the phone had begun ringing and Stephanie went to answer it.

"Hello, Bunker residence. Good morning, Mike! I'm okay thanks, in spite of everything. Everyone here is fine and awake. Yeah. Aha. Hold on and let me ask Gloria."

Stephanie turned and faced Gloria, who was still at the door.

"Gloria, Mike wants to know if it would be all right if they come by in a little while."

"Well, of course. Tell him to come with that big appetite of his. We have a lot of food."

Stephanie relayed the message then hung up the phone and resumed looking at clothes.

Gloria watched as the caterers came out of the van with a huge platter of sliced cheeses and different kinds of sliced meats. They also had different kinds of breads, sodas, juices, potato salad, macaroni salad, cole slaw, chips and dips, fruits, cakes and pies, plus hot food which consisted of roasted chicken, ham and roast beef. Everyone stopped what they were doing and stared at the caterers as they made their way back to the dining room table.

Once the table was set, Gloria began holding her stomach.

"My gosh! There is enough food here to feed Calcutta! I just don't know where we're going to put all of this!" Gloria couldn't take her eyes off the food on the table.

"I know where I am going to put it," commented Teresa as she stood next to Gloria and stared at the food. "I'm gonna put it right in here!" Teresa pointed to her mouth, smiling.

"Hear, hear!" responded Matthew heartily, with a smile also. He then went over near Teresa and gave her a high five.

Gloria turned and looked at Miles, who was not far away, observing the caterers and the table, making sure it was just perfect.

"Miles, why is there so much food?"

"Everyone and anyone that is associated with Mr. Hanley always have things done exquisitely and extravagantly and most importantly, to the utmost extreme. It's never too much when it comes to people, especially a woman."

There might not have been too much eating for breakfast, but that was different for this meal. Everything came to a complete halt while the family, Teresa and Faye attacked the table. Once they got theirs, the clothing staff got theirs. They ate an adequate amount but not like Gloria thought; even Matthew, who Gloria thought would devour the table, just had a plate full, but everyone looked satisfied. Once they finished, they all went back clothes shopping.

Twenty minutes after that, Gloria heard the sound of a cell phone. Out of the corner of her eye, she saw Miles dig into his pocket and pull his out, then look at the number on the display. He then sashayed over toward Gloria, who was standing near the rack that was by the basement door.

"Gloria, would you mind if I take a call in your kitchen? It is a private call."

"Of course not, Miles." She waved him off like it wasn't a problem. "Feel free."

Miles quickly made his way through the kitchen door as he began to answer the phone in a low tone. Immediately after that, the doorbell rang. Matthew was closest to the door, so he went towards it to open. Gloria figured that it might be Mike and Beth but when Matthew opened up the door, it was a deliveryman dropping off more flowers.

"More flowers, Ma!" Matthew yelled as he began to sign the receipt.

Gloria walked over towards the front door as the delivery man looked in, as he still held the flowers in his hands. He smiled at Gloria and nodded. Gloria smiled back and nodded also. Matthew gave the deliveryman back the receipt as the deliveryman handed him the flowers.

"Y'all have a nice day," the deliveryman said as he tipped his hat to them and then turned and headed off the porch.

While Matthew headed into the house with the flowers, Gloria continued standing at the door, contemplating whether she should invite the clothing delivery men into the house to fix themselves some food from the table. They had been sitting in the truck for hours. She thought that they must be hungry. They had been working hard and it was just way too much food, even if Mike came with a huge appetite. There would still be enough left over.

As Gloria thought about the food, she had to admit that in her opinion, it really wasn't that good. Presentation-wise, it was excellent. The way they had set up the table was just perfect, but the food wasn't seasoned and it wasn't cooked all the way through. The cake tasted doughy. So did the bagels and donuts earlier, and even though Matthew had packed his plate full of food earlier, he didn't even eat half of it, and neither did she. She barely had two forks-full of the French toast with syrup. It just didn't taste right, to her. Yes, it was hot. Everything was hot, but it just wasn't good. In her opinion, the only thing that was pretty decent that she ate without a problem was the sliced cheese and cold cuts on the huge platter. Gloria thought to herself that she could've done a much better job preparing that food and charged a lot less than what they were probably charging Rupert.

Gloria made up her mind and decided to invite the deliverymen to come in and eat, but before she had an opportunity to do it, she heard someone's voice calling her name from down the street.

"Gloria, hey, Gloria!" the voice cried in the far distance.

"Who is that calling me?" she asked herself as she began to look around.

The voice was familiar to her. It was a man's voice, but at first, she couldn't exactly identify the face to the voice because of the busy street. Cars were going up and down the street and people were going up and down the street and there was Chris in the distance waving towards her with a huge smile on his face and there was...

"There's Chris waving at me," she said happily. Then it dawned on her that if Chris came into the house the way that it looked right now, she would have a lot of explaining to do. So she did what any normal woman in her situation would do....she panicked!!!

Gloria ran back into the house then closed the door with a hard and loud slam. She then put her back up against it as if it was a dam and was about to burst. She extended her arms sideways making her body look like a trembling letter 'T'. Her eyes were bulging out as she stared from side to side with her mouth open. Gloria was confused and didn't know what to do.

Stephanie noticed how Gloria was behaving. As a matter of fact, when she slammed the door, everyone took notice and began staring at Gloria. They also all laughed, thinking that she was trying to be funny.

"Hey Gloria," Stephanie said. "If you wanna keep the door closed, all you have to do is turn the lock into position. It'll work every time." Everyone continued laughing at Stephanie's comment.

"Chris is out there and he's heading this way!" Gloria panicked, her chest heaving deeply.

Gloria's voice was cracking as sweat began pouring down her forehead. Everyone began looking at each other in perplexity.

"Yeah, so what, Gloria? Chris has been here at least a million times," Stephanie added as she tried to understand what the problem was.

"Yes that's true, Stephanie, but he has never been here while the living room was filled with racks and racks of clothes worth over a million dollars, and I do not feel like explaining to him why I have all of this in the living room!"

Once Gloria said that, Stephanie understood what the problem was.

"Oh my God, Gloria, what are we going to do?!" Stephanie was now panicking too.

Teresa and Faye, who had retired to the couch, were now standing, not knowing what to do. The twins just stared at their mother, looking concerned. The clothing staff started to look frightened as they looked at one another, then went to stand near the caterers, who were huddled up in the corner by the dining room table.

"Think, Gloria, think!" she kept saying to herself as she began to blink and snap her fingers fast.

While everyone looked confused, Stephanie looked around then suddenly blurted out the first thing that came to her mind as she stared at Gloria.

"What would Lucy do?!" Stephanie shouted right out of the clear blue sky, causing Gloria and everyone to look at her strangely.

The comment caught Gloria totally off guard, causing her to question Stephanie.

"Stephanie, my dear cousin, who the hell is Lucy?!"

"Ah, ah, Lucy!" Stephanie stuttered nervously. "You know, Lucy! Lucy Lucy. Lucy from *I love Lucy*. She is always in situations and predicaments like this and always seem to get out of them unscathed," Stephanie responded positively.

"Stephanie that is television. This is reality!" Gloria shouted angrily at Stephanie as she continued breathing hard and cutting her eyes at her.

"Listen, let's just think about this for a moment, okay? On television, if Lucy was doing something that she and Ethel weren't supposed to be doing and Ricky or Fred were on their way, about to catch them, what would Lucy do?"

Gloria lowered her head to concentrate for a few seconds as she thought, then lifted her head up quickly almost as if she was possessed.

"Okay, okay, I got it!" She shouted to Stephanie. Gloria looked towards the frightened caterers and clothing staff then calmly said, "I need each one of you to please do me a huge favor…"

They all nodded as they seemed to relax at the serenity of her voice.

"I need y'all to quickly take these racks," then she raised her voice as if the building was on fire, "and get the hell out of the house!"

The caterers and clothing staff nervously bumped into one another trying to get out of each other's path as they began grabbing things. Just as Gloria screamed this, Miles was coming out the kitchen through the door and was nearly trampled by the caterers who were rushing into the kitchen to start moving the plants to one side of the kitchen, along with the kitchen table. Matthew was right behind them to open up the back door. Zoe grabbed all the clothes, hers and her brother's, and then headed downstairs into the basement. Stephanie tossed her clothes toward Gloria who was making her way up the stairs to change her clothes, and Faye and Teresa didn't know what to do, so they started following Stephanie, waiting to be useful.

Everything was moving like Gloria's Rolex watch: precise, in order, and perfect. To Gloria, it was like everything was happening in fast motion, like she was in a videotape and someone pressed the speed button. One minute, she was downstairs, and then the next, she was in her room slipping off the dress, taking off the earrings, throwing on Archie's shirt that she had on yesterday and some jeans and slippers. The next minute, she was back down the stairs.

"Gloria! Meet him out on the porch! I'll let you know when we are done!" yelled Stephanie who, along with Faye and Teresa, were trying to put the furniture back in its places. The clothing staff members were trying to maneuver around Miles so they could roll the racks out the kitchen back door and into the backyard. They wanted to abscond to help the family out.

"Hey, what's going on here?!" shouted a confused Miles.

Miles had his hand over his mouth and one hand on his hip as he looked at everyone zooming all around him. Stephanie motioned to Gloria for her to go and that she would handle Miles. With that, Gloria quickly walked out the front door, just as Chris was approaching the house.

"Oh hi, Chris!" Gloria exclaimed as she tried to act surprised at seeing him.

"I saw you on the porch a moment ago talking to a delivery man and I called to you. Did you hear me?" Chris was now walking up the porch towards her.

"Well, you know, I heard something but I couldn't make it out."

"So what brought you back out here then?"

When Chris finally reached Gloria he gave her a kiss, which surprised her. She didn't have the chance to kiss him back because he pulled away, so instead, she rubbed his arm. She really did enjoy the kiss, though, and wished that if they were alone, he would do much more.

"Well, I came back out to ah..." *think, Gloria, think.* "Because I wanted to give the delivery man a tip." *That was a good one, Gloria.* "But now, it is too late. He's gone."

While this was going on, inside, Miles was having a hissy fit.

"Why are you moving everything around in such a rush? Where was Gloria going in such a panic? Is there something wrong?"

"Relax, Mr. O'Shea. Everything is just fine. We just have to do this till a guy that Gloria is talking to out in the front leaves, then everything will go back to the way it was before you went into the kitchen," Stephanie assured him. She was trying to calm Miles down.

"See, I knew it!" Miles said as he stomped his foot lightly on the floor. "I leave just for a few minutes and everything goes haywire!"

Miles looked disappointed, then he looked at Stephanie suspiciously.

"Who is this guy that Gloria is speaking with?" He sounded like a lawyer cross-examining a defendant. Stephanie didn't appreciate his attitude, comment or nosiness, but she had to ignore it for Gloria's sake because anything that happened in the house, she knew that loyal Miles would go back and report to Hanley.

Think fast, Stephanie, she said to herself. "He's, he's...he's m-my b-b-boyfriend."

"Oh!" responded Miles. "B-but if he's YOUR boyfriend, why aren't you outside talking to him?"

"Well, because, ah, well, he was upset the last time he came over because there were a lot of people in the house and he is quite jealous and he doesn't like me to be around a lot of people, so please, Mr. O'Shea, just go out till we get rid of him, okay?" Stephanie was trying to move him out the way of the moving racks, and she was trying to get him outside.

"Okay! But-but isn't he going to be upset if he sees these two ladies?" he asked as he pointed to Faye and Teresa.

"No, because he knows them, but he doesn't know you and everyone else, now please, Mr. O'Shea..."

"I know what will make him feel better," he said excitedly. "Give him one of these suits! You know that they say, 'music sooths the savage beast,' but after he tries one of these suits on, he'll be purring like a kitten!"

"He won't like these suits, Mr. O'Shea. He doesn't like to wear suits, or these types of clothes."

Stephanie was beginning to lose her patience. She had told him nicely that he had to leave the house but O'Shea was not paying her urgency any attention.

"Well, what does he like? I'm sure we could get it from the truck."

"He only likes corduroy and polyester." She was nudging him on his back to leave.

"Oh dear God!" he responded in shock. He put his hand on his chest as if he was about to have a heart attack and as if it was the first time he had ever heard profanity.

"If you just fix him a huge sandwich, that usually calms down anyone with bad tempers and attitudes. You know what they say, 'The way to a man's heart is through his stomach.'"

Stephanie put her hands down at her sides and balled up her hands into fists then closed her eyes tightly and yelled, "Get out, get out, GET OUT!!!"

Stephanie couldn't get any clearer than that and finally, Miles got the hint. He jumped as if he was startled then zoomed through the kitchen door, then out the back.

Back at the front porch, Gloria continued talking with Chris casually as they smiled and flirted with each other. He stood very close to her, blocking the wind blowing on her. Although nothing was blowing on her, she had goose bumps all over her body just being close to him. Pleasure filled her from head to toe as she looked up in to his eyes while his manly voice talked.

"Actually, Gloria, to be honest with you, I was coming out of my house from down the street and something just told me to look up the block towards your house. I had thought about you anyway while I was in the house, just thinking how good it was to see you again and to hear that you were single." He laughed impishly. "Well, when I looked this way from my house, I saw the huge truck in front of your house then I started to think stupidly. I was thinking that you were moving everything out of the house because you decided to sell it. Just call me crazy."

Gloria didn't interrupt him. She just listened to him speak and watched his eyes sparkle.

"I stood there, in front of my house, waiting to see activity up this way but nothing was stirring, not even a mouse, until I saw the deliveryman come up your porch and then Matthew opened the door. Once I saw you, well, that was when I decided to come by just to say hello... Well...hello."

Gloria couldn't help but stare at him, and she quickly checked him out from top to bottom. To her, he had definitely aged like fine wine and looked even better outside, where the sunlight could really illuminate his features. Gloria was also able to feel his sexy stare pierce through her eyes right to her heart and soul. She was definitely elated to see him, but this was his second bad time encounter, but oh how soft his manly expressions were when he smiled. She couldn't imagine knocking that smile off his face by telling him about why she couldn't see him last night, or letting him come into the house with all those racks of clothes. The less he knew, the better.

"Well, Chris, I am happy that you've come by. You know that you are always welcome here."

"Well, is that right? Well, that makes me feel good, but I have a question for you. When you say that I am welcome, do you mean, welcome here in your heart..." Chris pointed to her heart area, "...or welcome in your house?"

When he made this comment, it totally caught Gloria off-guard. She was speechless. This was a personal and private moment, but she didn't want to open herself up to everyone walking up and down Hauser Street. Even the deliverymen were facing in her direction. But why would it bother her if she had feelings for him? When she was going out with Mike when she was younger, she would kiss openly on that very porch in that very spot for the whole world to see, including Chris, who was now willing to express his feelings right then and there, not caring who was there to see or hear.

"Gloria," he continued quickly, not giving her a chance to respond. "Ever since I saw you yesterday, I have been feeling strange. Gloria, I've missed you and thought about you often. I was wondering if..."

Chris was just about to touch her hand but before he had a chance to finish what he wanted to say, Stephanie opened up the front door fast, which startled both him and Gloria.

"Oh there you are, Gloria. I've been looking for you everywhere." She said as she huffed and puffed like the big bad wolf, then she looked at Chris. "Oh hello, Chris, how are you doing? Why are y'all talking on the porch? Come on in!"

"Yeah, Chris, let's talk inside."

Before Chris could say anything, he was being pulled inside. Chris looked a tad annoyed because he wanted to say something from his heart to her in private at that moment but was stifled.

As Chris came in, to his left was the living room sofa in front of the window and sitting down was Faye who he had known for years, and another woman who looked vaguely familiar. He could not picture or remember where he had seen her or when was the last time that he had seen her.

The Life and Times of Gloria Bunker

"Hey Faye, how's it going?" he asked pleasantly as he smiled to her, then rubbed her back. He then went to extend his hand to Teresa who was smiling widely.

"Hello, ma'am, my name is Chris." When he finished saying this to Teresa, he just stared at her trying to figure out how he knew her. He was looking confused. "Excuse me but I, ah, don't I know? Ahh!" Finally, he remembered where he knew this woman, so his facial expression changed from confusion to absolute delight. "T-T-Teresa! Teresa is that you?!" he yelled loudly as Teresa nodded and stood up from the couch to greet him.

Chris walked toward her quickly and once there, hugged her tightly. "Oh my God, Teresa, I haven't seen you in decades!"

Gloria and Stephanie looked on and just smiled at Chris's and Teresa's reunion. He was very excited to see Teresa again.

"Oh, Chris!" Teresa cried happily. "You definitely are the sightless for the blind eyes!"

Teresa couldn't help but to continue checking Chris out from head to toe. Gloria looked at Faye then at Teresa.

"You mean that he is a sight for sore eyes, Teresa!" Gloria interjected as she laughed.

"That too!" Teresa as she wiped the tears from her eyes.

Chris was so happy at seeing Teresa that he forgot how frustrated and annoyed he was before while he was on the porch with Gloria. Chris hadn't noticed the dining room table that still had all the food on it, but Gloria noticed it and nudged Stephanie, who began looking in the direction that Gloria was looking.

Stephanie just shrugged her shoulder as to say, 'I don't know. We just overlooked it.' Gloria began to think how she was going to explain all the food on the table, but she had been doing well so far; this shouldn't be a problem.

After Teresa and Chris finished greeting each other and quickly catching up on old times, he turned to face the area which was filling his nose with different mouth-watering aromas.

"Hey, I knew my nose wasn't failing me," he exclaimed as he sniffed with a smile. "Look at all that good food on that table."

"Its food, all right, but good—I'm not too sure about that," Stephanie mumbled but Gloria heard her and poked her in the side.

"What did you say, Stephanie?" he asked.

"Oh, I said that you are more than welcome to help yourself. The sliced cheese and cold cuts are absolutely delicious." When Stephanie said that, the other three encouraged him to try them.

"Well, I would love to, ladies, but unfortunately, I didn't come by to socialize. I only stopped by for a few minutes, just to say hello, and I'm glad that I did."

He turned to Teresa when he said this, then he turned back to Gloria. "I sure have good timing, don't I?"

"Impeccable, Chris. Absolutely impeccable."

Chris began walking over towards the dining room table to get a better observation, feeling drawn like a moth to a flame.

"The table does look very appetizing but you know something, I will help myself to a New York cup of coffee."

"Via Colombia," Gloria quickly interjected, causing everyone to chuckle.

"Good choice!" Faye quickly yelled from the couch as Teresa quickly poked her.

"What was that, Faye?" Chris asked as he reached for a cup to pour the coffee into.

"Good choice, ah, er, um, I think the brand is 'Good Choice' coffee," Faye responded as she tried to cover up her words.

While Chris fixed himself a cup, Zoe came downstairs. When she saw him, she smiled and walked towards him to greet him.

"Hey CB, how are you doing?" Zoe was now standing next to him, smiling.

"Hey Sunshine, how goes it?" he responded happily and brought her close to him with one arm and hugged her.

"What did you call her, Chris?" Gloria asked with surprise.

"Oh? Oh, I called her Sunshine." He responded nonchalantly. "Yeah Ma, Sunshine." Zoe echoed.

The name surprised Gloria because Gloria also called Zoe that as a nickname.

"Wow, that's really peculiar. Why do you call her Sunshine?"

"Wow, Gloria; does it bother you that I call her that name?" Chris asked, looking concerned.

"Yeah Ma, is there a problem?"

Gloria quickly responded to assure the two.

"Oh, not at all, guys. I just wanted to know why that name. That's all."

"Well," Chris poured milk into his coffee then stirred it. "It was when she was maybe two years old and her hair was really blond, like your hair was when you were real young; and if you do remember, I used to call you Sunny because your hair was so bright, like the sun."

Gloria began to feel weak in the knees as Faye and Teresa sighed and smiled at each other. She had totally forgotten that he used to call her that when they were small children.

"So I guess that when I saw her looking so much like you, it brought back memories and ever since that moment, I've been calling her that."

Chris then looked down at Zoe who was now looking up towards him with a smile, then they both gave each other another hug.

"I didn't know that you used to call my mom that name, Chris. I guess that I was so used to you calling me that name that I never asked you the history of it. I just accepted it for being special like it is." She then looked at her mother. "Now that I know that it was because I reminded you of my mother, the name is even more special now." Zoe started to get emotional; she had tears in her eyes and almost started to cry. Gloria just stood there, almost in a daze, as Chris started to look at tad embarrassed.

"So, Ma, why do you call me Sunshine? Is it for the same reason?"

When Stephanie asked this, Chris's expression went from embarrassed to surprised.

"Is that true, Gloria? Do you really call her that also?"

"Well, believe it or not, I do call her Sunshine, too." Gloria nodded and smiled.

"No!" he responded with surprise, then drank some of the coffee as he smiled also.

"Yeah, I sure do. I've been calling her that since she was a baby too, haven't I, Zoe?"

"Uh-huh," she replied, walking over to Edith's chair.

"Ummm! This is some good coffee. Hey, did you have all this catered?" Chris asked as he looked at a stunned Gloria, who didn't know what to say.

"Well, ah, er," Gloria was lost for words but before she could think of something to say, Matthew came out of the kitchen.

"Triple H is the greatest WWF champ in wrestling history," he remarked, walking towards Chris, who instantly started smiling at the comment.

"The Rock is better, if you smell what I am cooking."

"No he's not!" Matthew got up in Chris's face.

"Yes he is!" Chris bent down in Matthew's face, then they playfully threw fake punches at each other, then hugged each other as they laughed like little kids. This made everyone start smiling laughing, as they were amused by the men's theatrics.

"Don't get in the way of these two wrestle-holics," Stephanie said to Gloria. "When these two get together, it is like show time at Madison Square Garden! One is totally addicted to it and the other one can't stop watching it. They are made for each other."

"I must admit, I have never seen my children act like this with anyone," Gloria said with much surprise and happiness.

"What?!" Stephanie exclaimed with surprise. "Are you kidding me?! These guys are totally uncontrollable when they are together. Sometimes I forget who's the kid and who's the adult."

Gloria couldn't hide her joy by watching her kids show so much love and interest to Chris. It made her even more attracted to him. She could imagine the four of them going places together as a happy family and doing things at home together. Seeing Chris interacting with her children lifted her spirits and grasped her heart. Gloria could stare at them all day. Then somehow, her thoughts returned to when they were on the porch and he asked her if he was welcome in the house or her heart. She wanted to say, 'both' but he didn't need to be welcomed into her heart because he already resided there. He had a huge part of her heart, the size of a mansion, but she had to tell him this. He'd never know unless she spoke up. All she was thinking about was telling him how she wanted his lips, his touch, and how she wanted to surrender herself to him and allow him to take charge over her.

After Chris finished talking with Matthew, he'd totally forgotten about the question that he'd asked concerning the table. She was happy about that, but he wasn't finished asking questions.

"I know that tomorrow is the funeral. Do you think that we could get together today?"

That is what Gloria wanted to hear.

"Sure Chris. I really do wanna see you."

"Hey then." He said happily. "When will it be good for you?"

"Well, Mike and Beth, his wife," Gloria noticed that Chris smiled when she said the 'WIFE' part, "are on their way over. I'm going to spend some more time with the ladies, then after that, I should be free."

Chris began to drink more coffee then looked at the table.

"Well, I guess that we can find somewhere to talk, being that I can't take you out for a bite to eat. You are already fully loaded!" he said as he chuckled. "What's the occasion for, anyway?"

"Oomph! He remembered," Gloria said to herself as she began to panic. "Well, her, ah, a friend of the family decided to surprise us with the food. It was a total shock, but we appreciate it." *Good Gloria. You didn't lie. You just didn't say who the friend was.*

"Well," he said as he looked at all the food, "they sure spent an arm and a leg on this."

Faye leaned over to Teresa and made a remark, hoping that no one heard her.

"It tasted like arms and legs but I don't know from which animal."

Once again, Teresa poked her, but this time they both chuckled. Gloria caught a glimpse of this but didn't respond to it.

"There is enough food here to feed all of Astoria!" Chris chuckled again as he finished his cup of coffee. "Gloria, I really hate to drink and run but I have to drink and run." He began to head towards the door quickly as he said goodbye to everyone.

"Chris, I'll give you a call later." Gloria said as she walked behind him to the front door.

Chris stopped at the door and turned to look at her.

"I'll be looking forward to it." Then he opened the door, waved goodbye to everyone and then he was gone. When Gloria closed the door, she leaned up against it and smiled widely as everyone started clapping and cheering over a plan well executed.

"Oh, Gloria, everything worked out perfectly!"

Stephanie was elated as she ran into the kitchen to let everyone back in through the back door.

"Oh, Gloria, you are right. He is absolutely gorgeous! He hasn't changed," Teresa replied.

"Didn't I tell you?" Gloria was nodding excitedly. "We are going to see each other later," she said proudly as the other women congratulated her.

By this time, O'Shea and the whole crew were making their way back into the house very cautiously.

"Are you sure that it is safe for us to come in here?" Miles was looking around as if he was on safari as he looked out for any wild animals to come pouncing down on him.

"Don't worry, Mr. O'Shea. The big bad wolf has gone and won't be blowing down the house with his huffing and puffing."

Everyone started laughing.

"Thank you, everyone," Gloria said as she addressed the room. "Thank you for your fast work and your cooperation. I really do appreciate it very much."

After everything was moved to make room for the racks again, Gloria went to the porch and invited the deliverymen to come into the house to partake in the food on the dining room table. The deliverymen all humbly accepted.

While this was going on, unbeknownst to Gloria, Chris had walked a few blocks down from the house, but he realized that he had left his beeper sitting near the living room couch in his house. He turned back around heading towards his house and stopped as he looked ahead up the block and he was able to see Gloria come out of the house onto the porch then motion for men in the big truck in front of the house to come into the house. Chris could see that they were dressed in uniforms. He had found this odd because Gloria hadn't mentioned them before when he commented earlier about the truck. He wanted to know what was going on but decided that it really wasn't his concern, but he still was eager to know. He stood there in the distance, watching while waiting for them all to go into Gloria's house so he could continue to his house.

A half hour later, after the deliverymen ate their food and everyone finished trying on their clothes that were on the racks, the last rack was being rolled out of the house and down the porch, straight into the trucks, and the staff were putting the last pieces of the furniture back into their correct spots. When they finished, they said goodbye to everyone and walked out of the house. All the while, Miles stood someplace nearby supervising everything and everyone.

Once Miles was satisfied with the way everything looked, he was ready to leave, also. As he made his way, sashaying to the front door, he turned and said goodbye to everyone also. Gloria was right behind him to let him out.

"Thank you so much, Miles and I mean for everything. Everything turned out just perfect. Make sure you tell Rupert that we all said thank you again." Gloria extended her hand out to Miles, who took hold of it limply.

"Oh I will Gloria, I won't forget. I just hope that you and your family and friends will remember this special day," he said, smiling, then the next second, he was looking very serious.

"I know I will. I guess that I should also say thank you for a quite interesting morning. For a minute there, with all the racks outside in the back, I thought we were about to have a yard sale." Miles looked at all the women and began squinting at them in an accusing manner.

"Oh, it wasn't that bad, Miles." Gloria lightly hit him on his shoulder to relax him.

"If Rupert had seen you today, he would have been so very proud of you, the way you supervised the whole operation. You ran it as if you were the head of a well-oiled machine, nice and smooth." Gloria was laying the butter on pretty thick because she didn't want Miles to go back and give Rupert any negative report.

Gloria saw that her comment was stroking his ego as he began to smile, but the smile quickly disappeared when he looked at Stephanie and remembered what had happened earlier between the two of them.

"Yes, Gloria, but- but-but she yelled at meee!" Miles sounded like a spoiled child as his voice went up two octaves. He pointed at Stephanie then folded his hands around his chest and tapped one foot. He looked like he was about to cry. When Stephanie saw his mini-outburst, she teased him by making a kissy face at him, then she winked.

"Oh, don't pay her any mind, Miles. Stephanie is harmless." Gloria then moved closer to him as if to tell him a secret.

"Hey, Miles, between you and me..." Gloria then looked from side to side. "I really think that she has the hots for you." Gloria was barely able to keep herself from cracking up laughing, but she played it off quite well.

Miles put the palm of his hand on his chest and took a deep breath, looked Stephanie up and down, then rolled his eyes.

"I think that I better get going," he said as if he had been insulted, then he left quickly.

When Gloria closed the door, she burst into laughter, which made everyone else laugh, too.

"Hey Ma, what's so funny?" Zoe asked as she gathered up more clothes that she had taken off the rack with Matthew.

"O'Shea was mad because Stephanie yelled at him, then I told him that Stephanie liked him. You should've seen the way he zoomed down the porch stairs!" Gloria laughed as she held her gut.

"Oh, great, Gloria, you just scarred that gay man for life," Stephanie said.

"Ma, you are so bad," Zoe replied as Matthew and she headed for the basement.

"Hey Matthew, let's try on our new clothes!" she said excitedly as she rushed to the door. Matthew was right behind her, eagerly looking forward to trying on his new clothes.

As Zoe went down first, Gloria called out to Matthew before he disappeared.

"Hey, Matthew, don't you wanna take some food downstairs to eat? As you can see, there is plenty left over. I am surprised that the deliverymen left so much food. I thought that they would demolish it but they didn't. Oh well. There is more for you."

Matthew turned and looked at the food then curled his lip up .

"No…thank…you," he responded almost in disgust, and then he was gone.

CHAPTER ELEVEN:
Hanging with the Girls

Now that the twins, Miles and the staff were gone, the four grown women were able to talk freely. Stephanie was heading upstairs to put her clothes away as Gloria made her way to the chair where her clothes were.

"Stephanie, would you mind?" she asked, holding her clothes up to her to take them upstairs.

Stephanie nodded. Gloria gave her the clothes then she disappeared up the stairs. Gloria then sat down in the big chair looking towards Teresa and Faye as if she was exhausted.

"What a morning!" Faye exclaimed as she shook her head back and forth. "I feel like I hit the lottery." She began looking at the clothes lying across her lap and on the armrest of the couch. Teresa sat next to her nodding her head in agreement.

"Yeah, girl, this is the best surprise that has happened to me since Hector surprised me with front row middle seats to see my favorite singer, the king of salsa, Marc Antony, perform at Madison Square Garden. I still haven't come down off of that high. Now this! I'll probably come down from this high when my youngest is a grandmother!"

Teresa too began looking at all the clothes that she had picked out.

Faye and Teresa couldn't stop thanking Gloria for everything. They were very appreciative for being able to share in her joy.

"Now, girlfriend," Faye said as she put the clothes over the arm rest. "You have a lot of explaining to do. Who, what, when, why and how did all this come about? Did you rob Saks since we saw you yesterday—not to mention a huge breakfast and lunch catered personally?"

"Yeah Gloria, what is going on here? Inoculating minds want to know." Teresa got comfortable in the couch and leaned forward to hear every juicy detail.

"You mean inquiring minds want to know, Teresa." Gloria laughed with Faye. "Inoculating means to put a virus into the body in order to immunize."

Teresa just shrugged off what Gloria said.

"Inoculating, inquiring—whatever! Spill the beans, toots!"

As Gloria was about to tell everything to the anxious women, Stephanie came back down the stairs and went to sit down in Edith's chair to hear the juicy details, too. Once Gloria started telling her story, all eyes were glued on her, barely blinking, as mouths fell to the ground. Gloria was very animated with her story as she relived every moment. She made facial expressions to show how she had felt at that moment, which really made the women enjoy the story even more. No one moved from their spot or position as Gloria spoke. Faye and Teresa were occasionally shaking their heads in disbelief, fascinated by what they were hearing. Gloria was doing such a good job telling and reliving the story that the women were feeling her emotion as if they were there with her. When she finally got to the end, the women weren't satisfied. They wanted to hear more. It was all very exciting to them to hear. All three leaned back in their places and fanned themselves with one hand as the other hand went on their chest as they sighed. They all looked up as they seemed to be in deep thought.

"Will somebody please get me a fan? I feel like I am going to faint," Faye exclaimed happily.

"Will somebody please get me a handkerchief?" Teresa cried as she sniffled. "That is sooo romantic that I could cry. I thought chitterlings was dead, but I guess that I was wrong." Teresa was now wiping tears from her eyes with the back of her hand.

"You mean, chivalry, Teresa. You thought that chivalry was dead," Faye corrected.

"Yes, that too, honey." Teresa replied. "Oh boy, I can't wait to get home to see mi novio, Hector." She began hitting her two hands together with a serious expression on her face.

"Only thing free from his heart that he gives me are rides on his route or a metro card to travel on public transportation. The last vacation he took me on was to the hospital when I got food poisoning and I stayed there overnight. He didn't even stay. He had to go to work. He got there late, though, but he still left."

"Oh, girls, it's not just the money. Money is nice, yes, of course!" Gloria was now standing up and looking towards the ceiling as she smiled widely. She then started spinning around joyously, as if she was in heaven. "It's the love and the attention and the fact that he treated me with total respect of a gentleman. He was elegant, classy, debonair, flamboyant, loud and obnoxious, but all in a fun way. He just enjoys life and wanted me to share in that with him. And girls, when he took my hand…" The women looked on intently. "When he took hold of my hand and stared into my eyes, I don't know how to describe it but, but it was like I, I just couldn't swallow or speak—I, I mean like it stirred a spark of life in me. To be honest with y'all, I wanted him to do so much more. My body quivered and then came to instant attention. I had to struggle to keep my composure and it was hard, girls, very hard. I had to behave in the way that he was treating me... Like a lady. I was literally and totally swept off my feet. It was beautiful and magical and breathtaking and heartwarming and exciting and enchanting!"

Gloria went on and on and on then she plopped back into the chair looking exhausted. "And it was so overwhelming and in excess to the point where I was drunk—not the kind of drunk that you might be thinking of, oh no." Gloria started shaking her head. "The kind of spaced-out drunk you might feel after you reached that, that, that..." Gloria began blushing.

"Say it, Gloria!" Stephanie yelled in anticipation as she stomped her feet like a spoiled kid.

"Yeah, girl! Don't leave us in suspenders!" added Teresa as Faye started nudging her.

"You mean, suspense, Teresa, not suspenders," she corrected as she rolled her eyes at her.

"After you reached that perfect, perfect, purrrrr-fect orgasm."

Gloria looked at all three women then put her face in her hands, hiding her embarrassment. All the women fell back in their spots and moaned and sighed. Once she recovered, after the women moaned with delight from her description, she continued, "I was literally knocked out. I didn't want to do anything. I just wanted to lie back and remember the whole experience over and over again." For a few moments, the women just sat there quietly as each and every one of them imagined what Gloria had experienced. Each one was staring into space and each one of them looked like they were in a trance, the way children look when they go to a circus or a carnival for the very first time: totally overwhelmed. They were so happy that words couldn't describe what they were feeling. They were just reveling in the joy of it all.

"Girl, Gloria, I am so happy for you. I am totally blown away and speechless. He is tall, dark, handsome, caring, witty, classy, *and* rich? Talk about a total package. And girl, you said that he has a nice strong body and he only has eyes for you? Child! See if you can clone him. Forget that. Find out for me if he has a black brother. Hell, find out if he has ANY brother. I could be down with some jungle fever if I had to. I wouldn't even care if it was jungle pneumonia. I ain't lying!" Faye then snapped her finger, crossed her leg and rolled her eyes with a New York attitude. Teresa began slapping her on her arm as she laughed vigorously.

"Look at you, Gloria. Some women have all the luck," Stephanie said with joking envy. You come back to New York to find two men who want your attention. Yesterday you only had to think about Chris coming back into your life and…"

"Oh?" Faye looked surprised; she didn't know about their past relationship.

"Yeah, Gloria and Chris were childhood sweethearts but she dumped him for Mike. She hadn't seen him since she broke up with him decades ago, and now ever since he saw her, I think that he wants to try and maybe get that spark burning again. Gloria felt the same yesterday but that was before she ran into Warbucks."

"Oh my God, Gloria, you got yourself one hell of a problem." Faye looked panicked as Gloria nodded.

"Tell me about it."

"Now hold on here," Faye interrupted as if she was trying to explain the theory of relativity.

"Gloria, Chris is fine." When she said this, they all nodded in agreement. "He also has the physical, athletic body like Hanley, too, and Chris is classy and respectful and caring, plus he is a pillar in the community. Everyone knows and loves Chris. I've never heard anyone say anything negative about him. I've known Chris for ten years and I've seen his business prosper, so I know that he ain't poor. He has that big store over on the avenue with all those workers and THEY love him. Girl, he's a good catch!" she assured.

"Everything that you've just said is 100% true. They are both gorgeous in looks, in physical fitness; both are successful, even though one is richer than the other. They're both exciting to be around, but I just don't know. I care for and I am not going to lie, I desire both of them, but I know that that is not fair. No matter whom I choose, one is going to be hurt. I've already hurt Chris before. I cannot afford to hurt him again. Plus, I might not even move back to New York. I don't want a long distance relationship. At least if I choose Rupert, he would have no problem wherever he is, just jumping on an airplane and coming to me. He travels to different countries, cities and states the way your novio, Hector, travels from Flushing to Jamaica and back. I don't think that Chris would be able to do that."

"But Gloria, if you love Chris, you would stay," Teresa replied. "Love is a sacrifice worth taking. Mr. Hanley can fly you off somewhere at a drop of a dime, but if what Faye said is true about Chris being successful, he'd do that for you, too, if you wanted him to."

"I know. You are right, Faye. I just don't know what to do. Do y'all wanna hear something strange? While I was out with Rupert last night, I thought about Chris. My feelings for both men are battling one another inside my heart."

"Well, Gloria, the candidates didn't go out during election time trying to win your vote, then turn around and cast their ballot for the opponent,"

Stephanie added. "He goes full force, doing whatever he has to do to win you over. He goes out there for a purpose; to be victorious. Even though Chris and Hanley don't know about each other, they want you before anyone else decides that they might be interested in you."

"Gloria, you are going to have to choose, girl. Who are you willing to spend your time with?" Faye asked.

"That's the same thing that O'Shea said to me. Who am I going to choose?"

"Gloria, I thought that O'Shea didn't know about Chris," Stephanie said as she looked confused.

"Oh he doesn't. I just had a strange dream and he was in it. See, in the dream, Rupert and Chris were hanging from branches that were being lowered into a pit of quicksand. I had to save them, but O'Shea said that whoever I saved first would be my true love. There I am standing between the two, not knowing who to save first, but as I waited, they continued sinking! If I don't hurry and make up my mind, they both will die or I would save one and the other might die."

"Oh my God, Gloria, what did you do?" Teresa asked as she started biting her nails nervously.

"Well, the last thing that I remember was O'Shea telling me to follow my heart."

"So you never had a chance to save them either?" Faye asked.

"No." Gloria shook her head. "When I woke up, my heart was beating fast. It was so real."

"I bet. It sounds like you are locked between a rock and a heartbreak."

"Teresa, it's 'caught between a rock and a hard place', but you are definitely correct about the "heartbreak' part. Someone is going to be hurt. It is either feast or famine with me. I go for years without having anyone in my life to having two men to choose from and not knowing what to do." Gloria sucked her teeth then shook her head.

"Gloria, I wish I had an answer for you, girl, but I'm having problems just trying to find one."

"Ain't that the truth, Faye," Stephanie replied. "Here we are trying to find a halfway decent man, and my cousin here wasn't even looking and they fall right into her lap—two, no less!"

Gloria just smiled modestly as Stephanie teased her, all in good fun.

"So, here my cousin has two extremely handsome men vying for her attention, and get this, I might add, they are intelligent, well respected and successful. What are you doing that we don't know about? Tell me, teach me. I'm a fast learner."

"Me too, girl, I wanna know your secret."

"I don't know. I am just being me, I guess." She said a tad bashfully, but then her demeanor changed. "But being me right now is not a good thing to be. I'm coming with a lot of baggage and a lot of confusion. With Daddy being gone and this house and his business that I might be selling, everything is moving so fast around me." Gloria then put her hands on her head and rolled it around to emphasize how she was feeling. She then shouted out, "Can someone please just hit the pause button or slow-mo for a moment! I need to catch my breath!"

Stephanie was able to relate because she also lost someone that she loved, her Uncle Archie. As Stephanie nodded, Faye and Teresa looked at each other as they felt their pain.

"But I am not going to spoil the mood in here, ladies," she said, trying to cheer up as she noticed everyone started looking sad. "I am happy, though. Now I have two men that relax my mind and spirit. Thank God at least I have two winners instead of losers to choose from." Gloria then put her hands up to the heavens as if she was praising God.

"Amen!" shouted Faye.

"And they both care a lot about you. I guess it's never too late to find Mr. Right."

"Well, I can honestly say that it is never too late. There is someone out there for everyone."

"Well that is encouraging, because I am still waiting," Faye exclaimed as she began to stand up. "I just hope that these,, she pointed to her firm and nice-sized breasts, "and this," she then took her two hands and grabbed a handful of her perfectly round rear, "will hold on just a little bit longer. It is hard, though, and I am not talking about my breast or ass. I mean that it is hard out there. I've been trying. It is not like I haven't. I haven't asked God for too much in a man. I didn't request Denzel or Cuba or even Wesley, but he at least gotta have a job. I mean, what's with all these guys with all this expensive jewelry and clothes and fancy cars, but still live at home and ask their parents for gas money? Oh no, honey! Ain't no man with ten fingers and ten toes going to be lying up in my bed talking about, 'I'll see you later, Faye. I'll be here when you come from work!' I'm sorry. Not in Faye's lifetime!"

"Or what about this, girls?" Stephanie knew what Faye was talking about and had to comment. "They ask you out for a nice meal then you accept and you both go out and everything is perfect. The food is excellent, the restaurant is fine; oh, the ambiance of it all! Even the conversation is flowing well. Then the bill comes."

As soon as Stephanie said this, all the women started looking at each other and started nodding their head with a smile and began murmuring.

"Then the bill comes!" they said in unison.

"One of two things happens. One, he starts patting his clothes for his wallet and realizes that he must have forgotten it—so he says." When Stephanie said that, the women started laughing.

"Or the check comes and you notice that he is not reaching for it. You know what he does? He looks the other way then starts whistling." Stephanie began leaning over the chair towards the three women. "The nerve of these guys! They ask you out then they want you to pay!"

When Stephanie finished speaking, Teresa looked like if she didn't say what she wanted to say, she was going to overflow like lava coming out of a volcano.

"Oh, girls, I gotta get a piece of this enchilada!" she cried. "Or they tell you that they wanna take you out and you accept the offer. You think that you will be going someplace nice. He picks you up in the car. So far, so good. Next thing you know, he's making a left turn into the drive-thru at the neighborhood White Castle, McDonald's or some other fast food hole in the wall. He then thinks that he has done something special because he supersized the order!"

"Teresa, Hector did that to you?" Stephanie asked as tears rolled down her eyes from laughing hard along with Gloria and Faye.

"No. Hector knows better than to do that to me. It was a date that my oldest had gone out on a while back. She came back and told me about it. She was furious!"

"What about this one?" Stephanie added. "He calls and invites to take you out. You accept his offer. You go out and everything is going well till the bill comes. Surprisingly, he digs into his pocket and starts taking out money. Once he takes some money out, he puts his wallet back into his pocket then he says, 'Your half comes to...'"

"Oh, nooo!" Gloria shouted as she laughed with the other two.

"Oh, yes!" Stephanie replied. "Of all the dates I've been on, that one is my all-time favorite."

"I remember one time when I was helping Daddy out at the bar and this customer came in. He was quite handsome, I must add. I went to him and I gave him a menu. Our eyes met each other as we started flirting with one another. Well, it was slow so as I did the other tables, doing my hostessing duties, I kept going by his table talking with him and bringing him food and drinks. He ate and drank while he talked with me. I found him quite appealing and a pleasure to talk with. Well, to make the story shorter, it was time for me to give him the bill. When I placed the bill in front of him on the table, he looked at it in shock, as if it was food covered with maggots or something. I looked back at him in shock, as if I had done something wrong. He then said to me, as he looked at the check then at me then back at the check. 'What's this?' and I said, 'Sir, this is your bill.' I was looking at him strangely. Do you know what he said to me? He said, 'Oh, now my name is sir, but during our whole date, you were calling me by my name. Now you want me to pay, right?' He sucked his teeth, slammed down the money on the table with an attitude, then said before he left, 'I never wanna see you again!' Can you believe that? Just because I was being friendly with him, he thought that I wanted to be his date right then and there, and that he was going to get a freebie. No wonder he kept ordering food and drinks!"

"Girl, you gotta be kidding, Gloria!" Faye said. "The nerve of him." She then shook her head.

"I kid you not. I had never seen him before in my life, and he thought we were dating. You know, there have only been four men in my life—Chris, Mike, Ray and Rupert—and I've never been disrespected or mistreated by any of them. I never had to go through what you all have experienced."

"Consider yourself lucky, Gloria." Stephanie put her hand on Gloria's back. "And be happy that you never had to deal with the dreaded booty call."

"The booty call!" Faye echoed.

"What is the booty call?" Gloria asked innocently.

"Let me break it down to you, my dear cousin of mine. The booty call comes hours later, after a lousy evening when you thought that you were going to be wined and dined but instead you ended up being pooped, scooped and duped."

Gloria began laughing as she listened intently like a child to a grownup reading a fairy tale.

"He brings you home…"

"Early!" Teresa added as she jumped into the conversation.

"Yes, early!" Stephanie said as she pointed to Teresa. "And reluctantly you give him a kiss good night. You are now home, ticked off and…"

"You know good and well that he wasn't heading back home!" Faye interjected.

"Yeah, yeah, that's right!" Stephanie pointed and nodded towards Faye. "So you go to bed after you call your girlfriends and tell them about your loser date and how you never wanna see this clown again. So, you are hot. While you are steaming mad, you drift off to sleep. Hours pass by and it is about two or three in the morning and your phone starts ringing. You don't check your caller ID because you are half asleep. You reach over for the phone in the dark then you say, 'Hello?', like, whoever is calling, this better be important. Then you hear on the other end a man's voice that sounds like the loser that you went out with earlier who made you pay for the meal. He says in his most romantic voice, 'Hey, baby. Whatcha doin?' So you tell him…"

"I'm sleepin', fool!! Remember, you brought me home early? What else am I supposed to do?" Faye had her hands on her hips, pretending to be angry as she interjected. Gloria was enjoying this.

"So he says, 'How about I come over there and keep you warm?'" Stephanie was making her voice deep like a man's voice as she told the story. "So you reply in not so kind words…"

"That is why I have JC Penney blankets on my bed and a twenty-five dollar vibrator in my dresser drawer. You blew your chance, loser!"

When Faye said this, the other three women looked at each other with their eyes wide and mouths open, looking astonished, then they laughed hysterically like a bunch of hyenas.

"Hey, that's right. I said it. Ain't no shame in my game. Hey! When in doubt, use it. It'll make you scream and shout!" Faye had the women in stitches. Teresa had her head lying on the armrest with her eyes closed and her hands on her stomach laughing. Stephanie fell out of her chair and was lying totally on the floor rolling in laughter and Gloria looked like she was about to slide out of the chair, as she had her eyes closed with tears pouring out of her eyes. Faye just sat there, unashamed by what she had just said.

Once all the ladies calmed down and were able to catch their breath from laughing so hard, Gloria wiped her eyes and turned to Teresa, who was still trying to sit up after laughing. This was the hardest and the longest laugh that the women had had since Gloria came back to New York.

"See, Teresa, I told you that she is sexy, she is sassy and she is raw!"

"Just like that chicken that was served to us by the caterers over there on the table." Faye blurted out, then snapped her finger. When she realized what she had said, she quickly covered her mouth but she knew that it was too late. Teresa had also poked her before she had finished her sentence, but the words had already come out.

After Faye made her comment, it had gotten so quiet in the living room that you could've heard a pin drop. Faye felt embarrassed and ashamed for what she had said. The last thing that she ever wanted to do was to hurt Gloria's feelings. Faye lowered her head in guilt. She had offended a friend that had been so very nice to her. She wanted to crawl away somewhere and hide. Teresa felt for Faye because she knew also that the food hadn't been that good and she knew that Faye didn't mean to say what she had said, so she lowered her head, too.

Gloria could see that Faye showed remorse and regret for making that innocent comment. Gloria couldn't help but burst into laughter as she looked at Faye's face, which looked like she had just got caught with her hand in the cookie jar after she was told that she couldn't have any.

"What's so funny, Gloria?" Faye asked as she sat there looking very uncomfortable. "I just insulted the food and you crack up laughing?"

"Faye, girl, I'm not offended by your comment." Gloria began waving her hand as if to brush the comment off. "To be totally honest with you, that food was really bad, and I am being polite when I say this. The people who prepared that food should be arrested for impersonating chefs."

When Gloria said this, Faye and Teresa began to relax and feel more comfortable.

"I thought that I was the only one. I'm glad that you noticed and said what you said."

Faye felt relieved and her shoulder that was once slouched down was now straight up.

"Oh, Gloria, thank you." Faye said with all sincerity. "You know that I would never want to offend you, and that is the truth."

"Oh, I know that you wouldn't, Faye. Don't even worry about it. No harm was done by your word—only to our stomachs by that food."

"So, the dildo said to the vagina…" Faye's joking broke the tension and started everyone laughing and hooting up a storm again. "I'm only kidding, guys, only kidding!"

Faye began waving her hands in front of her face and shaking her head as if she went face-first into a spider's web.

"Well, I am not kidding," Stephanie added. "I didn't want to offend you either, Gloria, but I gotta be more descriptive. That food, although very beautifully decorated on the table, tasted bland and unfresh; and what kind of seasoning was that, if any? It tasted like pure crap!" Once again, there was high laughter at the caterers' expense. "If Matthew didn't eat it or eat a lot of it, it had to have been pretty darn bad."

"It's true. I've seen him in action. I'll tell you one thing, Gloria. That boy is not allergic to a fork and knife," Faye added.

"Gloria, I didn't want to say anything either but I definitely second the commotion of what Stephanie just said." Teresa was nodding her head.

"You mean that you second the emotion, Teresa," Stephanie corrected. "See! I told you that I didn't wanna say anything."

"I gotta ask y'all a question." Faye said with a totally serious expression. "For such a fancy caterer, how in the hell could they screw up the pate and crackers?!"

A roar of laugher filled the living room again.

"Oh, you girls are making my stomach hurt!" Gloria hollered with glee.

"Just like that ham did to me! Aye Dios mio!" Teresa cried merrily as she held her stomach, pretending to have a stomach ache.

"Oh ladies, it has been such a pleasure spending time with you all and having y'all around me. All three of you have been such a comfort," Gloria added. "I don't remember the last time I had so much fun with sisters."

"Oh, please, Gloria, allow me to second that commotion," Stephanie joked as gaiety, happiness and laughter overtook the four women. They continued sitting and conversing with each other, lending each other their undivided attention.

"Gloria, it is a shame that all that food is going to go to waste," Faye said.

"What makes you that that? Thank God those wonderful deliverymen took a lot and don't forget that Mike will be coming over, probably with

Beth. If he won't eat a lot, then this world is coming to an end. He can eat, y'all. He hasn't changed. His appetite is still just as big as it was when we were married plus, with Stephanie's expertise and my magic hands, we will turn those leftovers into meals fit for royalty," she exclaimed proudly.

"Yeah," responded Stephanie. "The only thing that the food needed was some good seasoning and someone who knew what they were doing in their kitchen."

"You know what? If I gave that table to you right now, Faye, you would be able to make a huge gourmet buffet, huh?" Gloria asked.

"Girl, with a snap of a finger and a blink of an eye!" Faye replied with no hesitation.

"Hey, Gloria, you know, your mother was the queen of gourmet leftover creations. Boy, did she know her way around that kitchen, rest her soul. And she was always so patient. I remember when she first took interest in teaching me how to cook. I was so bad that I could burn Kool Aid! She would always say to me, 'Teresa dear, no wonder you are so skinny. You've been cooking for yourself. If you continue cooking for yourself, you are going to wind up in an early grave, but by then, there won't be anything left of you to bury." Teresa chuckled as she thought back with fond memories. "But with constant practice and determination, and I won't forget the encouragement from your mother, I could have taken horse meat and make it into horse dovers."

"Teresa, I do think that you meant to say hors d'oeuvres. It is French," Gloria corrected.

"Or what and who is French?"

"No, no, Teresa," Gloria tried to explain. "The name is called hors d'oeuvres."

Teresa sat there for a few seconds trying to grasp what Gloria was saying. "Okay. Now I understand. Oh boy! I can barely speak English; now I'm rushing to learn French!" Teresa rolled her eyes as she sounded out of breath. "I can't believe myself sometimes."

The telephone rang while the women continued with their interesting conversation and Gloria got up to answer it on the third ring.

"Hello, Bunker residence. Oh yes, hello, Mr. Kindred. I am just fine, thank you. A-ha, yes that is true. Well to be honest with you, I have company right now. Well, sometime this afternoon. Unfortunately since the funeral is tomorrow, I have a lot of last minute things to do, so I can't give you a set time right now. Can I call you? Thank you for your understanding. Yes, I do. I have your number close by. Yes, sir. See you then. Bye."

All conversations stopped while Gloria went to the phone. When she hung up, she went back to the chair.

"Gloria?" Stephanie said inquisitively.

"Oh, that was Kindred. He wanted to know what time he could come over concerning the house. I told him that I'll call him later. Thank God for Rupert, though. He saved me a lot of money by being so generous in letting us shop till we drop for free. We all don't have to worry about clothes for tomorrow and because we got the clothes early we don't have to meet at the bar this afternoon. That saves me a few hours to deal with last-minute things like Mike, Beth and Chris. Thank God that I have Stephanie here to help too."

"Well, like we said yesterday, Gloria, Teresa and I are willing to help you out with anything. We know that it is rough for the both of you—heck, the four of you—right now. Remember that we are here to help relieve any pressure you might be going through."

"Oh thanks, you guys. We appreciate that, you know, but I think that we have everything pretty much under control."

"Yeah, all the funeral arrangements have been taken care of," Stephanie interjected. "We don't even have to worry about that. Limo service and all of that is all taken care of. The very few personal friends and family all know about the funeral. They confirmed their attendance, plus all of Queens and the outer part of the state know, so I would say that it is going to be a huge turnout. The Reverend Felcher is ready. He has a whole service prepared for him, so everyone is prepared. Even the plot is re-dug and ready."

"Right next to Mommy."

"Yep, and the weather is supposed to be absolutely beautiful. Uncle Archie will be pleased."

"You know, Archie spent so much time at the bar; he would have been pleased just to have everyone have a toast to his name, and he would have…"

"What did you say, Faye?!"

Faye's comment sparked interest in Gloria.

"Did I say something wrong?" Faye asked, wondering if she offended Gloria.

"No, not at all, Faye. As a matter of fact, you said something right!" Gloria looked into the distance, nodding.

"Well please, girl. Tell me what I said."

"Everything is prepared for the funeral tomorrow but we overlooked one thing…"

"What did we forget, Gloria?" Stephanie asked.

"A reception after everything is over!" Gloria said excitedly. "Faye is right. There should be a meeting place where everyone can come and relax and to hear stories, good or bad, about Daddy and to just eat and drink and socialize, and that should be done at the bar. We don't know. Archie Bunker's place might not reopen. This will give people who knew him a chance to just say goodbye and to toast to his memory."

"Oh, Gloria, that's a wonderful idea! I can't believe that we forgot all about that. But how are we going to let everyone know?"

"What are you going to serve? Gloria, there's going to be a lot of people at the funeral."

"How are you going to have all this done before the funeral?"

The women became quiet for a few moments as they tried to come up with an idea or a plan. Every now and then, one would look at the other then they would shrug their shoulder, till Teresa began sitting up straight, eyes wide like an owl.

"I got it, ladies. I got it!" she screamed enthusiastically. "What have we been talking about since we have been alone? We've been talking about catering!"

"We don't have enough time to get a caterer, plus I don't have a lot of money."

"Hey! If we all chip in to get a caterer...," Faye suggested.

"No ladies. You are missing the point and it is staring you right in your face!"

"What, Teresa? Just say it!"

"Us!" Teresa had her hands out in front of her as she looked at the women.

"Us?" Gloria repeated, looking confused as she tried to understand what Teresa was talking about.

"Yes, us!" Teresa opened her eyes wider to emphasize what she was saying, plus she nodded.

"I get it!" Faye said excitedly. "We can prepare the foods ourselves!" Faye then turned and gave Teresa a high five. "Good thinking, girl."

Gloria looked at Faye and Teresa, who looked like they solved the riddle to a puzzle, as she shook her head and looked doubtful.

"But girls, I don't have a lot of money. We might as well forget about it." "Gloria, the bar is packed with food. You don't have to buy anything. Everything is there!"

"Oh, Faye, once again, you are absolutely right. And if this is the last time Archie Bunker's place is open, let's let it go out in a blast!"

"So what's the plan, Hannibal?"

"Okay. Mike and Beth are coming over, right? I have to meet with Mr. Kindred and I definitely have to squeeze in Chris. I just have to figure out what time we could meet at the bar." Gloria stared straight ahead as she began thinking to herself.

"Well, I want you to know that I am available anytime that you need me."

"So am I. I'll be picking up Teresa, anyway. We'll come together." Teresa nodded with Faye.

"I got it!" Gloria cried as she clapped her hands one time. "Mr. Kindred told me to call him at any time. I'll call him once Mike and Beth leave. I don't know how long they will be staying. I don't plan on spending too much time with him."

"Good!" Stephanie interjected.

"What's wrong, Stephanie? I know that you don't want me to get rid of the house, but we have to face facts. I might not be moving back. It's just better to be on the safe side."

"Well, you are definitely correct about me not wanting you to sell, but that is not why I said 'good' when you mentioned spending time with Kindred. Not for nothing, Gloria, but I don't like him and for some reason, I don't trust him."

Stephanie had the same expression on her face when talking about Kindred as she had when she told Gloria about the catered food that she had eaten.

"Oh?" Gloria responded as she cocked her head to the side and faced her.

"It is true, Gloria. There is just something about him that screams 'sneaky'."

"Oh, Stephanie, that's just your imagination. I never got that feeling about him."

"Because all your attention was being soaked up by Mr. Hanley." Faye and Teresa laughed when she said this.

"There is something about those eyes of his that just ain't right, and I am usually good when it comes to judging people. Remember that I am in the entertainment business. When I say that I know, believe me, I know. He's up to something, but I just don't know what it is."

"Oh great, Stephanie. Like I don't have enough to worry about," Gloria commented as she sucked her teeth and rolled her eyes. Gloria stood up and paced back and forth nervously. "Now I have to worry if Kindred is up to no good."

"I'm sorry, Gloria. It's just a feeling that I have. I wanted to tell you how I felt but got so bombarded with things that I forgot."

"Honey, I appreciate how you feel and I respect your opinion, but I'm just going to hear what he has to say, that's all. I won't be signing anything. You don't have to worry about that."

That comment seemed to have relaxed Stephanie some, but Gloria was still concerned.

"Well, back to what I was thinking," she said, then turned to look at Faye and Teresa. "Ladies, how about early evening?"

Faye and Teresa both looked at one another, then shrugged. "That is fine with us," Faye said. Teresa agreed.

"Oh that is great!" Gloria exclaimed happily. "Daddy is going to be so pleased!"

"He'll be even more pleased if you forget about Cali and come back home," Stephanie added.

"Please Stephanie, not now. Let's talk about that after the funeral. Look, you know that I love you. We are pretty much all that we have left: me, you, the twins and Joey. We aren't close with the distant family. I know that our roots are here in Queens and I will really take that into consideration when I make my decision. Trust me, cousin, okay?" Gloria then smiled warmly.

Gloria knew deep down inside that there was nothing wrong with Kindred. Stephanie just didn't want to be alone in New York without any family. Ever since her father literally dropped her off and never looked back, Stephanie had always felt alone. Well, who could blame her? Mother died when she was young, father left her when she was young, Edith and Archie were gone, and now Gloria and the kids were in another state. Gloria would admit that she too would think of any excuse to prevent her and the kids to return back to Cali, even if she had to do a little manipulation, but Gloria didn't have time to worry about that. She had other matters to deal with at the present time, like the food preparation for the funeral.

The women spoke a little longer, then Faye and Teresa rose off the couch to get ready to leave.

"Okay, you guys. Stephanie and I will meet you all at the bar. Y'all get home safely."

"Oh, we'll be just fine, Gloria. Again, I wanna thank you for the clothes," Faye said smiling.

"Yes, Gloria. I..." Teresa hesitated for a moment then spoke. "I second, ah, er, ditto!" she exclaimed proudly because she got the word right. "I thank you and my girls thank you and even mi novio Hector thanks you."

"Why does Hector thank us, Teresa?" Gloria was bracing herself, because she knew that Teresa was about to say something funny.

"Well, Hector thanks you because he didn't have to spend any money on clothes, but what he doesn't know yet is that there is a gigantic television and VCR at JC Penney's with my name on it!" Teresa then snapped her finger. "He ain't getting off the hook that easily!"

All the women started laughing at Teresa's comment as Faye and she made their way to the door. They both bid Gloria and Stephanie goodbye. Faye was the first out the door and down the porch. Teresa was the last to leave. She stopped before she walked out onto the porch then turned to Gloria, pulling on her sleeve.

"Gloria, please give Mike my regards. I really did wanna see him and surprise him. Wait till he gets a good load of me!"

Teresa started laughing as she walked onto the porch, then down the stairs, following behind Faye. Gloria just stood at the door, smiling and shaking her head.

No sooner had the two walked upstairs to their room to admire their new clothes, the doorbell rang. Gloria was the one who headed downstairs to answer.

As Gloria opened the door, standing in front of her were Mike and his wife Beth. Mike was totally bald on the top and some down the back. He had the rest of his hair cut very short, making him look much younger than his actual age; his skin was still smooth with only tiny crows' feet around the eyes. He also had a beard and mustache which was darker than the hair on his head.

"He is dying his beard," she thought to herself. Much heavier now than he was when she was married to him, he still wasn't considered obese, but she could definitely see that everything had gone totally to the stomach, not the legs, chest, butt or arms. Mike was never big on fashion and that hadn't changed even when he married Beth. He had on jeans, dungaree shirt and a corduroy blazer, brown, just like his shoes. Gloria thought that he really did look like a professor. The only thing that he needed was the glasses hanging around his neck and some books or a little attaché case. Replacing the attaché case at the present moment were flowers that he was holding.

Beth was a few inches taller than Gloria. When she had first met Beth, Beth was a blond, but once she and Mike got married, she had been a red head and she wore it well. Sometimes it was short, sometimes long; right now, it was short but fuller on the top, with a little bit of bangs in the front that fell over her forehead. The red hair complemented her skin tone, which was a natural olive, but her skin had a healthy tan to it and Beth didn't wear a lot of makeup. She looked glowing with her flawless complexion and European features. She had big blue eyes and a straight nose like Glenn Close, with little freckles on it and she had a pencil-thin mouth with a strong chin and cheekbones. She was considered an attractive woman. She had on a beautiful multicolored sundress with a red light sweater that wasn't buttoned. She wasn't wearing stockings, showing a pair of beautiful tanned legs, and she was wearing open-toe shoes. She looked much different than the last time Gloria had seen her. She looked more relaxed, more serene. Maybe it was because she was away from all the smog, Gloria thought.

Mike was first to come in and give Gloria a kiss, then Beth came in with a huge smile on her face. She gave Gloria a sincere hug and a greeting and Gloria responded by doing the same.

"Oh, Gloria, it is good to see you again," Beth said as Gloria welcomed her inside of the house.

"It is good to see you too," Gloria responded graciously.

Gloria showed sincere gratitude on her face to see them.

"Once again Gloria, like I said on the phone, I'm really sorry to hear about your father," she said in a low tone full of sincere remorse. "It is much better to say it in person."

"Oh, thank you so much, Beth. I appreciate that. Come and have a seat," Gloria suggested in a cordial tone, then pointed her to the couch as she closed the front door, but before Beth sat down she nudged Gloria, then nodded her head towards Mike, who introduced himself to the dining room table and the food that was on top of it. Within seconds of walking through the door and to the table, he had a sandwich prepared and had already taken a huge chunk out of it, showing no mercy. He was facing the kitchen door and was nodding his head up and down in enjoyment as he chewed. Beth pulled on Gloria's sleeve then leaned her head towards her as she kept her eyes on her husband.

"Look at this, Gloria. Once a barbarian, always a barbarian. We've been up and down Main Street, Flushing, touching everything on the street from A to Z, then we get on the wrong bus thanks to Mr. Navigator here. I told him it was the wrong bus, but does he listen? I would say no. He has dirty hands, but he still makes a sandwich."

She was smiling and shaking her head in disbelief. Gloria looked on and laughed and shook her head, too.

Mike heard the women giggling in his direction so he turned around to face them and started mumbling, with a mouthful of food, then smiled and took another chomp of food.

"Him barbarian. Him say something. Him eat now!" Beth started beating on her chest, sounding nothing like Tarzan, but it still made Gloria laugh more.

Beth and Gloria made their way to the couch; once seated they looked back in Mike's direction. Beth was now pointing as she stared forward.

"Gloria, do you see the big pot of flowers that Mike simply plopped down in the dining room chair there? Well those are from us to you," Beth said proudly.

Mike had now turned around and was facing back towards them. "And this is also for you."

Beth dug into her purse and pulled out an envelope. Gloria knew that there was a card in it with some cash. She was able to tell by the thickness.

"Thank you so much, Beth." Gloria graciously accepted it as Mike mumbled something again with a mouth full of food.

"Oh, thank you too, Mike," she added, then both she and Beth laughed more at Mike's expense.

Mike then swallowed, which allowed him to speak coherently.

"Well, you said come with an appetite, so knowing me to be the gentleman that I am…" When he said this, the two women looked at each other then playfully yawned. "I didn't want to offend you by just nibbling. I'm starving. I haven't eaten all day."

"Mike, she said come with an appetite, not with that thirty pound spare tire around the hips," Beth quipped.

Mike waved Beth off then turned back around and began eating more. Beth continued shaking her head. "Can you believe this sight?!"

"Oh, it is okay, Beth. We ate till we almost exploded. Mike can eat to his heart's delight."

"Did you hear that, Mike? Gloria said knock yourself out."

When Beth said this, Mike opened his eyes wide, then actually got a plate and started loading up, looking like a pig in hog heaven.

"Would you care for something to drink, Beth? How about something to eat? You better get some before the human garbage disposal hogs it all."

"I would love to, but I just wanna relax for a few minutes." Beth sounded out of breath. "That is a beautiful table, Gloria. Did you do it?"

"No!" she said quickly but with a lot of force behind it, causing Beth to jump. "I mean, ah, I can't take credit for the food. It was a gift from a dear friend."

"Oh, how very nice. I can't wait to sample everything. It all looks so yummy!"

As Beth looked at the food, she licked her lips once.

"Believe me, sister, you can wait," Gloria commented to herself, but then she looked towards Mike, who wasn't doing any complaining or slowing down. "Maybe his taste buds went numb once the meat of the chicken touched his tongue."

"Well Gloria, you look good despite the circumstances." She was looking at her from head to toe. "I guess that New York has been wearing on you well."

"Well, I can say the same about you. I noticed it at the door. You look so, so, so, different."

"Well, I slept well on the flight in, I slept well at the hotel and we had a nice walk on Main Street. It looked like Chinatown over there. They have all kinds of stores and deals everywhere. Despite taking the wrong bus, which was another reason why we took so long."

From the dining room area, Mike mumbled something about Flushing Meadow Park and Shea Stadium and Willets Point, where they play tennis, as the women looked at each other peculiarly.

Beth leaned forward in Mike's direction then playfully squinted her eyes as she tried to understand what Mike was saying.

"Honey, I'm sorry but Gloria and I can only speak one language. We already know that you speak two, English and Foodian." After Beth teased Mike, she started laughing then slapped Gloria on her leg, which of course caused Gloria to laugh. Not at the corny joke, but at the fact that Beth thought it was funny and wanted her to think that it was funny also. Mike looked at Beth then mocked her laughing as he continued eating, not in the least bothered by the comment.

Gloria could look at both of them and see that they were very much in love. Gloria could honestly admit that Beth was good for Mike. She was strong-willed, intelligent, somewhat funny, liberated and very caring. Plus, she was Polish like him. There had been a time when Mike had been solo and wasn't very happy and Gloria had felt badly for him, but once he met Beth, she had turned his life around and had really made him happy. She had moved in first with Mike before they had gotten married, but once they did, it was as if Mike was a new and changed man. He could still put an all-you-can-eat buffet restaurant out of business, though. Gloria knew that that would never change. She was happy, though, that she and Mike had remained friends all these years despite what had happened in the past, and that he was happily married.

Ten minutes later, Beth was at the dining room table fixing herself a plate of food and something to drink. A few minutes after that, Gloria told them to come into the living room and bring the food with them. Beth sat back on the couch in the corner. She put her plate on the coffee table. Mike was about to come and sit down in Archie's chair. Gloria went back and sat on the other side of the couch.

Before Mike sat down in Archie's chair, he looked to his left and right, then sat. Gloria stared at him while he did his little ritual and found it odd. She began looking at him strangely.

"Well," he said, as he made himself comfortable in the chair. "This is a moment in history. I looked around to see if someone was going to take my picture. God rest Archie's soul, but this is the first time ever that I am going to sit in his chair without hearing, 'Hey, Meathead, get the hell out of my chair!'"

Mike even did a good imitation of Archie. Unbeknownst to Mike, Stephanie had quietly made her way down the stairs and sneakily walked up behind him, hoping to scare the pants off of him. Before trying to scare him, she looked towards the two women sitting on the couch for approval. With approving nods from Gloria and Beth, Stephanie sneaked up closer to an unsuspecting Mike, who was eating his food carefree and contentedly.

"Hey, Meathead, get the hell out of my chair!" Stephanie yelled in a deep voice, trying to sound like Archie and causing Mike to jump and nearly spill his food. Mike was going to make sure that he saved his plate.

The three women roared with laughter. Stephanie fell to the floor laughing and Beth and Gloria held their stomachs and rolled around on the couch.

Mike stood there red-faced, looking embarrassed, not really knowing what to do.

"Very funny, Stephanie!" Mike responded embarrassedly, then went towards the dining room table. "You scared me so much that I have to get another plate."

Beth stopped laughing and sucked her teeth and rolled her eyes concerning her greedy husband.

"There is always some kind of excuse for you to eat more."

Beth also began wiping the tears from her eyes from laughing so hard.

Once everyone finally calmed down, Stephanie went to introduce herself to Beth.

"Stephanie it is so nice to finally meet you. I have heard so much about you. You are absolutely beautiful."

"Oh, thank you so much, Beth." Stephanie's voice went up a few octaves higher. "It is nice to meet you too." She then went over to Mike who was bent over the table loading and eating and she put her arm around his shoulder.

"And how are you, Mike? It is so good to see you again." Mike stood up and gave her a hug and kiss with his mouth full of food. "Sorry that I scared you like that. It was too easy, Mike. I couldn't resist!"

Mike mumbled something again then smiled as he chewed.

Stephanie then looked at Mike's girth with surprise then rubbed it lightly.

"Hey, man! When is that baby gonna pop out?!" She was bulging out her eyes with a smile.

"In about five months!" Beth shouted, then all the women started laughing again. Once again, unabashedly, Mike mocked the women's laughter then continued eating.

It looked like Mike wasn't going back to the big chair any time soon, so Stephanie took his spot.

"So, she is not only beautiful, Gloria, but she has a good sense of humor."

"Yeah, this is true. She has always been funny. She is just a natural. She has kept her Uncle Archie on his toes and in stitches for ages. I think Stephanie and I were the only two people who had his number."

"I would have loved to have met him," Beth said casually.

When Beth said this, the two women looked at each other then started laughing as if Beth was out of her mind. Even Mike chuckled at the comment while he kept his head down eating and looking at the dining room table.

"Are you sure?" Stephanie asked as they all continued laughing.

Mike ended up taking residence at the dining room table. When he heard the women laugh, he thought that they were laughing at him, so he turned to them and mocked them.

"So Stephanie, I heard that you are a singer," Beth said with wonder and excitement.

"Well, I've done some singing work, and I aspire to be a singer but nothing yet, but I believe that my luck is going to change. "Stephanie was nodding her head.

"What have you done that I might have heard or heard of?"

"I've done voiceovers for local kiddie shows here in New York, and one of the nationwide commercials was for Genesis Insurance." She said nonchalantly.

Beth sat up straight in excitement and with a smile on her face. "Oh, was that you?" Beth was looking surprised.

"Yep, that was me." Stephanie was being very modest about the whole thing.

"What do you mean, 'was,' Stephanie!" Gloria responded. "That commercial still airs around the country. She gets a nice piece of change every time it airs." Gloria said proudly. "She also does background vocals on demos that are given to big name musicians. Her voice can really tear the roof down. She has performed at Daddy's place many times to SROs"

"SROs?" Beth asked as she looked perplexed.

"Standing room only," she explained. "I think that the first time that she performed, she was still a little girl and she sang and even danced. There's not a shy bone in her body, at least not when I last saw her perform," Gloria declared. "Give her a stage or a microphone or both, then stand back and watch out! She is like a firecracker."

Stephanie looked like she was about to blush. She felt happy because Gloria was proud of her accomplishments.

"That is so nice, Stephanie, not to mention brave. What made you wanna do that line of work?" Without thinking, Stephanie immediately answered.

"I love to see people happy and smiling."

"Happy and smiling," Beth echoed and nodded as she thought about what Stephanie said.

"I give you a lot of credit, Stephanie. I think that I have a good voice but I get so nervous singing and talking in front of people. Last month at my niece's third birthday, I got nervous just singing happy birthday," Beth remembered.

As the three continued chatting away, Mike eased up from the table and was heading towards Edith's chair. His plan was to get revenge on Stephanie while she had her back to him and was facing the two women on the couch, who saw what Mike was trying to accomplish but were not saying anything.

While Stephanie was in the midst of telling a story, Mike was able to sit down in the chair without getting her attention. He then slowly extended his hand and was just about to shock her by putting his hand on her but Stephanie responded.

"Good try Mike, but don't eeeeven think about it!" Everyone was in total awe and amazement that she caught Mike without even turning around.

The Life and Times of Gloria Bunker

"Now, how in the hell were you able to do that without turning your head? Oh, I know." He nodded and looked at the two innocent women accusingly. "The women gave you a signal, right?"

"You are absolutely incorrect, Mike."

"Well, how did you know, then?" He asked suspiciously.

"I smelled the onion and garlic on the food that you are eating." Then she laughed, causing the other two to laugh also. Mike rolled his eyes, then threw his hands up in the air.

"I give up!" he said then went back to the table.

"Ladies, I've laughed so hard that my stomach hurts." When Beth said this, Mike turned and looked at her with concern.

Before Mike sat down at the table again, the phone rang. Gloria was the one who got up to answer the phone on the third ring.

"Hello, Bunker residence. Oh, hi, Joey, where are you? Oh. When are you leaving? Aha. Did you bring a suitcase with you to work? Well, I don't think that you need to pack too much stuff because I have a lot of clothes for you, new clothes and shoes. Calm down, Joey, calm down. I'll explain everything when you get here. By the way, your father and stepmom are both here."

Stephanie liked the fact the Gloria referred to Beth as Joey's stepmom. That was a sign of respect and approval of Beth and it made Beth part of Joey's family.

"I'll tell 'em, Joey. Where else? Downstairs in the basement. Yes, Stephanie is here too. Okay, I'll tell her, too. See you soon. Love you too. Bye." Then she hung up.

As Gloria walked back to the couch, everyone was staring at her.

"Oh, wrong number," she joked. Everyone started moaning. "Okay, okay. That was Joey. He will be leaving shortly and should be here tonight, if there are no delays. He told me to tell you all and the twins that he loves you. That was it. He sounded well."

"Oh, that's good." Beth said. Then she looked around like something just popped into her head. "Speaking of the twins, I haven't seen or heard them. Are they here?" She was sounding a tad anxious and concerned.

"Oh, they are down in the basement. Let me call them and let them know that you all are here."

Gloria got up from the couch and headed towards the basement door to call the twins. Once she was by the door, she opened it and called down to them.

"Hey, guys. Mike and Beth are here!"

While she called them, Stephanie and Beth continued talking as Beth also ate.

"Okay, Ma!" Zoe cried back. "We'll be up in a moment. We are still in the new clothes!"

When they said this, Beth perked up again as she did when she heard that Stephanie was a singer.

"Oh? New clothes? Oh, I love new clothes!" Beth cried, sounding like a little girl who had been asked if she wanted some candy. "Gloria, tell them to come up and let me see what you bought them." Beth quickly took two forks full of food as she looked excitedly towards her.

Gloria really wasn't in the mood to explain about the clothes or her situation with Rupert right now, but she knew that once the twins came up with the new clothes on, she was going to have to do a lot of explaining. She was going to try to talk her out of it by making up some excuse.

"Oh Beth, I don't think that they..." But before she could even finish talking, Beth interrupted.

"Oh, come on, Gloria. It'll be fun. It'll be like, like...twin models. They'll look so cute, too. How many outfits did you buy them?"

"Well, actually, I..."

"Yeah Gloria, send them up," Mike interjected. "I'd like to see what you got them, too, and I heard you on the phone saying you got Joey a lot of stuff. I'm impressed. I would like to see what you got him, too."

Gloria looked to be out-voted. She looked towards Stephanie, who could only shrug her shoulders. Gloria was really showing her reluctance.

"Oh, come on, sister. Stop being so bashful. I'm sure that what you got them is nice."

"Okay, then." Gloria was defeated. "Hey, kids, come up now, okay? No need to change. They wanna see the new clothes!"

Gloria knew that the minute that they came up with those expensive clothes on, she would be bombarded with a lot of questions.

But Gloria didn't understand why she didn't want Beth and Mike to know. Any other woman would be proud to show off their kids with new clothes on. Any other woman would've been proud to announce to the whole world that the man of her dreams had finally materialized and wanted to have a meaningful relationship with her. Even if she wasn't interested in him, she could always brag at least, but not her. Gloria knew that the Stivics knew she didn't have anyone in her life. She was sure that she knew that they would want her happy. They would rejoice to know that there were two people interested in her and that one was a famous, very rich, real estate mogul and the other was a successful business owner and former love. This was nothing to be ashamed about. She should be flattered. Gloria didn't know how she should feel, but at the present moment she was definitely confused.

Mike had stopped eating as he stared towards the basement door, and Beth had put down her fork and was smiling with anticipation. Gloria began to walk back toward the couch, so all the attention would go to the twins once they made their appearance.

The Life and Times of Gloria Bunker

A few seconds later, there was a rumble from downstairs. It was the twins making their way up to show off their new duds. Gloria heard giggling, which she knew was Zoe. They were on their way, talking low to one another and chuckling at the same time. Once they walked through the door, Gloria was surprised to see that not only were the twins dressed in the new clothes, but they also brought up handfuls of the other clothes too. She guessed that they thought when she had said that the Stivics' wanted to see the new clothes, they had meant all the new clothes. She couldn't fault them for that.

When the twins finally reached the middle of the living room and put the new clothes on Edith's chair, Mike's eyes bulged out as if he was the only person inside an all-you-can-eat for a dollar McDonald's fast food restaurant. He stood up and walked over to them. They greeted each other as he began examining the clothes. Gloria noticed that Matthew looked uncomfortable in the new clothes and looked uncomfortable modeling them in front of everyone. One the other hand, Zoe looked to be in hog heaven. She loved modeling the new clothes as she turned and held her head up high and sucked in her cheeks as she pretended to be a runway model. This caused Gloria to chuckle.

As Mike checked out the name tags and the prices, he had to do a double-take just to make sure he was seeing what he was seeing.

"So Mike, how do you like it?" Zoe asked as Mike checked out the outfit and the name tag.

"Gloria, these are name brand clothes with names and labels I cannot even pronounce........And I am a teacher, no less." Mike couldn't believe his eyes.

"Oh here," Mike said as he was examining one of Matthew's suits. "I see one I can pronounce. Versace?!" Mike looked at the clothes in front of him, then at Gloria, then at the clothes again. "Gloria, the jacket alone costs seven hundred dollars!"

"I know, Mike. Don't it just rock!" Matthew smiled widely. "Yeah, it is a little stiff for my liking but after I wear it a few times, I can grow to like it."

"Now me too, me too, Mike! Now check out these. You haven't seen these yet!" Zoe couldn't be left out as she jumped in front of Matthew and Mike so she could be the center of attention.

Gloria glanced at Stephanie, who nodded towards Beth, who was facing the excited twins with her hand over her mouth in total shock, awe and amazement. Beth didn't know what to do or say. Even when they said hello to her, the only thing she could do was lift her hand slightly and give a little wave with a smile.

Mike continued looking through the clothes.

"Lulu Couture, Gloria?" Mike commented in disbelief. "I didn't know that they made clothes for teens." He was now examining the name tag on the dress she had on, then looked at Gloria. "Gucci!" Mike was acting as if it was all an illusion, that his mind was playing tricks on him.

"Yes, Gucci!" Zoe screamed as she began spinning in circles merrily. "It is magical. I feel like those girls from the Valley! You know the ones. Those snobby stuck up ones. The ones that when you talk to them, they look at you like, how dare you even form words in their presence. The only difference is that I'm not a snob. I could do this every day and remain exactly the way I am but now, I might act snobby towards those snobby, stuck-up girls."

"Gloria, how were you able to afford all these expensive clothes?" Mike was still looking through Matthew's and Zoe's clothes. "Plus you have a lot of clothes for Joey? Oh, Gloria, please tell me your secret. Did you hit the lottery and didn't tell anyone?" Mike asked in a joking manner.

"Oh, Mike, come on!" Beth responded quickly. "You know that she is a real estate agent. She probably sold a multimillion dollar house out in the hills and received a huge commission and bonus right, Gloria?"

Gloria smiled embarrassedly, then swallowed. "Well, guys, I cannot take the credit for this."

"Sure you can, Gloria. Stop being so modest. Hell, I'm going to become a real estate agent right after I..." But for some reason, she didn't finish her comment.

"Right after you what, Beth?" Gloria asked.

"Probably right after we return home, right, Beth?" Mike said.

"Well, maybe. Maybe not right after, but some time down the road."

"Well, I can't take credit for the clothes because I didn't buy them." When Gloria said that, Mike and Beth looked at a quietly sitting Stephanie, who was just watching everyone interact.

"I changed my mind about real estate, Mike. Hell," Beth said, then started rubbing her vocal cords as she prepared herself to sing. "Mi, mi, mi, mi, do, ray, mi, fah, so, la ti, do!"

"Sorry, Julie Andrews," Stephanie replied as she stared at Beth, 'but I can't take credit for the clothes, either." Stephanie was now shaking her head.

"Well, can you put us out of our misery, as the suspense is slowly killing us, because I know that the twins didn't buy them?" Mike said forcefully.

"Hey, watch your tone, Mike Stivic," Beth replied. "Gloria doesn't have to explain anything to you. She is not your wife anymore."

"Thanks, Beth. It's okay. I want to explain," Gloria said. "It was given to us by a gorgeous billionaire tycoon who likes me and I like him back and he surprised us this morning. He is also the one who surprised us with that elaborate table full of food. Not to mention...the huge breakfast feast that's still in the kitchen, clothes for Stephanie and clothes for Joey and me." It was out. She said it, she did it, she was relieved.

Beth and Mike stared at Gloria for a few seconds then stared at each other then stared back at Gloria, but to her surprise, they burst into laughter. "Okay, fine, Gloria. If you don't wanna tell us, that's fine."

"Yeah, sister stop trying to be like Stephanie. You did pretty well, though; straight face and all."

"She's not lying, guys. She is very serious." Stephanie quickly came to Gloria's defense. "Everything that Gloria is saying is true."

Both Mike and Beth stared at Stephanie and Gloria for a few seconds to see if they were joking but to their surprise, Gloria and Stephanie looked very sincere.

"So, who is this billionaire who lavishes you and the family with clothes and an abundance of the most delicious food that I have ever tasted?" Mike was still teasing both women, not giving in to the fact that they might be serious.

For a quick second, her mind jumped to what Mike had just said about the food being delicious. Beth wasn't doing too badly on her plate before her.

"They like that crap!" she said to herself, and she was wondering if Stephanie caught her vibe, so she looked at her. Stephanie looked back but Gloria couldn't read her, then her mind went back to the question that Mike mockingly asked her, but before she could respond, she noticed that Beth felt like getting a little heckle in, just for laughs, too.

"Well Mike, why don't you guess? Gloria did say that he's a billionaire and gorgeous. That leaves Bill Gates, Ted Turner and Donald Trump off the list."

"It's Rupert H. Hanley." Gloria was finally able to say above all the joking and laughing.

"Rupert H. Hanley," Mike echoed. "I was just about to say him." Mike was still joking with Gloria but noticed that as he and Beth stared at the two women and the twins this time, they were serious as high blood pressure.

Beth didn't notice before that Gloria had that very expensive watch on; then she realized that what Gloria had said was true. She stood up, her eyes drawn to the watch, almost hypnotized, then touched it.

"Mike, Gloria is not joking. She is serious. Am I right, sister?" When Beth asked this, Gloria nodded her head bashfully.

Mike and Beth hesitated at first, then screamed for happiness for Gloria. They had screamed simultaneously and so loud that everyone in the house became startled for a moment.

"Oh, Gloria, this is absolutely wonderful news! Mike, Gloria really does have a boyfriend. Sister, I am so happy for you!"

Beth was leading her back to the couch.

"Gloria, you really hit the jackpot. How long have you been going out with him?"

"Well, it is kinda weird, actually."

"Hey, guys. We lived it," Matthew said as he and Zoe picked up their clothes. "We already know the story, so Zoe and I are going back downstairs, okay?"

"Yeah" Zoe added. "We'll see you later."

Mike was really interested in hearing the story, so interested that he left his food on the table and sat down in Archie's chair. Stephanie took Edith's chair and the two women returned to the couch, where Beth began eating again.

"I only met him yesterday. Not even twenty-four hours ago. But I've been in his white stretch limo, private jet, private helicopter, his penthouse in Miami and at his beachfront resort. I haven't even been back in New York for twelve hours yet."

"Oh Gloria, that is so exciting!"

"How did you meet him if you only met him yesterday?" Mike asked.

"Well, the real estate company that Daddy had been talking to about selling the house…"

"Selling the house?!" Mike responded as he interrupted Gloria.

"Yeah, I thought so also, but anyway, I had an appointment to see one of the agents that runs Rupert's Queens Office. Rupert wanted to come along for the ride, so when he came into the house and saw me, the rest is history."

"Oh, it had to be more than that, Gloria."

"No really. That's it. Stephanie was right there. She can vouch for me."

"It's true. She didn't do anything out of the ordinary but just say hello." "That must have been some hello," Mike exclaimed.

"Yeah, it must have been because my hello has gotten all of us free good buys."

"That was a good one, Gloria," Beth replied as she pointed at her.

"Thanks, but seriously, the money is nice. I am not going to lie about that, but I didn't spend time with his money. I spent time with him and you know what? He is a wonderful human being and I like him a lot. Even if I had met him and he wasn't a billionaire, I would have been very interested in him. I'm sure that there are plenty of rich men out there who are total losers and don't know how to treat a woman, but not Rupert. Rupert is a total gentleman and he reeks of class and style. When I was with him, I felt so light. I never thought that my feet would even hit the ground again."

"Gloria, you look like you are glowing as you talk about him," Beth remarked.

"Oh, Beth, I can talk about him all day and never once mention that he is rich."

Gloria had just happened to look over towards Mike, who was smiling in her direction.

"Gloria, I must admit that I find this whole fascinating story terribly romantic. Love at first sight, and what makes it really sentimental is that he cares for you just for being yourself. I could just cry." Beth then looked towards Mike and leaned her empty plate towards him. "Mike, would you mind bringing me some more that delicious food?" She then looked at Stephanie and Gloria. "I'm sorry, ladies. I guess that I am on the Mike Stivic's Sumo diet."

"The Mike Stivic's Sumo Diet?" Stephanie asked. "Yeah gimme..."

"Gimme sumo this and gimme sumo that!" Mike interjected by beating Beth to the punch line as he stood up and headed to the dining room table.

While loading up on food for Beth, he quickly ate some food off of his own plate.

"That's Mike for ya," Beth commented pointing towards Mike, who had a mouth full of food once again. "He always thinks about my needs first, before he thinks about his."

Beth was being sarcastic. "He is so caring, so thoughtful and would do anything for me."

Gloria and Stephanie both giggled.

"Well, you know, Beth, Gloria here..."

"Oh no Stephanie, don't!" she said to herself. "Please don't tell anymore!"

Gloria tried to get Stephanie's attention by cutting her eyes at her, but Stephanie wasn't paying any attention to her. She was too busy facing Beth and talking to her.

"Not only is a billionaire interested in her, she also has another man who is also caring, so thoughtful and would do anything for her."

"Oh no, Gloria!" Beth exclaimed. "How were you able to find the time? Wasn't the billionaire enough?!"

Mike was making his way back to the couch, handing Beth's plate to her, then he went back to pick up his plate to bring over to the big chair, so he could continue to eat.

"So, who is this other guy, Gloria?"

"An ex-boyfriend that I had before Mike and I started going out back in the day"

"Chris Barlow?" Mike asked with amazement.

"Yep. I saw him yesterday. He came over and we chatted for a while. We have a date, er, ah, get-together sometime today."

"Hey, Gloria, you sure know how to be at the right place at the right time. What does he do and how does he look?" Beth had begun eating the food off of her plate ,and so had Mike.

"He still looks exactly like he did back when we were dating. Tall, dark, handsome, still kind and still respectful and..."

"He still has feelings for her. He never got over her."

"Thanks, Stephanie!" Gloria playfully cut her eyes at her. "And what does he do for a living?"

"Something concerning construction, carpentry, electrical and plumbing something or other. Stephanie said that he has a big store not too far from here."

"Actually Faye said it, I think, but I knew about it," she leaned over and told Gloria.

"I remember Arch mentioning Chris in my presence. I remember the year he had done the basement downstairs, remodeled it and everything. I forgot what holiday it was but Gloria had to work and I was coming to New York to spend the holidays with some friends in Astoria. I volunteered to bring the kids here and when I got here, the kids greeted Stephanie and Archie, then they all zoomed downstairs."

"I remember that, Mike."

"I said to Arch, 'Where are they going and why are they heading to the basement?' and that was when he gave me the whole tour. Chris did a magnificent job to that basement and he had completed the basement quickly. Arch had said, 'Hey, Meathead, if my little goil had married Chris like I had always thought she would before she met you, I wudda got the job done cheaper than I was charged. Thanks a lot, Meathead!' Arch always playfully reminded me of that." Mike chuckled then his voice went very low as if he was talking to himself. "Boy, do I wish that I could hear him say that again." When Mike said this, it became so quiet that you could hear a pin drop. "I remember one time at the house—it might have been that same day when Stephanie, Joey and the twins were downstairs playing around—I forgot what I was doing..."

"Probably eating, knowing you." Beth interjected to lighten the mood and got a good chuckle.

"Anywaaay...," Mike continued as he playfully gave his wife a dirty look.

"I started hearing in unison as a song, 'Meathead, meathead, meathead' over and over again but I paid it no mind, but I saw Arch come by the basement door. He heard it then went down the stairs. I heard him call the kids to him. Arch said in a very loving, tender and caring voice, 'I want you little guys to do your Grampa and Uncle Archie a favor. I don't wanna hear you use the word 'meathead' anymore, ok? The reason why is because that's a special word that I use for Mike, see, so if you use it, it won't be a special word anymore."

Oh, Mike, I remember that too." Stephanie's eyes began to well up as she talked low. The memory was making her feel Mike's sentiment.

"He said to them, 'Meat, er, ah, Mike is special to me, so therefore he has a special name.' When he got finished speaking to the children, he came up the stairs. I remember when he saw me, he noticed that I was staring at him and he said, 'Hey, Meathead, whatever you heard downstairs...Dummy up, you!' Then he speedily disappeared as fast as he appeared."

The Life and Times of Gloria Bunker

Mike started smiling as he ended the story. "Hey, by the way, come to think about it..."

"You were eating!" all the women shouted in unison as they all laughed.

"Archie would tell all of you, maybe I'm getting this feeling because I am sitting in his chair, but...Stifle there, why don't you'ze!"

"This whole thing concerning the billionaire and the ex-boyfriend reminds me of that song, 'Torn between two lovers, feeling like a fool, la, la, la, la, la..."

"Beth, you should feel like a fool, singing like that," Mike jokingly commented.

"Listen here, Kielbasa head...," Beth uttered loudly.

"You mean, Meathead, Beth," Gloria corrected.

"Well, I got the 'head' part right. I didn't mean to insult the Kielbasa by comparing it to him." Beth looked at Mike, smiled then winked at him.

"Love you too, babe." Mike smiled then gave her a pretend kiss from the chair.

"So, Gloria," Beth said as she turned her attention to her. "Speaking of love and speaking of 'two,' meaning the number, what are you going to do about these two loves of yours?"

Gloria sucked her teeth and rolled her eyes.

"Oh, Beth, I wish that it was an easy choice but it isn't. I don't know what I am going to do. I don't want to hurt either of them. They are both so sweet. Part of me wishes that I'd never met Rupert. That way I could give all of my attention to Chris. But there are other parts of me that wish I'd never seen Chris. That way I wouldn't have an opportunity to hurt him again, just in case I wanna be with Rupert."

"You have a dilemma, Gloria, and I wouldn't want to be in your shoes."

"Well, I promised myself that when I meet Chris today, I am going to tell him everything. I feel badly because when I originally agreed to go out with him, I had told him that I was single. I didn't know about Rupert at the time, and I had also told Rupert that I was single but all through the date with him, I kept thinking about Chris."

While they continued talking, the telephone rang. Stephanie volunteered to get the phone because Gloria was the one who was in mid-sentence. When she got up, she faced the kitchen.

"Hello, Bunker residence. Oh, hello there, Mr. I-wont-forget-to-call-early!"

Stephanie was talking angrily, with one hand on her hip.

"Hold on!" she ordered.

Stephanie then turned and looked at Gloria, who had stopped talking and was facing her. Stephanie motioned to Gloria that she was going to pick the phone up in the kitchen and if she would hang the phone up once she got in there. Gloria already knew the routine. Stephanie laid the phone down on the table then walked through the kitchen door. Gloria heard Stephanie pick up the phone then yell, 'Okay, Gloria. I got it!' then Gloria hung the phone up and came back and sat on the couch.

Gloria shook her head with a smile on her face towards Beth and Mike.

"That has to be Jerry she is talking to. That's her agent/manager, what have you. The way she talks to him, sometimes I think that it is much more."

Mike started fidgeting in his chair and kept looking at the food on the dining room table anxiously. Gloria noticed his movements then decided that she should release him from his pain.

"Go ahead, Mike. Go and get more food before you develop a rash on your tush. You know that you want more. It is calling out to you. Eat and enjoy yourself." Gloria motioned with her hands for him to go to the table.

Without hesitation, Mike jumped up out of the chair and headed back to the table contentedly.

"Gloria, I don't know what it is about this food. It just tastes so good!" he remarked.

"It is true, Gloria," Beth added. "Whoever prepared the food should be commended."

"Or committed!" Gloria replied only to herself, but then she looked at Beth. "Well, that food sure was something." That was the best that she could say.

"Mike dear, bring me some dark meat from the chicken, please!" Beth called out, and he nodded.

Gloria could understand Mike's appetite. She was used to it, but she had never seen Beth eat like she was doing, especially with a meal that really wasn't well prepared. Maybe it was because both of them hadn't eaten anything that morning before they arrived at the house.

This time, Mike prepared Beth's food first, then brought it to her. He even brought her more to drink, which she happily accepted, then he went and got his food and drink and was heading back to the big chair. Mike was looking awkward in the chair, trying to get comfortable and eat. Actually Gloria thought it was a funny and pitiful sight all at once.

Gloria got up from the couch and made her way to Mike and put her hand on his back.

"Mike, go sit next to your wife on the couch. You'll have more room there, plus you can put your food on the coffee table." After Gloria said this, Mike nodded, then switched.

Gloria watched them for a moment as they ate quietly and occasionally looked up towards her and smiled. Gloria had to admit that they did make a beautiful couple. Gloria decided to get herself a cup of coffee then come back and finish enjoying the chatting.

When Gloria came back into the living room, she noticed that Mike and Beth were in a conversation and they were laughing with each other. Gloria almost felt awkward coming to the chair and interrupting them so she kept quiet and watched. Gloria noticed how Beth's eyes sparkled as she looked at Mike, almost flirting with him and how Mike looked like a young boy with his silly school crush grin on his face. Mike and Beth looked the way she and Chris looked after they seen each other earlier. It also was that same look that she and Rupert had last night as she spent time with him. Gloria noticed that they looked so comfortable with each other, so in love, so right in knowing that this person is mine and will be mine forever, despite the faults, the looks, the attitude, mood swings, and such. I love this person and we are compatible.

Gloria looked at Mike, her former husband, the one who gave her a beautiful, healthy son, Joey. A man she loved and adored and who she would have done anything for. Now when she looked at him, all those past feelings were gone. She saw in him a dear, close friend that she could confide in and tell her problems and thoughts to, like a brother that she never had. She didn't desire to have any, 'Let's do it one more time for good ole time sakes,' or wish that she and he were still together. She had long gone buried all of that. She had moved on. She had to admit that it was a long time coming, though. She had forgiven him for her past hurts and pains when he cheated while still married to her, but did she cheat too? Not physically like Mike had, but mentally she had. Tons and tons of times, over and over again, and it was always with that same person…Chris. And she had enjoyed it and she enjoyed it immensely. Many times she had regretted marrying Mike, but she wanted to stay in the relationship because it was the right thing to do. Her mother had stayed together with her father and she wanted to do the same, but it wasn't meant to be for her and Mike. Oh, how she longed for Chris while married to Mike. How she wanted to be snuggled in his embrace, to have him firmly hold her and caress her. How she wanted him inside her and how that feeling hadn't changed, even to this day. She could only imagine Chris's gyrations and him thrusting his machine smoothly and rhythmically in and out of her as she brought him closer to her. She wanted to hear Chris grunt as he made passionate love to her. She wanted to hear him call out her name. She wanted to touch Chris in all the right places and have him smile with pleasure and have him release himself in pleasure also. It would be a raucous sound even though the lovemaking would send them to another plateau.

Gloria's mind had drifted so far away from the present that she had forgotten that she was sitting in the living room in the presence of Mike and Beth. Although she may have been staring at the two and maybe even smiling and nodding, in actuality she was high in the heavens, frolicking in the clouds while her body was in bed with Chris lying next to her, gently running his hand through her hair as she stared into his eyes, his other hand cupped and fondling her soft breast.

"Well?" Mike asked as she was snapped back into reality by the sound of his voice.

"Yes, well. Most definitely well," Gloria responded with a smile on her face.

"What? What are you talking about, Gloria?" Mike was perplexed by her comment.

"Oh, I'm sorry, Mike. What did you say?" Gloria instantly turned crimson red.

"You know that she has a lot on her mind, Mike," Beth said in her defense.

"I had said, if you decide to sell the house, which I particularly think would be a bad idea, what will happen to Stephanie?"

"Ooh!" Gloria exclaimed. "Oh, don't worry about Stephanie. Although she moved back in when Daddy asked her to awhile back, Stephanie still has an apartment in her agent/manager's apartment building. It is a beautiful one bedroom apartment. It originally was a warehouse in Long Island City by the number seven train. But the neighborhood started having a new wave of young corporate types come in and upgraded the whole community by making old ugly and empty warehouses into lofty expensive co-ops and condos."

"Well, how can she afford to live there and here at the same time?" Beth asked.

Gloria started smiling widely as she looked towards the kitchen area, where Stephanie was loudly talking to Jerry. She leaned in toward them in order to talk low.

"Stephanie won't tell me. I don't know why, but I know that Jerry is her boyfriend."

When Gloria said this, Mike and Beth perked up as their eyes got wide.

"Stephanie has a boyfriend. Isn't that cute!" Beth remarked as Mike smiled and nodded.

"I think the reason she won't tell me is because she probably lives with him there and she would think that I would be upset with her because she is not married."

"Yeah, I think that something is up too." Beth was looking towards the kitchen area also. "You don't talk to your agent or manager like that unless you are being intimate."

"He's really a nice man, also. I met him once when Stephanie put on a show at Daddy's place. He was standing with his hands crossed with his head nodding, smiling like a Cheshire cat. Just the way he looked at her, anyone could tell that he was interested in her. Daddy knew also, but he didn't know about them living together."

"Well, Gloria, how can you be so sure?" Mike asked.

"Mike it doesn't make sense that every time that I called to check on Stephanie, he was always in the background. I would say, 'Stephanie, what's that noise in the background?', and she would say, 'Oh, it is only Jerry. I have a problem in the kitchen and he is checking the pipes.' Yeah, checking her pipes, I'm sure."

Mike and Beth chuckled at that.

"If that wasn't giving the relationship away, she would say something like, 'Jerry is here because I'm showing him some new ideas I wanna do for the show.' There was always some kind of excuse or other. But what really gave it away was when I called her late one night and Jerry picked up the phone. I could hear that he was dazed from being in a dead sleep and being woken up quickly. He slurred his words when he said hello. Not the kind of slurring from drinking; it was the kind that you get when you are tired. Boy did I shock him when he found out that it was me and that I was requesting to speak to Stephanie. I wish I had been there to see the expression on his face!" Gloria began to chuckle.

"Wow! That must've really shocked him!"

"It did, I'm sure," Gloria responded as she giggled. "His excuse was that Stephanie had accidentally left her cell phone in his apartment when she came and picked up some music material. And if the call was really important, he would go downstairs and take her phone to her. He had planned on giving her the phone in the morning, anyway. I wanted to laugh and tell him that that was the lamest excuse I had ever heard, but it was a pretty good one for someone who was just woken up out of a comatose sleep. I knew that Stephanie was right there snuggled up to him in dreamland, too. I told him that it wasn't important and that I would call her some other time. I wonder if they really thought that they got away with something, because that was so far from the truth." Gloria said in a sneaky manner. "Oooh, I can only imagine Stephanie's reaction to Jerry for answering her phone when I hung up. I am sure that she gave him a good tongue lashing like she is giving him in the kitchen. When she finally called me back, she repeated the same thing that Jerry had said to me when I called late in the night. I am sure that she had her story already planned even before she called me. I just played along with her as she explained to me about the phone that was left at her manager's place."

"Aah yes! Young love. Oh, how so very charming," Beth exclaimed. "What they won't do to hide a relationship.

"Yeah young love my foot!" Gloria replied quickly. "Jerry is much older than Stephanie. He is thirty-six or thirty-seven, but you could never tell it if you saw him. He is quite handsome, too. He has a good head on his shoulders, not to mention that he has a wonderful youthful body and he is a good businessman too. He is into all the promotion stuff. Stephanie is not his only act. He manages a few boy groups, young and old, solo acts and girl groups; even comedians. That's very popular these days. He also hires a lot of the famous celebs to perform for him, then he rents out clubs and restaurants and charges patrons to see the celeb in person. You name the artist and he can get them." Gloria said proudly.

"Wow, Gloria. It seems like Stephanie has a good man."

"Well, I think so, but the way that Stephanie yells at him sometimes, it would make anyone think that Jerry doesn't do anything for her, when he really does. That's how I know that the relationship is much more important than she is leading me to believe. I believe that with his looks and brains, he's going to be extremely successful and he is going to make Stephanie a star."

"So, you sound like you like him, huh?"

"Yeah, Mike. I do like him. I'm just waiting for her to tell me officially what I already know. I want her to know that I already know that they are an item and I will not judge her for what she does with her life. If she doesn't tell me by the time I head back to Cali..."

"If you go back to Cali" Mike quickly interjected.

"Yeah, if I go back—I am going to confront her on it myself."

"Gloria, you sound to me like you wanna go back to Cali."

"Gloria, to be honest with you, Beth and I actually thought that you would be moving here after the funeral and all."

"Oh, Mike, I don't know, man." Gloria looked frustrated. "One minute I wanna go back then the next minute, I wanna stay here. I can't answer now. I just can't answer. I feel like Scooby Doo, with my body going in a million different directions all at once. I'm extremely saddened about my daddy being gone, I'm extremely happy about a newfound love, I'm sad because I might have to tell him that I can't see him anymore. I'm extremely happy about an old flame that I am very interested in, I'm sad because I might have to tell him that I can't see him and break his heart twice in his lifetime, I've been treated like royalty all in a few hours and my family treated to lavish gifts. Also, I have to deal with the house, worry about my father's business and bury him, and all of this is on my back. I don't know if I'm coming or going."

Gloria was on the verge of crying but she was trying to hold on. She was trying to stay strong and brave but it was a struggle.

Beth got up from the couch and made her way to her.

"Oh, dear, I know that you are going through a lot right now and we are here for you. We feel your pain. We don't wanna see you hurting. That's why we are here for you. We love you and the family, you know that." Beth had her arm around Gloria, comforting her while patting her in a loving manner. Mike wasn't too far behind to lend his support.

Gloria smiled and nodded that she was holding on well and that she appreciated Beth's words..

"Thank you guys. Thanks so very much for your support during this hard time, but I'm ok and I'm going to stay this way. It's a struggle to keep everything together, but I'm doing it."

"Yes you are, and we are very proud of you. You are holding on and doing a terrific job," Beth said with a lot of encouragement. "I have to be strong for my family, you know. I can't afford to fall apart."

Mike and Beth looked at each other and smiled.

"Yeah, we know, Gloria— family. It is very important."

"I'm concerned about all of my family members. I worry about Stephanie and if I do go back to Cali, I'm really going to worry about her. Even though she is my cousin, she is also like my first child, my first daughter. I wanted to take her to Cali when I moved back out there, but that would have broken Daddy's heart. He loved her so much. When she had gotten older and moved out, I asked her to come and live with me and the kids then, but she wanted to have her independence. I couldn't blame her. Now, she has Jerry, even though she hasn't told me that yet. She won't be going. I worry so much about the twins and what they are doing. Thank God that I have the best kids any parent could ever have. They are blessings from up above. They have never given me a day's or minute's worth of problems. Oh, and Joey, my Joey. I really worry about him so much." Gloria sucked her teeth then shook her head. This comment caused Mike and Beth to look at each other.

"Gloria, why do you worry about Joey? Joey is doing just fine." Mike chuckled as if what Gloria had just said was a tad strange.

"Well, because he's been through so much in his lifetime: Mommy's death, your uncle's death, our separation, Ray's death and now Daddy. That's a lot to deal with and most of this happened when he was very young. Daddy's death has just happened and only God knows how he's going to deal with that. He adored his Grampa, talking to him for hours on the phone long distance."

Gloria looked up to the heavens as she remembered fondly.

"Gloria, Joey is going to be just fine. He's an intelligent and respectable young man," Mike assured her as he made light of what she was saying.

"Yeah, on the outside, Mike, but inside he is hurting."

"Oh, Gloria, you are just being overprotective, that's all."

When Mike said this, Gloria sat up straight and looked him straight in the eyes. She didn't take kindly to his callous attitude.

"Mike, I know my son. I've raised him all these years by myself when you weren't around. I dealt with his mood swings and his sadness and his loneliness. I had to deal with the 'Mommy, how comes?' and 'But, mommy, what ifs?' Did you know that for a long time he blamed himself for us not being together?"

Mike stiffened as if a volt of lightening went through him. Mike then looked toward Beth as he turned crimson red from embarrassment. Beth had already known that Mike had cheated on Gloria and wasn't in Joey's life for a long length of time.

"'Is Daddy going to come to my birthday party? Mommy, did you tell Daddy about my birthday party? Mommy, can you call Daddy to see if he can come and see me perform in the play at school? Did you send Daddy those new photos of me? If you don't have the money to buy me that new bedroom set, can you call Daddy? Maybe he has money to help us out.' Or what about the dreaded, 'Mommy, how come Daddy doesn't see me? Doesn't he want to see me?' He would always say with giant tears running from his big, sad eyes. You don't know how much that broke my heart to see him look like that. Mike, I had to deal with that on a constant basis. He understood that you and I weren't getting back together but he never understood why you divorced yourself from him. I never told you this, Mike, so now you know why I act so overprotective, as you say."

Mike lowered his head in shame and guilt as Gloria continued talking.

"Mike, have you noticed that Joey has NEVER had a successful, healthy relationship with a girlfriend? He is always in and out, in and out of relations, and when the girl is gone, Joey doesn't care or worry about it. Joey dumps them and will have another one very quickly. It's like he doesn't have empathy for these females—for his family and the females in it, yes, but for his relationships, no."

When Gloria finished speaking, Mike, still looking ashamed, began to clear his throat.

"Gloria, you are absolutely right. I haven't always been in Joey's life and when I finally did get into his life, I only saw him on weekends and he was much older then, but what I do know about Joey is that he has a good head on his shoulders and he will survive anything."

"Mike, how can you say this when he shows no emotions? Yes, he smiles and greets people in a kind and courteous manner and he has an excellent demeanor, but have you ever seen him cry?"

Mike stared forward as he tried to remember if he had.

"I can answer that question for you. No. You've seen him laugh and show that million dollar smile and those beautiful eyes get all bright and shiny but when he hurts, you'll never see it because he will not show it. He did when he was very young, but he got immune to hurt. You might hear it if he slips and forget to close the door but he holds most of it in. I need to stay in Cali to be near him if he needs me." Gloria nodded as if she positively had just made up her mind.

The Life and Times of Gloria Bunker

"Well, Gloria, Joey is a grown man. One thing he doesn't need is a mother still holding his hand. He has an excellent job teaching and the faculty likes him and he has his own apartment. What he doesn't need is a mother looking over his shoulder, making sure he crosses the street safely."

"Mike, I will always be there when he needs me. He doesn't have anyone else."

"Excuse me, Gloria!" Mike said as if he was offended. "What do you mean that he doesn't have anyone else? Are you trying to say that I don't mean anything to Joey? That I don't matter?"

"No, Mike. That's not what I am saying and maybe it was wrong for me to say that, but he doesn't come to you with his problems. He doesn't come to you for advice. He comes to you to hang out, talk politics, go to game or other guy stuff..."

"Gloria, don't underestimate the relationship that I have with my son. I love him and he knows that, and he could come to me anytime if he has a problem."

Gloria was listening to what Mike was saying but was quickly ready to give a truthful response to whatever he had to say.

"Mike, I know that he can come to you and yes, he also knows that he can come to you, but the question is, DOES he? Does he feel comfortable coming to you if he has a problem and if he does, ask yourself when the last time he did was. If you ask me the same question, I can tell you the day and the time."

Gloria was really letting Mike have it and putting him heavily in his place. He was so stunned that he didn't know that to say, and he didn't dare look in Beth's direction.

"Mike, it's easy for you to say, 'Go and move back to New York. I'll still be in Cali if Joey needs a parent in his life,' but he needs me there. Even if he never comes and visits me or even calls me, he would always know that his mother has never left him alone and will always be there when he needs her. I've never left him in the past and I won't start now."

"So, Gloria, does that mean that you are going to sell this house and not see Chris? You are going to put your life on hold just to worry and follow around a grown man who has flown the coop to make it on his own, mistakes, calamities, bad relationships and all? So forget about the twins, who are actually living under your roof. Focus all your energy on Joey. Does that make any kind of sense? Joey wouldn't want you to do that. Joey would want you to go on with your life and be happy. Allow Joey to be an adult."

"Mike, you will never understand how I feel. I've raised Joey and I've always been in his life, through every skinned knee and runny and bloody nose; through every spelling bee and school play; through every graduation, from pre K to college. Me. I was there. There is a special bond there, a bond that no one could break. When you have that experience with a child, then you'll know what I mean; plus, if we leave Cali, Joey wouldn't see his siblings. That's not fair."

When Gloria said that, Mike and Beth looked at each other then held hands tightly then looked at Gloria again.

"Gloria," Beth said, finally getting into the conversation, finding that this was the opportune time to say what she had been meaning to say but was just waiting for the right moment. "We're pregnant."

CHAPTER THIRTEEN:
Gloria Meets with Mr. Kindred

"That's right, pregnant!" Gloria screamed happily into the phone an hour later, after Mike and Beth left. "I nearly fell out of Daddy's chair. I was shocked at first because I didn't expect Beth to tell me that, but when it finally registered in my head what she had said, the only thing I remember is screaming, jumping off the chair and running over to them both and hugging them. I was crying tears of joy. She was crying tears of joy and Mike just sat there looking very proud, and he should be. I knew something was different the minute I saw her. She had that, that, that, look. She was glowing and her face looked very beautiful and full. At first, I thought that she had put on weight, but I had no idea that she was a few months pregnant. I should've known that she was pregnant the way she was enjoying that nasty catered food I was telling you about earlier, but it just went over my head. She actually did beat around the bush, you know, giving me hints, but I didn't catch on. She didn't want us to know till the whole family was together in one spot. They were just waiting for Joey to arrive. Everyone was happy for them, but we promised not to tell Joey. We're leaving that for them to do. He's going to be that baby's sibling, anyway.

"Mike definitely wouldn't mind if I told you the good news, Lionel. So, when are you going to be heading out to catch your plane? Aha, first class, Mr. rich tycoon?" Gloria teased. "No, that's okay, Lionel. We have all of that plus millions of beautiful flowers. Yeah, aha, okay then, Lionel. See you then. Oh, yeah, by the way, tell Jenny that I'm looking forward in seeing her and that I brought her that sweet potato pie that she likes so much, and give my regards to your daughter and the boys. Too bad that they won't be coming with you. The kids were looking forward to seeing them again. Tell your father that I said thanks for his words. Bye for now."

Gloria headed to the couch, where Stephanie was sitting at the other end, relaxing with the television on but watching Gloria.

"So, how is Lionel?"

"Fine, just fine. He just called to see if we needed anything before he left for the airport. He and Jenny won't be leaving till this evening but wanted to touch base with me just in case I would be going out. He called at a perfect time."

"What was his response concerning Mike being a father again?"

"He screamed for joy. You should've heard him. He was very happy. Joey is going to be thrilled to be a brother again, too. He had always wanted to have a lot of siblings, someone that he could look after and protect. He loved being a big brother for the twins, always there when I needed him. Yep, he was there to help change diapers and wipe runny noses. He also helped with the feeding, not to mention helping with the burping, but never once complained. He was such a little man, but his heart stood twenty feet tall," she said proudly.

"Speaking of Joey, while I was on the phone talking to Jerry, I heard you and Mike go at it pretty good. Was it bad? Because the way you told me when they left, that was the feeling that I got."

"We went at it, but very civilly, though. I had to set the record straight about how strong Joey's and my relationship is and unfortunately for him, I had to remind him that he wasn't always in Joey's life and I did it in front of Beth. It's not as if Beth didn't know. Beth knew of it anyway. She hadn't heard anything that she had never heard before."

"But you told me that you told Mike that you were going to stay close to Joey. Joey is not going to come to New York since he has that great job in Cali, so that means that you are going to be staying in Cali?" Stephanie was looking a tad disappointed.

Gloria waved that comment away and rolled her eyes.

"Oh, I just said that to Mike because he was making light of what I was saying about Joey and he said that I was being too overprotective and so on. He really got my goat, I tell ya. I just said the comment about not moving back to New York to show him how important Joey and his feelings are to me, that's all. Hopefully he got the point."

"So, you still don't know what you are going to do?"

"Girl not in the least; one minute, I am going, then the next minute, I am going to stay." Gloria sighed. "But I do know that I am leaning towards…"

"I don't wanna know because then I'm going to ask you again later and your answer will change. I wanna know when you finally make your decision."

When Stephanie said that, Gloria nodded.

"So, what time did Kindred, Mr. Sneaky, say he would be here when you called him?"

Gloria waved her hand at Stephanie again.

"Oh you!" She shook her head. "He should be here very soon. When I called him, he said that he was at a closing and would head straight over afterwards. He told me that Rupert ordered him to only stay a minute due to the funeral tomorrow. I think the truth was that Rupert didn't want him staying long because he didn't get a chance to see me today. He doesn't want any other man to be around me longer than him." Gloria chuckled proudly as she blushed.

"Wow! Jealousy so very early in the relationship—isn't that cute!?"

As Stephanie teased Gloria, Gloria continued waving her off with a smile on her face.

"Okay, Gloria. When he gets here, I want you to check him out. Study him and then you'll see that I was right. He's sneaky, I tell ya. I would not do business with him."

"Stop it, Stephanie. It's only your imagination. He is a businessman trying to buy property. I'm not going to sign anything. Trust me. I just want to see what he is willing to offer."

Ten minutes later, the doorbell was ringing. Stephanie was at the dining room table with plastic containers, putting food in them. She also had a huge sharp knife that she had used to slice up the leftover meat and had already discarded the bones and fat. Gloria was on the telephone talking to an acquaintance who would be attending the funeral tomorrow.

Once Gloria heard the doorbell ring, she said goodbye politely then went towards the door but before she opened it, Stephanie called out to her as she waved the huge knife in front of her and squinted her eyes menacingly.

"Remember what I said about him, Gloria. Watch him. Keep your eyes on him. He is not to be trusted. I don't know what his motives are but I want to tell you something quickly. In the building where I live, I was bringing my garbage down into the basement and with all of the poison that was lying around, not to mention the traps, there were many dead mice and rats all about. It stank very badly. I smelled the same smell when I met that Kindred guy. I can smell a rat when I see one coming. You'll see what I mean."

While Stephanie was talking to Gloria, she was very serious in her tone, even though Gloria was paying her no mind as she continued. "But if he makes one false move," she warned as she raised the knife up. "I'll turn into Mother Bates from *Psycho*!" Stephanie then thought a minute then continued. "As a matter of fact, I'll turn into Kathy Bates when she played that crazy woman from Misery but the only difference is that he won't have to worry about his legs."

When Stephanie said this, she started to stab at the air, especially the area where Kindred's frontal private area was, causing Gloria to wave her off while she shook her head and opened the door.

As the door opened, Kindred was standing there and had caught Gloria laughing, but he didn't see Stephanie's imitation of the shower scene from *Psycho*. He was wearing a hat ,which made him look very distinguished. He took it off as he greeted Gloria.

"Good afternoon, Ms. Bunker Shaw. I'm glad to be catching you in a happy mood," he commented with a smile on his face.

Quickly Gloria checked his face to see if he looked the way Stephanie was describing him, but Gloria couldn't tell. She thought that he looked quite sincere, honest and businesslike.

"Please, Mr. Kindred, come in," Gloria asked very graciously. He nodded with a smile then entered into the house with his hat in one hand and the attaché case in the other.

Kindred noticed Stephanie at the dining room table packing up the food and he said hello to her. Stephanie turned with the knife in her hand and waved it at him and nodded then said hello with a fake smile on her face. He didn't catch on, and Gloria was happy about that. At that moment, she could've killed Stephanie. He turned back and looked at Gloria as he continued smiling.

"I see that you've enjoyed Mr. Hanley's little surprise, huh?" Kindred nodded his head happily.

"Little? No. Surprise? Yes." Gloria began to chuckle. "We've enjoyed it and all of Queens enjoyed it and we still have leftovers!" Gloria joked. "Please, Mr. Kindred, have a seat."

Gloria used her hand to point him to the couch. He nodded, then headed towards it and sat down in the corner, making sure Gloria had enough space to sit down, also. He placed his hat to his left side and he laid the attaché case on the coffee table. Once Kindred sat, Gloria sat down next to him.

"Mr. Kindred, before we deal with the matters at hand, would you care for refreshments? Some coffee, tea, punch or soda? We have anything that you like."

Gloria was just about to get up and head towards the kitchen to get him something, but Stephanie turned from the dining room table and interjected.

"Yes, Mr. Kindred, we have all that but if you want a sandwich, we have cheese, sliced cold cuts, chicken, ham, roast—we don't have any fox, though, but we can spot one a mile away."

When Stephanie said this, Gloria was shocked. She gave Stephanie a very evil look that could have killed her dead if Gloria had that power. Stephanie was pretending she didn't see what Gloria was doing. Gloria was relieved that Kindred didn't catch the meaning, or if he did, he didn't say anything. He just smiled kindly and waved his hand in a kind gesture.

"Thank you, ladies. Thank you for your generous hospitality, but no thank you. I had something at my closing and I am full." Kindred patted his stomach, which did look a tad bloated, then he laughed a few ho ho ho's like Santa Claus.

"Are you sure, because…" Stephanie still had the knife waving at him making Gloria upset. She was getting fed up with her behavior.

"He said, no thank you, Stephanie!" Gloria snapped at her as she squinted her eyes. "Don't you have a lot of food to put away?" Gloria asked as she tried to get Stephanie out of the room, feeling like she was going to mess up the deal on the house.

Gloria's voice was harsh this time. Stephanie just shrugged her shoulders then put a smirk on her face and started taking the food into the kitchen. Gloria was thinking of ways she could carve up Stephanie and put her into tiny plastic containers.

"Besides," Kindred had turned his attention back to Gloria, "I have strict orders from Mr. Hanley to be in and out. He is the boss, so what he says, goes."

"Yes, you did mention that on the phone," Gloria said. "Okay then, Mr. Kindred. Whenever you are ready, I am ready."

"Okay then. Let's get started," he responded as he turned back towards his attaché case to open it. Gloria looked at his hands. Kindred's hands looked like they had never done a hard day's work in his life. They looked smooth like a woman's hand: long fingers, with nails that looked like they were manicured. They were even glossy like they had clear polish on them. They didn't move nervously nor did his hand shake. He moved assuredly and confidently. She could tell that he was successful and lived a good life. He definitely knew what he was doing. She still didn't feel any underhandedness on his part at all.

As Kindred opened the attaché case, Gloria noticed a lot of papers inside a folder and wondered if all of it was concerning the house. When she saw the address on the label, she realized that it was all concerning the Bunker house.

Kindred dug into his blazer pocket to pull out his reading glasses. Once he got them out, he placed them onto his face. He opened up the folder and on the front page was the contract. Kindred lowered his glasses below his eyes and right on the tip of his nose as he glanced over it for a second just to make sure that everything was to his liking and in correct order, then started to speak before he showed it to her.

"Okay, Ms. Bunker Shaw, this is the contract." Kindred said very businesslike as he leaned over towards Gloria so she could see it.

"This is the estimated worth of the house, and this is the amount that we are offering to buy the house for. As you can see, it is quite a generous amount."

Gloria looked at the amount, and it was a nice piece of change. Kindred could tell that she was impressed because Gloria's eyebrows went almost over her forehead, but she didn't say anything. She just nodded with a serious poker face.

After Kindred finished showing Gloria the contract, he took it further by adding;

"Your father really liked the price. He couldn't believe that we would offer him this much for the place, but mind you, Gloria—if it is ok for me to call you that..." he said with a smile on his face.

"Sure, Mr. Kindred. Please feel free to call me that."

"...all contracts are subject to change."

When Kindred made this comment, Gloria didn't understand what he meant, but she still nodded.

Gloria still couldn't get over the fact that her father was thinking about selling the house. If he was thinking about selling, then he was probably interested in closing the bar also. If this was true, then where would he have gone? He had to live somewhere, but where? She was thinking that he probably had wanted to move to California to be near her and the family.

"Daddy, what were you trying to do and why didn't you just tell me?" she said to herself. "I know that you had a surprise that you wanted to tell me, but you wouldn't tell me even though I asked you over and over again. That surprise could have been anything from A to Z. I know that it was big if you kept it from me. That is why you kept it secret for such a very long time. I just hope that whatever it is, I make the right decision concerning the house."

Kindred then took the contract and put it back into the attaché case, which puzzled Gloria. He then started sifting through the papers again till he found what he was looking for.

"Aah!" he exclaimed in relief. "I found it!"

Gloria could see that Kindred had another contract in his hand and he was going over it with his hand before he showed it to her. He was looking so intensely, but he zoomed over it quickly.

"Now," he continued as he leaned over to her again, "this is a different contract. This is the one that I rewrote this morning, since that you are a very dear friend of Mr. Hanley," he said with a wink and a satisfied smile on his face, letting her know that it was going to be a substantial amount more than the original contract. Gloria now understood what Kindred had meant when he had said earlier that contracts were subject to change.

Kindred showed her the new contract, then put his finger where a new amount appeared, and the amount was much different from the original.

"This is the new amount that we are offering you for the house. As you know, your father liked the original offer but because of you, you are being offered so much more. Your father would've loved this!" he said enthusiastically.

The Life and Times of Gloria Bunker

When Gloria saw the new price, her eyebrows flew from the top of her eyes up past the forehead and hairline, past the top of her head, then down her neck. She tried to hold on to her poker face and she was fighting with her emotions to stay calm, but there was Mr. Kindred, looking at her and nodding his head as he smiled like a Cheshire cat.

"Huh?" he said with a grin on his face. "You like that? I told you that it was a substantially more than the original price."

Gloria was able to control her emotions and remained calm, cool and collected. She took a deep breath then swallowed then cleared her throat, but when she spoke, it came out sounding like Minnie Mouse.

"Well, Mr. ah, uh, er, Kindred, that is a nice fair amount." Gloria nodded as sweat started appearing on her forehead. At that moment, Mr. Kindred was the kindest, most honest, most handsome human being in the universe.

Mr. Kindred then handed the contract to her. "Here you go, Ms. Bunker Shaw."

"Gloria," she corrected.

"Sorry. Gloria," he echoed. "This is for you. It is a copy. You think it over, then let me know."

Gloria took the copy of the contract. Even though she controlled her emotions, her hands were shaking. She kept staring at the amount, thinking that number was a mistake but hoping that it wasn't. She was thinking that if she took her eyes off the amount, it would just disappear, but it didn't. It was right there in front of her in black and white and confirmed by the wonderful, delightful and pleasantly honest Mr. Kindred, who was closing the top of his attaché case and looking like he was preparing to leave.

"Well, Gloria, I kept my promise and please tell Mr. Hanley if he asks," he said as the attaché case snapped closed, "that I didn't keep you long at all. If all business transactions could run as smoothly as this did, this country would be a pleasant place."

"I agree, Mr. Kindred," Gloria responded as she continued looking at the copy of the contract.

"Take your time, Gloria. I know that this is a sad time for you, but if you don't mind me saying so, if I were you, I would sign the contract, get the money and move on with your life. The house has too many memories. I'm only thinking about you because of your relationship with Mr. Hanley. You'll be much happier, and might I say much richer, if you just get rid of this excess baggage. I'm sure that your father would have wanted it that way."

"Daddy, oh my daddy," she repeated over and over again in her mind. "I'm getting such conflicting thoughts: Sell, move, sell, move, Rupert, Chris, Rupert, Chris, New York, Cali, New York, Cali. Boy! I have a lot to think about."

Mr. Kindred was rising up from the couch and picking up his hat that was to his left side. Before he picked up the attaché case on top of the coffee table, he extended his hand to Gloria.

"Gloria, it was my pleasure seeing you again," he said cordially.

"Likewise Mr. Kindred, I will think about the offer and will get back in contact with you when I make up my mind."

"That will be fine, but I hope the next time that I hear from you, you will tell me that you are willing and ready to sell"

"Well, whatever I decide, Mr. Kindred, you will be the first to know."

With that, Kindred picked up his attaché case off the coffee table then headed towards the front door behind Gloria, who was now opening it up. He nodded to her with a smile, then walked out onto the porch. Gloria watched as he walked down the steps and headed towards a late-model black Benz that was in front of the house. He didn't look back at her, but he kept that nice honest looking smile on his face right up until he got into the car and drove away.

Gloria quickly closed the door then ran toward the coffee table and looked at the contract again. She then called out to Stephanie.

"Stephanie! Stephanie!" she hollered, sending Stephanie charging into the living room with the knife in her hand as she looked around cautiously.

"Where is he?! Where's he at! Just point me to 'im, then I'll give him the point!"

Stephanie went searching for him the way a dog might search for the cat when he knew that no one else was in the house to reprimand him for doing wrong.

"Cut it out, Stephanie!" Gloria said seriously.

"I'm trying to, but you haven't told me where he is!" Stephanie responded even more seriously.

"Come here and look at the contract and see how much money he's offering to buy the house!"

Stephanie sucked her teeth and rolled her eyes in disappointment, as if she would have had more fun hunting down Kindred to slice him up. She slouched over, then put the knife down on the coffee table before Gloria showed her the copy of the contract. Once Stephanie saw the price, she blinked her eyes rapidly, as if trying to adjust them, and she opened them widely.

"Gloria, am I seeing what I think that I'm seeing?" Stephanie asked, as if she doubted what her eyes were showing her.

"I had to make sure. That is why I called you into the living room. I guess you are seeing the same thing that I am seeing."

"I told you, Gloria, that Kindred is a very nice man, very nice. Salt of the earth, I tell ya."

"Oh, girl, please," Gloria said as she playfully hit her on her shoulder.

"Oh, Gloria, if you accept this offer, you will be on Easy Street for a long time."

"It is nice, I'm not going to lie, but money isn't everything. What's more important to me are you and the kids. There are a lot of comfortable and rich people in the world who aren't happy because they have no family, no one to care for them and no one for them to care for. Money is nice but family is more important."

"So, this amount of money hasn't shifted the scales as to what you are going to do?"

"To be honest with you, just a mega fraction, that's all. It is just one less thing to worry about and one more thing to cross off my agenda. Now that that has been taken care of, I still have Chris to deal with and get the food to get done for tomorrow, and it is still early."

"So what are you going to do now?"

"Well," she said as she started heading upstairs, "I have a long date with a tub right now."

CHAPTER FOURTEEN:
The Man of Her Daydreams

There was nothing else Gloria wanted to do more than to lie down, relax and put her head back in a nice hot steamy, bubbly, sudsy tub. She'd never had a chance for a bath since last night. Once she got up in the morning, she had been busy. She didn't like not cleaning herself, so she left Stephanie downstairs and zoomed up into the bathroom.

She began running the tap water, which had steam rising from it. She poured into the tub a scented, fragrant liquid that instantly filled the room with a relaxing aroma. She covered her hair with a plastic cap then took off the towel that was wrapped around her. No longer a size eight, she gazed quickly at her body in the mirror, looking at herself from head to toe naked, and was quite pleased with what she saw. Her skin was still nice and firm, breasts were still full and didn't sag nastily; hips, legs and thighs looked good and even the little extra pooch around the middle looked good. She nodded with a smile then took her foot and placed it into the tub slowly, testing the temperature with her big toe. When it was to her liking, she stepped totally into the tub then sat, leaning her head all the way back, facing up with her eyes closed. She sighed in relief and sank deeper into the water, trying not to think of anything. The only thing that she wanted to think about was herself and some tranquility.

Even though she knew that she still had a lot more things to do before the day was over, she decided that she wasn't going to rush. She was going to take her sweet time and not think about anything but relaxing. At that moment, Gloria needed some 'me' time and she wasn't going to let anyone take that from her.

While relaxing with her eyes closed, she listened as the water from the faucet dripped rhythmically into the tub. Gloria didn't realize that her two big toes were bopping each other under the water as she slapped her thigh lightly with her hand to the rhythm of the drip. In a very low voice, Gloria began singing a tune that she hadn't thought about in many years. At first, she was only singing the beginning of the song.

"Bah, bah, bah, bah, bah, bah, bah, baaah," she sang over and over again.

She had no idea why that song had suddenly come into her memory, but it went well with the sound and rhythm of the drip from the faucet. The whole room was filling up with steam, and Gloria looked like she was taking a bath high up in the heavens. When she opened her eyes and saw all the steam in the room, she was unconcerned, but even though the room was filled with the hot steam, she was still able to feel a little breeze coming from under the bathroom door on her breasts. She first took the water and splashed her chest, then she ran the water in the tub some more and sank deeper, till the water was up to her neck and her head was the only thing sticking out of the tub. At that moment, Gloria WAS in heaven.

Gloria closed her eyes again as she concentrated on her relaxation, then she heard a loving, soft and kind voice, almost sounding like a whisper.

"Hey, if you don't keep an eye on that water, it is going to overflow."

Gloria smelled cologne in the room, and it had a real rugged smell. It smelled as if it was right next to her nose. She could not recognize the brand of the cologne but she definitely was able to recognize the voice, even though it came to her only in a whisper.

"Chris!" she yelled in surprise. Then she opened her eyes and saw him kneeling down beside her with a finger in the water going back and forth. "What are you do...?"

Chris interrupted her by putting his finger to his lips.

"Ssshh, Gloria. Now, we can act out the scene from the Titanic or you can turn the water off."

Gloria lifted her feet out of the water and turned the knob off with her toes. Unafraid, she stared at him, not sure if she was having an illusion or not, but whatever it was, she was enjoying it.

"Chris, are you really here or am I dreaming of this whole thing?" she asked as she smiled.

Chris just stared at her, not taking his eyes off her.

"Well, either or, how would it make you feel? Would you be upset or would you just enjoy having me here?"

As he gazed at her, he took his hand and rubbed the side of her face gently and passionately. Gloria felt like she was burning up and her body would make the tub boil. When he asked her the question she couldn't even speak. She was too busy staring at him. He was so handsome and very youthful-looking to her. He sent her places where she hadn't been in years.

Chris was dressed all in white. He had a collared shirt on and the sleeves were rolled up. His skin was naturally tanned looking, and his hair was thick and dark. Unashamed by her nakedness, she reached over to him with her right hand, lifting her right breast out of the water, and ran her fingers through his hair.

"Oh Lord, if I am dreaming, please don't wake me up," she begged as she quickly looked up towards the heavens, then back towards Chris.

The look that Chris was giving her told her that he desired her just as much as she desired him.

"Gloria, you have always been the woman of my dreams and I have always loved you. There has not been a day since you left me that I haven't thought about you."

As Gloria stared into Chris's eyes, she could tell that as seriously as he was speaking to her, he looked like he had tears forming.

Gloria had a lump in her throat. The only thing that she was able to do was move her hand through his hair then down to stroke his smooth but strong masculine face. As she touched him, he closed his eyes. Gloria could only imagine what he was imagining.

"Gloria, I have loved you ever since we were little, and I always thought that you would be mine.

Gloria, after hearing those words, couldn't hold back her emotions. She started to cry.

"Chris, I am so sorry that I hurt you in the past, but I have thought about you too. Yes, Chris! Yes. I love you too! I love you, Chris, with every movement of my heart. I made a big mistake when I left you, and I know that I'll never be happy till you are totally in my life."

Chris wiped away Gloria's tears as she let them flow. He just smiled at her affectionately. Gloria let out a soft moan. Chris leaned towards her and kissed her lips as Gloria closed her eyes. Gloria then grabbed the back of his head and brought him to her, making the kiss more passionate. Gloria didn't want him to hold back.

"Yes, Chris, yes! I waited for this moment for oh so very long," she said as she was moving her hand from the back of his head to his neck. They were both enchanted being with each other and touching one another.

Chris grabbed hold of her hand and started kissing the tips of her fingers.

"I've kissed you a million times in my mind, Gloria, and now, having you here with me, I don't wanna let you go. I never wanna let you go, Gloria. I wanna hold you and caress you and keep you close to my heart forever."

"And I don't want you to let me go, Chris," she cried as she drifted off into her magic spell, saying over and over again, "I think I love you."

When Gloria finally opened her eyes, she was still neck deep in the tub, but the water wasn't running and the room was still steamed up from the heat. Her feet and hand were still bopping to the drip of the faucet. Then it occurred to her that she never had turned the water back on and therefore she had to have been dreaming.

Gloria began looking around the bathroom for any sign that Chris was there.

"Chris?" she called out hoping that he was amidst the steam. Gloria then sucked her teeth in slight disappointment.

"Oh, it felt so real having Chris right here next to me," she said. "That is such a bummer, but I am glad that I did imagine him here with me."

Gloria began sniffling, which meant that she had really been crying. She felt her eyelashes and eyes and they were indeed wet.

"I do love Chris," she exclaimed, as if this was a revelation. "When you dream, you always act and say how you really feel. And I even cried. If I had the opportunity to have dreamed that a million times, I would never get tired of it. It felt so darn real."

Gloria started feeling happy, but in the next instant, her mind shifted to something else.

"But I also care a lot about Rupert. Boy, do I! Plus, if I get all of that money if I sell the house, Chris wouldn't move to Cali but Rupert could pop up and be in Cali in no time, and not for nothing—if Rupert was touching and caressing me the same way as in the dream, I would have said the same thing to him that I said to Chris." Gloria was back to square one again.

"Oh, Lord, which one is the one for me?" she sighed.

Gloria was slightly worried because she was going to see Chris now. When she got out of the tub and changed into fresh clothes, she was going to call him, but she decided not to let that disturb her now from having a nice bath. She decided to block Chris out of her mind and to focus totally on finishing enjoying her bath, so the hands started slapping the thighs and the toes bumped each other as she 'bah, bah, bah, baah-ed' and drifted back into tranquility.

Gloria stayed in the hot soothing tub till her fingers started looking like pink raisins; even then, she still didn't want to get out. Reluctantly she rose out of the tub then started drying herself in front of the sink and mirror. She began frowning and making faces in the mirror. As she examined her face as she began putting on makeup for her get together with Chris, she exhaled.

"Life could've been so much easier if you were a twin. That way you," she said to the woman in the mirror, "could have one and I," she said, pointing to herself, "could have the other. We could be one big happy family, but nooo. You had to be the only child." She exhaled again as if very frustrated then she sighed. "I wonder if it is too late for cloning."

Gloria moved slowly in drying herself off then, once she was done cleaning up the tub, she headed with the towel around her to the bedroom. She wanted to find the perfect outfit and shoes to wear for her meeting with Chris.

Once she got into the bedroom, she noticed that the room looked like it had been hit by a tornado. It was still messed up from the previous night, when she was trying to find the right outfit to wear with her first date with Rupert. Outfits and the dress that she wore last night were thrown in different spots on her bed, chair, dresser, atop the television set and even on the lampshades. On top of all her old clothes were her new clothes that Stephanie had neatly laid on the chest at the end of the bed. They were stacked so high that if she put one more thing on top, like a feather, it would probably topple over. The clothes wouldn't hit the floor, though, because surrounding the chest on the floor were the new shoes that she had picked out.

Gloria didn't know where to begin. Should she wear one of her old outfits or should she put on something new? She didn't know what to do, but what she decided to do was to open up her suitcase and every item of clothing that she didn't want to wear, she was going to put inside the suitcase, and slowly but surely, she would be narrowing down her choices. Gloria did not plan on staying long in New York but she brought a lot of unnecessary stuff with her. When she was still in Cali and was making the arrangements to come to New York, she just opened up the suitcase and started throwing anything and everything into the suitcase. She wasn't thinking. She even threw in an outfit that she had not worn since Mike and she were together. She was surprised that she even still had it. It was so old that it was already back in style. She thought that later she would give it to Zoe, who had excellent fashion sense. She was sure that Zoe would get hold of it and design a whole new outfit or just add accessories to it. Into the suitcase went her sweat suits, nightgowns, slippers, t-shirts, stretch pants, leotards, etc.

"Leotard?" she exclaimed as she stared at them, shaking her head and making a face of disgust, then quickly threw them into the suitcase. "Tank tops, bras, pant sets, some blouses and skirts."

Slowly, the room started to look more organized. The clothes came off the lamp shades and the chairs. The only clothes that remained on the chairs were those that belonged to Joey. They were lying neatly over the top of the chair.

Gloria was finally able to see the blanket and sheets on top of the mattress. She had picked out two outfits that she wanted to wear, and she hadn't even gotten to the new stack of clothes yet. Once the suitcase was filled, she took it off the bed then started laying the new clothes in its spot. All the too dressy and expensive clothes went into one pile, sporty in another, casual in one and so on. Once she got everything into its pile, she started to eliminate clothes, and all the clothes that she eliminated were stacked on top of each other and placed out of the way onto the chest again. Out of the new clothes, there were two outfits that she wanted to wear, so now she had four outfits to choose from, two old, two new. She decided to put away the old clothes and kept her eyes on the new stuff. She wanted Chris to see her in something new, even though he had never seen her in the other outfits.

Both of the new outfits looked nice, and they were very expensive. One outfit was a red dress with gold lining around the breast area and it was fringed at the bottom and at the cuffs. She liked that one because it showed a sufficient amount of leg and it hung in the front to show enough cleavage. She decided that she would pass on that because it was a tad too much for a woman who would be burying a loved one the next day, so she went with the other new outfit. It was definitely more appropriate.

Gloria decided to wear the black skirt with the black leather belt, and white silk blouse with a turned up collar. It had black-trimmed, elbow-length sleeves. The blouse had red designs in it and the shoes were also red. She wore no stockings, which would show off Gloria's pretty legs. It was a casual outfit, expensive but not overdressed. It was a perfect 'hangout' outfit to wear to be with Chris. She was going to wear the same jewelry that she wore the previous night plus the Rolex. She was not going to take off that beautiful, expensive Rolex.

Gloria's makeup was perfect and so was her hair. She was ready to head downstairs. She looked good, felt good and to top it all off, she squirted herself with White Diamonds so she knew that she was smelling good. She was ready to see Chris. She couldn't get any better than the way that she was looking at the present time. She was hoping that he liked what he saw when he saw her. She knew that whatever Chris had on, she was going to like it when she saw him, even if it was jeans, boots, plaid shirt and all. In her eyes, Chris could wear holey ripped pants, ripped-up dog-bitten sneakers, a polka dot t-shirt and a little hat with a propeller on top of it, and he would still looked like a centerfold for Playgirl magazine.

Gloria checked herself out one more time before heading downstairs. She then gave herself a stamp of approval with a smile and a nod. She even threw herself a kiss in front of the mirror, then headed out the room, making her way down the stairs.

As she started walking downstairs, Stephanie was lying on the sofa watching television. She was really into the show until she looked over her head as she heard Gloria descend the stairs. When she saw what Gloria was wearing, she sat up and smiled as she checked Gloria out from head to toe.

"Well?" Gloria asked as she walked off the steps, then around in front of the couch. Gloria turned and stopped like a model, then turned the opposite way and stopped, smiling widely.

"Oh Gloria, you look so beautiful, even in a casual outfit. You are still working it, girl." Stephanie snapped her finger after she said the remark.

"Thank you," Gloria said as she continued modeling. "Are you sure this is not too much, Steph?" Gloria asked with slight concern.

"Gloria, it is just right for the occasion." Stephanie was nodding her head. "Stop worrying, cousin. He is going to love what he sees," Stephanie assured her.

Stephanie was now sitting up on the couch as Gloria sat in Archie's big chair.

"You were upstairs for so long that I thought that you got sucked down the drain," she joked.

"Oh, I was just enjoying the ambiance of it all" she said as she smiled, stretched and put her hands behind her head. "It was so peaceful, soothing and relaxing. To be perfectly honest with you, I really didn't want to get out. I drifted into another dimension."

"Like the twilight zone?" Stephanie asked as she tilted her head to her side slightly. Gloria started smiling naughtily then did a Groucho with her eyebrows.

"More like the erogenous zone." Gloria blushed over what she had just said. Stephanie shot up as if stuck with a cattle prod.

"Gloria!" Stephanie was definitely surprised by the comment. This only made Gloria giggle and turn more crimson. "What were you doing up there?"

"I, my dear cousin, was just taking a nice hot comfortable steamy bath, till I drifted off into a daydream, and was awakened by the soft sexy voice of…"

Gloria hesitated as she built up the anticipation from Stephanie, who looked like she was about to bust a lung if Gloria didn't hurry up and tell the outcome.

"Chris."

"Chris!" Stephanie echoed as she put her bare feet on the couch and started stomping. "Gloria, what is it with you and these dreams?"

"Girl, I don't know, but they could keep on coming."

Stephanie sat up with her feet on the floor, then looked at Gloria with her eyes wide and smiling.

"Okay. Spit it out. Tell me all about it and don't leave anything out. I wanna hear everything, all the sordid details."

Stephanie now was the one who was doing the Groucho.

Gloria sat sideways so she could have all of Stephanie's attention as she began to tell the story.

"I had the whole bathroom fogged up. It looked like I was in a cloud or something and there was Chris kneeling down beside me saying sweet, loving and caring words to me. Stephanie, his smile, girl! It's enough to give you goose bumps, the way it dimples in the corners—and those beautiful eyes of his. They cut right to my heart. I'm not going to lie. He smelled so good too. Yes, girl, I could actually smell him; and I didn't care if I was lying in the tub naked. I..."

"Oooh yes, Gloria!" Stephanie yelled as she interrupted. "You were in the tub naked; so sexy. So erotic. So kinky! Tell me more!" Stephanie screamed as she sat at attention at the edge of her seat.

"Stephanie, I wanted him to see all of me. I lay in the tub unashamed. I wasn't timid or bashful in the least. I was ready to face my encounter with him. Whatever was going to happen, I wanted to happen at that moment. I just didn't care. I knew that whatever was going to happen, it was going to be beautiful, just right."

Stephanie closed her eyes then shook her head back and forth as she smiled.

"Stephanie, he grabbed my fingers and kissed them repeatedly. He touched me..."

"He touched you!"

"Oh yeah, girl, he sure did touch me. I felt tingly all over. It took a lot of control on my part not to pull him into the tub with me."

Stephanie was totally speechless but she still wanted to hear more.

"He ran his fingers up and down the side of my face and I ran my fingers through his thick hair as he closed his eyes and enjoyed the touch. My breast even came out of the water and I wanted him to see it and to touch it, too."

"Oh, Gloria, this sounds so romantic, so sensual, so-so unlike you." Stephanie sounded surprised as she said this. She was almost shocked.

Gloria looked at Stephanie as if she was bewildered by Stephanie's behavior.

"Why are you acting so surprised, Stephanie? I am a mother of three and I have needs, too. How do you think that I got my children? Little elves came down from wonderland and planted them into my stomach until the stork came and took them out?" Gloria joked. "I am a mature woman who loves sex and to be touched and caressed and soothed by a nice, handsome, strong man. Stephanie, I may be your cousin, but I am a human being, too."

"I know, Gloria. It's just that I have never heard you talk or act like this before."

"I guess that I never had a reason in the past to act any other way than the way I had been acting. Now, I am having romantic dreams. I cannot even remember the last time that I had one of them, and it was very romantic. Chris told me how he felt for me and that he loves me and wants me. I could've listened to him talk all night. The only time that I took my eyes off him was when I blinked and I tried not to even do that. He even made me cry, Stephanie."

"He made you cry? Well, that doesn't sound romantic," she commented angrily.

"It does when he tells you that he has always loved you and never stopped loving you."

Stephanie thought about what Gloria had just said for a few seconds then she responded.

"In that case, then you are right," Stephanie replied as she nodded.

"Stephanie, when he said those sincere words; those loving words to me, I had no other choice but to become emotional."

"So, what did you do after he said all these sweet words to you, besides cry?"

At first, Gloria didn't answer. She just stared straight ahead in a daze, as if she was entranced.

"Gloria?" Stephanie asked again, trying to snap her out of her catatonic state.

"Yes?"

"What did you do?"

Gloria turned red and she looked like she was getting ready to cry. Her lips started quivering as she was trying to get ready to say something but knew that it wasn't going to come out the way she wanted it to. She concentrated on what she wanted to say, so maybe the emotions that were building up inside of her wouldn't erupt in the form of tears.

"I told him that I love him and that I always loved him and that I made a big mistake by marrying Mike and so on." There. She said it and the tears didn't come. Yeah, the voice quivered a tad but it came out better than she had thought.

Gloria was still looking dazed as she faced forward, but then she turned to face Stephanie to continue talking to her. To her surprise, Stephanie was biting on the pillow, red faced, with tears flowing down her cheeks. Her voice started cracking as she began to talk.

"You told him that you love him. Oh, Gloria, I'm so happy for you, to finally let it out."

"Stephanie, you're forgetting something, dear. It was only a dream!" she reminded her.

"I know, silly, but at least you know how your heart feels. The heart doesn't lie. We might lie, but not the heart."

"You're right, Stephanie, for this reason, I cannot wait to see him to let him know how I feel but first he has to get a much-needed and overdue apology. I'm just glad that he has turned out to be such a good person. He could have harbored resentment and bad feelings, not to mention jealousy and even rage, but he remained a man, a gentleman, through it all. Stephanie, I have died a million deaths every time I think about how I just swept him under the carpet without even a reason, an excuse, a lie, anything. Stephanie, people sweep dirt and dust under the carpet, not a person or a person's heart or feelings. Too bad that it has taken me decades to own up to what I did. Thank God I have a second chance to right my wrong; to make everything right."

"Well," Stephanie said after she cleared her throat and wiped her eyes. "You may have swept him under the carpet, but that was so long ago, but not for nothing, Gloria. There might even be an opportunity for you to get swept off your feet. It's never too late for love."

"Thank you, Stephanie." Gloria said smiling towards her. "Hopefully you are right."

"So, what is your plan for today with him?"

Gloria lit up like an alcoholic on St Patrick's Day as she went over and sat next to Stephanie. She then grabbed hold of her hands.

"Listen, girl, I need your help on this."

"What do you need me to do? Whatever it is, just ask."

"I know that you just put all that food away beautifully in the fridge..."

"And in the big freezer downstairs," Stephanie added.

Gloria didn't realize that there was still that much leftover but she had forgotten for a moment about breakfast being catered also.

"Don't tell me that you wanna eat more food!" Stephanie responded as if he was surprised.

"No, Stephanie. I need you to prepare me up something. You know, add some good seasoning to it and make it taste good and appetizing."

When Gloria asked this of Stephanie, she put a huge, proud smile on her face and stuck out her chest as she faced Gloria.

"Well, today is your lucky day because while you were upstairs in your tub acting out the scene from *From Here to Eternity*, I had left a nice piece of the food to the side and I had already seasoned it and it tastes great, if I do say so myself. I really would have hated to see that food go into the freezer, then eventually into the garbage."

Gloria clapped her hands together one time happily.

"Good! That's one less thing to worry about. Well, my plan is this. Meet him down at Daddy's bar with the food and set a nice table up with just us two. No distractions, no interruptions, just me, him, the food, jukebox and stimulating conversation. No one will bother us because I'll still leave the gate half down with the closed sign on the door. By the time we finish, the girls should be arriving on time so we can start preparing the food for the reception."

"Oh, Gloria, that is an excellent plan."

Stephanie was now making her way off the couch and toward the kitchen.

"I'm just glad that I didn't put all that food away. Don't worry; I'll fix you something good."

"Nothing too fancy!" Gloria yelled in her direction. "Maybe some sandwiches and stuff. It will be just light eating while we are having light talk."

"Trust me, Cousin. You'll like what I am going to prepare." Stephanie assured her confidently.

Just like that, Stephanie went through the kitchen door, disappearing from Gloria's sight.

Gloria's heart began beating faster as she thought about being alone with Chris after all these long years. She was excited. She was very excited and looking forward to it, also. She just wanted everything to be right, so perfect. She was going to make sure nothing messed it up.

A few minutes later, after Stephanie finished in the kitchen preparing the food, Gloria had called Chris and he had agreed to meet her over at the bar in about a half hour. Gloria would be there well in advance and to have everything set up perfectly. She was almost ready to leave for the bar; she was just waiting for Stephanie to finish wrapping everything up.

While waiting for Stephanie to prepare the food, Gloria had gone back upstairs and gotten one of her father's shirts, her sneakers and old jeans that she could wear once Chris left and she began to prepare the food for tomorrow after the funeral. She had put all of the clothes near the front door so she wouldn't forget to take them when she left.

As Gloria paced back and forth anxiously, she heard a rumble coming from downstairs.

"The kids must be coming up from the basement," she said to herself.

She was right. Right after she said this to herself, Zoe and Matthew walked through the door. When they noticed her standing in the living room, they looked at her with happy, surprised faces and smiled as they walked towards her, checking her out from head to toe. Matthew was nodding and Zoe had her hands folded up under her chin.

"You look beautiful, Mommy, absolutely beautiful. Doesn't she, Matthew?" she remarked.

"You sure do, Ma. That is a beautiful outfit. C.B. will be a fool if he doesn't like the way you look. You know what you look like? You look like those movie stars on television just lounging around casually, but their clothes are still fancy. That's what you look like to me."

"Well, thank you, Matthew. I feel like a movie star right now, and I am about to go out with my leading man," Gloria responded as she chuckled a few times. She then gave Matthew a kiss on his cheek, causing Matthew to blush.

"Ma, you are simply a raving beauty!" Zoe commented proudly. "I am sure glad that you are my mother."

"Wow! Thank you, Zoe." Gloria was smiling from ear to ear as she gave Zoe a kiss also. "First, I am a movie star now I am a raving beauty. I'll take it. I'll take it all. Y'all know something. If you two weren't my kids, I would definitely adopt both of you."

Gloria gave them a hug and a kiss again, then quickly checked herself out one more time in front of everyone.

"You guys sure it is not too much? I mean, we're just going to eat and talk, that's all."

"Ma, it is perfect." Matthew replied as Zoe nodded her head.

Right after Matthew complimented his mother, Stephanie made her way out of the kitchen. She had a shopping bag filled with food wrapped in aluminum foil. It looked heavy, but the bag had handles on it.

"Here you go," Stephanie said walking towards Gloria. "Nicely and tightly wrapped."

Stephanie took out one piece of food that was wrapped tightly in aluminum foil and showed it to a satisfied looking Gloria, who was nodding her head in satisfaction.

"Thank you so much, Stephanie," Gloria said appreciatively. "I don't know what I would do without you."

When Matthew saw the bag, he became concerned.

"You are going to carry that all the way to Gramp's bar?"

"Yeah Matthew," She responded. "This bag and that bag over there."

Gloria used her chin to point to the first bag, then nodded towards the bag that was by the front door. This wasn't setting well with Matthew. He didn't feel comfortable having his mother doing all of that walking with no one by her side.

"Ma, I'm going to walk with you down to the bar, and I am going to carry a bag. You are on a date. You are not supposed to be carrying anything heavy or awkward. You are a woman," he said sternly. Zoe agreed with him and nodded.

"Yeah, Ma, Matthew is right. If you carry those bags to the bar, you are going to be all shiny from sweat coming down your forehead. You are not supposed to be sweating on your date. Let the man do that," Zoe said seriously. "You don't want to be all shiny on your date with your ex-boyfriend, do you, Ma?"

Gloria chucked as she got a kick out of how her children were acting toward her.

"Oh, of course not, Zoe, but I do think that it is a good idea for you to come with me, Matthew."

"I wanna come along and help too," Zoe quickly suggested. Gloria looked at her two children proudly.

"Well, yes of course. You can come along and help too, Zoe. Thank you. I appreciate that, guys. Are you ready to go?" she asked. "We should really get moving. I don't want him to beat me there. I wanna have everything set up before he arrives."

"Have a good time, Gloria," Stephanie said. "Joey and I will be awake when you come back tonight. Be prepared to tell us everything," she ordered.

"I will, Stephanie," Gloria replied.

Matthew took the bag out of Gloria's hand, then Zoe went for the other bag in front of the door. Matthew was next, then Gloria. Zoe opened the door and walked out. Matthew was next, but before Gloria walked out, she turned to Stephanie with a smile and with a bit of nervousness. Stephanie looked at her and smiled a smile of encouragement, then gave her two thumbs up. "Have a great time, Cousin. Go spend some you-time alone with your man."

After Stephanie said that, she gave Gloria a wink. Gloria did the same, then walked out and closed the door.

As Gloria walked off the porch and down the steps, Matthew and Zoe were on the sidewalk waiting for her patiently. They looked at her with such love and respect. She was happy to have them. They walked together down the street, one on each side of Gloria, telling her what she should and shouldn't do, and what kind of music to have playing in the background. Gloria just smiled and nodded in agreement. She was getting a kick out of how her children were so overprotective of her. They were also telling her how much they cared for C.B., Chris, and how much fun he was to be around. Gloria had already known that. She doubted that he would have changed. That doesn't disappear. Gloria had never been bored with Chris, and he had always been exciting to be with. Gloria's anticipation turned into anxiety.

CHAPTER FIFTEEN:
Finally Alone: Time with Chris

When the three arrived at the bar, there were more flowers and cards up against the gate. Once Gloria had the door opened and alarm turned off, the twins came in, then closed and locked the door. Matthew brought in the flowers and cards and placed them on the counter of the bar. Gloria then turned the lights on as Zoe looked around the empty bar and sniffed the air.

"Whenever Matthew and I would come here with Gramps, the bar would be empty just like this and it would have that lingering beer smell in the air too."

"Yeah," Gloria agreed. "I thought the same thing yesterday when I came in with Iggy."

"But this is a perfect spot for a quiet get-together with someone that you care for," Zoe continued as she spun around joyously. "Your own private meeting place."

"Ma, this was a good idea that you planned here. C.B. is going to be surprised and he's going to just love it and love you for it."

"Oh, it's not that big a deal, Matthew," she said modestly.

"Humph!" Matthew exclaimed as he sucked his teeth, causing Zoe to laugh. "Who are you kidding, ma? You did tell us that we were born at night, but it wasn't last night! You put a lot of effort into this to make sure everything works out just right. No one does this kind of planning half-heartedly. You like him and you want him to know it. Just like what Mr. Hanley did for you. You wanna make sure that Chris is going to feel the same."

"Man, Matthew," Gloria said as she rubbed quickly the top of his head. "I can't put anything over on you." The comment made him smile.

Zoe grabbed Matthew by his arm and started pulling him towards the door.

"Okay, Ma. You got here fine and we don't wanna hold you up. We'll see you later."

Zoe and Matthew gave Gloria a kiss and left her alone so she could set up the way she wanted to. Gloria made sure that the gate was halfway down and then she locked the front door and made sure the closed sign was in the window. She quickly went into the kitchen with the shopping bags and got out plates and cutlery, then started putting everything nicely and neatly on a table. Even though it was the same food from the caterers, Stephanie did do amazingly well with it. As Gloria looked at the food, it didn't even resemble what it had looked like earlier, when it first arrived at the Bunker residence. Gloria could smell the aroma of the newly-seasoned food, and it was filling the bar up. To an excited and anxiously-awaiting Gloria, it smelled quite tasty.

Gloria was ahead of schedule. She still had ten minutes to spare. Everything was in its right place and to her, everything looked perfect—just the way she wanted it to. She was hoping that her time with him would go the same way.

Gloria looked happy, relaxed and satisfied as she looked around the bar, nodding.

"If this doesn't show Chris how sorry I am about the past and how much I care for him now, I really don't know what else to do. But I'm sure, knowing him, he'll be happy." Gloria began smiling and nodding as she thought about this.

If Gloria had anything to do with it, which she did, the whole get-together was going to be a beautiful, enjoyable and memorable one. Even though the date would have to end before the women arrived, she was going to do all and say all in their time with each other. She looked towards the table again happily.

"I don't wanna be anywhere else in the world right now than right here. I don't wanna be with anyone in the world right now than with Chris."

Gloria's mind must've drifted away somewhere, because the next thing she heard was the knocking on the door. Gloria looked at the time on her Rolex, then nodded her head.

"It is Chris, all right. He is right on time," she said in a positive manner.

All of a sudden, her heart began pounding so loudly that she thought all of Queens, New York could have heard her. She began getting control of her breathing.

"Gloria," she said to herself, "the time has come. You have been waiting to be alone with him forever. Don't make him wait any longer."

Gloria mustered enough courage then turned around from the table and headed towards the glass door. It was Chris standing there with a huge smile on his face.

"Hello, my beautiful man," she mumbled so he wouldn't hear her.

Chris wasn't dressed up but he looked casual. He had a jeans outfit on with a Polo shirt under the jean jacket and black shoes. He had the sleeve cuff rolled up about twice with a watch showing on his left wrist. Gloria liked what she saw, and from the way that he was looking at her through the glass door, she could tell that he liked what he saw also.

When she got to the door and opened it, he walked through and greeted her with a hug. That was the first private hug that he had given her since they were boyfriend and girlfriend. He was drawn to her look, her smell and what she was wearing.

"Gloria, you look absolutely beautiful."

Chris then took her by her hand and twirled and twirled her, causing Gloria to squeal happily.

"And that is also a stunning outfit."

Even after Chris had let go of her hand, she kept spinning then began modeling the outfit like she had done earlier for Stephanie and the twins.

"Oh this old thing," she responded jokingly. "Oh I saw it in my closet and just threw it on."

"Well, Gloria, the way you look, you probably could make a housecoat look like something from a fashion magazine," he commented, and all of his comments were making Gloria blush.

"Oh, Chris, you are so sweet, but look at you!" Gloria was now pointing to him the way Vanna White points to the letters on *Wheel of Fortune*. "Talk about eye candy! You look so good that you could put a girl into a diabetic coma!"

The comment really made Chris laugh and he even blushed also. Gloria did like the way he laughed. It was a strong, masculine laugh that didn't linger on unnecessarily.

When Chris stopped his laugh, he told her, 'Thank you.'

"Now," he said, "being that our faces look like we just got in from Miami…"

"Who told you?" Gloria responded quickly in shock and uneasiness, catching Chris off guard.

"Huh?" he asked with surprise. Chris didn't know what she was talking about and that was what Gloria was sensing, so she had to act quickly and get herself out of this bind.

"I meant to say," she said as she laughed nervously. "What did you mean by that?"

"Oh." Now he understood what she was talking about. "I mean that we both blushed when we complimented each other."

"Oh, now I understand," she responded as she nodded.

Gloria was happy that she was able to get out of that tight squeeze. She then noticed that Chris began looking around the bar and spotted the table with all of the food prepared and fixed so perfectly. His eyes opened wide as his mouth looked like it was about to drool.

"I knew that I smelled something good and tasty in here besides White Diamonds."

Gloria was impressed that he knew his perfumes and that he liked White Diamonds.

So far, she had recovered well from the Miami comment, he loved the way that she looked and smelled, and he liked her food presentation. Everything was going her way.

Gloria put her hand on his back to lead him towards the table graciously like a hostess.

"I hope that you have a good appetite because that food is waiting for you. It is calling out your name. Can't you hear it?" she asked jokingly. "Come on and have a seat. We'll eat and chat."

After she said this, Chris nodded with a smile as he stared at the table full of delicious food.

"Gloria, everything looks so delicious," he commented once he sat down. "I don't even know where to start." Chris looked at the table from left to right, then looked up to her as she stood next to him. "Aren't you going to join me? I would really hate to eat alone."

Gloria was noticing the way that he was looking up to her. The bushy eyebrows really brought the colors of his eyes out more. He looked like a little boy: so young and innocent.

"Chris, why did you have to be so damned good looking?!" she commented to herself.

"Yes, I'm going to sit, but I have to do one more thing before I do."

Gloria turned and walked over to the jukebox, plugged it in and pressed a selection. Once the song came on, she walked back to the table where Chris was sitting and was about to sit down, but Chris quickly jumped up and pulled the chair out for her to sit.

"Allow me, Gloria," he said with a smile.

"Thank you, kind sir," she replied as she nodded with a smile then sat. "You are such a gentleman, you are."

"Well, I have to be when I am in the presence of a beautiful woman such as yourself."

"Chris, you've always been such a flatterer with your words."

Gloria was placing her napkin on her lap as she prepared to eat.

"Well, my mother taught me to be honest with a beautiful woman. When you see one, let her know. She has always given me good advice. I'm sure that you always get compliments, huh?"

"From your mouth to God's ears," Gloria replied in a low voice, then she started to laugh.

"What did you say?" Chris asked looking a tad confused.

"Oh, Chris, nothing," she said as she waved him off. "You are totally embarrassing me!" Gloria was now showing her Miami tan as she began to turn crimson red again. Gloria was thinking that was what Chris wanted her to do—to cause her to blush—and it was working.

"Come on, Gloria. Answer me!" He was now egging her on as they both smiled.

"No!" she cried, looking down from side to side trying to hide her blush.

"Yes! If you don't, I will not let up! I will keep on till you are so red that I can put you atop an ice cream sundae and call you a cherry!"

"Okay, okay," she finally yelled jokingly as she put her hands up in surrender. "Chris, to be totally honest with you, I don't get a lot of compliments.

I do get some compliments every now and then, but it doesn't mean anything to me unless it is said in honesty by someone that I truly wanted it to be said by."

Gloria wasn't looking down blushing anymore. She said this boldly to him, with confidence.

Chris was stunned at first and didn't know how to respond. Gloria could tell that he was very pleased by the comment because he nodded as if it was something that he approved of hearing.

"So, by your reaction, does that mean that it meant something when I said it?"

This was time for Gloria to start letting her feelings come out as she stared into her ex-boyfriend's loving and sincere eyes.

"Very much, Chris." Gloria's heart was beating the samba while she wondered if he heard it. Gloria didn't bring Chris there to beat around the bush. She was going to tell him how she felt and get everything off of her chest.

"It makes me feel good that you still think that I look good; and by the way, Chris, you look damn good yourself."

Chris and Gloria stared at each other, not saying anything, just gazing into each other's eyes lovingly. Neither wanted to move, almost not believing that the other one was actually there. Gloria was more emotional than Chris and felt some tears building up, so before they started to come down, quickly she snapped them both out of the trance and back to reality.

"Well, now," she said, coming back to planet earth reluctantly, "let's eat, drink and be merry."

The two began fixing their plates. Both started with the salad and worked their way up to the meat, both glancing at each other, smiling and flirting with each other.

Once their plates were full, they began pouring themselves something to drink. Gloria poured herself soda and so did Chris. Gloria had remembered that Chris didn't drink alcoholic beverages. After Chris poured his glass, he extended it towards Gloria, and it got her attention. He cleared his throat before he spoke, never taking his eyes off her.

"Gloria, before we eat, usually people make a toast, but I would like to do something different. I wanna thank God for this food and for finally being able to lay my eyes on you again and having the opportunity to spend quiet and meaningful time with you, besides just eating. He has answered my prayers."

After Chris said his speech, he took a drink of his soda and started to eat his salad, almost as if he was nervous to have kept his eyes on Gloria, just in case she didn't feel the same way. Gloria felt his uncertainty and wanted him to know that she was thankful to be there with him, too, so even though he put his glass down quickly, she added so he could hear and know how she felt.

"Yes. Thank you, God, for answered prayers."

Gloria began eating her salad, too, but looked at him from the top of her eyes as she had her head down and she noticed that he smiled in relief.

"You are doing good, girl," she said to herself. "Keep up the good work."

The meal was going fine, with nice light conversation as they ate. They laughed and teased and joked with each other as they remembered incidents from the past. They talked about, 'What ever happened to?' and 'Have you heard from?' and 'Have you seen?' They even did a few 'Did you knows?' and 'I heard thats' which just kept the conversation flowing nonstop.

After the two finished the meal, Chris took a break and sat back in the chair and patted his stomach with a satisfied smile. As he nodded his head, he smiled and looked across to Gloria, who was just admiring him.

"You know something, Gloria? I could do this every day."

"If you did, Chris, you would be big as a house! You sure know how to put it away," she commented jokingly.

"Oh," he said as he looked at his plate. "This is true, but that's not what I would do every day."

"What do you mean, Chris?" she asked, somewhat confused.

"I could just stare at you every day. As a matter of fact, I could just stare at you for a lifetime."

Gloria was starting to feel like mush again, melting in the presence of Chris and his kind words.

"Oh, thank you so much, Chris. I feel the same way," she added.

"And Gloria, that meal was really good. Everything tasted so perfect; so delicious."

"Well, I'm so glad that you liked it, but remember, there is still dessert. I hope you have room."

Chris looked at her and did a Groucho, moving his eyebrows up and down.

"Weeelll, I think that I can make room for that, right after this food goes down."

He then patted his stomach again, then blew air out his mouth like he was blowing a bubble.

Gloria noticed that Chris did eat a lot, but to her, it looked as if the food went to his muscles.

The last song on the jukebox was just finishing and the next song was about to start. Chris heard the slight static, then the song began playing. The song was, Abba's *Dancing Queen*. He perked up when he heard the beginning of the song, as if he had won Bingo, then stood up. He started singing along with the music, then reached his hand out for Gloria to come on the dance floor with him.

"The dance floor is a little bit crowded, but there is enough room for us to squeeze in. Why don't we show these amateurs how to do it?"

Without waiting for a reply, he had Gloria on the dance floor dancing along with him. He and Gloria were doing an excellent job. Both were pleased with each other's dancing. Gloria remembered that Chris was a great dancer back in the day, and he hadn't lost a step. Gloria was a great dancer, too, spinning and twirling, putting her hands in her hair and tossing it ever so perfectly. They looked like teenagers at a ball, and that's how they were feeling. Gloria shook and shimmied and wiggled her hips, while Chris snapped his fingers, moved his arms and hips. They both felt comfortable and secure and confident in each other's presence.

Chris tapped Gloria on the hand then nodded towards the empty tables and chairs. Gloria looked but didn't understand what Chris was trying to tell her.

"Look at all those jealous guys looking at me like that," he said jokingly. Look at them with their arms folded across their chests as they shake their heads from side to side. They're jealous because I am dancing with the most beautiful girl in the whole room. In fact, they are jealous of me because I am dancing with the most beautiful girl in the whole world."

Chris then took her hand and gave her a spin.

Gloria smiled at him and realized that he was in a silly and giddy mood. She wasn't going to let him have all of the fun. She was going to get in on it, also. She pretended to see the men sitting and staring unkindly at him.

"Boy, if looks could kill, Chris, you would be dead!" Gloria added, making him laugh his masculine laugh. Then Gloria tapped Chris and nodded behind her.

"Psst, look at that girl sitting at the end of the bar." Gloria was almost whispering.

Chris looked at the end of the bar, knowing that no one was really there, but he saw that she was in the mood to play along.

"Yeah, I see her." Chris said as he curled up his lip in disdain.

"Well, she's been giving me the evil eye since you asked me to the dance floor."

"The nerve of her." Chris said sucking his teeth and shaking his head. "Well, you have nothing to worry about, because all my dances are for you."

"Well, I truly hope so because there is no one else in here that I wanna dance with or spend my time with," Gloria said as she moved in closer towards him.

"Well, that's what I want to hear."

Chris was accepting her new position.

Just as things were going so well and everything was getting kind of deep, the song ended. They stopped, laughed and hugged each other.

"Oh, that was fun, Gloria. I forgot what a good dancer you were."

"Well, you are not too bad yourself, Mr. Disco Inferno!"

Gloria and Chris were about to go off the dance floor when another good song came on. It was Michael Jackson's *Thriller*.

"Whoa! You can't sit down now!" he said in a playful panic. "The party has just started!"

Chris's eyes were sparking like stars.

"I agree," she added, dancing her way back to the dance floor. "Let's show these two left-footers how to dance!" Gloria was very enthused and excited.

They continued dancing, talking and laughing as the song played.

Song after song continued to play and the two just continued dancing, just being in the moment and with each other. Gloria hadn't thought once about Rupert, and she had blocked out that she still had to prepare the food for tomorrow after the funeral. Just like when she was in the tub and only wanted to think about the hot soothing water over her body, she just wanted to focus all of her attention on her and Chris.

After ten songs played, the two decided to take a little break. They headed back to the table. Chris again escorted and helped her to her chair as she fanned herself. He headed to his side, but this time, he took the chair and moved it closer to her, instantly making her feel tingly inside.

"You know," he said as he began reaching for a dessert plate, "that dancing caused me to work up an appetite!"

Chris then got a plate for him and one for her.

"I know what you mean!" Gloria said in agreement as she accepted the plate. Chris reached for a blueberry Danish while Gloria requested an éclair, chocolate.

Chris and Gloria were really enjoying each other's company. Gloria couldn't remember the last time that she planned something special for a man besides her father. It had to have been when the twins were young and her husband Ray was still alive.

While they ate and talked, Chris looked at Gloria seriously and asked her a question.

"Gloria, there is something that I need to try to see if I'm correct—may I?"

Gloria didn't know what it was but she said yes. The next thing she knew, Chris leaned over and kissed her on the cheek. Gloria couldn't hide the fact that she liked it by blushing and smiling.

"Now what was that for, Mr. Barlow?" she asked suspiciously.

"Well," he said as he licked his lips. "I wanted to see what tasted sweeter: my blueberry Danish or you."

"Well, what's the outcome, professor?"

"It wasn't a fair test."

"What do you mean?" she asked.

"Well, I've been eating the Danish for awhile. My kiss took only a second or so. I need to do it again," he said playfully, sounding disappointed. "It's only fair that I get to do the test again."

"There goes that impish Groucho again," she said to herself. "Well then, professor," she said as she put down her éclair and wiped her mouth with a clean napkin. "I think that you should do it longer but this time, try the lips. You'll get better results."

Gloria leaned towards Chris as he met her halfway, then the two began kissing each other passionately. It was light at first but after they both tasted each other, they began kissing longer and more passionately. Gloria took hold of the back of his head like she did in the dream and kissed him harder. She closed her eyes and drifted high into the heavens, past the stars, floating weightlessly like a balloon.

When they slowly and reluctantly stopped kissing, which they had done for awhile, Chris spoke but it sounded more like a whisper.

"You are most definitely sweeter than any ol' Danish. I had to be sure, but I have to be honest with you. I knew that you would be sweeter."

"Well, professor, I am glad that you used me for your case study and I'm glad that I passed the test," she said very seductively.

"Oh, you did. With flying colors."

The meal had started out with light conversation but now had turned into a romantic exchange of sentiments and feelings, and it didn't stop even after they finished eating.

When the two finished kissing more, slow music came on the jukebox. It was playing, Sade's *Is it a crime*. Chris closed his eyes, smiled then bobbed his head from side to side.

"Ooh, Sade," he exclaimed, almost in a trance. "No one has a deep, melodic voice like hers."

"I agree." Gloria took hold of his hand as she rose from her chair. "Would you care to dance with me, Mr. Barlow?"

"It would be my esteemed pleasure and honor, madam," he replied as he began rising up.

As Gloria led Chris to the middle of the dance floor, he held his arms out to bring her to him, and she was about to enter into his embrace when she stopped.

"I have to do something," she said as if she forgot something. She went over to the wall and touched a knob that lowered the brightness of the lights, dimming them.

Gloria was then satisfied what she'd done, nodding her approval. She quickly walked back over to where Chris was waiting for her.

"Now, this is much better," she said as she looked up at him.

Gloria took hold of Chris's hand as she took his other hand and put it down at her waist. She then leaned in towards him and put her head up against his chest. She was able to hear his heart beat quicken.

After a few seconds went by and she thought that it was safe to go to the next base, Gloria let go of his hand and she put both of her hands around his shoulders.

Oh, my! He is so hard and muscular even in the shoulders! she thought to herself.

While this was going on, Chris had both his hands around her waist.

"Sorry Chris," she said as she looked up to him. "It's much more to hold onto than years ago."

Chris put an impish grin on his face as he looked into her eyes.

"Oh, I like what I am feeling, Gloria. I love a woman with meat on her bones. Believe me; you won't hear me do any complaining."

As they held each other, they swayed from side to side with the music. She could feel Chris's breath on top of her head then, after a few more seconds went by, he had his head on top of hers.

Oh, if I could just drift away at this moment, she thought to herself. *Just Chris and me alone with no one to bother us.*

Chris's heart was pounding so hard and low that she thought that it was practicing for a solo part in the song they were swaying to. She looked up to stare into his eyes and he raised his head back up then looked back at her.

"How are you feeling right now?"

"I feel like the luckiest man alive." When he responded to her, Gloria smiled at him, satisfied.

Gloria snuggled back into position against his chest and he put his head back on top of hers, while he held her tightly up against him causing Gloria to be able to feel his manliness through his pants. Gloria had already known that he was quite well endowed and wondered if he had gotten more endowed as he got older. Gloria purposely ground up against it and she was able to feel it throbbing through the jeans.

You are a naughty girl, she said as she playfully chastised herself.

When her mind told her that, that was when she knew that she better control herself, but while she thought this, Chris must've realized what she was doing when she grinded up against him. He decided to be a little naughty himself and moved his hands past her waist and took a few squeezes of her butt. She didn't show any sign of disapproval until he removed his hands and went back around her waist. When he did that, she took her hands from around his shoulder, took hold of his hands and lowered them back on her butt.

"Now, that is much better," she commented as he chuckled and got the hint.

After Sade's *Is it a crime* went off, the next song was Sade's *Sweetest Taboo* then *Nothing will come between us.* A few more slow songs followed those, and then and only then was when they decided to sit and give their feet a break. When they sat back down, Chris's chair was right against Gloria's and she was leaning her head on his chest as he had his hand around her shoulder. They were both staring straight ahead contently, enchanted by the whole evening. They both began to speak at the same time, then they laughed. They both then started telling each other to speak first but Gloria won when she told him to go first.

"Gloria, this evening couldn't have been more perfect than it turned out to be. I've been dreaming about you for years, wondering how you were, how Mike was treating you, if you were happy and if you ever thought about me.

I never thought that I would ever see you again and ever since I have, I haven't been the same. It is like I've been reborn."

Chris's voice was soft and soothing, so sincere and honest.

Gloria began feeling hot again and she started to feel her emotions stir deep inside her soul, rising up and headed to come out in the form of tears. She felt the same way that Chris felt, but she had to tell him about Rupert. She had to tell him about everything, but she really didn't want to hurt him. With any luck, he might not take it so badly.

As Gloria was listening to Chris pour his heart out and as she waited her chance to say what she needed to, he switched the conversation so quickly.

"I remember when we were teenagers and you had the biggest crush on…"

"Keith Partridge from the Partridge family!" Gloria yelled excitedly.

"That is right." Chris laughed. "David Cassidy." He was nodding his head up and down.

"Oh, Chris, I was crazy about him, wasn't I?"

"That's an understatement!" He laughed a little louder. "You were totally gone for him. Didn't you use to always write him?"

"I sure did," she replied proudly. "Twice a month for a long time."

"Well, do you remember the time when…"

"Oh, Chris, I know exactly what you are about to say," she said as she gasped in remembrance. "I haven't thought about this story in decades!" She was squeezing his hands as she remembered.

"You are remembering the incident when it was my birthday, right? No, no, it was some holiday, right?" Gloria asked as she tried to remember.

"No, it was the summer. You and I were junior counselors at Elmhurst Summer Day Camp."

"That's right, that's right! How could I have forgotten that? I would make little presents and beads so I could send to Keith, er, ah, David. He used to wear the band around his neck, too, but I wanted him to wear one of mine. I would have died if he had worn it on the show."

"And what was your favorite song that year, if you do remember?"

"It was..." Gloria began looking up as she tried to remember far back to the seventies.. "I think that the song was *I think I love you*. I still have that album somewhere collecting dust and cobwebs next to Mr. and Mrs. Potato-head and a box full of broken slinkies and Etcha-sketches" She chuckled. "I remember that that was the year when we took the little kids on the camping trip upstate and somehow I developed a very bad case of..."

"Poison Ivy," Chris interjected quickly.

"That's right. Poison Ivy. Oh, Chris, I was in such pain that year that I cried like a baby. I had scratched till my skin turned raw. Mommy had kept telling me not to scratch it, telling me that if I did scratch, it would leave a scar and I would have the scar forever. I tried not to scratch it. It felt so good to scratch but later, it sure did remind me. It had spread all over."

"I remember. You looked like a blond pizza. You kept telling me, 'I have Poison Ivory, Chris,' in the saddest voice I had ever heard from you. You looked so cute then."

"Yeah, cute, all right," she said sarcastically. "Cute with raw skin. I must've looked like a chicken who had all its feathers plucked off."

"Don't forget the blonde hair," he said as he teased her.

Gloria playfully slapped him on his hand.

"Oh, you!" she exclaimed as he chuckled. "I remember that I had to stay in bed till I healed because I had it so badly. I was pink from head to toe, covered in pink anti-itch medicine. Even though I looked like a mess, you came to visit me every day. You've always been so good to me."

While lying with her head up against his chest, she took her right hand and touched his left hand that was hanging from her shoulder. He gave her hand a little squeeze as he held it.

"Being that I had to stay in bed, I didn't know what was going on for awhile and you didn't tell me anything different, so there I was lying in the bed feeling sorry for myself, looking like a pizza, like you said, thinking that I would be scarred for life. Even thought I got twenty-five cards from twenty-five little campers saying, 'Get well soon,' I was down in the dumps. Boy, Chris! At that time in my life, that was the worst thing that I had ever experienced."

"Yeah, I know. You were not a happy camper. I was just happy that you wanted to see me despite the way that you looked."

"And why shouldn't I? You were my boyfriend. You better have come to see me!"

Again, playfully, she hit him. He loved it. To him, Gloria hadn't changed. She used to do the same thing to him now that she had done back in the day. She was sassy, vivacious, funny and not hung up or even stuck up about her looks. She was a sweet woman with a tender heart, like her mother. He just continued holding her hand as she was snuggled up against his chest, listening to her reminisce.

"I remember the day when I was in my room sleeping and Mommy came and woke me, telling me that you were downstairs. I didn't even hear the doorbell ring. I was so out of it."

"Yeah, I remember. By the time that I got up to your room, you looked like a deer staring into headlights of an approaching car."

"Yeah." She chuckled. "I was still dazed, but I perked up when I saw you."

"Yes, you did." You could hear the pride in his voice.

"I remember that you had a newspaper in your hand when you came in my room."

"Yep, it was the Long Island Press."

"It sure was, and you wanted me to see an advertisement, showing me that Keith Partridge, David Cassidy, would be doing a promotional tour and would be at the old Elmhurst Movie Theater, which is at that big ol' mall on the avenue."

"Yep, that's right."

"I was so mad with you the way you came into my room that day, saying, 'Gloria! I got something to show you!' then BAM! The article. It was a one day thing and then he would be gone, and that day was the day he was supposed to be there. My heart dropped to the floor because I knew Mom and Daddy wouldn't let me go. But then..."

"That's right. But then." Chris echoed, smiled and nodded his head.

"I start hearing from the hallway, 'I think I love you and what am I so afraid of. I'm afraid that I'm not sure of a love there is no cure for.'" Gloria sang a part from the song. "Next that I know, Keith, er, ah, David comes walking into my bedroom! I could have just died! Thank God I was red all over from the cream for the poison Ivy, because I was blushing badly. I remembered that I screamed."

"Yep, you sure did scream. When I told you that I brought him here for you and that I told him that you were his number one fan, he wanted to meet you, plus the fact that my dad knew his manager personally, it was quite easy. That surprise was planned way before he came to your house. Just that you got Poison Ivy at a bad time. When I told my pops that you were crazy about David Cassidy, he called the agent and he said that when David was in New York, he would stop by and surprise you."

"And what a surprise it was! He took a whole roll of film with me. Twenty-four pictures of him and the pizza-faced girl. I looked awful, but you guys didn't care. He stayed for awhile chatting with us, just being regular. It was great. He had given us autographed pictures of him and photos of everyone on the show. I slept with that under my bed for months. I didn't think that life could've been any better than that moment. I just can't believe I forgot about that."

Gloria sucked her teeth and shook her head.

"That's why I brought it up, Gloria. I wanted you to know that I had never forgotten. When David Cassidy sang 'I think I love you,' he was singing from MY heart. He was singing words that I wanted to say to you at that time. I couldn't have said it any better than when he sang that song to you. Whenever I hear that song on WCBS.FM, or other oldie stations, or even watch an old episode of the show, I thought and think about you and how much you mean to me. Gloria, back then, you knew how I felt about you and you knew that I loved you, but I want you to know this day that I never stopped loving you and I still love you. I tried to tell you this on the porch, but got interrupted. I'm glad that I told you here."

Gloria was tired of listening to him talking to the top of her head. She wanted to see his face as he talked to her. She sat up and turned to him with glassy eyes, because the tears were definitely going to be flowing now. She grabbed hold of both of his hands, closed her eyes and took a deep breath before she spoke. Chris just stared at her with loving and adoring eyes, waiting to hear what she had to say.

"Chris, please listen..." she pleaded after she exhaled and opened her eyes, but he interrupted her.

"Look, Gloria, just because I..." he interjected, but Gloria quickly stopped him. She took her finger and put it over Chris's mouth, then she brought it back to her lips, telling him not to speak. She was nervous as she shook all over, but she had to get what she had to say off her back before the pressure of it broke her down.

"Chris, let me talk," she asked lovingly. Chris just looked on and kept quiet.

"First of all, I want you to know that I have thought about you at least a billion times over the years. What I did to you when we were young was wrong. You had always treated me so well. You didn't deserve what I did to you. Oh, Chris, I'm so, so very sorry."

"Gloria, you don't have to do this." Chris wanted to assure her that everything was ok and left in the past.

Gloria could tell that by bringing up the past, Chris was looking uncomfortable and wanted to avoid thinking about what had happened, but she was determined to say what she had to say.

"Chris, please, listen and let me talk. This might be uncomfortable for you, but imagine how I must feel having to say it. I have to release it and let it go, so please give me a moment."

Chris seemed to relax as he stared at her seriously and gave her his full attention. Chris could tell that this was very important to her.

"Chris, I have waited so long. I'm not a kid anymore. I am a mature woman who is trying to correct a mistake that was done so very long ago. I avoided you, Chris after I met Mike." She cried as tears rolled down her face and squeezed Chris's hand tighter.

"I don't know why I chose Mike over you. I knew then that it was wrong. I think that I did it to tick Daddy off because Mike was everything Daddy didn't like: long haired and hippie, hair on the face, Polish, etc—just the opposite of you. I didn't agree with Daddy's vices and I think that Mike was my way of getting back at him. I couldn't get back at him with you because he liked you a lot, but whatever my excuse was, I should have told you about him. Chris, I loved Mike but not the way a wife was supposed to love a husband. I was in love with someone else and that someone else was you."

Good girl! You said it! You finally said how you really felt! I'm so very proud of you! she congratulated herself.

When she said this, all the weight that was on her lifted off like leaves blown away by a gust of wind. She felt lighter than a crackhead with AIDS. She looked at Chris with her tear-drenched eyes and she was able to see how pleased and relieved he was to hear what she said.

"So what you are telling me is…" he said with pleased eyes that were burning her soul.

"I was in love with you." She inclined her head as she squeezed his hands even tighter, almost cutting off his circulation. "I've avoided you all these years because I was ashamed of what I did, and I would have continued avoiding you if Stephanie hadn't invited you into the house yesterday. I'm so glad that she did, though."

"Well, in that case, I am glad that she did, too, but I have a question to ask you. You said that you have been in love with me in the past, but how do you feel about me now?"

Gloria knew that he was going to say that and that was the problem that she had been trying to avoid. At this moment, everything could fall apart. She hesitated before speaking.

Make sure what you say is right, Gloria. You won't be able to take it back once you say it, she warned herself. *This gorgeous hunk of a man just told you that he still loves you and he has every right to know how you feel toward him.*

Gloria wanted to kick herself for not practicing what she was going to say before seeing him.

Gloria opened her mouth to tell him everything; about how she felt about him now, about meeting Rupert, about her confusion—everything. She took a deep breath, held it, then glanced at his handsome masculine face. She let go of one of his hands because the other hand was getting comfort from his and ran it through his thick hair then down the side of his face. He closed his eyes as she did this.

"Though I cannot deny that I have terribly strong feelings for you, I've always had. I would like to tell you more than that in detail, but I believe that I can't tell you more than that right now."

Huh? What the hell was that? That's not what you were supposed to say! yelled her inner voice.

No, I am definitely not saying that. She shook her head and removed her hand from his face. Why was this handsome man making it so hard for her to say what she had to say?

Gloria didn't feel right. She felt strange, like she was on fire. It started all the way down at the tip of her toes and worked its way up. It was causing her body to feel tingly and shaky. She was almost shivering on the outside, but there was an inferno building up inside her. Was it passion? Desire? Was it confusion? Did it feel good? Bad? She couldn't explain it.

All of a sudden, Gloria started thinking what if those feelings going on in her body were the desire to have him right then and right now? What about his sensuous touch; and his big hands touching her in all of those sensitive spots on her body which hadn't been touched like that in such a long time. She yearned to be explored by him; to have him touch her.

"So Gloria, what is it? You are not attracted to me intimately?"

"I can definitely say that that's not it, Chris, but..."

"Gloria, I haven't changed. I am still that same Chris that you knew when you were younger. Only that I am older now. Gloria, I love you and I want to spend the rest of my life with you. Too many years have gone by that I want to make up for. Gloria, I am a successful man. I can give you a good life, whatever you want. I have to let my feelings known right now, Gloria. I might not have another chance to do it. I can't lose you again. Unless..."

"Unless what, Chris?"

"Unless you desire to be lost to me," he responded sadly and in a low voice.

"No, Chris. I don't desire that at all. I do desire you in my life."

"Then why can't you answer my question?" he countered. "If you feel the same that I do, and desire me in your life, why can't you tell me if you are still in love with me?"

"Because," she said, hesitating. "I-I-I, oh, Chris...please don't think badly of me."

Gloria put her head down as the tears flowed harder and she reached for a napkin off the table.

Chris leaned towards her and comforted her while rubbing her back.

"Gloria, I could never, ever think badly about you. At this very moment, I love you more than ever. I just need to know how you are feeling about me now—if I still have a chance in my lifetime to have you again as my own, and me, your own."

"Of course you do. I do want you to know that," she said, sounding muffled under the napkin.

"Then why don't you want me to know more, Gloria? Why don't you want to let me know if you want to spend your life with me and that you are still in love with me?"

Chris wasn't giving up. He was being more persistent. Gloria swallowed then dabbed at her eyes.

"Chris, I didn't do all of this for a hi-goodbye. I did this because I want you back in my life and I wanted you to know that I had made a mistake years ago, a big mistake. Oh, how things could have been different."

Gloria was trying to muster up enough courage and tell him that there was someone else in the picture that she had feelings for and that she wasn't ready to give that up yet. Maybe he might understand, but probably he wouldn't. He might just get up and walk out angrily, never wanting to see her again.

Taking a deep breath and then exhaling, she decided to be more firm.

"I'm sorry, Chris. As much as I would like to satisfy your curiosity right now, I just can't. You will just have to take my word that I will tell you everything you want to know. I just need a little bit more time."

"Gloria, how much more time are you going to need?" Chris asked with slight agitation. "You might be selling the house, and then where will that leave me? Knowing what the answer is ten minutes before you head towards JFK and out of my life?"

Gloria knew that Chris was one hundred percent right. It really wasn't fair to make him wait, no matter what the outcome would be. Gloria would win out and one would be hurt. Gloria was making it more convenient for herself, holding on to both men, then when she decided what she wanted, bye-bye second guy and that second guy just might be Chris.

Gloria started thinking that her love for Chris would outweigh anything from Rupert because of the dream that she had while bathing in the tub while the room was filled with steam, when she confessed her feelings to Chris about how much she loved him, but all of a sudden, she started to remember all the bopping of the toes and slapping of the thighs and the bah-bah-bah-bahs while lying in the tub. The song that she was singing in the tub was the song that David Cassidy had sung when he surprised her the year that she had caught Poison Ivy! The surprise that Chris planned especially for her! Why would she have had that dream, and why would she have sung that song after not thinking of it in such a long time, only to have Chris all of a sudden mention it later on during their date? Not only that, the name of the song was *I think I love you*. And those were the words that she had said in the dream to Chris. Maybe God was telling her the answer, giving her hints to let her know that Chris was the one for he,; that he was her true soulmate. At that moment, she didn't know. She couldn't think straight. Her mind was spinning. Not realizing it at first because she didn't hear herself say it, she cried out as she put her hands on her temples.

"I'm so confused! I'm so confused! I'm so confused! I wish that I could give you an answer right this very moment, Chris, truly I do, but I just can't!"

Gloria began sobbing heavily. As Chris stared at Gloria as she sobbed, he felt horrible for making her cry. He felt responsible for it. He then realized that Gloria had come back to New York not for pleasure. There was a very good reason for her to be back. Her father, whom she had loved so very much, had just died. He started to feel selfish at putting his needs before hers. Obviously she had a lot on her mind: the funeral, her children, the burial, the planning of the food and what was going to happen to the house and bar.

THE BAR! he thought to himself.

Despite what she was going through, Chris started to realize that Gloria still took time out of her busy schedule to spend time with him and made sure the evening went perfect, and she apologized for the past; and there he was pushing her for an answer and giving her more added pressure and stress, even after she had told him that she would give him an answer when she was more up to it.

"Oh, Gloria, I'm sorry," he said in a soft, mellow voice. "I didn't mean to make you cry. That was not my intention. I know that you have a lot on your mind with the funeral, the planning and all. It was wrong of me to push you. It was very selfish on my part."

Chris then took his hand and put it under Gloria's chin to lift her face up so he could look into her eyes, which were soaked in tears from crying so much.

"Can you forgive me?" he asked apologetically.

When Gloria lifted up her head to look at Chris, it was all that she could do to keep from grabbing him again and just kissing and holding him tightly. She saw that he was hurting for making him cry.

Gloria nodded sincerely to let him know she accepted his apology.

"Chris, I'll give you answers to your questions, j-j-just give me a little more time."

Chris held one hand out making a stop motion with it.

"Gloria, please take your time. I don't wanna rush you. When you are ready, you will tell me."

"Chris, really, I don't mean to make you wait. That wasn't my intention. It is just that…"

"Look, Gloria, you don't have to explain anything. You are not Burger King."

When Chris said this, Gloria looked at him with confused eyes.

"What I mean to say is that I can't have it my way just because I ask for it, like at Burger King. I know that you will tell me all in good time. You are more like Dunkin Donuts."

When he said this, Gloria started to cheer up and smile.

"How am I like Dunkin Donuts? Round and sweet?" she joked. "Or am I a Munchkin?"

"No, you are like Dunkin Donuts because you are worth the wait."

Chris started smiling, which lightened the mood for both of them. Chris sighed a sigh of relief. "Now, that is more like it. I always hated to see you cry. I'd rather die than see you cry."

"Then where would that leave me, Chris? You'd be dead but I would still be crying. I would be crying because you were dead. I wouldn't want that to happen because that pain would kill me; then we would both be dead."

Chris didn't know if Gloria was trying to be funny or not, but he laughed, causing her to laugh.

"That is kind of romantic, though. Like Romero and Juliet—an older version."

"Yeah." She added, looking normal and happy again. "An older version but without the poison. Oh, gosh! How painful. In the movies they make it look so easy and wonderful, but it is not!"

Gloria had Chris cracking up laughing as she continued talking.

"You don't just simply close your eyes then slowly fade into blackness. I remember when I babysat over at Iggy's house when he was a little boy. He had a dog by the name of Shadow…"

"Oh, I remember that dog named Shadow. He was like a German Sheppard mixed with retriever. He was a beautiful dog," he recalled.

"Yeah, he sure was. That was before…"

"Before what, Gloria?" he asked.

"Well, Iggy's mother had laid down some poison because the City was repairing some pipes in the street and mice were running rampant, going into people's houses. Well, when she laid down the poison, she forgot to keep it out of reach of Shadow, and later that night while we were going over Iggy's homework, we started hearing gasping and choking. It was awful. The dog was writhing in pain, flipping and everything. When Shadow threw up before he died, there were the half-digested pellets. Just thinking about it just-just... yech!"

There before Chris was the Gloria that he knew and loved. Chris just smiled and shook his head back and forth at her natural comedic ranting.

"Well, what was so romantic about the story was that one couldn't survive without the other; same with *West Side Story*."

"And *Earthquake*., Gloria added as she nodded her head.

Chris began looking at Gloria with a confused face to see if she was actually serious or if he was hearing things.

"*Earthquake?*"

"Oh yeah. *Earthquake*, with Charlton Heston and Ava Gardner."

"I don't remember any romantic sparks in that movie, Gloria, between those two. As a matter of fact, if I am not mistaken, they were either separated or divorced and Charlton Heston was sleeping with a young girlfriend; not to mention that Ava Gardner's character was a spoiled lush."

"But the ending, Chris, the ending. Don't you remember when they were underground and the water level was rising and Charlton Heston was rescuing everyone by helping them up the ladder, including his girlfriend and Ava's character? Don't you remember when Ava's character was climbing up the ladder, either a pipe or someone stomped on her hands—I don't remember—then she fell into the water, screaming and crying in pain?"

Chris had always loved to hear Gloria tell a story. She would always become so animated as she got into it, using her hands, body gestures and facial expressions. He could listen to her talk or explain something all day.

"That's right, Gloria. I do remember now," he blurted out.

"There was Charlton's character on the ladder, just a few feet away from safety up the ladder or take a chance to save his wife and risk his life. It was a test of who he really loved. It was romantic, Chris, because he couldn't go up that ladder, oh no." Gloria was shaking her head. "Yes, he may have saved the girlfriend and got her up that ladder but he really loved his wife despite her manipulative, spoiled ways and being a lush, and he jumped in after her and they died together. At least Ava's character died knowing that her husband really loved her."

Chris thought about what Gloria said then nodded in agreement.

"I think that you are absolutely right. I had totally forgotten about that, but I wanna tell you something, Gloria, and I don't want you to forget. I would die for you in a heartbeat; regardless of what your answer will be to me whenever you tell me."

It was so amazing to Gloria how Chris was able to manipulate her emotions just by saying something. Everything that he seemed to say put her in another state of mind. Before she had an opportunity to respond to what he had just said, he looked down at his watch then opened his eyes wide in surprise.

"Boy, where has the time gone?! It seems like I just walked through the door of the bar. Now it is almost time for you to get ready to start cooking and preparing for tomorrow," he said in a disappointed manner.

Gloria was the next to jump in surprise as she looked at her watch. He was right. It was almost time to start cooking, once the girls arrived.

Gloria sighed in disappointment and frowned. "Well, Janet Jackson said it best in that song, *Funny how time flies when you're having fun*."

As Chris got up, reluctantly, he looked at Gloria's watch as if it was the first time he had seen it the whole night, opened his eyes wide and whistled.

"Wow, Gloria. I just noticed that beautiful Rolex on your wrist. That is an expensive watch. You must be really doing well in the real estate business, huh?"

Gloria dared not say anything, so she just smiled and shrugged her shoulders modestly. "Well, I do pretty decently."

"Decently is not the word. That is absolutely beautiful. Is it new?"

"Yeah. I just got it recently." She was hoping that he didn't ask any more questions. She lucked out. That was his last comment about the Rolex.

When Chris stood up, he held his hand out to Gloria to help her out of her seat.

"I want you to know that the whole evening went perfectly. It couldn't have been any better."

"Chris, believe me, it was my pleasure."

"I do wanna say that I am happy that you came back to New York City, even if it might only be for a short time. I'm sorry you had to come back under such sad circumstances."

Gloria didn't respond. She just nodded.

"Thank you for taking time out of your busy schedule to make time for me."

"You are welcome, Chris. A lot of stuff was said today between us and I know how you feel. Don't think that I am going to forget anything."

"Well, I hope not," he quickly responded. "Can I call you later or tomorrow maybe before the funeral, just in case you might need me for something?"

"Well, let me call you. I know that I am going to be exhausted when I get home and Joey will be up, and I am going to spend some time with him before I go to bed, and you already know about tomorrow. I'm going to be quite busy."

"I understand." He nodded with a smile, even though deep down inside he was a tad disappointed. "If that's what you want."

"But I promise that I will call you as soon as I have a chance; plus I'll see you here tomorrow, anyway. We'll spend some time together then. Sound good?"

"Sounds perfect." He smiled again then they both hugged each other and kissed passionately.

After they finished kissing, Gloria walked him to the door. No more words were said. Only facial expressions and eye contact were given. Gloria opened the door and Chris was just about to walk out, but first he turned and looked at her one more time, stared for a few seconds, then gave her a wink and walked out.

Gloria watched as Chris quickly disappeared out of sight. She then locked the door and leaned up against it, facing the bar as she closed her eyes peacefully.

"Oh, thank you, God. Thank you so much for such a beautiful evening. At one point it was touch and go but I was able to recover quickly, thanks to David Cassidy...David Cassidy, Lord?" she asked as she laughed. "David Cassidy?"

CHAPTER SIXTEEN:
Three Women and One Big Kitchen

Gloria glanced down at the Rolex again to see how much time she had before the women arrived. She saw that she had enough time to change her clothes and warm up the ovens and stoves. There was still food left on the table that they could nibble on while they were preparing. She had contemplated packing it up but changed her mind at the last moment.

Ten minutes later, Gloria was already in the kitchen boiling eggs for the deviled eggs, macaroni salad, egg salad, and tuna salad. They were in a huge pot on the stove. In some other big pots, she had potatoes and pasta boiling. She kicked herself for not starting these food items earlier. It would have saved her some time, but her mind was too busy focusing on Chris and making sure everything was right for him.

Gloria moved gracefully through that kitchen, knowing where everything was. She was at home in that kitchen, just as if she was in her own house or at the house on Hauser Street. Edith had taught her well. Gloria had helped her daddy out plenty of times working in the kitchen at the bar, so she was used to cooking and preparing meals for one or over one thousand people.

Right on time, Gloria heard a knock at the door, then heard the keys turn in the lock.

"Faye and Teresa are here," she said as she headed out the kitchen to greet them.

"Hey, guys," she yelled happily, as if this was the first time she had seen them in a long time.

The two nodded and smiled as they came in and greeted her back in the same fashion. One of the first things the two women did was lay their things on the counter then sniff around before eyeing the table with the food on it.

"Umm!" commented Teresa. "It sure smells good in here."

Faye nodded in agreement. She then looked Gloria up and down and frowned.

"I know that you didn't wear THAT when Chris was here." When she said this, she had one hand on her hip and the other hand pointing to the outfit that Gloria had on.

Gloria looked at her clothes innocently, held her hands out at the sides and spun around as if modeling the outfit.

"What's not to like?" This caused the two to start chuckling. All three headed over toward the table.

"If you wanna eat something before we start, just help yourselves."

"Well, it looks like the same food from earlier, but it sure doesn't smell like it."

Faye and Teresa were both picking up plates to sample the food. Faye bit into a sandwich, and looked at Gloria with surprise.

"And it definitely doesn't taste like the food from earlier."

"Well, you can thank Stephanie, who did a miracle on it and saved it from being a meal for the garbage can."

Teresa was biting into her sandwich and some potato salad and nodded.

"Totally different than earlier. So Gloria, Stephanie is home?"

"Yeah. She wanted to be there when Joey arrives." Gloria looked at her watch. "In about an hour, hour and a half."

The three sat around the table for a few minutes before they headed into the kitchen. Gloria told them that the eggs, potatoes and pasta were on the stove cooking. Faye and Teresa were reaching for cups to pour themselves something to drink.

"I haven't eaten since I left the house and I had only nibbled then because it was bad. I saved my appetite for now. I am really hungry."

"Me too." Faye added, "Although I did stop at the store for a pack of Tic Tacs to get that nasty tasting food out of my mouth, but that doesn't count as a meal. I'm famished myself."

"Well, help yourselves. Eat till your stomachs burst. I did and so did Chris."

"Oooh, Chris!" the two said in a teasing manner. Gloria just waved them off with a smile.

"So?" Teresa said grinning widely. "How did it go with you and Chris?"

"Yeah, how did it go? Did you tell him about the billionaire playboy? Inquiring minds want to know, girl." Faye then took another hearty bite of her sandwich and washed it down with some punch.

"Everything went just perfectly," she said proudly as she thought back on the evening. "We laughed, talked, ate and drank, danced, ate and drank, slow danced, hugged and kissed…"

"Now ya talking, girl!" Faye interjected.

"Yeah, that's what we wanna hear. The gooey stuff!" Teresa was nodding he head.

"You mean juicy stuff, Teresa." Gloria corrected.

"Yeah, tell it. Tell it all—Juicy Goosey, Gooey Louie—we wanna hear it!" Gloria and Faye smiled and shook their heads.

"Well, I want y'all to know that the mood had become quite romantic once the slow songs started on the juke box. Slow song after slow song, we danced and held each other closely. Girls! He even copped a feel!"

"Copped a feel!" Faye started jumping around in her chair and lightly slapping Teresa who was smiling widely and nodding her head.

"Wait a minute," Faye said as she looked at Teresa. "You know what 'copping a feel' means?"

"Aah, nope!" she responded innocently as she shook her head.

"Then why did you—" Faye shook her head. "Oh, never mind. Anyway, it means that he reached out and touched someone, which used to be AT and T's slogan." Then Faye demonstrated by lifting up her butt cheek from the chair and squeezing it with her hand.

"Ooooh!" Teresa nodded with a smile. "Now I understand. Chris squeezed the Charmin!"

"And that's not all. As he reached out and touched someone by squeezing the Charmin, he became like Mrs. Butterworth when he took his own sweet time!"

"He also boldly went where no man has been for quite some time!" Faye added, causing everyone to burst out laughing. "You did it fiercely, girl!" Faye exclaimed as she gave Gloria a high five.

"You sure worked it, chica!" Teresa added as she gave a high five too. "Girls, I'm not gonna lie. The last time I had my Charmin squeezed, mi novio Hector bought a roll from the supermarket!"

"Well, that was as far as it went. The whole date, he was nothing but a true gentleman. And the way that he held me in his arms? Girls!" she exclaimed. "I wanted him to take me right there on the dance floor!" When Gloria said this, the other two's eyes bulged out. "To be totally honest with you, ladies, I wanted him to take me right there on the counter or even on this table."

"On this table!" the two screamed out in unison.

"Wow, now you are getting kinky!" responded Faye, with an impish grin on her face.

'Oh, you are a naughty girl, Gloria," added Teresa nodding.

"Once we sat back down and Luther, Michael Bolton, Sade and Anita Baker serenaded us, we just sat in the chair with the lights dimmed and drifted off into our own thoughts. I'm sure that he was thinking about me just as I was about him." While she spoke, Faye and Teresa listened intently.

"And then you told him about the rich guy?" Teresa was reaching for another helping of food.

Gloria smiled embarrassedly as she began looking at both of the women, not knowing what to say. Faye and Teresa stared back at Gloria as they waited for a response. When they didn't get one, they looked at each other then looked again at Gloria, again waiting for a response.

"Wait a minute, Gloria," Faye said as she sat up straight with her eyes wide. "Don't tell us that you didn't tell him about Mr. Hanley."

"Well, I'm trying not to tell you. That's why I'm just smiling."

"Oh, Gloria!" Teresa shouted in disbelief and disappointment.

Gloria stood up from her chair and started pacing back and forth, looking confused. "I couldn't do it, I tell ya. I just couldn't do it!" As she was saying this, Faye and Teresa began rolling their eyes. "He was talking all sweet and looking all oh-so-fine with his jean suit on and Polo shirt. He smelled oh-so-good, too. And that masculine voice of his when he laughed—it wasn't fair. Chris had an unfair advantage. He kept telling me how much he loved me and that he had always loved me and has never stopped loving me. How could I have told him? I just couldn't. Girls," Gloria was pleading her case as if she was on trial talking to the judge for understanding and leniency. "Do you all know what made matters even worse? He even said that he would die for me. Come on now. What would you have done if you were in my shoes?"

Faye and Teresa both looked at each other in silence. They couldn't answer the question.

"That's not it. He even said that he wanted to spend the rest of his life with me. He would have married me right here if there was a minister present, but then he asked me how I felt about him."

"Well, that was your opportunity to tell him about Hanley, Gloria!" Teresa said in frustration.

"Yeah, girl." Faye added in agreement "He gave you a chance to tell him everything."

"Well, girls, I didn't bite the bait. I passed on it. I became a chicken; a coward; I really did mean to tell him, but I didn't have the guts."

"So what did you tell him?"

"Yeah, how were you able to get out of that spot?"

Gloria took a deep breath then exhaled. "It wasn't easy, girls, but I told him that I have deep, strong feelings for him, but for all the other feelings, I couldn't give him an answer right now. I told him that I needed more time. He wouldn't give up. He was relentless in his questions. He wanted an answer right then and there, but I couldn't give it to him. When he kept pounding me, I did what any other woman would have done."

"And that was...?" Teresa asked.

"I cried."

"You cried!" Faye echoed as she clapped her hands together and nodded. "Yep, that'll do it."

"Or show him a breast. That'll make him forget what he was talking about all together. As a matter of fact, it'll make a man forget his name or where he lives!"

"Well, it didn't have to get that far, but once I cried, he realized how stressed I was and backed off. From there, somehow we started talking about Romeo and Juliet and poison. then Iggy's dog, the babysitting, all the way to the movie *Earthquake*. This saved the date. That was when he said he would die for me."

"Oh, that was so romantic." Faye said emotionally. "Stuff a man full of food, give him a handful of bootie, give a little bit of the water works and the man is ready to die for you."

"Now just imagine if you had taken out a breast!" Teresa added.

"You know, I wasn't even paying attention to the time. He was the one who ended the date after seeing what time it was. He was mindful of the fact that you two would be coming over to help me prepare for tomorrow, so he left, giving me plenty of time to change my clothes and to start some of the food; and concerning any answer to his question, he told me to take my time giving him the answer. He knows that I'm being bombarded with a lot of things right now."

"So, when are you going to tell him?"

"If you sell the house, is that when you are going to tell him?"

"Those are exactly the same questions that he asked me, but I decided to tell him sometime in the next few days. You know, like when things slow down around here and I am able to concentrate and get my mind in order."

The two women nodded in agreement.

"That sounds fair. By then, you should have enough guts to say your true feelings to both," Teresa replied.

"Or you'll still be a chicken and Chris will get his answer by seeing the tail lights of the taxi driving you and the family to the airport heading back to California."

"No. He definitely will have an answer by then," Gloria assured them.

Gloria decided that while the two were eating and drinking, she could go for some more soda while she waited for them to finish, so she reached for a glass and started to pour.

"So, enough about me and my very mundane life." She chuckled. "What happened when y'all got home with all the clothes?" she asked, then took a gulp of the soda.

"Well, when I got home, I had a date with a mirror and I paraded around it wearing the new clothes, thinking that I was Halle Berry. Girl, let me tell ya, I looked good!" Faye said with pride.

Faye was now reaching for a refill and another portion of food. "Now, the only thing that I need is a good man to come and ask me out. You noticed that I said a good man, not a handsome man. A handsome man can be and most likely is a dog, but a good man is right to the point. A...good...man... Shoot! I don't even care if he's a leper! I don't mind walking around with some lotion for his skin and a bag just in case something falls off, if he would know how to treat me good!"

Teresa nearly choked on her sandwich and Gloria nearly spit out her soda laughing so hard at what Faye had just said. Faye just sat there, looking at the girls seriously.

Once the two calmed down, Teresa began telling them what happened when she got home.

"Well, when I walked in the house, no one was at home. Everyone was out. I thought that Hector would have been home because he worked late last night. Well, I was able to go to the girls' room and put their clothes on their beds and then I went about my business, watching a recording of a Novella that I missed the other day. Well, one by one, they all started arriving, starting with Hector. He passed by the kids' room and saw the clothes. At first, he thought that it was old clothes, stuff that he had bought them awhile back, but when he got a closer look, he noticed that they weren't anything that he had bought. Once he checked out the fabric and stuff, girls, I thought that New York had been invaded the way he screamed and shouted. He threatened to take away the credit card and how could I have done this knowing that we are moving and yadda yadda yadda and blah blah blah." Teresa waved him off to the two ladies then she rolled her eyes as if she wasn't worried by Hector's rantings and ravings. "You should've seen the vein bulge out in the middle of his forehead as he turned cryptic red!" She laughed as she pointed to the middle of her forehead to show the women.

"Teresa, you mean to say 'crimson red,' not 'cryptic,' Gloria corrected.

"Whatever the word is, he was like a strawberry, I tell ya!" Teresa adjusted her body in the chair.

"Once he finished acting like Ricky Ricardo after Lucy pulled one of her crazy red headed schemes, I innocently and calmly told him everything. You should've seen his face then. I said to him that it was a gift from you to the family, then he started acting the way Ralph Kramden did on the *Honeymooners* when he did something stupid to Alice. He couldn't apologize enough. When the girls came in a little while after and saw the clothes, the place sounded like an explosion hit it!" She exclaimed with a lot of enthusiasm.

"The girls came running into the living room to me and dove on me like I was a hotplate at Yankee Stadium!"

"Home plate, Teresa."

"Hotplate, home plate—whatever. At least I got the 'H' right," she countered. "They told me to tell you thank you and that they'll personally thank you tomorrow."

"I can't wait to see them tomorrow."

"Gloria, they are beautiful girls. I met them." Faye commented. "Well-mannered and polite."

"And they looked beautiful in the clothes, too, Gloria. Thanks again. So every time they tried on an outfit, they came and modeled in front of me and Hector. He loved the way they looked, too. He kept asking me about my new clothes. I told him that I got the outfit for tomorrow plus one other for special occasions, then he said that he was happy that I didn't get him anything and that he was happy that I kept my word and yadda yadda yadda…"

Teresa then hesitated for a moment to take a bite from her food then she drank some soda. "So then I went into the bedroom and gave him his clothes."

Gloria and Faye both started laughing.

"I don't pay that man no never mind when he speaks to me. In one ear and out the other," Teresa commented as she once again waved off Hector.

"So, what did he do when he saw what you brought for him?" Gloria asked as she wiped the tears.

Teresa started smiling impishly before she was about to take a bite out of her sandwich.

"Well, remember that I just told you about Yankee Stadium!" she said as she did the Groucho with her eyebrows and smiled, showing teeth like a Cheshire cat.

"Ooh, you little vixen, Teresa!" Faye shouted. "He gave you some!"

"Home run!" shouted Gloria as she high fived Teresa.

After Teresa let the two women know that she and Hector got intimate after he had received the clothes, they all continued talking for another ten to fifteen minutes, then they cleaned off the table before they headed to the kitchen. Faye and Teresa had come prepared, dressed in old but clean clothes. Faye was used to working in the kitchen because it was her job. She began showing Teresa around the kitchen as Teresa nodded. Once Teresa got familiarized with the layout, all three met in the center of the kitchen.

"Okay, girlfriend, I am ready to get busy. What do you have in mind?" Faye asked eagerly.

"Well," Gloria exclaimed as she tapped her lips with her hand and thought about it. "We'll put some of the tables together, right, and lay two tablecloths, one red and one white. In the center, we'll make a huge fruit display. Are you familiar with that?"

"Yeah, I'm a master at that," Faye said proudly.

"Well then, I'll leave that up to you." After she said this, she turned to Teresa. "Teresa, you could start making some cakes and stuff. I know that you are a master of that."

"You got it."

"Then maybe when we all get finished with these things, we can all start cleaning the meats and stuff and have that ready to go in the oven tomorrow."

"Well, Gloria, all the ovens have timers on them. We can season all the meats and program the ovens to start baking when we want them to, so by the time we get here, they would already be done."

"Oh, that's great!" Gloria exclaimed happily. "I had forgotten about that! That'll save a lot of time and hassle."

When Gloria said this, Teresa and Faye nodded in agreement. "Okay, girls, let's get going."

Faye headed for the walk-in refrigerator and began taking out boxes of apples, bananas, oranges, grapes and watermelons. She got a huge platter and bowl and some sharp knives in all different sizes, spoons, ice cream scoops and other utensils. After that, she got some smaller bowls. She cut the watermelon on the sides and top to make a design then scooped out the inside, making watermelon balls, then she filled the hollow watermelon shells with the watermelon balls and the other fruit with the big bowl. She decorated it by putting fruit inside and had the grapes dangling all around the sides of the bowl, then she stacked the fruit up like a pyramid. Faye was moving like she had done this kind of work every single day. She was done quickly. Gloria had no idea that Faye would've completed that job so very fast. Faye even made a huge salad.

Gloria also watched Teresa move. Once she was shown where everything was, she never asked another question. She moved around the kitchen like she was born there, singing to herself and smiling. Teresa poured bags of flour and sugar and eggs into the huge mixer along with water and vanilla extract. She greased up some huge bake pans then scooped in the moist liquid ingredients. After that, she popped them into the huge oven, then she even made homemade frosting. When she was done with that, she started on making miniature Danishes and donut sticks. Teresa was like a kid in a candy store who had the run of the whole place.

Teresa looked like she was enjoying what she was doing. She had the same look Gloria's mother Edith had when she baked in the kitchen at home. Needless to say, with Teresa's experience with Edith and working at the bakery, she was done quickly also.

As for Gloria, she was moving at a steady, rhythmic pace. By the time she had come back into the kitchen after Faye and Teresa had eaten, all her food that was on the stove was already done. The only thing she had to do was drain and season the pasta, which she would do when it cooled. The eggs and potatoes were run through the cold water till she was able to peel the shells and skins off. Once she did all of that, she got out the huge bowls they would be going into. She then got her mayo and mustard and seasonings and onions all ready, then one dish after the other, she began preparing her salad dishes. She was also done quicker than she had thought. They were all working as a team and no one got in anyone's way. After all three women finished their easy tasks, Gloria began taking out meats and when she was done, they all began cleaning and seasoning. Once that was done, all the food was rolled into the refrigerator till tomorrow. Teresa went to where they were sitting at in the dining area and joined a few tables together. Gloria had given to her tablecloths in red and white to cover the tables. Faye was behind her with stacks of paper plates and plastic forks and knives, and she had plastic cups for people to drink from. They then laid out everything on the table and nodded with their tired hands crossed around the waist.

"That looks pretty good," Teresa commented with delight.

"It'll be better tomorrow when everything is laid out nicely."

Gloria came out soon afterwards and looked at the table and nodded.

"Girls, we did real well tonight. The good news is that we'll still be home at a decent time."

Gloria looked at both women and gave each one of them a hug and a high five, as she showed her gratitude to them.

'Yeah that's good," Faye commented as Teresa nodded. "We'll be able to have some good sleep."

"Gloria, everything is going to be just perfect. Mr. Bunkers would be proud."

"I think that you're right. I just hope that there will be enough food for everyone." When she said that, the two looked at each other and just laughed.

"Gloria, what are you talking about? There is enough food to cater Madison Square Garden."

"Faye, what do you mean? It's more like the Houston Astro Dome!" Teresa interjected.

"You guys are forgetting three very important things: Mike, Joey and Matthew. Those three together could bankrupt Fort Knox if it was filled with food."

"Well then, in that case, we'll just make it," Faye said after she stopped laughing.

"Listen, Gloria, you're going to be very busy tomorrow so what I'm going to do is come back here and put the food in the oven, then return to the funeral. I'll set the timers and everything. It'll work out fine," Faye assured her.

"You'll do that for me? Oh, Faye thanks a lot. That will definitely be a load off my back."

"I can come back with you and help you set up," Teresa said to Faye, who nodded in agreement.

Gloria suddenly became overwhelmed with everything and started to cry.

"Thank you so much, guys." Her voice began to crack. "I don't know how to thank you. You both are heaven-sent. You've been so very helpful that I just don't know how to repay you."

The two went and embraced her, showing comradeship, compassion and sisterhood. They patted Gloria and even began to cry with her because they had known Archie also and would miss him, too. When they finally were able to regain their composure, Gloria began to speak, sounding like she was trying to catch her breath.

"The next time that I come back in here, my daddy will be in the ground forever."

As quickly as she said that, Teresa was ready to respond to try to cheer her up.

"Oh, Gloria, you can't look at it like that, honey. His body may be in the ground but his body was just a house. His spirit has moved out and is now living in a mansion in heaven with Edith."

"Yeah, girl. Your father is up in heaven right now, driving Jesus and God crazy."

When Faye joked to prevent Gloria from being sad, it lightened the mood and they all smiled.

"Yeah, you know something, guys? You are right. My body just felt a little guilty for not crying over daddy all day. It was too busy having fun and it wanted to really remind me why I was here in the first place."

"But knowing Archie, that's not what he would want you to do."

"Yeah, Gloria. He would want you to remember him happily. That is why we put this whole thing together: to remember his life, not the fact that he is no longer with us," Teresa added.

"Thank you so much again for your kind words. I really do feel so much better." The two smiled when she said that.

"Well, that makes us feel happy then," Faye said, as Teresa nodded.

After this was said, the three did some last minute preparations before they left. The bar was already clean, so they didn't have to worry about cleaning it, and the women had cleaned up in the kitchen when they had finished their jobs. They were all ready to leave after Gloria picked up her bag with her dress that she had worn earlier in it, and the two took their stuff off the bar counter. Faye knew the procedure, to wait for Gloria outside while she locked up, then once outside, since it was late, Faye drove everyone home, starting with Gloria.

CHAPTER SEVENTEEN:
Speaking with Rupert and Spending Time with Joey

It wasn't quite midnight by the time she reached the porch. Most of the lights were out on the block and the lights at the old Jefferson's house went off just as she arrived.

"Someone in there is about to go to bed," she mumbled as she looked in that direction. Gloria had noticed that the twins' lights in the basement were out which meant that they were probably sleeping. The lights were out in the living room, and the only light she saw in the house was the master bedroom, where she had laid her clothes.

Joey must be up there waiting for me to come home, she thought.

As she opened the front door and went in, she noticed that everything was quiet on the main floor but she heard a television on upstairs. It was either coming from the master bedroom or Stephanie's room. If everyone were in their room, she would be able to call Rupert without any disturbances. So far, no one in the house had even noticed that she had even come in, so she decided to go and talk in the kitchen, where it would be real private. She brought the bag into the kitchen with her just in case someone decided to start walking around and noticed the bag on the floor, and she left the light off as well. There was enough light coming from the back window.

As she went in, Gloria could still smell Stephanie's food aroma lingering in the air. She smiled as the aroma went up her nostrils, then made herself comfortable in the kitchen chair. She began rummaging through her purse for Rupert's private number. Once she found it, excitement went through her body. Chris was slowly disappearing from her mind. She was anxious to speak with Rupert. She made herself comfortable and grinned eagerly as she began punching in his number on the telephone and waited for him to pick up the phone on the other end. The phone rang three times before she heard his voice. The sound of him made her smile more.

"Hello, you have reached the most charismatic, world renowned, handsome and modest billionaire in the entire world; not to mention the best body and all around hell of a good guy, Rupert H. Hanley. The 'H' is for hello, lovely Gloria. How are you this night?" He then burst out with a happy, hearty laugh as if he had just heard a joke.

"The 'H' is for how you can be so full of energy so late at night?" she asked as she laughed.

"Well, that's an easy question, my beautiful lady. Because when it is almost hours before a child's birthday, he can't sleep. He's excited because he imagines opening up his presents and seeing the wonderful gifts and toys and all."

"Rupert, you didn't tell me today is your birthday, you slickster," she chastised him playfully.

"Well, my dear, it is true. I am a slickster, but it is not true, judge, that today is my birthday."

Gloria then sucked her teeth.

"Then what is this talk about a child and birthday and yadda yadda yadda?"

"Well, Gloria, I am the child and you are the birthday gift and I was looking forward to hearing from you, so I couldn't sleep or just sit around looking bored or tired. I've been on fire, anxiously waiting for your call. You do that to me, Gloria. You make me feel like a kid again. You make me feel so, so happy and drunk on life!" he said with excitement.

"Well, you do the same with me, Rupert. You make me feel special and needed, and you make me feel in ways that I can't explain because no one has ever brought those feelings out in me."

"Well, believe me, Gloria, the pleasure was all mine. I'm going over the quarterly reports concerning one of my hotels and looking at the profits. That is the best thing about being me—the profits." He laughed again.

"Well, I think that the best thing about being you is your sense of humor, style, charisma, your unpredictability and charm."

"Oh, you're only saying this because it's true," he joked, then laughed. "I knew there was a reason to stay up late for your call; to have my ego blown up more than it already was!"

Gloria's heart was aflutter for this man. "Do you think that it is too forward of me to you where you are?" she shyly asked.

"Well, would you think that it is too forward if I answered you?" he joked. "Oh, you!" she exclaimed.

"Well, I am in the white stretch heading to my resort in sunny Mexico. Well, actually, it is not sunny; it is night and it is Acapulco," he said nonchalantly.

"Oh my gosh, Rupert. I can't even afford this call!" she exclaimed in a panic.

"You don't have to worry about that, Gloria. That is why you have my personal line. It will be a local call when your bill comes," he assured her.

"Wow, Acapulco! You sound like you are right down the street. The call is crystal clear."

"It better be. I pay enough for it. Speaking of paying, how would you like to come down to Mexico with me?"

"Oh, gosh, Rupert, you know that I would love to, but I have the you-know-what tomorrow. Believe me, I would rather be in Acapulco than going to my father's funeral."

"Oh, Gloria, I am so sorry for that, but I wasn't talking about tomorrow. How 'bout when all of those matters have been taken care of and you are just hanging around being bored?"

"Then of course I would love to, Rupert. I would enjoy spending more time with you."

"Well then, we have another date," he said enthusiastically. "So, what did you do after I spoke to you earlier? Probably sat and ate up all the food on the table, huh?" Rupert was joking, sounding like a person catching another person with the hand in the cookie jar.

Boy, did Gloria really want to tell Rupert just how bad-tasting that catered food was, but she didn't want to look at a gift horse in the mouth. It wasn't his fault that the food was bad. She should tell him so he wouldn't waste his money on those caterers again. She thought about it but decided not to say anything after all. It's not the gift but it is the thought that counts.

"Well, the food went to good use. The rest went into the fridge. We even ate it at the bar."

"Huh?" Rupert asked. "We? Bar?"

"Oh, I'm sorry, Rupert. I need to explain. Some lady friends and I decided that after the burial tomorrow, we should have a big get-together to celebrate my daddy's life instead of mourning his death, so we went to the bar and started cooking and baking up a storm."

"Oh, Gloria, you could have told me. I could have had the caterers prepare the same food, enough for about a thousand people. It wouldn't have been a problem."

"No!" Gloria shouted quickly and loudly, which totally caught Rupert off guard.

"Whoa Gloria, what's wrong?" he asked, sounding very concerned.

"Nothing, Rupert. I didn't mean to sound like that. I apologize and appreciate your thinking of me. I just meant to say that it was something that we wanted to do ourselves, that's all."

"Oh, okay Gloria, I understand. That must've been pretty hard for you. Catering like that really takes some time to plan."

Gloria put her hand over her mouth, trying hard not to laugh.

"Well, we think that we did a pretty good job. We think that everyone should enjoy it."

"Well, that sounds nice that you did that. I commend you all."

"Thank you, and by the way. Matthew, Zoe and Stephanie said hello. They've been on highs ever since receiving the clothes. Teresa and Faye told me to tell you once again thank you for allowing them to pick out clothes, too."

"Gloria, it was my pleasure. I enjoyed making you and your friends happy."

"And my kids," Gloria added.

"Oh, oh yeah, your kids too. Speaking of them, how are they and how do they like their new clothes?" His question stunned Gloria. It was as if he didn't hear what she had just said.

"Rupert, I just told you that my kids and Stephanie said hello and that they've been on a high since receiving the clothes."

"Oh, I'm sorry, Gloria. I must've gotten distracted when you said that part. So anyway, what time will this get-together at the bar be?" Rupert changed the subject quickly and Gloria knew.

Gloria was still thinking about when he had become distracted when she had mentioned her kids and Stephanie. How was he able to hear the names of Faye and Teresa but not hear her when she mentioned the kids and Stephanie? Was it because when she said their names and said that they said hello, that he didn't remember the names as being her family? Maybe when she had said all the names, he had assumed that all the names had been friends. Maybe she was wrong and he really got distracted, but she soon forgot about it and answered his question.

"I figure that the get-together will be some time around two or three and it'll go on till I throw everyone out," she said, then chuckled.

"Well, I'll make sure that I speak to you some time tomorrow if that is okay with you."

"Oh, you don't need to ask me that. I just wish that I could give you more of my time, but right now, I can't," she said sadly.

"But Gloria, I really do understand. I'm patient. They say it is a virtue or something," he joked.

"Rupert, I want you to know that you have really been a blessing to me since you came into my life. You really are a special person. There's not too many of those anymore."

"Gloria, if you keep flattering me like this, I'm gonna make you my wife!"

"Oh, you!" she exclaimed laughing, but she noticed that he wasn't laughing back.

"Rupert, are you there?" she asked seriously.

"Oh, I'm here, Gloria. I haven't gone anywhere. I meant what I just said," he said seriously.

"Oh, Rupert, I don't know, I mean, you don't know how much, er, ah..." Gloria couldn't talk. All of a sudden, her throat swelled up.

"Gloria, I don't expect an answer from you now, nor do I wish to pressure you. I just want you to know how I feel. Like I said before, I am a patient man."

"Oh, Rupert, you sure know how to sweep a girl off her feet."

"Gloria, I am just being me."

"And that is what I love about you."

"Wow! That is what I want to hear. Thos gushy love words!" He then chuckled. "Listen, my dear lady, it is late and believe me, I can talk to you all night, oops! Its morning. I will talk to you sometime today, much later."

"Sounds good. You have a good, profitable day, okay?"

"I will try, and, Gloria, I will be thinking about you, and praying."

"Thank you, Rupert, Good night."

"And good night to you, Gloria." With that, Rupert hung up his line.

Gloria sat in the now-dark kitchen, absorbing what Rupert had just said. She smiled and fanned her face with her hands. She was flushed. When she arose from the chair, she realized that she wasn't just flushed, she was exhausted. She walked slowly out the kitchen then stopped by the basement door and listened. She didn't hear anything, so she walked through the living room to the stairs. Tired, she began walking up the stairs. Once she reached the hallway, she realized that the television was on in her room. The door was cracked open and she knew that Joey was in there because from the hallway she was able to see his huge toes wiggling on the bed. As she walked into the room, he saw her and jumped off the bed to greet her.

"Hey, Ma, how ya doing?" he asked with sparkling, loving eyes as he gave her a hug and kiss.

"Hey, kiddo, how are you?" she responded back as Joey smiled.

Joey was checking her out from head to toe, observing what she had on and vice versa.

"Hey, look at you! You look good. Have you grown since the last time that I seen you, even though it was just the other day?" she said jokingly. Gloria slapped him on his shoulder lightly.

"Oh, come on, Ma. You know that I look the same." He responded as he blushed.

"Everyone is knocked out?" she asked as she dropped her bag on the floor near one of the chairs.

"Well, I know that the twins conked out maybe about two or two and half hours ago. Stephanie tried to wait up for you to hear all about anything and everything, but her eyes were too heavy."

"Yeah, they all had a quite busy day," she recalled as she took off her sneakers and socks and plopped herself down on the bed, exhaling loudly in exhaustion.

"Talk about a busy day," he said smiling. "You've been going all day, I heard."

"Pretty much. Everything is done down at the bar. Believe me, I didn't expect to be back this early but we all worked as a team and got everything done pretty quickly."

"Well, I'm glad that you are home safely. I'm not used to hearing that you are out so late. Is this a New York thing?" he asked, then started chuckling and laid his head on his mother's lap. Gloria began rubbing the top of his head. He loved every bit of it.

"Oh, you..." she said as she chuckled back."So, tell me how your ride was coming in."

"Nothing special. Everything moved swiftly and the airplane left on time. I got out of the airport quickly and had no problem getting a taxi. I was going to stop by the bar but then I said to myself that I would only distract you. You know that I can't help in the kitchen. I can barely boil water!"

Gloria playfully popped him on the top of his head over his comment.

"It is not like I never tried to teach you. I don't know where you got the lack of cooking skills from because your father and I are both excellent cooks."

"Maybe we had an ancestor who didn't have any arms," he said jokingly.

"Your problem is that you are looking for that woman who is going to do all your cooking for you. I think that I spoiled you with that. You would come home from school with a cooked meal. None of that fast food junk, wasting money and stuff. Now that you are on your own, you live in those 'hole in the wall' burger or pizza joints. I don't like this fast food business that you are doing everyday. You need to eat a decent meal like the ones that I used to cook for you."

"I eat decently." Joey rolled his eyes. Gloria didn't see that but she heard him suck his teeth.

"Well, I don't consider an 'everything pizza' a decently made meal."

"And why not?" he asked as he pulled her leg. "It has all the major food groups in it: meat for protein, cheese for calcium and veggies. What's not to like?"

"Okay, Joey. Remember that your genes are half Stivic and you know what your daddy..."

"Father," Joey interjected.

"Father looks like now," Gloria finished her sentence.

Joey opened his eyes wide as he stared at the television and thought about what his mother had just said. He didn't respond, but Gloria knew he was thinking about it.

"So how is...?" Gloria was actually talking about Joey's ex-girlfriend. Gloria didn't say a name because Joey always had someone new in his life.

"Jennifer, Ma. Jennifer."

"Yeah, Jennifer. How is she?"

Joey hesitated before answering her.

"I don't know. I don't go out with her anymore." This comment made Gloria suck her teeth.

"Who would have guessed!" she said sarcastically.

Joey just chuckled. "She didn't have any goals." He said nonchalantly.

"Well, she must've had something because she lasted most of the summer. You had to know about this while you went out with her."

"I did but I dealt with it till it got on my nerves. When that happened, I had to let her go." Joey was talking as if it wasn't a big deal to him.

"So, who is the girl this week?"

Joey chuckled again. "No one. I decided to go single for the moment. I don't need the headache of breaking in a new girlfriend while I try to deal with Gramps being gone."

Joey's voice got real low when he said this.

"What you need is a good girlfriend who would be by your side comforting you instead of you handling it all by yourself."

"I'm fine," he responded, being abrupt with her.

"You always become so withdrawn when calamity comes, and you wanna be alone."

"I know, Ma," he uttered, sounding annoyed. "I like to be by myself when I am feeling moody."

"Joey, sometimes I think that you just don't like people."

"That's not true!" he uttered raising his voice, then turned on her lap to face her.

'I love you, the twins, Stephanie, my father and stepmom dearly."

"Oh, we know that, honey, but you don't care anyone else. Maybe you are afraid."

"I can take care of myself, Ma." He flexed his muscle to show her how big it was.

"Honey, I'm not talking about that kind of afraid. I mean that you are afraid to get very close with a friend or a girlfriend because you are afraid they might leave you."

When Gloria finished saying this, she left him with that to ponder.

"Oh, come on, Ma," he said, sounding annoyed. "I am not in the mood to hear criticism."

"Oh honey, you are getting it all wrong. I'm not criticizing you. I'm just trying to tell you that you can put down the boxing gloves and let your guard down. I want you happy. Boy, do I want you happy; and I wanna see you smile that handsome smile of yours, huh?"

"Look, Ma, I don't agree with what you said but I will be more mindful, all right?"

"That would make me feel much better...plus, I am ready to be a grandmother. I don't know how long I can keep up this beauty," she joked making him laugh.

"Ma, you'll be beautiful forever." He playfully slapped her on the legs. "Beauty or not, I still wanna be a granny."

"Yessss, ma," he said in a playfully annoyed voice. "That's enough about me; let's talk about you. How was your date with C.B.?" he said innocently.

"Oh, so you call him C.B. also?" she asked with surprise.

"Yeah, why?"

"Because I think that Stephanie and I are the only ones who don't."

"Well actually, Ma, it is only you, because she calls him that too."

"She never told me that. I just assumed that she..."

"Nope, she calls that that, too. She just called him Chris in front of you. I don't know."

"Well, does he have a nickname for you?" Joey hesitated at first before he answered.

"Yep, it's 'The Stiv,'" he chuckled as he hid his blush from his mom."Can you believe that I am a grown man teaching students and he still calls me 'The Stiv' when he sees me! I love that guy," he commented fondly as he smiled and shook his head.

"Don't tell me that Stephanie has one also!"

"Okay, I won't tell you," he said, then Gloria pinched him on his ear, making him chuckle and hit her hand. "Okay. Her name is 'Doe eyes.'"

"He gave the whole family nicknames, huh?"

"Yep. So, what's your nickname from him?" he asked as he turned and narrowed his eyes.

"Well, he hasn't given me one that I know of, but I sure wouldn't mind one from him."

"So does that mean that everything went well on the date?"

"Yes, Joey. It was a wonderful date. He was a gentleman and he treated me with respect. Joey, I want you to know that Chris loves me and is willing to spend the rest of his life with me. I already know that he loves you guys and you guys love him and your gramps loved him."

"And I guess that the only questions would be do you love him and are you are willing to spend the rest of your life with him, right?"

"That's right, honey, I've always loved him. He was my first love. Now we are both single and have a chance to have a life together, but someone else is in the picture now."

"Yes," he said as he smiled widely. "The world famous Rupert H. Hanley!" He screamed and started rolling back and forth on the bed, causing Gloria to laugh and look at him like he was bonkers. He jumped off the bed and went to the chair where his clothes were that she picked out for him and held them up against his body looking in the mirror and turning around, smiling at her.

"Oh, Ma, thank you for the clothes! They are wonderful. These are all the latest styles and these clothes are very expensive. I've tried them all on over and over again, and they are a perfect fit. I couldn't contain myself when I saw them."

Gloria was enjoying seeing Joey smile. He didn't do it much and it concerned her. Just seeing him happy and being joyful, looking like a delighted child, almost brought tears to her eyes.

"I'm glad that you like them."

"Oh, that's an understatement, Ma. I don't just like them. I love them. I've never had expensive designer clothes before."

Joey was heading back to the bed after putting the clothes back on the chair, then he lay back on Gloria's lap, looking at her sincerely.

"You know, Ma, I know that it hasn't been easy raising us on your own and a lot of times you went without things just so we could have, and I want you to know that I appreciate everything that you've done for me. You've given me a good life, a humble life, and I have always had clothes, nice clean clothes and shoes. I have never 'wanted' for anything because of you or desired anything that you couldn't give me, but it's nice to have the new clothes, though. I just want you to know that."

"Oh, honey, don't feel badly because I see you happy over something I couldn't give you. Just think of this as an early Christmas." She was rubbing his head again as she was able to feel the heat of excitement escape through his body. "It does my heart good to see my children overjoyed. I don't care how old you are."

For a few moments, both just stayed on the bed quietly. in their own thoughts, till Joey spoke. "So?" he said as he stared at the television.

"So what, honey?"

"So, what about this rich guy? How do you feel about him?"

Gloria looked up to the ceiling and smiled. "I like him a lot, not just because he is a billionaire. At my age now, I don't need much. Just some grandkids," she said as she pulled on his ear.

"Ma!" he yelled as he got the hint.

"Materialistic things don't do much for me, but they are nice to have, though. What I need is someone who is going to treat me nice and love and respect me and you guys because if he is in my life, he is going to be in yours also."

Joey nodded in agreement when she said this.

"So, your problem is that both of them treat you good, both are successful, both are respected and respectful, both are fun to be with and I heard that you find both attractive."

"Extremely."

"Well then, what does your heart say?"

"There are so many parties on the heart line lately that it is hard to make out all the voices. All parties are talking at once. Some parties are louder than the other. One minute, I think that my heart says Rupert, but after spending time with Chris, my heart is saying Chris. I really don't know, Joey. I told Chris that I need some more time because of the funeral and all. He respected me enough to understand my feelings. He told me to take my time in answering him but I'm going to tell him my decision after the funeral. Thank God that both don't know about the other."

"I agree," Joey said as he nodded.

"So, I heard that you got a good offer on the house. What side are you leaning towards?"

"I'm still right in the middle. New York 50%, Cali 50%. I just don't know, Joey. You know, I feel like I'm on a game show, and Bob Barker is the host."

Joey chuckled as he imagined his mother being on a game show in front of millions of people all staring at her, cheering her on.

"I can almost hear Bob Barker say, 'Gloria, you have ten seconds to choose. Either go back to Cali as a rich woman and enjoy an excellent life with a billionaire or lose all that money, stay in New York and work in real estate or your father's bar. Gloria, you can give both choices away for what's behind the mystery door. So, what do you choose, Gloria? The clock is ticking and you're almost out of time."

Gloria was even sounding like an enthusiastic charismatic host. Joey even clapped over her impersonation. "Joey, I just can't do it. Whatever I decide, someone is going to be hurt and I don't want either of them hurt, especially Chris."

Joey turned back to face his mother, who was looking very worried. She had her eyes going in all different directions and she was blinking rapidly. Joey wished that he could take her pain away but didn't know how and that was bothering him.

When Gloria saw Joey looking at her with concerned eyes, she smiled at him with that motherly, loving smile of assurance.

"Don't worry, Joey. I'll be just fine. If I stay in California or if I stay in New York, it won't matter because I'll still have you all. That's what's most important to me."

"Of course, Ma. Even if you decide to stay, I'll still keep in touch and let you know how I am."

"Joey, I would hate to leave you in California all alone," she said sadly, almost pitifully.

"Huh?" he said, looking shocked at her comment.

"Well, you'll be all alone while the twins and I are in New York. I would worry about you so much—if you are eating well, if you are happy. I wouldn't be able to check on you to see if you are okay."

When Gloria said this, Joey rose off his mother's lap and sat up straight on the bed, looking extremely serious.

"Ma, first of all I want you to know that I love you so very much. If I was dirt poor without a cent to my name and I had a choice to live with a rich family over you, I want you to know that without hesitation, I wouldn't leave your side, and I mean that. Now, that being said, I think that I need to remind you that I am a full grown adult—a man—a man who has moved out on his own. I have my own place and an extremely excellent job and I am happy, very happy, despite my up and down relationships. I am not a child anymore and I don't need my mommy worrying about me. It would be different if I was a woman, but a man does not need his mother looking out for him."

Joey lovingly took hold of his mother's hand and said very earnestly to her, "Ma, please, whatever you do or whatever decision you make, don't stay in Cali because I would be alone so far away. Ma, I may be alone because that's the way that I like it. Alone is one thing, but I am far from being lonely."

"Son, you don't understand. You are not a woman and you'll never be a mom. You don't know how we feel." Gloria was almost developing tears in her eyes.

"Ma, when I was a little boy and Grammy was alive, did she say the same to you?"

Gloria had to think about that for a moment. "She did," she said. "So did your gramps."

"But, Ma, it was like what I said earlier. You are a female. Family usually keeps a closer eye on females. Now, answer me this. When Ray was alive, how did y'all feel when 'The Mrs. Shaw' used to say sappy things to him like, 'You are my little boy' and, 'You won't be able to make it on your own without me'?" He was squeaking his voice and whining as he imitated Agnes. "And, 'If you love me, you would always stay close to me.' How did you guys feel?"

"Joey, it would drive us absolutely crazy!" Gloria responded angrily as she balled up her fists and gritted her teeth. "She wouldn't let him grow up, even after we were married."

"I remember you discussing her with him, saying how she always tried to manipulate him and make him feel incompetent or like a little boy who needed to be guided by her."

"That's true—she did that the way that she babied him. Boy! He hated it. He hated it with a passion, but he loved her dearly despite her ways. He knew that deep down someplace in that so-called heart of hers, she meant well for him. He was a successful professional still being coddled by his mother. If she had a choice, she would've kept him as a child forever. That mother hen wouldn't let that birdie fly away from the nest unless she was close by."

"Ma?"

"Yes, son?"

"Do you see any similarities in you two?"

Gloria began thinking about what her son had just said to her and what he just asked her. She hated the way Agnes was and Ray hated the way that she had treated him despite the fact that he was grown and with a family besides her. Gloria hated everything about Agnes and despite the fact that Ray was dead, this woman was still in her life, causing double the problems because she was kin to her twins. Gloria was wondering if she was turning into Agnes by being so possessive of Joey. Maybe Mike might have been right. She wasn't sure, but she knew that she didn't want to push Joey away from her. Maybe Joey was seeing something in her that was developing and he wanted to bring it to her attention. She had to admit that if she really thought about it, she would realize that Joey was right. She was being overly possessive.

After Gloria thought about it, she began nodding slowly as she looked ashamed. "Oh, Joey, I am so sorry. You are absolutely right. I do see the similarities. I'm going to try not to turn into Agnes, with your help, whether if I stay or if I leave. I will try to cut the apron strings. I don't mean to be possessive but it's just that..." "Ma, you don't have to explain," he said as he held his hands up to her. "I understand. There is no reason to be ashamed and feel uncomfortable for showing you your love for me. I just wanted you to see it now so you don't become a bitter old lady like The Mrs. Shaw, without a life and living with only memories of your child, or children, who tried to run from you and you just following behind, making their lives miserable, even though you could never do that to me or the rest of the family," he assured her.

Joey kissed Gloria's hand and lay back on her lap. Gloria resumed rubbing his head.

"So, son, if I do decide to stay here in New York, with the twins, will you come, too?"

"No Ma, I have a wonderful job in California. I've put New York behind me. I consider myself a Californian, through and through."

"I had a feeling you would say that, but it didn't hurt to ask."

Once again, the two became quiet for awhile as they watched television, until Joey mumbled something that Gloria couldn't understand, so she asked for him to repeat.

"I said are you ready for the funeral today?"

"Well, like I said earlier, the food is all ready and..."

"No Ma, I'm not talking about that. I'm talking about emotionally."

Gloria was quiet before she answered. "I guess I am, as ready as I ever will be. It is time to let Daddy, er, ah, your Grampa go and move on. I know for sure that that is what he would want. Not just for us to mope and always be sad. He would say something like, 'Listen here, you guys there. I don't want all the crying there for me, ah, so, shed a few tears there and stifle all that mopin' nonsense, geez!' she said in her Archie Bunker voice and dialect. Joey loved when she did her imitations.

"But I'm going to miss him, Joey. Very much, I'm going to miss him. Now, I don't have a mom or a dad and the family is very small and I don't have any brothers or sisters. I was spoiled, Joey, and you were right when you said about family keeping eye on their girls. Although I didn't appreciate it then or even understand it, I definitely understand it now. I would do anything to have him back right here and right now."

"Me too, Ma," he responded in an unhappy utterance.

Joey took hold of his mother's hand, kissed it, and then wrapped it around him for comfort.

Once again, Gloria and Joey became quiet, lost in their own thoughts and feeling the loss of a loved one. Ten minutes later, Gloria heard Stephanie's door open and she then came into Gloria's room, looking very sad.

"Sorry, guys, but I heard the television on and decided to come in. Is that okay?" Stephanie looked like she was on the verge of tears.

"Of course, honey." She had her hand out to her, motioning for her to come to her, which she did. Joey moved down towards Gloria's knees as Stephanie climbed into the king-size bed with her and silently wept. Strangely enough, after about five minutes, Gloria heard footsteps coming up the stairs, then through the bedroom door came Matthew and Zoe. They didn't say anything, but Gloria knew what they wanted. She motioned with her hand for them to come to her and they did. Stephanie was on Gloria's left, Zoe to Gloria's right, Joey by Stephanie's legs and Matthew by Zoe's legs. They all faced the television but no one was watching it. Gloria knew that they were all thinking about the funeral in just a few hours. Slowly, one by one, they fell asleep on the bed, no one moving and in the same position, all comforting one another.

CHAPTER EIGHTEEN:
Time to Say Goodbye to Daddy

Morning came quickly for the family. Everyone seemed to wake up at the same time, but everyone was reluctant to get up and move about. The morning hit the clan with the sun shining through the windows and the sounds of birds in the trees. The morning breeze felt comfortable as it circled its way through the room. It was the kind of morning to remind you that summer was still around, the kind of morning to say, 'Hey, go put your shorts on, and that tank top, and head for a picnic, barbecue or beach, even the nearest pool.' It wasn't the kind of morning to scream, 'Hey let's all go to a funeral,' but that's where they would be going, to put Archie Bunker to rest.

Slowly and reluctantly, one by one, they got up quietly, not saying a word, looking exactly the same way they did when they went to bed hours before. Zoe was the last member still in the bed snuggled up next to Gloria.

"Honey, you awake?"

"Uh huh," she said muffled behind her. "You ready to get up?"

"No, I wanna go back to sleep. That way, I wouldn't have to say good bye to Grampa."

"Come over here," she told Zoe. She climbed over Gloria and curled up in her bosom, almost in a fetal position as Gloria wrapped her arms around her for comfort. Zoe felt protected, like she was in heaven. She closed her eyes as Gloria's love encircled her.

"Honey, there's a time to laugh and there is a time to cry, there's a time that we die and there is a time we have to say goodbye. This is the time where you have to do all. It's only right. Daddy was there to say hello to you when you were minutes old. Now it's your time to say goodbye to him. I know that he is going to look down from heaven and have his heart touched by seeing you one more time, don't you think?"

"Uh huh." Zoe could barely speak through her sobs, which were starting again. Gloria started to hear them as Zoe sniffled and trembled slightly. Gloria started kissing her on her head.

"Oh honey, it's gonna be ok. We all must go on. He would want it that way."

"Oh, I know, Ma. I'm just going to miss him so," she cried as her voice cracked.

"I know you will, and he knows that, but don't you think that you should say it to him?"

"Uh huh, I do. And I will. Now I don't have any adult male figure in my life that I'm close to who isn't my brother," she said sadly.

"You don't need anyone else. Those two are the best adult male figures you can have."

"I guess you are right, Ma." Zoe then became quiet for a few seconds to think. Then she spoke again. "Well, I still have C.B."

When Gloria heard her say that, she quickly responded, "Yeah, and you have Mr. Hanley." Gloria wasn't ready for Zoe's response to that.

"Well..." Zoe said then hesitated. "I'll still have C.B. even if you get with Mr. Hanley. C.B., I know. Mr. Hanley is nice, but he's more for you."

Wow! This comment would've floored Gloria if she wasn't already lying down. Gloria was shocked and speechless, but she wanted to hear more from Zoe. When she recovered from the initial shock, she curiously asked her, "Zoe, if Mr. Hanley and I decided to become very serious, do you think that you would ever be able to accept him as part of the family?" Again, Gloria was surprised by Zoe's reaction and response.

"Ma, I wouldn't have a problem but would HE be able to accept US as part of HIS family. That is the question. Obviously, he loves you. There's no doubt in my mind about that, but could he be a stepparent the way Beth is with Joey? I truly doubt it. Sorry, Ma. Don't mean to hurt you, but it's only my opinion."

"Honey, what makes you think that?" Gloria asked with an embarrassed laugh.

"Mommy, anyone can see that he only has eyes for you and you only. Mommy, when he was here, he tuned everyone out and only focused on you. A bomb could've gone off but he wouldn't have noticed. He was too busy looking into your eyes." Zoe chuckled.

"Wow, Zoe. I didn't notice that," she said in surprise.

"Of course not, Ma! Cupid had shot you in the tush, too!" Zoe reached over Gloria and popped her on her butt a few times. Gloria playfully started to tickle her to really get her laughing. When they calmed down, Gloria continued speaking.

"So, how do Matthew and Stephanie feel? Do they feel the same way?"

"Ma, I can tell you this. The two just want you happy. We all like Mr. Hanley and think that he is a terribly nice man. Marriage material? We don't think so. He'll treat you like you deserve to be treated. He would probably even do things together with us as a family, but they also don't think that he'll make a good stepfather who would show us love and stuff. We all might be wrong but from first impressions, we don't think so."

Zoe's words were really making Gloria think. All of a sudden, it snapped back in her mind when she mentioned to Rupert earlier that her family had said hello and mentioned the clothes, but Rupert didn't even remember their names. Should she make a big deal over that or was it just a one-time mistake? He had said that he must've gotten distracted. That could happen to anyone. He did say that he was in a stretch limo going over some figures. It could happen to anyone. As she continued making excuses for Rupert, Stephanie yelled from the kitchen downstairs.

"Hey guys! Coffee is brewing and breakfast should be ready in about fifteen minutes!"

Voices from all over the house shouted back to her in acknowledgement.

Fifteen minutes later, everyone were down at the table getting ready to eat, except Gloria, who had gotten a telephone call from Chris to see if everyone was okay and if they needed anything. Immediately as she hung up the phone, it rang again. It was the attorney, Mr. Rabinowitz who was calling to say that he was going to try and make it over to the house some time that day to read the will. Gloria was fine with that. He said that he would also try his best to get to the wake or the burial or even the reception but he had just gotten back into town and had a lot of things to catch up on before he saw them. Gloria understood. After she finished talking to him, she began heading down the stairs to eat a little breakfast with the family.

Gloria didn't have time to think about what Zoe said earlier because she had gotten distracted by the phone calls. Now she had forgotten about what Zoe had said and began focusing on other things, like breakfast and the funeral, reception, the will, etc.

Once she made it downstairs to the table, Gloria noticed that everyone was sitting around the table waiting for her and they all looked like zombies, expressionless and in their own sad worlds. Heads were down and shoulders were slouched. Gloria knew that she had to do something to get them going, to start everyone's motor, so after she poured herself some coffee and everyone started passing food around and serving themselves, she began to speak.

"Well!" she exclaimed as she put a slight smile on her face. "Matthew, is your special thing that you have for Grampa ready?" She then took a gulp of her coffee. This seemed to perk him up a tad and she saw some life in his eyes as he began to speak.

"Yeah, it is all ready. Zoe helped me with some words that better described how I felt, so it sounds real good. I have something else planned, too, that everyone should like."

"Are you going to give us a little hint?" Stephanie asked as she put jelly on her bagel.

Matthew shook his head with a smile on his face. "Sorry, Stephanie. It's a surprise."

"But I know what it is. I know what it is!" Zoe sang in a teasing tune. "But I'm not telling!" Zoe's little teasing antics got everyone at the table laughing.

Now that was what Gloria wanted. Gloria wanted the mood lightened up. Now everyone was talking and moving around with energy.

Joey was eating some cereal and chomping on some bacon and toast. When he came up for air he began to speak to Gloria.

"So, Ma, anyone important on the phone?" After he said that, he tore back into the food as if he didn't eat it right then and there, it was going to run away from him.

"Well, Chris called. He told me to tell you guys, hello and that he will see you all later."

"Hi, C.B!" they all yelled and lifted their cutlery up in the air as if a goalie had just scored, then they immediately went back eating without skipping a beat. Gloria looked in amazement for a few seconds then continued as she shook her head and smiled.

"And Mr. Rabinowitz called and said that he would try to make it over here today to read the will. He just got back in town and had a lot of things to do before he had to see us."

Everyone nodded their head as they continued eating. They continued with their light conversation until breakfast was over.

As the inevitable quickly approached, the last-minute telephone calls and doorbell ringing rapidly came and went as the family prepared to finish getting dressed. The two men of the family were the first to be ready and sat in the living room watching the television till the three women were ready. They were watching the television but weren't really paying attention to what was on. Zoe was the next member of the family to make her way into the living room. She went and sat next to her big brother Joey on the couch. Stephanie was ready after Zoe. She went and sat in Archie's chair, next to Matthew, who was sitting in Edith's chair. A little while after that, Gloria was the last one to come down the stairs. As soon as she reached the bottom step and was about to head into the living room to sit on the couch next to Zoe, the telephone rang. Gloria then pivoted and went to answer the phone.

"Bunker residence," she said in a monotone voice. "Okay, thank you. Goodbye." When she was done, she hung up the phone lightly. She then exhaled deeply and sighed. Everyone turned to look at her with curious, sad eyes before she spoke.

"That was the funeral home. They called to say that the limousine is waiting. It's time."

Everyone looked at each other, no one moving, looking as if they were about to walk the long corridor to the electric chair for their execution. Gloria had to initiate the first move so she started to give orders to get things in motion.

"Matthew, honey, go and check and make sure the back door is locked. Zoe, do you have your little purse? If not, go get it. Stephanie, Joey, all ready?"

When she had told Matthew to check the back door, obediently, he stood up and headed for the kitchen to check. Zoe had forgotten her little purse, so she headed down to the basement to pick it up. She even decided to take a light shawl just in case it got breezy. Stephanie and Joey had nodded reluctantly that they were ready to go. Once Matthew and Zoe were back, Gloria opened up the door and one by one ,starting with Joey, they all headed towards the black limousine that was parked in the front. The chauffeur was a tall, blond female, about 26 years old, very pretty, dressed all in black–cap, too. She was standing by the limo door with her hands patiently folded down in front of her, waiting for the family to come out so she could open the door to let them in the back. Once the family all met on the porch, they waited for Gloria, who was the last to come out of the house, to lock the door, then they all headed towards the limo.

As they walked toward the limo, the pretty female chauffeur smiled and greeted the family with a polite nod of the head. They smiled back and said thank you as she opened up the limo door. Stephanie was the first to get in. Zoe was next to get in, then Gloria, Matthew and Joey. The two men sat on one side of the limo and the women sat on the opposite side, with Zoe in the middle with her head on her mother's shoulder. Gloria and Stephanie had put dark glasses on to cover their sad eyes.

All three women had little handkerchiefs in their hands to wipe away tears. The chauffeur closed the door and made her way back around to the driver's side.

Once inside, the chauffeur lowered the glass partition to ask the family if they were comfortable and ready to go. Everyone nodded except Gloria, who sat behind her, who said yes.

The limousine wasn't going far because the church and the funeral home were right next to each other, less than two miles away. For a beautiful Saturday morning, traffic was very light. It wasn't lunchtime yet, when it would be pretty busy, but it definitely was a 'hangout at a park' kind of day or even a 'let's go shopping at the mall' kind of day.

As the limousine began approaching the funeral home, Gloria started noticing a lot of people all dressed in black standing and talking in front of the building. Traffic was starting to build up there as cars lined up waiting to go into the parking lot.

"The funeral home must have more than one service going on," she said in passing. "Look at all the people."

The chauffeur heard Gloria's comment and decided to interject.

"Excuse me, ma'am, but there is only one service going on now and that is for Bunker."

Gloria had a look of surprise as she glanced at the family, who had the same expression on their faces.

"All these people are here for Daddy?" she commented in disbelief.

"People started arriving early. I guess that they knew it would be packed," the chauffeur replied.

"And here I thought that we would be early." As Gloria spoke, the rest of the family was speechless. No one could believe that all those people came to say good bye to Archie.

"No one has been inside except for the immediate family—not that many, though."

"Oh, that's just the funeral family," Gloria said causing the chauffeur to look curious.

"A funeral family, ma'am?" she asked.

"Yeah, the funeral family. We only see each other during funerals." After Gloria said this, the chauffeur nodded in understanding. "They are so far removed that they have to tell me how we are related. These people right here in the limo are truly his immediate family," Gloria exclaimed proudly.

"Well, I would personally like to give my condolences to you and your whole family. I knew him because I have eaten there tons of times. We were on a first-name basis."

"Thank you for your sympathy," Gloria said as the family said thank you also in low tones. "Do you mind if I ask you your name?"

"No, not at all. It's Billy. My real name is Belinda, but it didn't sound right to be called Belly." Everyone laughed slightly. "So they just call me Billy," she said pleasantly.

"Well, it's nice meeting you, Billy," Gloria said, then she started to introduce the family.

"Thank you. It's nice to meet you, too; unfortunately, we have to meet under these circumstances but I'm sure that we'll see more of each other since you'll probably take over where your dad left off, huh?"

Gloria began shaking her head. "I don't know what I am going to do concerning the bar. Right now, everything is at a standstill till I get all other matters taken care of first."

"Oh, I truly understand. He will be missed. Everybody knew Archie Bunker. He definitely was a-a-a..." She was looking for the right word to describe Archie.

"A character!" Gloria and the family replied in unison as they laughed, while Billy nodded.

"That's it! That's the perfect word to describe him," she said as she chuckled and made her approach to the front of the funeral home. Once she parked and radioed inside that the family had arrived, an usher soon came out and approached the limo.

"Are you all ready to go inside or would you like to wait a few minutes?" Billy asked.

The family looked at each other then at Gloria, letting her know that they were ready.

"Billy, we are ready to go inside," Gloria said as her voice cracked. Billy nodded and made her way out of the limo.

Gloria's body began tensing up and shaking as she felt all different kinds of emotions, but they were mostly sad. Zoe almost made it, keeping a stiff upper lip, but she started weeping on Gloria's shoulder. Gloria and Stephanie both touched her on her leg for comfort. Matthew and Joey both looked to be in a hypnotic daze.

Billy made her way around to the sidewalk and opened the limo door. Once she did that, she held out her hand to help Stephanie out, then Zoe, then Gloria. Zoe was so distraught that she couldn't let go of her mother. Matthew got out next, then went and put his arm around Gloria, then when Joey got out he went to Stephanie and held her. She leaned toward him, as she was losing it now herself. Gloria was trying to stay strong but it was hard for her. Even Joey and Matthew had tears in their eyes as they followed the usher. All nationalities, races, creed and genders, young and old, watched in sympathy and compassion as the family made their way into the funeral home.

Once inside, Gloria noticed that the corridor was filled with people, just like outside. She felt proud that all those people came to pay their last respects to her daddy.

As the usher respectfully led them to the huge room where Archie was laid out, no one wanted to go in. Zoe was still buried in Gloria's bosom, shaking her head in disbelief.

"Mommy, please! I can't do it! I can't go in there and see Grampa lying in a casket dead!" she cried loudly.

By this time, Matthew had made his way from around Gloria to Zoe to comfort her, and he let his tears come down hard.

"Come on, sis. It is going to be okay," he assured her in a comforting manner as he held her tightly. "We have to say goodbye and we'll do it together, you and I."

With that said, Zoe nodded and the two bravely began walking down the aisle together, holding on to each other for comfort. Before Gloria had a chance to catch up to Joey and Stephanie, they were already right behind the twins, holding on to each other.

"Oh Chris, I wish that you were here to comfort me and walk me down the aisle to my dad so I could lean on your shoulder while we cry together," she mumbled.

As Gloria watched the family move down the aisle, she noticed that the room was huge. It was the size of an auditorium. She was sure that there should be enough seats for everyone who was waiting outside in the hallway and outside down the block.

The room had a reddish purple carpet with the same colored chairs, but the sides of the chairs were like a gold colored metal. There were huge flowers in the room, lining the platform, which looked more like a stage. There were about thirty chairs up there. Gloria thought it was probably for the choir because there were mics and there was a stand for Reverend Felcher to speak from. Archie's casket was in the middle, below the stage, and it was open. The lighting was good as it shined right on him. She was quite a distance away but what she was able to see made him look heavenly. Gloria began walking slowly down the aisle toward the casket. Gloria did see some funeral family members that she barely recognized. She hadn't seen some of them since she was a teenager and the others since the passing of her mother, but nonetheless, somehow they were her family. They weren't sitting in front row. They sat in the second row on the right side from where Gloria and the family would be seated. Mike and Beth were there already. They had stood up as the twins made their approach. They were seated in the front row. Lionel and Jenny Jefferson sat in the two end seats next to Mike and Beth. They stood also as the family walked down the middle aisle. All four were in the end chairs on the left side of the auditorium near the window. They would greet Gloria and the family after they walked past the casket. They, just as the funeral family on the opposite side of the hall, all had a look of sadness and sympathy on their face.

Zoe and Matthew reached Archie's casket and just stared, not believing what they were seeing. Zoe was shaking her head with her head down as Matthew rubbed her back and whispered in her ear. Stephanie and Joey soon arrived right behind them, and then Gloria came up next to them. They all just held tightly to one another and stared at Archie at first, not saying a word.

The family commented that Archie looked very elegant in his gray suit and purple shirt and dark purple tie with gray slanted lines going through it. His hair was combed back and his face was nicely smooth and clean-shaven. His hands were folded on top of each other and wrapped around a cross. On his wrist he had a watch and on the other wrist, an I.D. bracelet and his wedding ring to Edith that he had never taken off. Archie even had a closed, serene smile on his face.

"Mommy," Zoe commented with surprise, "Grampa looks like he's napping."

"Yeah, he looks so very peaceful," Matthew added.

"He looks exactly how I last saw him—just resting on the bed," Stephanie responded as she nodded her head and smiled.

"He actually looks quite handsome, doesn't he, Ma?" replied Joey.

"Yes he does," she responded as she reached into the casket and touched Archie's hands.

"Hi Daddy," Gloria said almost in a child's voice. "I'm here, Daddy. The whole family and I are here right by your side and we want you to know that we love you and are always going to miss you. You may be gone here on earth but we'll always have you as a part of us. Your legacy will continue forever."

After Gloria said that, it became too much for her; she lost it and began crying uncontrollably and the family had to come around her to comfort her and calm her down. Gloria was so overwhelmed with grief that she nearly fainted. The family led her to the front row to sit down, and the usher was there quickly to give her a glass of water that Stephanie took from him, then gave to Gloria to drink. She began murmuring, "It is okay, Gloria. Just take it easy and relax."

Zoe ran to sit next to her and laid her head on her mother's shoulder and wrapped her hands around her arm. "It'll be fine, Ma," she assured her as she squeezed Gloria's arm.

"I'm sorry," Gloria said after drinking the water and regaining her composure. "I'm okay now." She nodded and smiled to Stephanie and the usher as she gave back the glass.

"Don't be sorry," said the usher, as Stephanie nodded then sat on the other side of Gloria. Matthew went and sat next to Zoe after he said hello to the Stivics and the Jeffersons. Joey was still talking with his father and stepmother. After that, he was going to greet the Jeffersons next. Both families were going to greet Gloria and the girls later when they were calm, even though the funeral family got up from their seat and relocated themselves behind Gloria and her family after they hugged and tried to comfort them.

Once everyone was seated, the usher, who was still standing by, asked if it would be okay to start allowing people to come in, but Gloria said not yet. Gloria then motioned for Matthew to come to her which he did quickly.

"Honey, do me a favor and find Chris, Faye, and Teresa and her family and bring them in first," she asked. Matthew nodded then left quickly, then she looked up to the usher.

The Life and Times of Gloria Bunker

"You can start allowing people to come in once my son comes back with some of our close personal friends." When Gloria said this, the usher nodded then stepped back. A few minutes later, Teresa and her three girls came walking down the aisle slowly, all close together, comforting one another. They went right up to the casket and stood for about a minute as Teresa bowed her head, followed by the three girls, then said a prayer as the girls nodded. When finished, Teresa and the girls crossed themselves with their hands. Teresa then kissed the crucifix that she had on around her neck, as she whispered lowly and sobbed. When they were done, they turned to greet Gloria and the family. Gloria noticed that Teresa's daughters were absolutely gorgeous in person. She said this to the girls once they came to greet her, making them bashfully and modestly smile. They all hugged Gloria, Stephanie and Zoe. They didn't hug Joey because he was now talking with the Jeffersons but would give their sympathies to him later. Next was Faye, who stood by the casket, lightly sobbing and occasionally shaking her head and dabbing at her eyes with her handkerchief for about a minute. Once done, she then turned and greeted the family with a hug and an it's-going-to-be-okay smile.

The next thing Gloria saw was Chris coming down the aisle with Matthew. Once in front, Matthew made a detour to sit next to Zoe but left a spot for Joey next to him. Chris stood in front by the casket for about a minute as he talked to Archie. Once done, he turned to greet Gloria and the girls. He then sat behind them, but he sat next to Faye and Faye sat next to Teresa and her girls. Gloria thought to herself that Chris looked very handsome in his black two piece suit, black tie and shirt with matching black shoes and socks.

Gloria noticed that the usher was staring at her, waiting patiently to see if it was okay to start letting the mourners in. She nodded and the usher nodded back then turned to head out of the auditorium/hall to start letting mourners come in. By this time, Joey was making his way to his place next to Matthew. He turned around to face Teresa and the girls and greeted them with a slight but friendly smile. He then greeted Faye and then greeted Chris with a hug and a pat. While this was going on, the Jeffersons got up and went to greet Gloria and the rest of the family, followed by the Stivics.

Once the usher reached where all of the mourners were standing as they waited to come in, he gave instructions for them to walk down the left aisle, view the body then greet the family, and after that, have a seat. Everyone started coming into the auditorium/hall, doing exactly what the usher asked.

It was all done in a decent and orderly fashion. Once the mourners came in, another usher came out to the front to keep the line moving, as that there were a lot of people attending. Gloria had glanced up at the stage and noticed that the choir members were making their way out wearing their long fancy robes in reddish purple with gold colored lining. Gloria thought that they looked like proud eagles with their chests stickling out majestically and proudly.

Gloria also watched as the mourners came in. Everyone had solemn faces and looked gloomy in their black attire. Some mourners she knew vaguely but most she didn't. They all stopped near Archie quickly then kept moving. They all greeted Gloria and the family and introduced themselves saying things like 'He would want you to go on' and 'He is in a better place' and 'Be strong, sister. It is gonna be all right.' As these words were spoken, Gloria nodded with a slight smile of appreciation. There were a lot of handshakes, hugs, nods and a lot of sympathy and sentiment.

The choir was soon singing and swaying from side to side to slow hymns as the room began filling up. When most of the people were seated, Reverend Felcher came out from the side door that led up behind the stage. He had the same robe on that the choir had on. He was tall, in his late sixties, but very handsome and distinguished. He had a full head of white hair which had only slightly receded in the temple area, and it was parted to the side and he was wearing glasses and a heavenly, peaceful smile. He began shaking hands in the front row, making his way to Gloria, who looked up to him smiling.

"Hello, Gloria. I haven't seen you in such a long time. I know that we've spoken on the phone but seeing you again is so much different than speaking on the telephone."

'Yes it is, Reverend, and likewise. I just wish that it didn't have to be this way."

"I know, Gloria," he said with a kind nod. "But only God knows why things happen the way they do. At least God had blessed your father with a successful business, long life and you as a daughter." He then looked at her family sitting around her. "And a generation that will continue long after we are gone." When he said that, Gloria nodded.

While the two talked, Reverend Felcher went over the service with Gloria and she also had to tell him about some last minute things concerning the service, even though every mourner received a pamphlet of the service with Archie's picture on the front. She wanted the reverend to mention that there was going to be a reception at the bar after the burial, around two-thirty or three. He said that he would mention it at the beginning of the service and at the end, just to remind everyone. Once they finished their brief talk, he hugged her, then turned to be escorted to the pulpit by an usher who was standing nearby.

The service was moving by smoothly, elaborately and impressively for Gloria. When the choir sang, she bopped her leg with her hand or she nodded to the beat every now and then, dabbing at her eyes. She also patted

Stephanie on her leg and smiled at her to show her some encouragement and support, and she kissed Zoe on the head. Zoe was still glued to her mother for comfort as she continued to weep close to her bosom. Occasionally Gloria glanced at Matthew and Joey, then smiled and gave a nod or a wink just to let them know that everything was going to be fine. They responded likewise.

When Reverend Felcher started preaching, Gloria thought that he was excellent for his age. The spirit of God was really moving through him. There were a lot of 'hallelujahs' and 'amens' throughout the whole room and even an occasional roar of laughter when he said something funny, but mostly he spoke so charismatically that he could have brought the angels down from heaven above and had them hover over him and rejoice. Gloria thought that Rupert could give him a run for his money when it came to getting the Holy Ghost. This caused Gloria to chuckle and nod. This caused Stephanie to look to her, thinking that she was just chuckling over something he had said.

Time passed by and the choir was singing again. When they finished, Reverend Felcher said that there would be eulogies from the family. Stephanie was the first. She read two pages that she had written herself. Joey was after Stephanie. After Joey, it was time for Zoe to say something. Stephanie asked Zoe if she was up to do her eulogy for her grandfather and Zoe nodded yes. Stephanie gave her a nod of encouragement. So did Gloria. Zoe sat up straight, dabbed at her eyes then exhaled deeply. She stood up, fixed her dress then headed to the front in the middle and began speaking about this amazing person who she had known as Grampa. She did sob some, but she spoke so clearly and intelligently that it made Gloria proud. When she finished, she turned and looked at her grandfather, touched his hands and said that she loved him. After that, she came and sat back down next to her mother. Matthew was the next member of the family to get up to do his eulogy. He walked to the same spot where Zoe had stood and took out his two sheets of paper. He sounded eloquent, almost as if he wasn't reading; he never stuttered, muttered or mumbled once. When he was done, Gloria thought that Matthew was going to come back and sit down but instead he turned and looked up to the choir who had been seated but stood up when he cued them. He then casually walked over to the organ as the family looked on with surprise. The only one who didn't look surprised was Zoe, who leaned over towards her mother's ear.

"See, Ma. I told you that I knew what he was going to do," she said, very satisfied.

As Matthew made his way toward the choir then to the organ, the choir kept their eyes on him at all times. Gloria was watching with a very puzzled look on her face, wondering what he was up to and about to do. Once he got comfortable, he nodded to the choir. He then nodded to the lead singer, who nodded back to him with a smile on her face. She then began ad-libbing with her song for a few seconds. After she held her last note for a long time, Matthew began playing the organ with a musical piece that he had written. It was absolutely beautiful and heavenly. The family still couldn't believe what he was doing. Gloria leaned over to Zoe with a proud smile.

"Zoe, when did he have the time to do this?" she asked with her mouth opened, still looking at Matthew.

"He practiced downstairs in the basement playing by ear this song that came to his head that he thought would be appropriate for Grampa. You couldn't hear him playing it because he had the headsets on. He said that the angels gave him the song, words and melody and he learned it like in ten minutes."

"But honey, how come the choir is singing this song like they've been singing it for years?" she asked in utter awe.

"Easy." Zoe replied nonchalantly. "Unbeknownst to you, as a surprise, he had gotten in contact with Reverend Felcher's director of the choir, who has a computer which holds enough bytes for him to receive an email song from Matthew. Matthew emailed it to him and the choir has been practicing since the day we got here. Reverend Felcher and the director said that they would keep it as a surprise for you. They communicated via computer but when you went out yesterday they talked on the phone."

"How utterly sneaky of you guys," Gloria commented as she nodded to the beat of the music. "But I must admit that this is a pleasant surprise."

"Wow, Gloria. Look at Matthew play that organ!" Stephanie commented with surprise.

Matthew sang along with the choir and played the organ as if he had done this before.

"What is amazing about it is the fact that he never had any schooling in it and can play many other instruments by ear, too," Gloria said proudly. "And he can sing!"

When Matthew finished and the choir finished perfectly on time with him, he walked back over to the casket to the sound of loud applause and touched Archie's hand and leaned over towards him.

"I hope you enjoyed that, Grampa. That's from me to you."

Matthew's voice cracked as he hurried back to his seat while getting hugs and praise from the family. Finally, it was Gloria's turn to get up and speak. She also dabbed at her eyes and exhaled hard before she stood up.

As she walked to the front middle of the auditorium/hall, standing next to the casket, she scanned the whole room and saw all the seats filled, plus people standing up against the walls, even near the door.

"Well," she said as she exhaled again. "First, I wanna thank each and every one of you for coming today. To be honest with you all, none of us ever imagined that so many people cared enough for my father to come and bid farewell. We thought maybe about twenty people would show up. My gosh, this place is packed!" she exclaimed with an animated gesture that made everyone chuckle. "Despite how my daddy was, you all showed up anyway. You guys are absolutely nuts!" This comment got everyone escalating from chuckling to straight out laughing.

"Yes, Daddy was bigoted; yes, he was intolerable and yes, he was opinionated, always having something to say, but that's what we all loved about him. You either hated to love him or you loved to hate him, but one thing that he did do and that was keep you all on your toes. You all knew him as Archie Bunker, businessman, but we knew him as Grampa, Uncle and Daddy. He was a very caring, loving man who would do anything for his family, whether they liked it or not. I'm going to miss fighting with him and arguing with him and hugging and kissing him and twisting his ear when he ticked me off," Gloria said as the mourners began chuckling again. "I didn't just lose a daddy. I lost a personal dear friend." Gloria then turned towards the casket and touched him on the hand again. "You will always be my daddy and I will always be your little goil."

Gloria then smiled as the tears came down, then she went and sat down, being comforted by the family. Reverend Felcher asked if there were any other people who wanted to say a few words about Archie. People raised their hands, but before he started to call people up, he told everyone since there were a lot of people, they would have to talk quickly, but first, the choir would do another song.

When the choir began singing again, Gloria felt a hand on her shoulder. It was Faye, who whispered in her ear.

"Gloria, Teresa, the girls and I will be back. We're going to set up at the restaurant."

Gloria put her hand atop Faye's hand, nodded and said thank you. Once they left, the choir was almost done with their song. After that, people started coming up to say a few words. Everything was still moving quickly and smoothly, sticking exactly to the service program. Time was passing and all the people who wanted so say something had their opportunity. Last but definitely not least was Reverend Felcher, who wanted to say a few words about Archie. When he was done, the choir sang. Reverend Felcher had closing words then had everyone stand up and join hands to join in a prayer, then ended the service. Once done, he mentioned again about the reception after the burial, which would take place at Elmhurstdale Cemetery, about four miles away.

The choir continued singing as the family was led out the front and back into the limousine, where Billy was waiting for them.

They were placed into the limo as they waited for the casket to be wheeled to the hearse. People filed out of the funeral home quickly to get to their cars so they could follow behind the hearse and the limo.

CHAPTER NINTEEN:
Off to the Cemetery

Once the casket was loaded into the hearse, the precession started. Right behind Gloria and the family was the Jeffersons limousine. Gloria was happy to learn through Joey that yesterday when Lionel was able to speak to Mike on the phone, he volunteered to pick them up in the limo and take them to the funeral then after the whole evening was over, bring them back to their hotel so they didn't have to spend money on a taxi or public transportation. Gloria had offered Chris to ride with her in the limo but he had to pass, since he had brought some people along in his car who didn't have transportation. She had looked around for Iggy inside but couldn't spot him. She was hoping that he'd come to the burial and/or the reception after. For some reason her mind went to the neighbors next door. Out of everyone who introduced themselves to her, not one person mentioned that they were Archie's neighbor. If Archie had come out of that house a few times like Stephanie had said, they had to be at least acquaintances of his. She was wondering why they hadn't come or at least sent a card or something. She also began thinking about Faye and Teresa and her girls. She was hoping that everything was running smoothly for them at the restaurant and that they would get back in enough time for the burial. They've been gone for a long time now, but she was sure that everything was fine. Gloria then started thinking about Rupert, her big strong Rupert. She was wondering what he was doing. She also started wishing that he was there next to her with his arms around her and comforting her saying, 'Don't worry Gloria. I'm here to protect you. You'll never have to worry about anything ever again.' But then she realized that that would be a huge problem because Chris was there, too. What was she going to do? She had two lovers who could never find out about each other.

"Why can't I make up my mind t who I want to spend my time and life with?" she asked herself. "Yes, I did love Chris decades ago. Do I wanna get back with him just so the guilty feelings that I once had can be gone? Do I wanna get with Rupert because he can give me a lavish lifestyle?"

Gloria had promised herself that she wouldn't bombard herself with these questions because it wasn't important at the moment. She wanted her mind to be totally focused on her father and that alone, so she began blocking all of that out of her thoughts.

As the limousine approached the cemetery, Gloria noticed a lot of taxis inside the gate and outside, lining the sidewalk. Gloria was wondering what was going on. Once the limo pulled onto the property and made its way to the burial plot, she noticed that the drivers of the taxis all got out as the limo passed and started beeping their horns.

"Wow! They're so noisy that they could wake the dead!" Gloria exclaimed. Looking through the rearview mirror, Billy responded.

"I think that the noise is for you."

"For me?" she asked with surprise.

"Well, actually for Archie," Billy corrected.

And sure enough, Billy was right, because one of the closest taxis to the burial plot was Kenny Reed, the driver who drove her and the twins from the airport to the house.

As the limo approached, he got out of the taxi and began beeping his horn like the other taxis.. He wasn't dressed in black, probably because he was suppose to be working but decided to come and give his respects, then get back to work. He stood where he was till the limo stopped then waited for the family to get out, which took a few minutes because they were setting up the casket to be lowered into the ground. Once that was completed and everyone made their way to the seats, he nodded and smiled to her and the family. Gloria walked over to him with a smile and extended her hands to him, then leaned to him to give him a kiss, which made him blush through his brown skin.

"Kenny, you remembered and kept your promise. Thank you for coming."

"Yep, I'm a man of my word. If I say something or if I make a promise, you can best believe that I am going to do it."

"Well, it is real good to see you again. I really do appreciate it."

"You are welcome," he responded kindly as he continued smiling at her.

"Please," she said as she looked towards the burial site, "why don't you come closer? You are more than welcome."

"Well, that is nice of you but I am actually on the clock, plus I'm not dressed for it," he responded bashfully.

"Oh, I don't care about that," she said as she waved the comment away. "It is the fact that you came. I wouldn't have cared if you came in shorts, t-shirts and flip flops; besides, Daddy never was really into shirts and suits, anyway."

"Thank you though, really, but I can't. I can only stay for a few more minutes, anyway. Time is money, that's what they say." Kenny began glancing at his watch.

"Well, listen, there is going to be a reception at the bar right after the burial. Relay the message to all the guys. If you can, which I hope, stop by. It should start," Gloria glanced at her watch, "about two, two-thirty, three o'clock."

"So, you decided to stay and keep the bar open after all, huh?" he asked as he nodded his head in a I-told-you-so manner, but Gloria shook her head.

"Sorry Kenny. I still haven't decided yet. I just decided to have this big reception just in case Archie Bunker's Place does close for good. I want it to go out with a blast—you know, something that everyone will remember."

"Well, I think that's a great idea. I'll try my best to stop by, even if it's only for a moment. I'll definitely relay that message to everyone. I'm sure they will come.

"Well then, I'll see you later," Gloria said as she nodded to him. "Yes ma'am."

With that, Gloria turned and headed toward the family, who had stopped to wait for her as she talked. Once she got back with them, they all walked across the grass together and stood around the gravesite. Gloria had noticed something different about the size of the crowd. Back at the funeral home, the place was packed but only about half came to the burial site, but there still were a lot of people, not counting all of the taxi drivers who lined the path all the way out to the front of the cemetery.

When the burial service finally started, Reverend Felcher said a few words from the Bible while mourners stood around looking sad and weeping, shoulders slouched and heads down. When he finished, he led everyone in the Lord's Prayer. They joined in but spoke very low. When they finished, one by one, Gloria and the family took a long stemmed flower and waited for the casket to be lowered into the ground. When it was, Gloria and the family dropped the flowers on top of it. They then stood around in silence as the casket was covered with soil.

As the hole began to fill up, Gloria glanced around at the family. They seemed to be holding up well. Zoe, although puffy-eyed, hadn't clung to her since the limo ride. Gloria figured that Zoe had finally accepted the fact that her grampa was gone or either she had thoroughly exhausted all of the energy that she had that was stored up for this very day. Stephanie was standing next to Gloria and she occasionally took hold of her hand, then when Gloria looked at her, Stephanie smiled.

"Now Uncle Archie is really with Aunt Edith," she replied sadly as her voice cracked.

"Yeah," Gloria added as she stared at the pile of dirt that was piling up. "He's over her protecting her."

Matthew just stared at the mound of dirt, looking hypnotized as he had his hands folded in front of him, and Joey was standing next to his father Mike, who had his arm around him and was talking in his ear. Joey just nodded as he rubbed at his nose a few times. Gloria spotted Faye, Teresa and the girls, who were in the crowd. She tried to get their attention but they had their heads down in their own thoughts. Finally, she was able to spot Iggy, who was on the opposite side of her, facing her, but he was all the way in the back, to the side near the pathway, out of everyone's way. He had a suit on, too, with his head slightly down and his hands folded in front of him like Matthew. Gloria was wondering how he was able to hold his own hand with those muscles bulging out of his arms. Gloria thought that if he bent over any lower, he would burst out of the suit like the Incredible Hulk. He made her smile because she was happy to see him even though he reminded her of an iguana dressed in black and on steroids. There was someone else approaching that Gloria had seen as she was looking through the crowd. This person walked the pathway in his black suit then onto the grass, through the crowd and was heading in her direction slowly. He wasn't actually looking at her, she knew that for sure. He was looking at Stephanie. She didn't see it because she was looking at the dirt pile up. Gloria gave Stephanie a slight nudge, then when Stephanie looked up, Gloria whispered as she leaned toward her.

"Hey Stephanie, there's Jerry. He's headed this way."

When Gloria said that, Stephanie's demeanor instantly changed. She started looking around rapidly and moving her neck as if it was trying to balance the head correctly on top of her neck. When she finally spotted him, Gloria noticed that she instantly looked relaxed as she smiled and her eyes glittered.

Gloria nodded slightly at Stephanie ,but she didn't see her do it. Gloria was thinking, "I knew it! I knew it! Looking at those twinkles in her eyes gives her away. Why doesn't she just tell me that she has eyes for him? What is up with her? She is grown. She doesn't have to hide it like she is trying to do, not fooling anyone."

She did ask Stephanie a question, though, as they both watched him slowly work his way through the crowd towards them.

"Stephanie, I didn't know that Jerry was going to be here. Why didn't you tell me?" As if she didn't know. Gloria also thought to herself, *"I wonder if he is going to kiss her in front of me and give himself away."* She wanted to chuckle but didn't want to give herself away.

"Gloria, I had no idea that he was coming. What a surprise!" she said sincerely.

"That's sweet of him to come. I wonder if other agents would come to their performer's family funeral," Gloria said as she looked at Stephanie through the corners of her eye.

"Well, he's just that type of guy, I guess."

"You know something? He sure is. A very special guy, huh?" Gloria was really laying it on. If Stephanie caught on, she didn't acknowledge it. She didn't even answer Gloria when she asked the question. It was good for her because he was approaching them.

Jerry Foreman was a handsome 36 year old male. He was thin and stood about five feet eight inches tall. He had black hair which was cut close by the ears and full on the top, like a Guido-Italian style. His skin was a dark ivory complexion, like he might have Latino mixed in his genes. He had pencil thin eyebrows which were naturally arched like a cat's, long eyelashes and eyes the color of marbles. He wore a mustache which above his 'O'-shaped, full, kissable lips, the kind that girls go crazy for, and that at the present moment was in a slight smile as he approached Stephanie closer.

Once he got to a certain distance from her, he became reluctant, as if he didn't know if he should draw closer or just stay where he was. SInce it was a surprise visit, he really didn't know what Stephanie would want him to do. When Gloria saw him stop, she leaned over to Stephanie, who was just staring at him, pretending now that he was only an acquaintance that decided to come.

"Why don't you motion for him to come stand closer to you?" Gloria asked.

"Do you think that I should?" she asked nervously. Gloria was surprised by her reaction.

"Why not, Stephanie? Is he going to turn into a hideous monster or something?"

Stephanie chuckled but more in an embarrassed kind of way.

"Well, I was thinking that maybe, ah, er, actually…Yeah, why not?"

Once she was able to get his attention, she motioned for him, but the way she did it made it look like she was telling him that the coast was clear for him to sneak up into her room. Gloria was getting a kick out of the way they were acting. No one else caught on but her. She was wondering what was going on in both of their heads at that moment. What was he going to do? What was he going to say and how was he going to greet her? That is what Gloria was waiting to see. She also was going to keep an eye on Stephanie, too, to see how she was going to act.

Finally Jerry made his way to Stephanie. Gloria noticed that she was happy but was acting uncomfortable. He walked past her and went to Gloria and gave her a hug.

"Hello Gloria," he said in a low and sincere voice. "I'm so sorry."

"Thank you, Jerry," Gloria replied. "And thanks for coming."

Jerry nodded with a slight smile then worked his way down the line, hugging Zoe and shaking the hands of her brothers. When he was done, he walked back over to Stephanie.

The Life and Times of Gloria Bunker

Watch, Gloria. Keep an eye on them, she said to herself.

Once he reached Stephanie, Jerry hugged her then rubbed her back.

Hmm, Gloria thought. *The rubbing of the back; he didn't do that with me and Zoe.*

Jerry then held her hand and Stephanie began looking around nervously but he was not sensing it or either he didn't care.

Oh, he's giving himself away." Gloria sang in her mind.

"How are you holding up? Are you okay?" he asked, still in a low and caring voice, much different than when he talked to the rest of the family. When Stephanie nodded with a nervous smile, he was still holding her hands. He let one loose slowly, swung around to her side holding the other, then let go and stared with her at the mound of dirt getting higher. If that wasn't enough to give it all away, he put his left hand around her waist and brought her closer to him, then when he realized what he was doing, he let go of her quickly as if she was a porcupine who had or was just about to stick him.

Bingo! Gloria exclaimed to herself with a slight nod and a smirk on her face. *You can fool some of the people some of the time...*

Very slowly, people started to leave. The service was over once the family put the flowers on top of the casket after it was in the ground. Gloria began walking away and left Jerry whispering to Stephanie. Once she moved, all the rest of people began leaving. People began making their way over to her and the family to say a quick word or two.

Gloria was patient with everyone and showed kindness to each person who came up to greet her. Meanwhile, the rest of the family began breaking up and going into other groups who were greeting them. Zoe was talking with Teresa's girls, Teresa and Faye were talking to the Jeffersons, Chris and Iggy were talking to a group of guys, but they were actually waiting to be able to greet Gloria, Matthew was talking to Reverend Felcher, who was still there, and Joey was talking with his father and stepmom. Even though she was courteous and gracious to everyone there, her face kept turning back to where her mother and now daddy were laid with pounds and pounds of dirt on top of them, never to see the light of the day again. Part of her had died with them and been buried. She wondered to herself if she would ever be the same again. Who would she call when things got too rough, who would she argue with now that her daddy was gone? She'd never hear again 'my little goil' or 'hey little goil.' All she had now were photo albums and memoirs and video-tapes that she could relive over and over again. Part of her wanted to climb in the hole with them but another part of her, a big part, told her that she had to move on. She had to be strong, if not for her, for the family she loved.

Once the crowd and Reverend Felcher left, the empty seats, Gloria and the family were the only ones still there, staring at the pile of dirt. As the family headed toward the limousine, Gloria still stood almost frozen in her spot, facing the pile of dirt.

"Hey, Ma, are you comin'?" yelled Joey, who was the last family member about to get into the limousine, standing next to Billy, who he had been chatting with a few moments.

Gloria finally but reluctantly looked towards the limo then looked towards her mom and daddy. Gloria wanted to stand near them all day, just staring at them, but she knew that she had to go.

"Sorry, Mommy and Daddy. I gotta go now. At least now, you all are complete. Mom won't have to be lonely anymore. You two have a lot to catch up on. Me? Well, I have to go and be with my family. I will never forget ya's, ever. And I will take a little bit of ya's wherever I go. Be happy," Gloria then began wiping away the tears from her eyes and sniffled. "And I'll always love you." Gloria turned and began walking away, then stopped. She looked back one more time, smiled a slight smile, blew a kiss and waved. "Goodbye Mommy and Daddy." Then she headed to the limousine, not looking back again. She was met by Joey, who smiled at her, then helped her into the limousine.

CHAPTER TWENTY:
Eye-opening Conversation on the Way to the Bar

Once the limousine started heading out of the cemetery, Gloria looked at the family and she noticed that they looked absolutely drained—drained of emotions, drained of energy and drained of tears, just like earlier when they were sitting around the dining room table. Gloria thought that she should say something to get everyone's blood pumping through their system. They all needed to be revived.

"Well then," she said with a voice that cracked at first but got better as she continued to talk. "I don't know about you guys but I am absolutely starved!" She was sounding very emotional as she spoke. "I can't wait and see how nice the setup is at the bar. You know that Faye, Teresa and the girls went back to the bar and set everything up so we wouldn't have to rush getting there. They've really been a great help." She got a slight reaction from everyone but not much; just some slight smiles and nods. Gloria wasn't going to give up that easily.

Gloria then patted Zoe on the knee to get her attention.

"So honey, what did you think of Teresa's daughters? I saw you chatting up a storm with them," This comment put a little spark in Zoe's light bulb.

"Oh Ma, they were so sweet and caring. They complimented me on my looks, saying that I was pretty and how sorry they were about Grampa, you know. Stuff like that. They invited me over their place once they move but I told them that we might be going back to California. I told them that if we don't move, I would love to."

Zoe quickly looked at Matthew then back to Gloria and smiled.

"Hey, Ma, I don't know but I think that Matthew liked them, too. You should've seen how he was staring at them," she said in a teasing manner.

Matthew instantly started blushing, showing his Miami tan. He smiled and waved Zoe off while everyone ooohed and aahed at him.

"No, I wasn't. Don't start anything, Zoe," he ordered as he cut his eyes at her.

"Ma, I was watching," she added as if Gloria was a reporter and Zoe was a witness to an incident. "I saw the girls go over to him and tell him how beautifully he played the organ. By the way, you were great and you sang great, too," she added as she quickly turned to him then went back to Gloria. "Well, he instantly blushed like he is doing right now and he only smiled and nodded. When they walked away, he was drawn to them like Wimpy to a hamburger." As Zoe teased, everyone in the limousine started laughing.

"Aah phooey!" Matthew exclaimed, still blushing, as he waved Zoe off again.

"Oh honey, don't be bashful. Teresa's daughters are beautiful. There's nothing wrong with liking them," Gloria assured him.

"Yeah, there's nothing wrong with liking them. Just ask your big brother," Stephanie added, causing all the attention to switch from Matthew to Joey, who perked up and started looking very guilty. "I caught him, too, checking out Teresa's older daughter. I might be wrong, but if I'm lying why is he redder than Conan O'Brien's hair?" Stephanie caused everyone to start oohing and aahing as he waved everyone away while he smiled nervously, then he started nodding.

"Yeah, it is true. I was staring. I'm not going to lie. The girls are very pretty, especially the oldest one." He then looked toward Billy and mumbled under his breath, but Gloria was able to understand because she was looking at him. "But so is the chauffeur."

Gloria was so tempted to put Stephanie on the spot concerning her relationship with Jerry, like she had just done with Joey. It would be so easy. Just spit it out and see what Stephanie would say. She was going to confront her about it anyway so why not now.

The mood had lightened up and everyone was smiling, so why not just go for it? She started thinking that maybe she should do it in private, but then she started thinking that it was no big deal. He was a handsome man, not Quasimodo. She decided to go for it and tease her the same way that Stephanie teased Joey. Gloria waited for Stephanie's teasing with Joey to calm down then she jumped in without missing a beat.

"So what about you, Stephanie?" Gloria sang teasingly. "What is going on with you and Jerry? When she asked this playfully, Stephanie turned two shades redder than Joey.

"W-w-whatcha mean?" Stephanie asked nervously, which only caused everyone to laugh and tease her as she looked around the limousine in a confused manner.

"Oh come on, Stephanie. Stevie Wonder can see that Jerry has eyes for you and you for him. What's up?" Gloria was smiling at her suspiciously. "Aah, it ain't so fun when the rabbit's got the gun, huh, Stephanie?" Gloria continued teasing as she poked Stephanie.

"I don't know what you are talking about, Gloria!" Stephanie's voice went a few octaves higher, like she had sucked in helium, which only made everyone laugh more.

"Look girl, if you are going to make this difficult, I can play along, too. The way he held your hand, the way that you two look at each other when you are together. Girl, he put his hand around your waist and brought you close to him, the way you yell at him on the phone—spit it out, girl! You're not fooling anybody!" Gloria was sounding like a lawyer cross-examining a witness on the stand in court.

Stephanie hung her mouth open as she moved her eyes around at everyone in the limousine, as if she had done something wrong and had gotten caught.

"I-I-I..." was all that she was able to say as she still tried to deny it.

"Tell her, Stephanie," Joey said, trying to encourage her.

"Tell her what, Joey?!" she responded nervously as she smiled and opened her eyes wide. Joey sucked his teeth then waved her away. Gloria was loving this. She wasn't the only one. Matthew and Zoe had big grins on their faces as they teased her playfully.

"He's my agent, that's all. We are friends, okay? Now stop!" Stephanie couldn't help it; she burst out laughing, which gave her away as the oohs and aahs just got louder.

"Look Stephanie, I'm tired of playing this game because guilty is written all over your face. That man is your boyfriend." When Gloria finally said this, Stephanie gasped in denial. "You can gasp and look surprised all you want. Don't try it, girl. Like I said, Jerry is your boyfriend and he has been your boyfriend for some time now."

Stephanie tried to protest but Gloria put her hand up to interrupt her. "Now, since we know he is your boyfriend, the next question is why don't you want your family to know? That is one thing that I cannot figure out. Jerry is a handsome and intelligent man. You should shout it from the roof tops!"

"Come on, Gloria," she said with a serious straight face, really not wanting to talk.

"No. You come on, girl. What is there that I don't see that makes you wanna keep this man a secret? Is he a caped crusader? In the morning, he is a mild mannered promoter but in the darkness of night he prowls the streets looking for bad guys or something?" As Gloria joked and made her voice sound like an announcer for a television promo, the family laughed. As Gloria continued she became more animated.

"Look! Up in the sky! It's a bird! No, it is a plane! No, it-it-it is Promoter man!" Gloria announced in a deep theatrical voice.

"How about this one, guys?" Stephanie added enthusiastically, causing all of the attention to shift from Gloria to her. "Look up in the sky! It is a bird! No, it is a plane! No, it-it-it is a married man!" Stephanie also announced in a very deep voice, then she started laughing more as she looked at everyone's jaws that dropped to their laps and eyes all bulged out and went around the limo. Everyone was speechless.

"Oh my gosh, drama!" Zoe exclaimed with surprise. "My cousin is having an affair with a married man!" Zoe was shaking her head in disbelief as she stared at her with surprise..

"Oh no, I'm not, Zoe," Stephanie responded quickly, defending herself, then hesitated. "Well...yeah I am." When she said that, everyone gasped. "Well, actually, yes and no, but mostly no." Stephanie was all confused as she tried to make up her mind. "See, just looking at your expressions is the reason I didn't say anything about my relationship with Jerry before. You wouldn't understand." Stephanie then sucked her teeth and shook her head in discouragement.

"What's there not to understand, Stephanie? He's married and you're having an affair."

"Gloria, it is not like that." She took a deep breath then exhaled. "I didn't think that I would have to explain myself to my loved ones in a limo coming from my uncle's funeral." She chuckled.

"Oh honey, you don't have to explain to us. You are a grown woman. You can do whatever you wanna do."

"No Gloria. I do have to explain. I've been meaning to tell you all for so very long but just didn't know how to say it. It's not easy to do so and it is even harder to explain but here goes my best shot."

Stephanie dabbed at her eyes as she tried to gather the strength to talk.

"Jerry is married and has been married for sixteen years, but out of the sixteen years, he had only lived with his wife for a year and three months before her accident."

"Accident? She was in an accident?" Zoe asked in surprise as she interrupted her.

"Yes Zoe, she was in an accident, the kind of accident that could destroy a relationship—a relationship that he had with his wife for fifteen glorious months before she went into a vegetative state after bumping her head on the low ceiling in a house basement, the house that he had bought for her where they could raise a family and live the rest of their life together. When she hit her head, she laughed and cursed. They both got a kick out of it, but a little while later, she continued complaining about headaches but never went to the doctor despite constant orders from Jerry to go to the emergency room. She only took aspirin, unbeknownst to both of them that she was losing oxygen to the brain and lost a lot of blood that did not flow to all parts of the brain. Maybe doctors could have done something for her when she first started feeling the pain. Who knows, but once she went into the hospital, it was too late. There was nothing that they could have done for her. From that day forth, she never left the hospital."

"Oh, that is so sad," Gloria remarked as she took hold of Stephanie's hand. Everyone was looking at Stephanie with stunned and sad eyes.

"I didn't know at first. I had no intention of falling for him. He was just my agent. That was it, but as we spent more time alone together and got to know each other, we started falling for one another. That was when that turkey told me that he was married. Of course I wanted to break the relationship up along with his legs. I didn't want to be any man's mistress, some floozy. Uncle Archie didn't raise me that way. That was when he explained everything to me. When he told me, he cried something awful. He told me how beautiful she used to be and how much he had loved her and how much she had loved him, the plans they had, the places they would have visited and so on. All of that ended on the day that she bumped her head. He holds a lot of guilty feelings over that. He tells me that he relives that day over and over in his mind, and a little bit of him dies every time. He tells me that he is surprised that he is still alive. He said that I have a lot to do with that." Stephanie smiled proudly.

"He still visits her as often as he can. He still loves her but she will never get better and he won't pull the plug on her. He is her husband and has all say-so over what happens to her. He also still keeps in contact with her family, who hopes that a miracle will happen, but the damage is not reversible. She doesn't even know them or Jerry. Jerry has told me so much that I can go on and on, but you get the picture."

The family nodded that they understood what she was saying.

"Even though I knew all of this about his wife, for some reason, I still felt guilty, like I was doing something wrong and immoral. That is the reason I never told you, Uncle Archie, any of you. I didn't know how you would think about me. I couldn't have my loved ones thinking badly of me. That is the reason why I've kept our relationship a secret. He was the one to tell me to tell you guys everything. He said to me that if you all are as great as I said that you were, you all would understand, but I still didn't want to say anything. I just couldn't do it. No matter how many times I tried, I just chickened out. I'm so sorry." Stephanie lowered her head in shame.

Gloria reached over and gave Stephanie a big hug and kiss, then lifted her head up from under her chin with her hand.

"Oh, sweetheart, you have nothing to be sorry for."

"Yeah, why are you saying that you are sorry? There's no reason," Joey added.

"Stephanie, you didn't do anything wrong," Zoe assured her as she reached across her mother to touch Stephanie on the leg.

"We could never think badly about you. We love you too much" Matthew added.

"See there, Stephanie? You did all that worrying for nothing. Listen, don't you ever be ashamed or uncomfortable to tell me anything. You already know this. Good or bad, I'm here for the long run."

"You know, that's what Jerry said. He said that I was overreacting, but something just didn't feel right."

"Honey, it is not like he is cheating on her. I'm sure that she would understand. She would want him to go on. She wouldn't want him to waste away and just die."

"But he is still married to her, Gloria," Stephanie responded as she sucked her teeth and rolled her eyes in disgust. "It still bothers me. I can't help it that I have fallen for this married man. I really do care for him a lot. He treats me so well and would do anything for me. It really was a surprise to see him there. I really didn't expect him to show up."

"He really is a special man, Stephanie. I can see that."

"Yeah Stephanie, he's cool," Matthew added with a smile and nod, like Zoe and Joey.

"Oh, I know why you like him, Matthew. You both are into music. You love to play instruments and he deals with entertainment—perfect combination."

"Well, I can say the same with you," Gloria interjected. "You two make a good couple and don't you let anyone make you feel ashamed or embarrassed for what you are doing,"

Gloria wasn't saying it as a question. It was more of a polite order. Stephanie looked up at her, then smiled and nodded happily, all guilt feelings and embarrassment cleared from her face and lifted off her shoulders. Gloria noticed that she even looked more relaxed, at ease, at peace. This made Gloria feel good.

Since everyone was relaxed now, she slapped both her legs one time then looked around the limousine at everyone.

"Well, like I was saying before, I am absolutely famished!" As the family continued talking in the limo, Gloria learned that Jerry would be meeting Stephanie at the bar. Mike and Beth would be arriving at the bar with the Jeffersons, Iggy arrived on a motorcycle and would see everyone back at the bar and Chris would be returning after he dropped some of his riders back at home. Those people wouldn't be attending the reception due to prior engagements. Gloria invited Billy to come in and get some food and drink, and she accepted. Gloria's funeral family left after the burial. They shed tears, hugged and kissed Gloria and the family then promised to keep more in touch, as the family was getting so very small. Gloria knew that they were only talking, but she nodded in agreement just to be cordial.

CHAPTER TWENTY-ONE:
Archie Bunker's Place, Where the Truth Comes Out

Once they made it to the bar, Gloria saw that there was a huge crowd in front waiting to go inside. Gloria told Billy to park in the alleyway next to the bar so she didn't have to look for a parking spot on the street. As Gloria looked at the crowd, she knew that Billy would have had a hard time finding a spot to park.

"Man, I can smell the food from here!" Matthew exclaimed excitedly as he sniffed.

"Don't worry Matthew." Joey said. "I heard that Mom and the women made enough for a million people. You just might have about one plate, maybe a plate and a half once I get to it."

"Oh Lord," Gloria exclaimed as she rolled her eyes. "The battle of the stomachs!" Gloria began shaking her head back and forth with an Elvis curled-up lip.

"Don't forget Mike, Gloria," Stephanie reminded as if it was a warning.

"Forget that, Stephanie. Don't forget Iggy."

"Iggy!" everyone screamed in playful hysterics, which caused Billy to laugh.

As Billy attempted to pull into the alleyway, Gloria wondered why Faye and Teresa hadn't opened up the bar yet. It was two-thirty as she looked at her Rolex. She then figured that they probably didn't want anyone to come in till she and the family got there. She also noticed that, speaking of the devil, Iggy was standing up against the door of the bar in his black suit with his massive arms folded around his chest, controlling the crowd.

'Hey Ma, look!" Zoe yelled. "Iggy is a bouncer. We have our very own bouncer!"

The Life and Times of Gloria Bunker

Zoe began laughing as everyone in the limo started looking out the window toward Iggy.

"Oh, God bless him. He's keeping an eye on the crowd. Isn't that sweet?"

"Yeah Gloria, and he looks like he is taking the job seriously." Stephanie chuckled.

"Yeah, I wouldn't wanna be the person to tell that mountain to move." Joey was shaking his head as he stared at Iggy through the window. "No sirree, buddy."

"I wouldn't wanna be the person to tell that mountain to stay!" Matthew interjected as he looked at Iggy's intimidating girth, causing everyone to chuckle.

"Well, I think he is cute," Zoe commented in Iggy's defense. Everyone turned and looked at her with such a look that she instantly turned crimson and started laughing bashfully as she tried to hide her face behind her mother.

As Billy parked, the family was getting themselves ready to get out and enter into the bar through the alley door. Billy got out of the driver's side, then walked around to the door to let the family out. She nodded and smiled as the closest to the door, Zoe, made her way out, then Gloria, who was in the middle, then Stephanie. After that was Matthew, then Joey was the last, who then began chatting with Billy casually.

Gloria had her key out as she made her way to the alley door. She couldn't help but sniff a few times the overwhelming delicious aromas of the food coming from inside.

"Man, that sure does smell good," she commented as she began opening up the door.

Everyone came in as Gloria held the door open, As Billy came in, Gloria stopped her and said to her in a friendly tone, "Look here, girlfriend, you are officially on your lunch hour, so you can take your chauffeur's cap off and make yourself comfortable. That is how we do it at Archie Bunker's Place." Gloria then winked at her and nodded. Billy just looked at her, then Joey, then removed the cap and smiled as she nodded.

Everyone was met in the storage room by Faye who approached rapidly, eyes bulging.

"Oh my gosh! You guys scared the mess outta me!" She was breathing hard and holding her chest. "I heard some noise back here, not knowing what to expect. I was about to go Chuck Norris on some asses!" She got into a karate stance causing everyone to chuckle.

"Oh sorry Faye. It wasn't planned. Since Billy pulled into the alleyway, it didn't make any sense to walk all the way to the front."

"Yeah, that didn't make sense," she said as she nodded. "Well, come on in, guys."

As everyone headed towards the door to go into the lounge area, the lights from the lounge and the aromas hit everyone. Gloria noticed that Faye and Billy began talking.

"Wassup, Faye!" Billy greeted with a smile as she tapped her on the shoulder.

"Hey Billy, what's happening, girl? Come on in, take off your skin and rattle around in your bones."

"Take off your whose-its and rattle what around where?" Gloria asked as she looked at the two strangely, which only made them laugh.

"Gloria, I'm surprised that you didn't know that line is from an old Rolling Stones song. I pictured you as a Rolling Stones type," Billy commented.

"I'm more of a Rolling Gall–stones, if you know what I mean," she replied as she chuckled. "So you two know each other?"

"What?" Faye exclaimed. "Girl, Billy is one of our favorite regulars. Hey, I even know her favorite order: T-bone steak smothered in onions and mushrooms, baked potatoes with sour cream and chives, a chef's salad and loaves of buttered garlic bread," she said as she looked up and counted on her fingers.

"Oops! Don't forget the …" Billy added, as she pointed to Faye.

"Diet Sprite, no ice." Faye said quickly as she remembered.

"Bingo!" Billy gave Faye a playful pound on the shoulder, causing both to chuckle.

"Well Billy, we didn't prepare any t-bones today, and by the way, only God knows where you put it all, but we do have almost everything else."

"That's great. I'm starved!" Billy exclaimed as she rubbed her hands together and headed for the lounge with Joey as they continued talking.

As those two walked to the lounge, Faye stood near the door between the lounge and storage room as Gloria locked the door.

"I hope that you didn't mind us not opening up till you guys arrived. We didn't know how you wanted to do this—I mean, with the food and all—if you wanted us to serve it or just let them go hog wild."

"Oh no, I don't mind. Let me take a look at how well everything came out. Do you know that you can smell the food all the way into Manhattan? It just smells so good!"

"I hope it tastes as good as it smells." With that, Faye motioned for Gloria to come in.

Once Gloria walked in and saw the huge table with all the food, she was flabbergasted. There was even an area where all of Teresa's pastries and cakes were.

"Hey Ma, doesn't the table just look great! Yummy!" Zoe commented as she held her hands out to it as if modeling it.

Teresa spotted Gloria standing by Faye, looking totally surprised as her mouth dropped and eyes bulged.

"Oh Gloria, I hope you like it," Teresa said, looking a tad self-conscious over everything.

"Oh Teresa, it looks absolutely perfect. It looks so, so, so…" "Edible?"

"That too, but that wasn't the word I was looking for. I was thinking that it looks so professional, like the food had been catered. Oh Teresa, we can't do better than this."

Teresa could tell that Gloria was very satisfied with what she was seeing.

The way the women laid everything out was very elaborate. All the hot food was on one table, all the salads on another, and soda on another, along with the plates, cups, forks, knives and napkins. The fruit display that Faye designed was in the middle of one of the tables with the salads and one of the women prepared a huge punch bowl with punch mixed with fruit cocktail. That was on the table with the drinks. Gloria thought that the only thing missing was the huge ice sculpture of a fish or a naked Amazon woman covering her frontal area with a harp. She chuckled as she thought this to herself.

"Oh Teresa, I wish that I had a camera so I could take a picture of the table. I would love to look back and see how beautiful this table looked." As Gloria made this remark, Faye came up from behind.

"Did I hear someone mention that they are in need of a camera?" Faye continued walking past her and headed to the bar counter, reached behind it, then once she got what she needed, she held it up as if she caught the winning homerun baseball at the world series.

"Voila!" she exclaimed as she smiled a satisfied smile. "Archie always kept a camera on hand, just in case, for moments like this."

"Oh Faye, you are a dear." Gloria said.

Faye brought the camera to Gloria as she turned the camera on. As she waited for the 'ready' light to come on, she looked around the bar and saw the family mingling happily with each other and with Teresa's girls and Billy. She then heard a knock on the front door glass. It was Iggy looking in and smiling. Gloria noticed that he was so wide that he was bigger than the door in the arms and shoulder department. He was giving them a look as if he wanted to know when they were going to open up and let people in.

Gloria nudged to Faye and Teresa then nodded towards Iggy. Gloria held her hand up to him as if she was telling him, 'in a moment.'

"Okay. Which one of you two chained the pit bull to the front door?" she said jokingly.

Faye and Teresa both looked at each other then pointed at one another and laughed.

"He was a sweetheart, Gloria. He volunteered. His bouncer skills came in handy. I tell ya, when we got here, there were already tons of people waiting to get in, still dressed in black. They are probably people who didn't go to the burial. They were crowding in front of the door so much that we couldn't get in., Faye replied.

"That was when Iggy came and took charge, and immediately things became organized quickly. He was like Moses parting the Red Sea. He did it nicely and respectfully and got us in quickly to make sure everything was perfect. He's been out there ever since. Bless his huge muscular heart," Teresa exclaimed.

Once the 'ready' light on the camera came on, Gloria began taking pictures of the tables of food. Faye, Teresa and the girls had changed out of their funeral attire and had on casual comfortable clothes, so Gloria asked them to come and pose by the food, and they agreed. When done, Faye offered to take some pictures of Gloria around the tables of food, but she declined because she was dressed in funeral clothes. Faye explained to her that there was nothing wrong with taking pictures and smiling even though this was a funeral day, because the whole get together was a celebration of Archie's life, not his death. When Faye reminded Gloria of that, she talked Gloria into it, and she then allowed her to take pictures of her alone and of the family.

Once all the photos had been taken, Zoe and the girls volunteered to serve the food and give out refreshments. Matthew decided to lend a hand. This would allow the younger ones to socialize with each other and get to know one another and Gloria and all the adults could socialize with each other. Gloria liked the idea and accepted it. She then thanked the youngsters as they headed towards the bathroom to wash their hands. While they went to do that, Faye thought of something then turned to look at Gloria.

"Gloria, what about the hard stuff? The liquor and stuff? Are you going to give it all away or are you going to charge or what?"

"It is a celebration, Faye!" Gloria said gaily. "These people are always going to remember this day—the day Archie Bunker went out in a blast! Free drinks, girl! Everything is free!"

"Now girl, whatcha gonna do if you decide to stay and run the bar and there is no food or drink in the place?"

"Like I said before, Faye it is a celebration! Officially all cares and woes, all sadness and depression, all unhappiness and confusion were left outside that door in a garbage bag in the dumpster. I'm ready to move on. No more crying. Only happy thoughts and memories. If I decide to stay and it was meant to be, there will be a way for me to fill the place up with everything. If not, well, it just wasn't meant to be."

"You'll just have to turn it into a Starbucks and sell coffee for four or five dollars," Faye joked as they laughed. "Okay girl. Officially you are the boss." Faye began heading behind the bar to get ready to serve drinks once the door opened up. Teresa was next to come over to Gloria to talk before the door opened.

The Life and Times of Gloria Bunker

"Gloria, I'm gonna help Faye and the kids by giving out drinks or refills on drinks and food unless you need me to do anything special."

"Anything that you do is special, Teresa. That will be fine, but feel free to stop anytime you want and just socialize, okay?" When she said this, Teresa nodded.

"No, I'll be comfortable doing this. It'll keep my mind off of things," she said as she began walking away.

Gloria could see that Teresa was looking a tad down all of a sudden and she became concerned and decided to inquire about what was wrong.

"Teresa girl, what is wrong? Daddy is in a better place now. He is looking down right now happy as can be, especially at of all the hard work you have done for him. No need to be sad still."

"Oh, Gloria, that's not it. I loved your daddy, Mr. Bunkers, and I will miss him and I know that he is in a better place, but that is not why I feel the way I'm feeling."

"Well, what's wrong? You seemed fine yesterday. What's happened since then?" Gloria was very concerned.

"It is the new apartment and deposit and binder, Gloria." Teresa said uneasily.

"Why? What happened with it?"

"When I got back home, mi novio Hector told me that he had tried to get in contact with the staff at the new building but the number had been disconnected. Also, he went to the building and there were four moving trucks with families sitting in their cars, looking confused, scared and concerned. The building was closed. They were told that they could move in yesterday. They had no place to stay and their money was gone and the building was empty and the telephone number was disconnected."

"Oh my gosh, Teresa. That is absolutely horrible. There has to be some kind of logical explanation for that."

"I don't know, Gloria, but I know that Hector is furious and worried because we gave them a lot of our money and they cashed it, too. We didn't talk too much about it last night because I was exhausted when I got home and he had to go to work in the morning and wanted to get some sleep, but he wasn't going to sleep until he knew that I was home safe, God bless him—still concerned about me after all these years….or either jealous. Whatever the reason it was, I still find it sweet."

"Listen, we'll continue talking about this later, deal? I know that there is something we can do to find out what is going on at the building." Gloria assured her in a positive manner, making Teresa relax some. She didn't want Teresa all stressed out, especially after the funeral. Teresa then nodded in agreement and went behind the bar to give Faye a hand.

Everyone was in place staring at Gloria as she was about to open the door. She turned and gave them thumbs up. Stephanie was at her side, waiting for her to unlock the door.

Iggy heard the lock turn on the door then turned and looked at the women smiling.

"How you'ze guys doin? You'ze okay?" he asked with care and concern. "We're fine, Iggy. Thank you so much for your initiative and help." Gloria said appreciatively. Iggy began blushing slightly as he tried to hide it.

"Aah shucks, Gloria; anything for you'ze guys. So, ya ready for everyone to come in?"

"All ready, Iggy," Stephanie said, causing Iggy to nod.

He opened the door all the way till it stayed open by itself then he said to the women with much authority, "You don't have to worry about this. I got it." After he said that he began letting people in ten at a time. The line moved quickly and safely, although there were a lot of people.

Mostly everyone who came in, the two had already seen at the funeral or at the burial, but there were a few who weren't able to make either. One of those people was a little old Asian woman dressed in what looked like a black kimono. She was about sixty but because of a hard life or a lot of sun, she looked older. Her hair was curly, salt and pepper, and cut short, showing a lot of wrinkles on her forehead. She was also very thin—not a frail kind of thin but very thin in a healthy way. When she came in and saw the two women standing by the jukebox, she screamed out in exclamation.

"Glolia! Stephanie!" she yelled as she walked quickly over to them when they saw her.

"Mrs. Ling!" The two women exclaimed in unison as they met her halfway to greet her.

Once they got to each other, they embraced. She held on to Gloria first with her eyes closed and tears flowing. They both rocked each other from side to side. Mrs. Ling owned the coin operated laundry next door.

"Oh, I am so solly, Glolia. I'm so velly solly." Then she went and said the same thing to Stephanie. When she finished, she slapped both of them on their shoulder and stared at them, tears rolling down her face, looking like a puppy caught out in the rain. She then turned and glanced at the table full of food, drinks and pastries.

"Oh my God, look at the beautiful table. You are really sending Archie off in style."

"Would you believe that Gloria and the two women behind the bar prepared all of this last night?"

Mrs. Ling looked at Gloria then at Faye and Teresa with surprise. "Is this true, Glolia?"

Gloria started to nod modestly with a smile on her face.

"Come on over to the table and help yourself," Stephanie offered cordially. "It was made with love from us to you, in remembrance of Uncle Archie. I hope that you are hungry."

"Oh I am, I am, but I don't wanna eat anything quite yet. I have something for you." Mrs. Ling began digging around in her purse until she pulled out what she was looking for. When she found it, she smiled and nodded. "Ah, here it is. This is for you."

Mrs. Ling handed Gloria an open envelope with a card and a check.

"This is from me and Mr. Ling plus some of the other businesses on the block. I am proud to say that EVERYONE chipped in. Some gave cash and others gave checks. I took them all and just wrote out one big check. It is quite a substantial amount. Now you won't have any problems continuing on with the business with Archie gone."

"Oh thank you so much, Mrs. Ling, for what you've done here but I haven't decided if I'm going to stay yet."

"Oh?" she exclaimed in shock and surprise. "You mean that you might close the place?"

"Well, Mrs. Ling. I live in California. It would be a huge commute to work every day, plus quite expensive," she uttered jokingly, but Mrs. Ling wasn't smiling.

"Wow, I can't imagine Archie Bunker's place not in business. Everyone knows about Archie Bunker's place. Oh, if it closes, it will be missed for sure. Whatever would go here would never equal what Archie was to this community," she commented sadly.

"Oh, Mrs. Ling, that is so sweet to say."

"Well, Stephanie, couldn't you stay and run it?" she asked almost sounding desperate.

"That's a nice suggestion but I wouldn't be able to commit to it. I have my own career that I am trying to pursue."

"Oh, I understand," she uttered as she lowered her head sadly.

"Plus right now, we don't know what Daddy wrote in the will. We don't know anything."

"Well, I would hope that you would stay. It is the longest running business in the area. So many businesses have come and gone but he survived it all, thanks to Faye's magnificent cooking and Archie's personality. He sure was quite a character."

"Oh, that's the word we've been hearing lately, Mrs. Ling—character. He sure was quite a character."

"But what about you, Mrs. Ling? You and your family have been here long, too."

"Well, we've been here a long time but not longer than your uncle, and

I don't know if you know this but we are relocating farther down Roosevelt Avenue, where they have built all new apartment buildings and stores."

"Oh, you're kidding! We didn't know."

"Archie knew and gave us a beautiful figurine as a going away present. We only have a few more weeks left here. We should be in our new place by the first of October," she said proudly but a tad sadly.

"Well, I am happy for you, but I really hate to see you go."

"If you stay, you would still see me around. We own the building. We'll still be by checking on the place and eat some of Faye's food. She's the only person who cooks Asian food better than an Asian!" she commented as they all laughed. "That girl is phenomenal. I really think that you should think about staying."

"Oh I'm thinking hard, Mrs. Ling. The worst is over, and the worst was burying Daddy. It can't get any worse than that. If I was able to get through that and survive it with no scratches, everything else should be easy."

As soon as Gloria said that, in walked the Jeffersons, the Stivics and Chris, still looking very handsome in his black suit. As Gloria watched Chris, she turned to Stephanie and mumbled so Mrs. Ling couldn't hear her.

"Well, maybe I should say 'hopefully' everything else should be easy."

When Chris came in and saw Gloria talking with Stephanie and Mrs. Ling, he went to the corner of the bar with the two couples and sat till she had an opportunity to speak with him. He saw Gloria lead Mrs. Ling to the food table along with Stephanie, then she got bombarded by other people who wanted some of her time. Occasionally, Gloria would look over toward them and wave, then she would wave to him and he would just give her a smile. She wanted to go to him and have him hold her and kiss her and tell her that everything would be just fine. The worst was over. She knew that he would make her feel real good, at peace, comforted,; he had proven that last night when they were alone together in that very room.

As time went on, the Jeffersons and Stivics started socializing while people kept coming in and making their way to talk about Archie, even if it was only for a few minutes. Gloria noticed that the food was a success and everyone looked to be enjoying themselves despite the circumstances. The jukebox was playing but no one was dancing. There were a few chuckles but it was sporadic. It was almost like people felt uncomfortable about having a good time, and that wasn't what Gloria wanted. Gloria wanted this to be festive, like in New Orleans when someone passes away. People remember the good, not the bad and they dance and sing in the streets to loud and festive music.

As Gloria looked around at everyone who was there or walking through the door, all of them looked like they had just finished running a marathon in their black dresses and suits. Gloria could see that these people really were

The Life and Times of Gloria Bunker

going to miss her father. They looked tired and exhausted and didn't really know what to say or do. All around her people were in their own little cliques, shaking their heads in disbelief. People were talking about the food and weather, afraid to say something funny about her dad without feeling guilty. Gloria thought it looked more like an audition for extras in a new version of *Dawn of the Dead*. Why did her daddy have to be so popular? All she wanted was something small, maybe at the house, talk about old times with family and that's it. But nooo. She had what looked to be about three hundred people or more in the bar. It was packed and people were steadily coming in, and they all looked depressed.

Gloria walked over to Stephanie angrily and pulled her to the side so no one could see. "Stephanie, we gotta do something to loosen everyone up."

"Well, we gave them free liquor. They should be loosening up pretty soon," Stephanie quipped, but Gloria wasn't laughing.

"Stephanie, seriously though. This is not what I wanted. We didn't do all this cooking so people could be so downtrodden, and I don't want people to go home feeling the way that they did when they came in. What can we do to lighten up the mood?"

Gloria and Stephanie stood there for a few moments trying to think about something to make the people feel more festive.

"I got it!" exclaimed Stephanie with her eyes wide and a huge smile on her face, but it quickly disappeared. "I can't do it. I need Jerry and he hasn't shown up yet."

"What did you wanna do?" Gloria asked.

"I thought that maybe I might do a song to liven the mood, but Jerry is not here."

"Well you have Matthew, you know," Gloria reminded her.

"Hey that gives me an idea!" Stephanie commented as she snapped her fingers. "Matthew could do the song that he did today. While he is singing, I'll get the cordless mic and when he is done, I'll say something and he could accompany me, huh?"

"That is a great idea!" Gloria said excitedly.

Stephanie zoomed over to Matthew and told him the plan. He nodded and headed to the piano with no hesitation. When Stephanie went and killed the jukebox then Matthew began playing, instantly, people stopped talking then tuned their eyes and ears to his excellent playing and singing. When he finished, he didn't wait for the applause to die down. Quickly he went into a fast Stevie Wonder song, *I just called to say I love you.* As he played, Gloria looked to Chris who held his glass out to her with a smile. This was Gloria's chance to go to him while everyone was focusing on Matthew and the music.

"That is a beautiful song." Chris commented as she bopped to the music. "It reminds me of how I feel about you."

"Oh Chris," Gloria responded with a blush. "You look very handsome in that suit. You always look good in whatever you wear. You always have."

"Thank you for the compliment but you are beautiful also, and by the way, that is a very expensive outfit you have on. It's almost identical to Stephanie's. I didn't know that Gucci did dresses for funerals."

Gloria became nervous and didn't respond. She just smiled and nodded.

"You know, Gloria, I was quite proud of you today. Your daddy would be proud also. Everything was done so perfectly, even the reception. The table is beautiful. Did you and Faye and Teresa do all of this yourselves last night?"

Gloria nodded modestly. "And they did the food decorations themselves today."

"Well in my opinion, any catering company would be jealous if they saw this layout."

"Well, have you eaten yet?"

"No not yet."

"Well, why not, Chris?" she asked as she slapped him playfully on his arm.

"Well, because since I walked in I've been checking out another layout that filled me up."

At first, Gloria didn't understand but when she finally caught on, she turned instant crimson and lowered her head as she acted bashful.

"Chris, I don't know what I'm gonna do with you," she said after she sucked her teeth.

"I already told you what you can do with me, and it will make me the happiest man in the world. Marry me."

"Oh Chris," she said slowly, almost sounding exhausted. "I-I-I..."

"Look Gloria," he said putting his hand up. "I know you need more time and I'm respecting your wishes. I just wanted you to know that I haven't forgotten and I meant what I said yesterday. You don't know how I feel when I see you. I just wanna pull you close to me so I can hug you and take away all your pain. I don't care who knows, Gloria. I would shout it out right now to let everyone know. That is how much I love you and always have, Gloria. I know it is not the time or place, but I am burning for you, Sunny. Please don't head back to California to stay. Just go back and pack then come back to me. I want you and need you in my life. Hell, you can sell your house and move in with me, you and the kids. I have more than enough room. I love the kids too, Gloria. They have always been in my life. We can be a family, one big happy family—Stephanie, Joey, Matthew and Zoe, you and I," he said lovingly and tenderly. Taking hold of her hand, Gloria looked around nervously.

Gloria didn't realize that she was crying. She only noticed it when Stephanie started singing Anita Baker's song *Caught up in the rapture of love* and she got all blurry. She rubbed the tears away with her hands because she didn't think to get a napkin.

"You don't play fair, Chris. You're not making this easy on me," she said as she sniffled.

"I'm sorry, Gloria. Forgive me, but this is the way I feel. I don't wanna lose you again."

Gloria wasn't hearing what he was saying. She was still reliving the comment about one big happy family when he named the members of her family. Rupert didn't even remember. The phone call incident had brought itself back into her remembrance. Then she started thinking about what Zoe had said in the morning about Rupert only having eyes for her and him not accepting the family as his family. That concerned Gloria because whoever she chose, they would have to know that she was coming with baggage. The person she chose would have to accept all of her or nothing at all. Her children were her all, so they would have to be accepted sincerely, not just so the person could get close to her. They would have to feel needed and loved, not used. Could Rupert accept her family as his own? Could he get to know them and love them, not just buy them things and consider that love? Could he show interest in them instead of only her? Did he even know their names? Those were things she needed to find out. Gloria believed that Chris had a slight advantage over Rupert, because Chris had known her family their whole life, but she believed that Rupert had a slight advantage over Chris because Rupert was much more successful than him, a tad more unpredictable, exciting, flamboyant, carefree and eccentric. These were the things that Gloria loved. They both were equal when it came to caring and respecting and treating her special, like a queen, and she believed that they would do anything for her. Gloria did love all of the attention and all the special treatment from both men. What she didn't like was the fact that she had to choose one and hurt the other, and if Chris was the one who was going to be hurt, it would be the second time. She had to know for sure if she chose Chris that it was because she really loved him and cared for him, not because of guilty past feelings.

"Chris you promised me that you would give me time," she said, sounding frustrated.

"And I am a man of my word, Gloria. I'm just talking to you, that's all. I don't mean for my talking to sound like pressure." Chris even let go of her hand. "See Gloria—no pressure," he said with a smile and held his two hands up in a surrender.

Something came over her, a feeling that she couldn't explain; a burning, yearning feeling that traveled through the innermost parts of her body. Was it Chris's eyes or his voice or was it the fact that Chris let go of her hand and began playing fair? She didn't know, but what she did know was the fact that the feeling caused her mouth to have a mind of its own and it started to speak.

"Please, don't let go." When she said that, Chris wasn't sure what he heard. He looked at her in a perplexed manner. "What did you say?" He wanted to be sure he had heard what he thought that he heard.

"I said, please don't let go. Don't let go of my hand, Chris," she said almost in a whisper, very sincerely, then she smiled at him lovingly. Chris didn't have to hear any more than that. He gently took back her hand, then they both just stared into each other's eyes. "I don't know what has come over me, Chris. The wake, the burial—I just need to be comforted for a moment."

Gloria moved closer to him on the bar stool.

"Now, does it look like I am complaining?" "No," she said, smiling.

"If this makes you happy then I am happy. All I wanna do is make you happy."

"I know that Chris, and all I wanna do is make you happy. I would never want to hurt you. I cherish having you back in my life and I don't want anything to spoil that. Last night was special and magical and I don't regret any of it. I'm glad we stopped when we did because it was hard for me to contain myself. I was about to become a naughty girl." When she said that, he chuckled. "Believe me Chris; I share the same feelings you do."

"Well then, that makes me feel good. At least I know that, like the kids say these days, 'I'm in da house,'" he said proudly

You're also in the bedroom between the sheets! she thought to herself, but she just chuckled at his comment.

"For now, let's just enjoy each other, being together here with people we share one thing in common, and that is knowing my daddy, Archie Bunker."

"Here, here!" Chris exclaimed with a cheer. "Let us drink to that, okay?"

"Sure," Gloria responded as she nodded with an enthusiastic smile.

Gloria went and got herself a seltzer with a splash of flavored soda for taste. Chris called Teresa over to him and asked for vodka and orange juice. Gloria got her drink and came and sat next to Chris.

"I saw you talking with Teresa. What did you order?" She began sipping on her drink.

"A vodka and orange juice," he replied nonchalantly, then looked at her through the corner of his eye guiltily.

"A vodka and orange juice?!" Gloria echoed. "Chris Barlow, since when did you start drinking? You don't drink," she said in mock anger. She was more shocked than anything. Chris knew that he would get this reaction, so he smiled.

"I don't drink but this is a special occasion, like you said. I do drink occasionally, maybe twice every few years."

"Well then, shucks," she exclaimed as she exhaled deeply. "I want the same thing, too." She then hit him on his arm playfully. "Here I am trying to be all proper and ladylike for you and here you are playing dirty again!"

When Teresa brought Chris his drink, Gloria asked her to please fix her the same. As Gloria waited for her drink, she scoped the bar and saw the Jeffersons talking up a storm with Iggy, who had finally made his way in and was at the food table fixing something to eat. All of them were nodding their heads to the beat of the music that Matthew and Stephanie were doing. Mike was near Joey talking and eating up a storm, while Beth was chatting with Zoe, who was serving food to a couple. Everyone else looked like they were getting into the mood as they ate and mingled lightly. Gloria could see that their shoulders weren't drooped over like before. Now, shoulders were moving and swaying from side to side. She even heard laughter from a few people. That was making her feel good. What also made her feel good was the fact that Jerry was walking in. She immediately looked at both of their eyes—Stephanie's and Jerry's—and they lit up when they spotted each other. Stephanie's next song was *On Broadway*, in which everyone joined in with her. When Teresa came back with Gloria's drink, Gloria leaned over the bar towards her.

"Thanks for the drink, Teresa."

"Oh, you are welcome Gloria."

"Listen, don't you and Faye wanna take a break? Go and eat or drink something."

"Oh Gloria, I asked Faye if she wanted to take a break but she said no. I'm doing fine, myself. The way I feel right now, I just wanna stay busy. See, look at Stephanie up there." She nodded her head in that direction. "You see how she is dealing with her pain? She is entertaining; so is Matthew. He's playing his heart out. We'd all just rather stay busy right now, even our girls and Joey."

"You have a good point there, girl; when you are ready, don't you hesitate to stop, hum?"

"Okay Gloria." With that, she winked at Gloria then left for the other side of the bar.

Gloria just sucked her teeth and shook her head as she stared at Teresa. Chris noticed Gloria's mood change and decided to find out what happened.

"A dollar for your thoughts," he said as he sipped his drink through his straw.

"Oh Chris, I just feel so badly for Teresa and her family, that's all. She and the girls have been doing so well for me." Chris took a quick look in the three girls' direction and they were serving food. "They're been so helpful, but things aren't going well with them."

'Monetary problems, huh? Well, actually, that can't be it. The dresses that the girls have on cost a heck of a lot of money! Even the dress that she had on earlier, wow!" he remarked.

"Well in a way, it does have to do with money. See, Teresa and her family were supposed to be in their new location now, but apparently they are getting the run around. The staff at the new building apparently cashed the check and kept the deposit and binder and the place is not ready. They disconnected their telephone so there is no way for the family to find out about the apartment or their money. Get this! Teresa's husband went to the new building and there were four families in the front waiting to move in but the building was locked—no one there."

"Gloria, are you serious?" Chris asked in disbelief.

"I am serious as the plague, Chris. Now they are living out of boxes and the landlord has already rented out their apartment, and what about those poor people who thought that they would be in their new place? Oh Chris, it is just awful. I had a funny feeling about it from the get–go; I don't know why. People move every day, but when she told me that she had only seen a model of the apartment and never seen the pool that it's supposed to have, plus the other amenities, I didn't feel comfortable. But what really got me, I think, was when I heard that they asked for all this money up front—all this rent and security and deposit or binder, or whatever. If I'm dishing money out like that, I want a tour of the place. I might be wrong, but this is how I feel."

"Horrible! Absolutely horrible!" Chris looked at Teresa while she worked then shook his head. "So, where is this new apartment building? Down on Roosevelt where they are building all those apartment buildings and commercial property?"

"No. It is in Flushing; over by the Town Hall, Main Street, Northern Blvd, and Flushing High School."

Chris began to nod his head as he sipped more of his drink. "Yeah, I know the area very well." He sucked his teeth and curled his lip up in the corner. Gloria was looking at Chris and became concerned.

"Chris what is wrong?" She lightly touched his hand.

"I had an opportunity to meet some of those guys who were building those buildings. I passed on doing them. I would've made a hell of a lot of money if I had accepted."

"Really? So why did you pass on the job?"

"I passed on the job because I didn't like the way the representatives of the buildings wanted me to do the work. They wanted me to cut as many corners as possible. They wouldn't have minded if I just put up sheetrock and spit and just slapped on some paint. I couldn't have worked like that. Yeah, those buildings look nice on the outside but in a few years that place will be falling apart, but the landlord would've made a killing. The landlord probably doesn't even know about the shabby dealings going on in those buildings. Maybe he does know; who is to say?"

"So where does that leave Teresa and her family?"

"In the same situation she was at the beginning of the conversation, waiting. What these people probably did was cash everyone's checks and used that money to finish fixing up the building or put it in an account to immediately start collecting interest on it."

"That is really sneaky and underhanded business. Teresa gave them money months in advance and was promised that the apartment would be available on the first."

"Oh, it will be completed…Eventually, but at their leisurely pace. They already have Teresa's money. If she decided to take them to court, do you know how long that would take? Plus if she wins, the building would be completed by then and it could take forever before they even refund her money. It is just a bad situation."

"Well, is there anything we can do to help her and her family? She's been such a help."

"I don't know, Gloria. I would have to think about it for awhile."

The two sat quietly at the bar for a spell, thinking about how they could help Teresa and her family. Gloria heard a round of applause and whistles because Stephanie and Matthew had just finished another song. Matthew stopped and took a break as Jerry took his spot at the piano. Stephanie also took a break, as she talked with Jerry while he played. Everyone was becoming more alive and festive as time went on.

Finally Gloria perked up and sat at attention as she smiled at Chris. "I think that I have an idea," she said as she nodded her head.

"Okay, let me hear."

"Well, you know that I've been speaking with a gentleman who has been interested in buying the house. We hit it off real well and he offered me a lot of money for the house. Well anyway, maybe he might have some apartments available in one of his buildings!" she said excitedly but a few seconds later the smile disappeared. "Forget it. Even if Mr. Kindred was able to find them something, Teresa and her family would still have to come up with money for rent, security and everything else."

When Gloria mentioned Kindred's name, Chris looked like he had seen a ghost. His eyes got wide and so did his mouth, looking to be in shock.

"Gloria, did you say Kindred, as in Daniel Kindred?"

Gloria looked at him with surprise that he would know that name.

"Yeah Chris, why? By the way, how did you know that name?"

"Gloria, is this the Daniel Kindred from King and Duchess Realty?"

"Wow, you scared me at first, the way you were talking. No, the Daniel Kindred that I am talking about works for Maximum Properties," Gloria assured him.

"Gloria, I still believe it is the same guy. In about ten years, he's worked for so many real estate companies and has gotten fired for shady practices."

"Oh Chris, are you serious?" Gloria asked, sounding alarmed.

"Yes, unfortunately. He is sneaky and very untrustworthy. You would never be able to tell by looking at him. He looks so elegant and classy and businesslike but underneath all of that, he is a snake, a bum, a con artist." Chris was seething angrily in his seat.

"How do you know this, Chris?"

"Because I've done business with him in the past, but once I got to know him, I broke all ties with him. He never lasts long where he is at. He should've been a lawyer. I wouldn't be surprised that, what's the name of his company he's working at now?"

"Maximum Properties," Gloria said almost hypnotically, still dazed about Kindred.

"I wouldn't be surprised if Maximum Properties was the owner of all those buildings. I'm sure that they would love to hear about his reputation."

"Oh, poor Teresa. This is absolutely terrible news. Oh Chris, I can't tell her, not now."

"I think that you should tell her as soon as possible," Chris urged.

"And what about her money and stuff, even if I tell her? I know that she would probably rethink about staying in a place like that."

"But what about you, Gloria? Are you still going to do business with this guy? He is the scum of the earth. He doesn't care who he hurts, as long as he gets a huge commission."

"Wow! Just add this to more things that I need to worry about. Man! Stephanie was right. She told me that she didn't trust him. She couldn't put her finger on it but she told me to trust her on it. That girl was absolutely right. 'His eyes,' she kept saying. 'There is something about his eyes.' Wait till she finds out that she was correct in her feelings. Boy, how I wish that both of you two were wrong."

Gloria glanced at Stephanie, who laughed at something Jerry must've said, then she looked towards Teresa, who was working hard, trying to keep her mind off her pain.

"Such a good and caring woman and this has to happen to her and her family." Gloria just shook her head. She knew that she had to tell Rupert as soon as she spoke to him.

As Gloria and Chris continued talking, Stephanie and Jerry got the crowd going with the song *New York, New York*. Everyone had food and drinks by this time, so the kids were able to sit down and eat and drink without having to serve. The Jeffersons seemed to be everywhere, laughing and socializing. Everyone seemed to want their attention. They were like celebrities. Mike occasionally drifted away from the food table but not too far. Beth, on the other hand, was now sitting down, swaying to the music while she ate a plate of food and drank orange juice. After Stephanie and Jerry finished their rendition of the song, Stephanie bowed to a thunderous round of applause and cheers, then she and Jerry took a break and headed to the food table. Gloria soon felt a

hand on her shoulder but before she had a chance to turn around to see who it was, Faye leaned toward Chris and Gloria to get their attention.

"Excuse me, you two, but while there is food still left, I'm getting my pretty self over there and getting me some grubbage. Between us three, I heard that three fine and beautiful, not to mention young, women, made all that food!" She glanced at the table, then back at the two. "And you should be doing the same. I think that Iggy was just warming up. He's only had about six full plates of food. When he comes up for air and loads up again, we're gonna be in one heap of trouble."

She then looked in Iggy's direction, and when he spotted her looking at him, he smiled and nodded while he ate. This caused Gloria and Chris to chuckle.

"You know, Chris, from the time we left the cemetery, I've been saying how hungry I was, but I still haven't made my way to eat anything from the table."

"You know something, I haven't eaten yet either, and I am drinking alcohol. Isn't there a saying about not drinking on an empty stomach?"

"Yeah, let's go and eat," Gloria suggested as they made their way off the bar stool and headed towards the table. Faye had already beaten them there and begun loading up.

"I know that Teresa said that she didn't want anything right now but I'm still gonna fix her a plate and then I'm gonna see just how long she is going to try and resist it."

Gloria and Chris were just about to fix a plate when Stephanie called to Gloria.

"Gloria!" she yelled as she stood next to Jerry, eating. Gloria turned to look in her direction. Stephanie then nodded towards Teresa behind the bar. When Gloria turned to look at Teresa, she noticed that Teresa was trying to tell her something. She mouthed the words to her from the bar area.

"We need more beer," she mouthed with pure urgency, then held up a beer can with one hand and pointed to it with another. Gloria nodded and gave her the thumbs up.

"Chris, can you please give me a hand in the storage room?"

With that, she left the table before fixing anything to eat. Chris nodded then followed behind her.

Gloria led Chris to where the beer was in the storage room and then he picked up a box for her. Gloria watched as his arm muscles expanded and she even watched his butt muscles get tight while he was bent over. She couldn't help but comment.

"Oh Chris, you have a beautiful body. I love how your muscles just swell up." Gloria had to admit that she had that naughty feeling inside of her.

Being alone with him in the storage area and with people just beyond the door, she wanted Chris to take her and make love to her right there on top of the crates of beer. She could see that Chris felt like being naughty, also. He walked to the door quickly then put the box down and locked the door. He couldn't control himself anymore. Through his black pants, Gloria was able to see that he had an instant erection and it only excited her more. She didn't wait for him to come to her. She met him halfway. They rushed to each other, rubbing and kissing each other passionately. Gloria wanted him so badly but didn't say anything. She was just enjoying having him kiss her all down her face to her cheek, then chin, then neck. She moaned out softly as he had one hand behind her head and the other hand was gripping her buttocks. His touching made Gloria's eyes roll to the back of her head. Chris picked her up and led her back up against the wall, slowly lifting up her dress then all of a sudden he said...

"I'm vibrating!" he exclaimed as he had his face snuggled deep in her cleavage.

"Me too, Chris! I'm vibrating too!" she exclaimed with a smile on her face.

"No really; I'm vibrating—my damn beeper," he said in a disappointed manner.

Chris began digging into his pocket quickly then pulled out the beeper while Gloria began fixing herself up. As he looked at the number on the beeper, he became ticked off.

"Damn, talk about bad timing! And they put 911 at the end." Chris sucked his teeth then inhaled and exhaled deeply.

"What is wrong Chris?" she asked, looking very concerned.

"I have an emergency at one of my sites. I gotta go," he said with a frown. "I really don't wanna go but I have to."

"Chris, you know that that was a godsend," she said as she fixed his collar and moved her hands down his suit, feeling his chest and stomach muscles. "If you didn't vibrate, we would be doing the nasty right now and that would not have been appropriate."

"Yeah, you are right," Chris frowned but then he smiled. "But at least I know how you feel about me."

Without saying another word, he kissed Gloria, who stood there stunned, then he unlocked the door, picked up the box of beer and headed towards the bar area where Teresa was waiting. Once he put it on the bar area, he said something to Teresa, she waved him off with a smile then took the box and began opening it to stock up the beer. While this was going on, Chris quickly left the bar, leaving Gloria in the storage room, not believing what she was almost ready to do with him.

Girl, Gloria, you have absolutely lost your cotton pickin', rootin' tootin' mind! she said to herself. *You were going to do the nasty with him, right here, right now while all those people were out there. You've flipped!* Gloria began pacing back and forth with her hand on her forehead shaking it back and forth. With the other hand, she fanned her face, still crimson from overheating. *Girl, did you forget that today is the day you buried your father? What has gotten into you?!*

While she continued berating herself over her naughty behavior, Stephanie was making her way towards the storage area.

"Knock knock," she said as she peered into the storage room.

When Gloria saw her, she stopped rubbing her forehead but kept pacing. "Oh hi, Stephanie."

Stephanie noticed that something was bothering her. "I saw two people enter into the storage area and only one left, so I decided to come over just to check—making sure all was okay. By the way that you're looking, it seems like it's not. What is wrong?"

"Oh Stephanie, I'm just slipping deeper and deeper into utter confusion." Gloria was now sitting on some of the crates, being disgusted with herself.

"You were about to get busy with Chris in here, weren't you?" she asked with a sneaky grin as she nodded her head.

"Stephanie, how can you say that?!" Gloria looked at her in shock.

"Well, when you two came in here and he closed the door, I heard that familiar sound of the door locking; so I said to myself, 'Self, why would they go into the storage room to pick up beer but then lock the door?' then I said, 'The same reason you and Jerry have gone in there after you performed in the bar a few months back—to get busy."

Gloria jumped up and grabbed Stephanie by her shoulder. "Stephanie, this is so unlike me. I initiated it and was willing to go through with it, until he started vibrating."

"Now, that's a good thing, right?" Stephanie asked innocently. "What? Going through with it or vibrating?"

"Hell! Both!"

"Stephanie, that's a bad thing. Today is Daddy's funeral. Where's the respect? This whole thing—being back with Chris and him looking so damned good, and the house and Rupert and the bar, etc.—I am doing things that I've never done before. I don't like it, Stephanie. I just don't like it."

"Oh relax, Gloria. You are under a lot of pressure, the kind of pressure that you've never been through before. I think that you've been holding up excellently, and there is nothing wrong with you having a sudden lustful desire for a little bit of unplanned passion. I find the spontaneity of it all terribly romantic," she said in Gloria's defense.

'You think so, Stephanie?"

'Yeah, of course. Everyone has been tempted before in this area. You both are attractive and are attracted to one another."

"Stephanie, if his beeper hadn't vibrated, taking words out of Jerry Lee Lewis's mouth, there would've been a whole lotta shaking going on right now." Gloria was returning back to the crate to sit down.

"Well, like you said, thank God he started beeping, then. No harm done, so relax."

"Stephanie, that's not all…"

"More? More? Tell me! Tell!" she said with a huge smile on her face, anxiously expecting to hear something juicy. "I knew there was more! I'm all ears."

"Stephanie, it is not what you think. I found out some bad news and I must say that you were correct with your feelings."

"You are losing me, Gloria."

"Kindred. Daniel Kindred. He is a crook, a con artist, a low-down sneaky snake…"

"What did you find out?"

"Chris knows this guy. He has done business with him in the past but his scheming business practices caused Chris to stop working with him."

Gloria started explaining to Stephanie about what Teresa had told her and more about what Chris had told her. Stephanie was disturbed deeply, so disturbed that she was loss for words. The only thing that she was able to do was shake her head and clinch her fists.

"I could just kill him!" Stephanie finally said. "Are you still going to deal with him? I mean, he did make a great deal on the house if you do sell. That contract was legit."

"I shouldn't deal with him and I won't, but I'm definitely going to tell Rupert. I am sure he doesn't know. He wouldn't deal knowingly with a no good lowlife snake like that."

While Stephanie tried to calm Gloria down, a white stretch limo with gold designs all around it pulled up in front, beeping its horn to let everyone in the vicinity know that it had arrived. People in the bar all stopped what they were doing and stared out the window, wondering what was going on and who was about to get out of the limousine. Everyone commented about the beauty and the size of it. They were all wondering where the people inside the limo were going; if they were going to walk the avenue or if they were going to come into the bar. A minute or two passed by before there were any movements inside, then finally the chauffeur emerged from the driver's side and slowly made his way to the door in the back. A crowd of onlookers gathered in the area of the limo, just enough so they could see who was getting out.

When the chauffeur finally reached the door and opened it, out came Miles O'Shea, dressed all in black, with the covering going all the way down to his leg. He had a black handkerchief in his hand and he was wearing very expensive looking dark glasses. When he got out, he looked up and down the block in utter disdain, as usual, as he stood to the side so whoever else was inside the limousine would be able to get out, but next, a person didn't get out. A fancy cart was pushed to the door and the chauffeur leaned into the back of the limousine to take it out. The top of the cart had what looked like a tablecloth draped over whatever was hidden underneath it. Once the cart was on the sidewalk, Miles took hold of the handle and wheeled the cart away from the car door. Finally a man dressed all in black stepped out of the limousine with the help of the chauffeur. It was Rupert, smiling from Brooklyn to Bronx, with his dark glasses on.

"Hey! There's Rupert H. Hanley!" someone yelled from the street.

While the chauffeur closed the limousine door, Rupert waved to everyone as people cheered, gawked and clapped as if he was a movie star walking the red carpet at the Oscars. The chauffeur headed towards the front door of the bar and opened it up.

"Hey, who's that?" someone in the bar yelled.

"I can't see that well. Is it a movie star?" someone else asked.

When Gloria's children, Teresa and Faye saw Rupert, they all stared at each other. Zoe went to the storage room where Gloria and Stephanie were.

"Ma, Stephanie, you won't believe who just pulled up and is about to come inside.

Rupert was the first to strut through the door as he flashed his pearly whites, which lit the bar up. He had his hands out in front of himself as to say, 'You like what you see?'

Sashaying from side to side, pulling the fancy cart, was Miles, one hand dabbing at his eye and the other hand pulling the cart. Everyone was frozen and marveled at Rupert's presence. He was so intimidating as he walked in that instead of people going near him, they stepped back as if he wasn't really real. He enjoyed his entrance as the two walked in and the chauffeur closed the door and headed back towards the limo.

As Rupert exaggerated as he looked around making deep leans as he put his hand above his dark glasses and tried squinting, everyone was wondering what he was doing.

"Hey Miles!" he screamed so everyone could hear him. "I had heard through the grapevine that here at Archie Bunker's place they were having a celebration!" When he said that, Miles just nodded. "I heard that they would be celebrating the life of a dearly departed!" Again Miles nodded as Rupert preached. "Well now, in that case; I came to celebrate the life and not the death of a Mr. Archie Bunker!" The way Rupert was talking, you could almost feel in the air that someone was just about to shout out a few hallelujahs and amens. "For those here at this wonderful establishment who do not know who I am, ha-ha! I am the most hap-nin, charismatic, fun havingest, pearly white showing, the coolest, the foulest architect of amusement and excitement! Rupert! H! Hanley!" As usual, when he said this, he lifted up his head like when a wolf howls to the moon. "And by the way! The 'H' is for, 'Hey! How come everyone ain't celebrating?!'"

One thing about Rupert was that he had everyone's attention. Everyone was looking at him as if he was a brand new model Rolls Royce of their favorite color just rolled out on display. He dripped excitement and the air around him was so thick that a knife could have cut through it. The shock of seeing him and hearing his boisterous, pompous personality took a few minutes for people in the bar to get used to. He was like a very rare jewel that they didn't come across very much.

Rupert quickly walked over to the jukebox, unplugged when Stephanie and Matthew started performing. He bent over and plugged it in as everyone watched, and instantly a fast popular song came on. He first started bopping to the beat then he did a little shuffle to the music as he headed back to where he was standing. He then said, as he still had everyone's attention. "You can't celebrate without music, and you can't celebrate without..." When he said that, he snapped his finger to Miles who, right on cue, removed the white cloth over the cart ,exposing "...CHAMPAGNE!"

When everyone saw all the fancy champagne, everyone screamed and cheered as if their favorite boxing champ had defeated his huge and much bigger and stronger opponent.

As everyone continued staring at him in wonder, astonishment and awe, with huge smiles on their face, he addressed the crowd again.

"The champagne is on me. Why? Because I am Rupert! H! Hanley! And the 'H' is for 'How come y'all still just standing around? Come on and celebrate!"

While he was talking, right on cue, he popped the cork on one of the champagne bottles when he said, 'celebrate.' It was as if the sound released them from a hypnotic daze and the key word was said which would cause them to dance, laugh, scream, cheer and just be merry. In that instant, he became Simon Sez and they did what he said, which was to celebrate. Rupert then turned and looked at Teresa who was so stunned by his appearance that she looked like she was about to fall over the bar from leaning toward him.

"Hello, lovely lady," he said to her. This just caused her to blush and giggle, like a girl.

"H-h-hello Mr. Handsome, er, ah, Hanley," she finally was able to spit out.

Rupert then snapped his finger and Miles began carting all those bottles of champagne around to the door of the bar. "I'm sure that you could find some use for all this hooch, hmm?" He then flashed Teresa his smile, which nearly caused her to keel over.

"Y-yes Mr. Hanley, sir." Teresa was nodding her head rapidly with a smile.

"Please, please, call me Rupert," he insisted in a very charming voice as he handed her the open champagne.

"Rupert!" she yelled hysterically as she took the bottle from his hand and continued laughing. Everyone started laughing, too, at the way she was acting. Once he turned from the bar, that's when people walked up to him and greeted him. Rupert was charming, polite and friendly to whomever approached him but he was looking for just one person, and she was walking his way with Stephanie.

"Rupert you ol' devil, what are you doing here? I thought you were in Acapulco!" Gloria playfully hit him, then they both kissed and embraced each other.

"Well I was, but I had to come and support you on such a sad occasion. I thought about you all night and this morning. I wanted to come to the funeral, but like an idiot, I forgot to find out where it was." When he said that, Gloria was happy. She couldn't afford to have Chris and Rupert running into each other. That would have been disastrous.

"Oh I would've loved to have you there," she lied, but what the hell. It was over.

Stephanie, who was standing next to Gloria, coughed lightly to get her attention and to snap her out of the trance that she was slowly going into. When Gloria realized what Stephanie was doing, she quickly got the hint.

"Oh Rupert, you do remember my cousin." Then she nodded toward Stephanie. She purposely didn't say her name to see if he would remember.

"Oh-oh, of course," he said as he pretended to remember her. "It is good to see you again…" He was waiting for Stephanie to say her name but she decided to let him hang himself but to her surprise, he was able to say a name, 'Sheila.'

"Stephanie," she said dryly.

"That is right," he said as he sucked his teeth and snapped his finger. "Stephanie it is. It sure is Stephanie. How could I have forgotten such a beautiful, exotic name like Stephanie for such a beautiful, exotic looking young lady like yourself? Please forgive me," he asked oh-so-elegantly. Stephanie instantly started blushing and began to hide her face. He had won her over.

"Oh, it is okay, Mr. Hanson." She purposely said his name incorrectly, trying to prove a point. "Anyone could make a mistake like that. It is so good seeing you again and thank you in person for all the beautiful clothes." Stephanie then took hold of his hand and reached up to give him a kiss, then left the two of them and walked back over to Jerry.

Rupert failed. She didn't fall for the, 'How could I forget' line. If he noticed that she had called him, 'Hanson' instead of 'Hanley' he never let on. Gloria noticed it instantly but didn't comment on it. Rupert quickly decided to change the subject to get all of the attention back to Gloria.

"Speaking of clothes," he said, looking at her up and down. "For a woman in mourning; you look absolutely beautiful in your dress. It fits you perfectly."

"Oh thank you so much, Rupert. You look very dapper in your suit. There is something about a man in black that makes him so very sexy."

"Whoa!" he exclaimed as he started patting his blazer and pants pocket. Gloria looked puzzled.

"What are you doing, Rupert? She asked as she chuckled.

"I have to remind myself to talk to my tailor. Throw away all my suits and fill my closet up with only black clothes!" he chuckled as Gloria swatted at him with a smile, then waved him off.

"Oh you!" she exclaimed as she took hold of his hand and pulled him. "I want you to see what is left of our food table. Do you like it?"

Rupert looked at the table in awe. "Wow! You women did all this by yourselves?"

"Sure did," she said proudly as she stuck out her chest.

"Well, it looks absolutely beautiful. You did an excellent and delicious job.

"Let me take you over by the dessert table. I wanna introduce you to my son Joey."

As they approached, Joey stood up and extended his hand to Rupert.

"Hello sir, I'm Joey. Pleased to meet you," he said very courteously and respectfully.

"Well, pleased to meet you too, young man,; and please call me Rupert. All my friends do." He then turned to Gloria. "What a handsome young man he is," he commented.

Gloria and Rupert then went to where Zoe and Matthew were sitting and chatting comfortably with Teresa's three girls near the food table.

"My other children wanna tell you thank you for the clothes too, just like Joey."

As they approached, all five of them stood up and extended their hands to him and said thank you for the clothes. Rupert was very gracious to them. "Well, I'm glad that you liked the styles. It was my pleasure—a gift from me to you."

The kids all nodded and smiled when he said this. Soon after that, Zoe reached for a plate and looked to Rupert.

"Mr. Rupert, would you care for something to eat?"

"Well, you know something, er, ah, em, pretty lady, I think that I WILL have a bite to eat," he said a tad nervously because he couldn't remember her name.

"Mr. Rupert did you forget my name?" Zoe teased, but she wanted her mother to see that he didn't know.

"Of course I didn't forget, er, ah…" Boy was Rupert sinking.

"Sunny," Zoe interjected. Gloria's eyes opened wide as she smiled at Zoe.

"Sunny," he echoed as soon as she said the name. "I told you I didn't forget." He then nodded to Zoe then nodded to Gloria to show her that he remembered. Gloria wanted to laugh. She might not have laughed but the kids did. They found it amusing, so amusing that Carlotta decided to get in on the fun, too.

"Okay, Mr. Rupert. Did you forget my name?" When Carlotta said this, Gloria could see confusion all over his face. Gloria looked at Carlota, smiled and shook her head. She wanted to see what he was going to say. "Did you forget that it rhymes with Blue?"

"Now Sue, what would make you think I would forget you? With a beautiful face like that and a lovely name, you are not easily forgotten." Rupert really wanted to get away.

"What would you like to have, Mr. Rupert?"

"Oh, please call me, Rupert, She-er-ah-Sue-er-ah—-Sunny."

"Okay Rupert." Zoe was fighting not to laugh. "What would you care to eat?"

"Whatever your pretty, dainty hands decide is fine with me. It looks all so good."

Once Zoe finished fixing a nice plate, the two headed to the bar area where Gloria had been sitting with Chris. When they sat down and got comfortable, Teresa came over

"Mr. er, Rupert, my name is Teresa. I am Gloria's friend. I want to say thank you for allowing me and my girls to pick out clothes at Gloria's house.

You are a very special man," she said sincerely. "Dios te vendiga, which means God bless you."

"Pues, egualmente. El fabor es mio." Again when he talked, she blushed.

"So, how many daughters do you have, Teresa?" he asked as he took a bite of the food.

"Just three. My oldest is Izabel. She is twenty; Carlotta is nineteen and my baby is Yazmin. She is sixteen. You were just talking with them," she said innocently.

Rupert turned slowly to look at them and the three girls waved to him with a smile. Rupert instantly started coughing and choking as Gloria began hitting him on his back and Teresa started looking very concerned.

"A Dios mio, Rupert. Are you okay?" she asked worriedly. "Yeah Rupert, are you okay?" Gloria echoed.

"Yeah," he said as he began catching his breath. His face was crimson from choking and embarrassment. "I'm fine. I think that I just swallowed my foot when I put it in my mouth. It was a perfect fit but it just went down kinda hard."

Gloria started laughing with tears coming down her eyes. Teresa didn't catch on and really didn't want to know, so when she saw that he was okay, she left.

"Oh, I feel like such a fool," he said, shaking his head. "Oh Gloria, can you forgive me?"

"Oh of course, silly!" Gloria said as she continued laughing. "At first I thought it was a big deal, but you'd only met my family for a few moments. How could you really remember? I'm not mad at all."

"I kinda knew something was wrong. I didn't remember seeing three women. I did remember the young boy by the color of his hair but when the young girl asked me if I remembered her name, I thought that I was going bonkers. That young boy IS your son, though, right?"

"Yes, and HIS name is Matthew; and by the way, the girl who fixed your food…"

"Is not your daughter!" he said with surprise as he interrupted.

"No, she IS my daughter, but her name's not Sunny," she said, still laughing. "It is Zoe."

"Oh she got me good; they all did." Even he started laughing. "I guess I deserved that. I am absolutely bad when it comes to names. That is why my personal assistant, Miles, is always nearby." Gloria looked around and didn't see him.

"Maybe you might wanna ask him if he would like to eat something," she suggested.

Despite all of the noise in the bar, Rupert snapped his finger and Miles was right by his side, startling Gloria.

"Yessss, Mr. Hanley," he said dryly, much differently than he was yesterday at her house when Rupert wasn't there. "It is good to see you again, Ms. Bunker Shaw."

"Please Miles, call me Gloria. I asked this of you the other day."

"Yessss, Gloria. You look absolutely beautiful in black. It brings out your naturals," he commented as he looked at her up and down.

"You look nice too, Miles." She checked him up and down also and she nodded in approval.

"Thank you."

"Miles, Gloria would like to know if you would care for something to eat? If you do, go help yourself." Miles nodded then excused himself and headed toward the table.

As Rupert continued eating, Gloria thought that there was no better opportunity than the present to tell him the news about Kindred.

"Rupert, I have some news about your business that I need to talk to you about, since we are talking about names," Gloria said in a concerned tone.

The Life and Times of Gloria Bunker

Rupert seemed very interested in what she had to say. He put down his fork and knife then turned to face her. "Oh?" he asked as his eyebrows went up in alert.

"Rupert, this concerns Teresa over there." Gloria nodded in her direction. "And Mr. Kindred."

"Did you find out that they are having an affair or something?" Rupert looked in shock.

"No. Compared to what I have to tell you, you will wish that was it."

"Well, I am all ears," he said, looking very serious. Gone was the Rupert who was the joking, charismatic life of the party. He was now Rupert Hanley, the businessman, tycoon, entrepreneur, who dealt with many businesses and was successful at what he did. He didn't get where he was by allowing people to mess around or mess up his reputation or businesses. He was tuned one hundred percent to what Gloria was about to say.

Gloria didn't tell Rupert who told her the information but she told him that it was all found out by an casual conversation. Gloria explained everything to Rupert about Teresa's family and about the new building in Flushing and about the husband going to the building yesterday and seeing all the moving trucks in front of the building waiting to unload but unable to, the irate families, the disconnected phone numbers, the locked building, Mr. Kindred and Mr. Kindred's shady practices. Gloria asked him if he had known about this and he quickly said, "Hell no!" Gloria could see that he was furious. He snapped his finger and Miles instantly appeared with a small plate with a piece of cake on it. Rupert whispered something into Mile's ear, and Miles' eyebrows went up with a look of concern. He then nodded his head a few times and headed out the door and into the limousine, which was still outside waiting for them. Once inside, he logged on to the computer and turned on the printer. He typed in some information on the computer, then waited for all the information to come up on the screen. When it did, he must've found what he was looking for because he sucked his teeth then shook his head. He then pressed 'print' and waited for it all to print out. When it did, he headed out of the limo, back into the bar, and then to Gloria and Rupert. He handed the printout to Rupert and pointed to a line on the printout while one hand was wrapped around himself as he tapped his foot rapidly. Gloria could clearly see that he was upset and agitated. As Rupert checked over the printout carefully but not saying a word, Gloria continued talking to him about the situation. Rupert just nodded in understanding. When Rupert got finished checking over the printout, he leaned back over towards Miles and again whispered something into his ear. Again Miles nodded, pulled out a cell phone then walked away to talk in a more private and quieter area. When that was finished, Rupert looked at his plate of food then pushed it away from him as he exhaled deeply. Gloria could see that he could just strangle Kindred, but he was trying to control himself in front of her. She leaned closer to him and gave him a hug and a rub on his back.

"I am so sorry, Rupert. I hated to give you this bad news, but you had to know."

"Gloria, everything that you've told me was true concerning the building. Its right here in black and white." He was pointing to the printout which he was now folding up and putting into his pocket.

"Gloria, I can't believe that he told the renters that the place would be ready at the first of this month. That building will not be up to par till November—now later what you told me; if it's a Hanley building, it is supposed to be built with quality materials. No cutting corners. Gloria, you don't know how much you have saved my life. I knew that you were a very special person from the moment I met you." Rupert reached for her hand and held it gently in his.

"Well, I care what happens to you and I care for that woman with the sad face right there," she said as she nodded toward Teresa, who looked to be preoccupied in thoughts.

"Well, I think that I can do something about that sad face," he said as he began to smile.

Rupert called Teresa over to them. When she came, Gloria told her how she told Rupert about her dilemma and found out that the building was his but due to Kindred's shady practices she was having this problem about moving and money. When she mentioned Kindred's name, Teresa instantly knew him. Gloria saw anger on her face.

Rupert responded by telling Teresa how sorry that he was that she had been through the money and moving ordeal. He told her that she didn't have to worry anymore. He then pulled out his checkbook and wrote her a check to cover the money that she dished out for the apartment plus extra for pain and suffering. Again, he told her how sorry he was. Teresa leaned across the bar and gave him a big kiss after she let out a joyous scream.

"Oh Mr. Hanley, ah, Rupert, thank you so much!" Tears were flowing down her face as she cried tears of joy. This made Gloria cry, seeing her so happy. They both began wiping tears from their eyes. Rupert just looked so happy that he was able to help; but she knew that inside he was really angry. After Teresa got finished hugging and talking with Rupert and Gloria, she went back serving drinks, screaming, "Hey! I thought we came here to celebrate! Come on everybody, let's see a good time!" Then she did a shimmy and a jig behind the bar as she moved to the beat of the music. This got the crowd all festive again as the cheers and applause spread through the crowd like wildfire. Spontaneously, Gloria leaned over to him and gave him a big kiss on the cheek.

The Life and Times of Gloria Bunker

"Hey!" he exclaimed happily. "What was that for?" He began rubbing his cheek.

"That is for you just being you. Despite how ticked off you are deep down inside, you still get enjoyment out of making people happy."

"Well Gloria, I like to be fair. There are not too many fair and honest billionaires out there and as you know, there's not too many fair and honest people, especially businessmen, out there either. It does drive me insane when businessmen take advantage of clients. Why, Gloria? The clients are the ones that keep us alive. I never understood that; but I'll tell you this, there is one businessman out there we don't have to worry about anymore, and that's Kindred. As we speak, he is being replaced and being removed… Forcibly if necessary. I do hope that it is necessary. He's cost me a lot of money but I hope not my reputation. I'll make that money back quickly. I'm not worried about that, but what I am worried about is my reputation. You don't get that back quickly. Sometimes you don't get a good reputation back once it has been damaged.

"I'm glad that we were able to help Teresa, but I feel so badly for those other families who moved out of their places thinking that they would be moving into your building. I guess that you can't help everyone."

"Well, as we speak, Miles is on the phone trying to take care of that. At maximum properties, we really do care about the client. Maximum Properties is me. They are going to find out who those families are and find out where they are. I have people that I pay just for when problems like this arise. Don't worry about those families or any other family that's supposed to move into my building. Each and every one will be notified today by phone so they know the status of the building. It is better to do this now and prevent a lawsuit later. They'll have a choice to wait till the building is up to par, or a one hundred percent refund."

"Well in that case, I feel better," Gloria said, feeling relieved.

"How about anudda kiss, babe." Rupert then did a Groucho with his eyebrows.

"You got it; you tall handsome hunka man," she said sounding like Mae West.

Gloria gave him a big fat long kiss on the lips which really surprised him. Rupert put a huge satisfied smile on his face. "Your kiss could squeeze Skittles out of a rainbow, you know that?"

"Well, not everyone is worthy of a good kiss or deserving of one, but I think that your style, sex appeal and personality is definitely kissable worthy and deserving. You know why?" he asked, his voice getting louder. Gloria felt a preachin' about to happen, so she prepared herself as she started to chuckle.

"Why, sir?"

"Because! I! Am!..." Rupert was about to howl to the moon.

"Rupert! H! Hanley!" he and Gloria exclaimed loudly in unison.

"Do you know what the 'H' stands for?" Without waiting for a response, he took hold of Gloria's hand then got off the bar stool. "The 'H' is for 'Howz about a dance!?'"

Gloria laughed excitedly and got off of the bar stool and headed towards the dance floor, being led by Rupert who had already developed the Holy Ghost, as he shuffled his feet and arms to James Brown's *Papa Got a Brand New Bag*.

Everyone looked on and cheered as the two danced. Gloria was admiring his footwork. He really knew how to dance. Gloria wasn't doing too badly herself. She dipped herself and shimmied and wiggled from side to side and snapped her fingers while her feet moved to the rhythm. Rupert took hold of her hand and spun her out then brought her back to him. He then wrapped his arms around her and swayed with her then spun her back out. The crowd was going wild as they encouraged the two to continue on. As soon as that song ended, immediately, Chubby Checker's *The Twist* came on, causing everyone to get on the dance train. People were dancing and drinking, laughing and cheering. Everyone was merry, festive and jolly—just what Gloria wanted.

Even Teresa's girls and Gloria's kids got up and started dancing. Every now and then someone shouted out, "Long live Archie Bunker!" then everyone would cheer and chant, "Archie!" along with whatever song was playing. Someone else would add to the excitement by yelling, "And long live Archie Bunker's place!" which really got a huge ovation with everyone as they stared at Gloria, looking like they wanted her to acknowledge that she was going to keep the bar open. When this happened, Gloria simply smiled, put her head down and she ignored them, acting like she didn't hear what was said. After about fifteen to twenty minutes on the dance floor, Rupert and Gloria decided to take a break to sit down.

"Oh Rupert, I am having such a great time with you. I am sure glad that you came to surprise me. It really shows me that you care. That makes me more attracted to you."

"Oh so you do admit that you are attracted to me," he said, leaning close to her.

"Yes Rupert, I am very attracted to you, even more now than ever. See Rupert, it has nothing to do with the money. You are on my territory here and see how much fun we are having together. You alone without the money is an exciting person to be with. I am so happy just to have you here and see you."

As the two continued talking, Faye came by as she was taking a plate to go and get some dessert.

"Hello you two," she greeted cordially. "Hello Mr. Hanley. My name is Faye and I am a friend of Gloria's." She extended her hand for Rupert to shake it but instead he kissed it which caused Faye to become hot all over. "Oh, Mr. Hanley!" she exclaimed as she waved her hand over her face.

"Rupert, this is the other member of the triple threat who prepared the food table," Gloria commented proudly. "She is a culinary genius, learning how to cook on her own."

"And you did an awesome job, I might add." "Thank you, Mr. Hanley."

"Please, call me Rupert."

"Okay, Rupert," Faye said giggling like a little shy girl. "Ah Rupert, I would like to say thank you for allowing me to partake in the free shopping spree at Gloria's house. I really do appreciate it. It was very kind of you."

"Well, any friend of Gloria's is a friend of mine," he said graciously.

"Well, I just wanted to say that; didn't mean to interrupt your conversation. I'm just gonna go and stuff myself with some more calories."

With that, she left and headed to the dessert table. Once she got all the food that she wanted, she noticed that Gloria and Rupert were staring into each other's eyes lovingly and holding each other's hands passionately.

As Faye watched, she smiled happily for her, knowing that Gloria had been through so much. She headed back toward the bar when she happened to spot Chris making his way back into the bar smiling and casually greeting certain people. Faye's heart began racing and she didn't know what do. She looked at Teresa who was behind the bar dancing and preparing drinks, having a good ol' time. Stephanie and Jerry were too busy going goo-goo eyes over one another and the kids were in their own youthful worlds. She didn't know how to get Gloria's attention. No one saw what was going on but her. Somehow she had to warn Gloria. Without really thinking, she went quickly over to Gloria.

"Um, excuse me Gloria, but ah…" She didn't know what to say.

"Yeah, what's up Faye?" Gloria asked as she stared at Rupert.

"Um, ah, er…" Faye was having a hard time speaking as she tried to get Gloria to follow her eyes, which were looking at Chris.

"Faye are you okay?" Gloria asked with much concern. "What is it?" she asked again. "Faye?"

"What's the matter, Faye?" she heard Rupert ask. He then reached over and touched Faye's hand tentatively.

"Can you talk? I mean, is she choking?" she asked Rupert. "Are you choking?" Gloria was almost in a panic, with her eyes wide open and mouth dropping.

"Yeah, that's it!" Faye exclaimed as she began nodding. "I'm choking! I need to see you over here, and I mean right now!" They both eyed her suspiciously and with doubt.

"Now Faye, if you are choking, how come you are able to talk?" Gloria didn't buy it.

"I am too choking, Gloria." Faye sounded frustrated as she sucked her teeth and put her hands on her hip. "Look how I'm bulging my eyes out!"

Again Faye motioned with her eyes towards Chris, who was now heading towards them.

"Oh Gloria, please!" Faye begged with panic. "I need to see you in private!" she begged with a lot of urgency. Gloria looked at Rupert, then they both started laughing.

"Girl, whatcha up to?" Gloria stopped paying attention to Faye and took hold of Rupert's hand again then with the other hand touched him on his chin and smiled. "Faye is a big kidder. Not only is she sexy and sassy; she is also strangely funny."

"Oh Gloria," Faye said in frustration as her shoulders slumped in defeat and she stomped her feet, beating herself up because she was put on the spot and didn't have time to think of how to get Gloria's attention, which was now unfortunately too late.

"Oh hello Chris," Faye greeted before he approached, but Gloria was too busy swooning over Rupert to notice. Someone in the family gasped but Faye didn't turn around behind her to see who it was.

"Hey, wassup, Faye?" he said with a smile then, when he looked at Gloria and Rupert together, Gloria holding Rupert's face and hand as they stared into each other's eyes, the smile quickly disappeared.

Gloria was leaning into and getting ready to give Rupert a big kiss when Chris cleared his throat to get their attention. When Gloria looked up before kissing Rupert, she froze and didn't know what to do. It didn't stop Rupert, who had his eyes closed and followed through with the kiss. When he kissed her, Gloria still had her eyes on Chris, who looked like all the color had drained from his face. He just stood there watching, not saying a word. As Rupert kissed more passionately, Gloria tried to back up but it wasn't working. She had to pat him on the chest to get him to stop. Once he did, Gloria wiped her lips with her hand, looking very guilty, then looked towards Faye, who was giving her the 'I tried to warn you' look.

"Oh, ah, Chris," Gloria responded, but she couldn't keep her eyes on his face long.

"Hello there," Rupert said in a kind and friendly manner as he extended his hand.

"Hello sir. Chris Barlow," Chris replied in a friendly manner, shaking his hand.

"I'm Rupert Hanley," he said with a nod. "How can we help you, Chris?"

"Well, ah, I just wanted Gloria here to know that my emergency that was on my beeper was easily taken care of. That is why I'm back so soon."

After Chris said that, he quickly changed the subject. "Are you the Rupert Hanley of Rupert H. Hanley, Incorporated?"

"That is I. The one and only and in the flesh, ha-ha!" he exclaimed boisterously.

"Then I'm sure that that stretch out in the front must be yours."

"You are betting one hundred there, Chris," he responded proudly.

"Well, it is a pleasure and honor to meet you."

Gloria was so nervous that she wished that she was able to get away from the bar stool. Chris glanced at Gloria, who was looking like a sad puppy—a sad puppy who had wet the floor instead of the newspaper and knew it, then he glanced back at Rupert.

"So, what brings you to the bar? Did you know Archie?"

"Actually no. I'm here for Gloria to give her my support. Ever since I met her, we've been like love birds," he exclaimed proudly again. Gloria could have just died.

"Oh is that right?" Chris exclaimed, still looking very calm.

"That's right. I flew her to Florida in my private jet and helicopter, and how does she repay me? She robs me by stealing my heart, ain't that right Gloria? Ha-ha." He then took hold of her chin and brought her to him and kissed her. "She is very special to me," he proudly said. "So Chris, how do you know the family and Gloria?" he asked innocently.

At first, Chris couldn't answer because he was too busy staring at Gloria. When he finally spoke, he turned to Rupert and said, "Oh, ah, I've known Archie since I was young; as for me and Gloria?" He then looked back at her with a stone face. "Just passing acquaintances that hadn't seen each other in decades, just passing acquaintances."

Gloria dropped her head as she looked like she was becoming dizzy. Her whole world was coming apart right in front of her and her family. She had done what she had hoped she would never do again. She had hurt Chris for the second time. When she looked up, she looked towards Zoe who was watching. Zoe wasn't able to hear but she knew there was a problem. She was tearing up. So were Matthew, Joey, Stephanie and Faye. All were looking on. Everyone else was still being festive.

"Well," Chris said. "I'm sorry to have interrupted your intimate moment. It has been nice meeting you," Chris said as he extended his hand for Rupert to shake it, which he did. Rupert nodded with a courteous smile then Chris looked at Gloria, who was crying. "Have a good life, Gloria." Then he turned and started out of the bar, still very calmly. Someone gasped and yelled, "No!" but Chris kept on walking.

Gloria jumped off the stool and ran toward Chris. Rupert didn't seem suspicious in the least. He just figured that she had just remembered something that she had to say.

As she made her way through the crowd, she caught up to him and grabbed his arm.

"Chris, please! Let me explain! Don't go. Don't go like this. Look, look. I'm sorry. J-just give me a chance to..." But before she could finish her sentence, Chris just looked her in the face calmly.

"Not again," he uttered and shook his head once, then left her standing in the midst of everyone, frozen and lost for words. He walked out the door without looking back. Gloria was confused and in a daze. She didn't know what to do, say or where to go.

"Oh Gloria" Teresa exclaimed as she shook her head looking sympathetic.

Everything was spinning around her. She couldn't think straight. Instinctively she walked finally back to the stool where Rupert was waiting for her but before she was able to sit, the jukebox started playing KC and the Sunshine Band's *That's the Way I Like It,* which got everyone dancing. Rupert jumped off his seat excitedly and grabbed her hand.

"Come on, toots, let's show 'em how to shake our booties!" he said as he twinkle-toed to the dance floor, pulling her along. At first, she was hesitant and really quiet but then she started swaying to the music, not really getting into it. She still had tears in her eyes but she wiped them and tried to smile. After awhile, she started to laugh and really got into the song, still looking dazed. She wasn't looking at Rupert. She was looking through him and thinking of Chris. "Not again," she heard over and over in her head.

Gloria did hurt him and she was having a hard time dealing with it inside. The whole family and Teresa and Faye were very concerned for her but didn't know what to do. They saw her on the dance floor, dancing and smiling. To them, she looked okay on the outside but they were wondering what was going on inside.

A round of cheers went through the crowd and an "Archie" chant quickly followed at the end of the popular fast song. The next song got everyone mingling and taking a break from dancing. This gave Iggy his opportunity to do and say what had been on his heart. He walked over to the jukebox and unplugged it, getting everyone's attention.

"Attention everyone, I would like everyone's attention!" he asked loudly.

"And if you don't give it to him, he's gonna eat you!" someone heckled, causing laughter.

"Sheddep!" Iggy responded in jest. "Anyhoo, now that I got everyone's attention, I want everyone to know that this wonderful, delicious food that we have partaken in today was not catered by a caterer. That fancy table with all the meats and salads and cakes and pastries were all prepared by our very own Faye, Teresa and Gloria." When he said this, everyone in the place gasped in surprise and amazement. "Also, as y'all already know, they are permitting us to drink as much as we want to the memory of Archie Bunker."

The chant of "Archie" picked up again through the crowd. When it stopped, Iggy continued, "And let's not forget Mr. Rupert H. Hanley for his wonderful contribution of all the expensive champagne." All of a sudden, clapping went through the place. "I think that we should thank each and every one, including the youngsters at the table who served us." He nodded towards where the youths were sitting. "And don't forget Stephanie and Jerry," he then nodded to them, "for putting this whole thing together. How about a huge round of applause as they come up and take a bow. All of this was done to celebrate the life of Archie Bunker. Please put your hands together for them."

A thunderous round of cheers, whistles and claps echoed through the whole place as Iggy started motioning for all the people who had something to do with the planning and serving and singing to come near him to take a much deserved bow.

"Hey Iggy!" someone shouted. "Move out of the way. You're gonna block the entire family and everyone else!"

"How 'bout I knock your block off!" he responded jokingly while pointing his clinched fist at him. Both comments got a roar of laughter.

The family and Jerry, Faye and Teresa and the girls and Rupert humbly and modestly made their way around Iggy as the claps and cheers kept coming. Everyone around Iggy kept encouraging Gloria to come up, but for some reason, she was moving slowly. Finally she made her way there and stood next to Rupert who looked very comfortable in the limelight. Everyone around Iggy bowed and smiled as the chant of "Archie" broke out again. Suddenly Gloria became hot all over and tears started forming in her eyes. Her legs began shaking and she started to feel clammy all over. She tried to keep a smile on her face, but it wouldn't stay. Her lips started to tremble and her hand started shaking. A wave of fatigue suddenly fell over her and even though the crowd was chanting "Archie" the only thing she heard was, 'Not again.' She was so drained that her legs were feeling weak and her hands fell down limply to her sides. Lionel Jefferson was facing her, clapping, but he noticed that she wasn't looking right and he became concerned.

"Gloria are you okay?" He had stopped clapping and began moving closer to her. Thank God he did, because he was there just in time to catch her as she rolled her eyes back and almost dropped to the floor. Gloria had fainted.

Gloria was overwhelmed with everything— finding out about her father dying, traveling back to New York and seeing Chris again, meeting Rupert, flying to Florida and back, gifts of clothes and a Rolex, offer to sell house, wake planning, food preparation and burial, surprise visit of Rupert, hurting Chris twice plus the fact that she hadn't eaten since that morning—her body and mind just shut down.

When Gloria regained consciousness, she was in the storage room sitting in a chair with a cool wet cloth across her forehead. She slowly opened her eyes and stared at all the concerned faces looking at her. The first face that she saw was Lionel's.

"Lionel?" she asked in a low voice. "What happened?" She then saw Rupert, who was holding her hand. "Where am I?" As she looked around, Jenny, Mike, Beth, Stephanie and the kids and Joey were there all with concerned looks and tears in their eyes.

"You are okay, Gloria. You are in the storage room. You passed out."

"Yeah Ma, you fainted. Are you okay?" Zoe asked looking frightened as she sniffled.

"Yeah I'm fine." She slurred her words, sounding tipsy. She tried to sit up straight in the chair but was still dizzy.

"It is entirely my fault," Rupert said sadly. "I kept pushing her, not thinking that she should've relaxed."

"Oh don't blame yourself, Rupert." Gloria quickly interrupted. "If it is anyone's fault, it is my own, but I'm fine now. The only thing I wanna do right now is go home and rest."

"But Ma, you haven't eaten anything. The whole ride in the limo, you kept saying that you were hungry. Maybe if you eat something..."

"No Matthew, I'm really not hungry. I just wanna get back to the house and rest. I'm sure if I could do that. I'll be much better. Is Billy still out in the lounge?" she asked.

"Oh no, Gloria. She left a long time ago. She told me to tell you bye from her. You were too busy with..." She almost said Chris's name but Joey nudged her.

"Ah, you were too busy with greeting everyone." She said quickly and nervously.

"Rupert would you mind..." Gloria looked up to him and squeezed his hand.

Without hesitation, he interrupted her before she finished talking.

"Of course I will drive you home. I have to get going, anyway. I have an unplanned meeting at my Queens office, if you know what I mean." Rupert then winked at her.

"Well if it is okay with Mike and Beth, I guess that we are going to go now too, hmm?" Lionel said as he looked at the Stivics, who nodded in agreement.

"Well Jerry and all of us are going to stay to clean up, huh guys?" Stephanie said looking around the room. They all nodded in agreement. They were sure that Faye, Teresa and the girls, who were still out in the bar area, wouldn't mind.

CHAPTER TWENTY-TWO:
Looking for Mr. Goodbar-low

As the limo pulled in front of the house, Rupert was still being overprotective of Gloria. He snapped his finger a few times and there was Miles, who wasn't that far away, handing him a wet cloth, but Gloria shook her head.

"Oh Rupert, you are so sweet. Really, I am fine."

"That you are, very fine, but that doesn't mean that I'm not concerned for you."

"Rupert, it's just been a very overwhelming day, that's all. It coulda happened to anybody."

"It didn't happen to anybody. It happened to you, and that's who I care about. When I saw you pass out, and in the arms of that man, I felt jealous because he was there to catch you, although you were right next to me and I was helpless and didn't see that you were in need. I'm glad he was there, though; if not, you could've hurt yourself badly and that would've weighed on my conscience for a very long time. I don't want anything to happen badly to you."

"And I don't want anything to happen to you either. That's why I'm glad that I was able to give you all that information about Kindred today."

"And thank you so much on that again. You really saved my life and my rep, hopefully.

"You really don't know how much you have saved me. Now because of him, I'm going to be busy for the rest of the evening. I'm gonna take care of him; really take good care of him," he said angrily. "But you don't have to worry about your contract. It is legit if you still decide that you wanna sell. You also don't have to worry about any retaliation on his part. He'll never know that I found out about him through you. I'm taking credit for him being found out, then dumped. He's lucky if that's all I do to him.

When I'm good, I am real good, but when I'm bad—oh, you better watch out."

"He will get his, I'm sure, and I hope that it is soon," Gloria added.

"Well let me help you to your door." He nodded to the chauffeur, who quickly got out and made his way to the back door. When the chauffeur opened the door, Rupert pushed the fancy cart out of the way then got out first and held out his hand for Gloria to take it, which she graciously did. Together they slowly walked up the stairs and onto the porch then she began shuffling around her purse trying to find the keys. Once she got them, she unlocked the door then turned and looked at Rupert.

"Listen, I really want you to get some rest. You look out of it," he said worriedly.

"I am. I'm going to take a nice bath, then I'm going right to bed. I have so much running through my mind that I can't even concentrate. I thought that once I buried Daddy, things would get easier, but I was wrong. There are still a lot of things to worry about, but just in different degrees of stress."

"That's my life. Stress, stress and stress. I can relate. That is why I know that you need to rest. I don't mean to sound like a nagging old person but I care so much about you—you just don't understand."

"Thank you and I appreciate you and the fact that you drove me home and that you surprised me today and comforted me on one of the saddest days in my life. I will never forget this, never in the rest of my life," she commented sincerely.

"Well, I'm hoping that I will be right at your side for the rest of your life. I hope that you haven't forgotten what I said, Gloria. I still love you and wanna marry you."

"Oh Rupert, please..."

"No-no, I'm sorry. No pressure. I just wanted to remind you, that's all." He threw his hands up in surrender. "Well, shweetheart," he said, sounding like Bogey. "Parting is such sweet sorrow."

"Hey, since when did Bogey star in Romeo and Juliet?" Gloria asked as she chuckled.

"That *was* Romeo and Juliet, wasn't it?!" he asked, then he started laughing too.

"Oh Rupert, you are very special." Gloria took hold of his face and gave him a kiss.

"Whoa! These spontaneous kisses can really be addicting! I like them a lot," he commented

"You better get going and I better go lie down," she said as she began rubbing down his chest, then she touched him on his nose.

"Remember that I love you. No pressure. I'll call you later?" He began walking down the porch but still kept his eyes on her as she opened the door and was about to walk in.

The Life and Times of Gloria Bunker

"Okay," she replied as she nodded.

Rupert was heading back to the limo, but before he got in, Gloria called out to him.

"I love you too," she exclaimed with a slight smile, but she had a sad, tired and withdrawn look on her face. Rupert just looked up at her, first in confusion, then he smiled and nodded and got into the limousine.

Once inside the house, she started walking around exhaustedly. Being alone in the house caused her to be free to do and say what she wanted…loudly. She wanted to shout and scream but she just didn't have the energy to do it, so she just cried.

Gloria cried hard and she cursed and she cried and she stomped and she cried some more, all the way up to her parents' room, where she plopped down on the bed hard with her face in the pillow. She was really beating herself up for what she had done to Chris. She couldn't seem to shake it. Seeing that image of him while she was being kissed by Rupert, then afterwards when she ran after him trying to explain—he didn't even pull away from her. He just said, "Not again." and then left. "Why couldn't he have yelled or something? Why did he have to be so dignified? It is not fair! It is just not fair!"

Gloria finally sat up after some crying time and made her way to the phone.

"I gotta call him. I have to explain." She called him on his private number and she let the phone ring for a long time but he didn't pick up. Gloria expected that. She then started calling him on his other numbers on the card he had given her, but still no answer. "Oh please Chris, pick up the phone," she pleaded, but nothing. Gloria decided to get out of her funeral clothes and head for the bath tub to relax. When done and after putting on regular clothes, she tried calling the numbers again, but still nothing.

"Chris, Chris, I'm so sorry. Please let me talk to you. I need to hear your voice and see your face," she pleaded, but the only response she got was a ringing sound from the phone.

Gloria dabbed at her eyes, wiping away the tears, then sniffled a few times and headed down the stairs with her keys in her hands.

"If Chris won't answer the phone, then I am going over to his house," she said with determination in her voice.

Gloria put her dark glasses on and headed out of the house and a few blocks down to Chris's house. There were no lights on in the place or any sound coming from inside. That didn't mean anything, because he lived by himself and could be lying down. She prayed first before she rang the doorbell that he would be there then she rang. She waited but nothing happened. No one came to the door. She rang again and again but still nothing. She even rang it for a long time but that didn't work. She banged on it in frustration and said, "Dammit Chris, open up! I know that you are in there!" The tears flowed but it didn't do any good. If he was in there he wasn't answering.

Gloria took out her phone and began calling his numbers again and even heard the phone ring inside the house.

"Hmm, a busy man like Chris doesn't have an answering machine? That is strange," she said suspiciously. "He turned it off because he probably knew that I'd be calling him. He really doesn't want to speak or see me." Gloria wasn't going to give up without a fight. She wanted to see or speak to him and she was going to do whatever it took to do it.

After some time at the door, she turned around and sat on the top step. She started to remember years ago when she and Chris were in elementary school and it was summer and the Mr. Softee Ice cream truck would come down the street and would stop in front of that very house, and Mrs. Barlow would buy two ice cream cones for Chris and her. She liked chocolate with multi sprinkles and Chris liked chocolate with vanilla sprinkles. They would sit on that very stoop where she was sitting now and share each other's ice cream and talk about their lives together. They had thought that they would be together forever and have children. She wanted to be a nurse that week and of course, he was going to be a doctor. They were going to fix and heal the world. The only thing Gloria wanted to do was heal everyone in pain. She had no idea that years later she would end up doing the hurting to the one she had vowed to do the healing with—twice, no less. Oh, how Gloria yearned for those innocent days when life was so much easier, when the knight in shining armor saved the damsel in distress, the handsome prince rescued the princess and kids would fly like Peter Pan. As she thought back on these memories, it only made her more depressed and upset over what had occurred earlier at the bar as she watched the people go up and down the block and cars zooming to God knows where. She continued trying to reach him by phone.

Gloria sat on Chris's stoop till she saw Faye's car zoom down the street, heading to the house. Gloria figured that Faye decided to drop off the family first, then go back and drive Teresa and the girls home since they lived close to each other, but just because she saw them didn't mean that she was leaving that stoop. She hadn't tried to call for awhile and began calling again. She was getting frustrated but she wasn't going to stop and so far Chris wasn't going to stop not answering that phone. As soon as she hung up, the phone rang. Gloria couldn't believe it. Happily and quickly she answered, hoping that it was Chris. If he had caller I.D. he would know that she called and had been calling.

"Hello!" she answered anxiously, trying to find out who was on the other end.

"Hey Gloria, where are you?" Stephanie asked with concern.

"Oh, hey Stephanie," she said with a slight sound of disappointment in her voice. "I'm just a few blocks away sitting on Chris's porch."

"Oh that's great. You guys have made up." She sounded happy and relieved.

"No Stephanie. I am sitting on his porch. He is nowhere in sight. I tried calling him but he won't pick up so I came here to his house to see him. He is either not home or just won't open the door or pick up his phone."

"Well how long do you plan on staying there because Mr. Rabinowitz has been trying to call and…"

"Oh Stephanie, I totally forgot about him." She then hit her forehead. "The reading of the will."

"Yeah, the will. Should I tell him to come over now, to cancel for another day or…?"

"Okay, you can tell him to come over now. I'll be there in a few." "Okay then. I'll see you in a few…and Gloria?"

"Yes, Stephanie."

"How're you feeling?" she asked with concern.

Gloria exhaled deeply. "I'm just running on cruise control right now. My body is here but my mind is very active, going here and there rapidly. I think the best way to describe it is when you channel surf the television with your remote from channel one through channel four hundred over and over again; never really focusing on one show."

"I know the feeling Gloria, but not to your extent. Well, we have some food for you. We know that you have not eaten. That should relax your mind some."

Gloria didn't want to leave the stoop, so she stayed till she thought Mr. Rabinowitz would be almost at the house, but before she left, she rang the doorbell again and called. She still got nothing.

CHAPTER TWENTY-THREE:
The Reading of the Will

As Gloria made her way to the front of her house, a car pulled up. As the person got out, she noticed that it was Mr. Rabinowitz, the attorney. He was wearing black pants, a black vest, and a white shirt with a black tie. He also had black shoes on and he was carrying a briefcase. He had Jewish features with a red beard and mustache, and thin red hair on the sides and back of his head but no hair on top. Gloria noticed that for a man in his sixties, he had no gray. She wondered if he dyed it. As he walked around the car and approached the sidewalk, he called out to her.

"Gloria? Gloria Bunker, er, ah, Gloria, is that you?" he asked cheerfully.

"Mr. Rabinowitz, good to see you. How are you?" she extended her hand to him once they met, but he hugged her instead.

"It has been so very long. Hey, excuse me—as you can see, I tried to make it, really I did, but it has been such a madhouse in my life these last few days."

"Tell me about it," she mumbled.

"My black blazer is in the car. I'm so hot from rushing that I had to take it off."

"Daddy would have been proud. Everything turned out perfectly."

"Well that is good to hear," he said. "Shall we go in?" he asked as he led Gloria up the steps, as if the house was his. She was right behind him.

Once inside, after all the greetings ceased, Mr. Rabinowitz sat in Archie's old chair while Gloria, Zoe at her side, Matthew and Stephanie sat on the couch. Joey sat in Edith's old chair. Mr. Rabinowitz popped open the briefcase on his lap and put on his glasses and started picking up the first sheet inside the folder which she saw held quite a few.

"As you already know, you have all the originals in your possession, but I still have copies for you that you can compare them to. Whatever you need to sign today has a carbon copy. Would you like to get Archie's papers now or later?"

"It is not necessary to do it now. We'll do it later," Gloria said as she became nervous.

"Well, okay then, shall we start?" he said, as he was ready to start.

"I, Archibald Bunker, being of sound mind and body, as of August 20th of this year of 2001, bequeath the following."

"August 20th 2001—that was a little over two weeks ago," Gloria said with surprise.

"Yes, well, a lot had happened to cause him to update the will before he died."

Stephanie and Gloria looked at each other with confusion and wonder. Rabinowitz then looked back down at the sheet of paper that he was reading from and continued.

"I leave all of my worldly possessions to my daughter, Gloria Bunker Shaw." Gloria started to wipe at her eyes as the tears fell. Zoe leaned her head on her mother's shoulder then rubbed her leg, comforting her.

"I also leave all of my real estate and commercial property to my daughter, Gloria Bunker Shaw." When he said that, Gloria looked at him, puzzled, then to Stephanie. Everyone had the same look on their faces.

"All? How much property did Daddy have? I only knew about this house."

"Well, Gloria, that is why the will had to be updated. It was updated a few times in the year. Yes, one of the properties is this house but your father bought the bar's building."

"Daddy bought the whole building?" Gloria couldn't believe what she was hearing. The family began to comment excitedly over this news.

"Your father also bought a burned up building next to the alleyway…"

"I saw that building the other day. That is Daddy's building?"

"No Gloria, that is yours," Rabinowitz answered with a smile. Stephanie, Joey and the twins started screaming in happiness over the news.

"Gloria, your father also just bought the house next door…" he said as he nodded.

"Oh my God!" Gloria exclaimed as she held her face. "I can't believe this!"

"Gloria, you're a real estate mogul now!" Rabinowitz commented excitedly.

"Ma, now we gotta stay in New York!" Zoe exclaimed as she slapped Mathew a high five and began hugging him.

"H-h-how am I going to be able to afford to pay for these places?" Gloria asked; but she was still thrilled.

"They are all fully paid for and I have the contracts and deeds to prove it. I represented him at the closing. The only thing you have to pay for are the taxes and you can make that from the bar alone, plus tons more. The bar is a gold mine."

"Oh Gloria, this is great news!"

"And there is more," he said.

"There is more!" echoed the family excitedly as they continued screaming joyfully.

"I also leave 49% of my stocks to be split in equal shares to my niece Stephanie Bunker..." When she heard her name mentioned she instantly stopped shouting and froze, with tears streaming down her face.

"I love you, Uncle Archie," she cried, then she wiped the tears away with her long shirt that she had put on when she got home.

"...Joseph Stivic, my eldest grandson..." When Joey heard his name, he just lowered his head and stared at his feet and twiddled his thumbs.

"...and my twin grandchildren, Matthew and Zoe Shaw..." When they heard their names, they leaned their heads on each other and wept.

'I also leave 51% of my stocks to my daughter, Gloria Bunker Shaw."

Gloria was numb. The only thing that she could do was shake her head in disbelief.

"Mr. Rabinowitz, I have some questions to ask you after you finish reading the will."

"Well, that is pretty much it, besides the bank accounts and money from his insurance policies. He left all of that to you."

"Well that's what I mean, sir. Where did Daddy get all this money from?"

"Yeah, and if the house next door to Gramps is his, who has been living in there?"

"No one to my knowledge, Matthew."

"Well, someone has to be staying there. We hear noise coming from the house, plus someone gave me fifty dollars." When he mentioned this, Rabinowitz perked up.

"That was you?" When he said this, Matthew looked puzzled. "Let me explain about that. Someone from the office has been stopping by just to keep an eye on the house till the reading of the will. He told me that while checking the house the other day, a young boy was cleaning the back yard, so he decided to give him money for the work. He had no idea that the young boy was you, Matthew. Now concerning the noise; the television set is on in the house. We didn't want people to know that the house was empty. There is even a timer on, too, to shut on and off the lights."

"So why didn't he just tell me instead of having someone come by and check on it?"

"Because, Stephanie, Archie said that you can't keep a secret." He started to chuckle. Everyone nodded in agreement, including Stephanie, who nodded unashamedly.

"No wonder I saw him going in and out of the house," Stephanie added.

"He wanted to buy the place and fix it up so you all would come back to New York."

"Daddy wanted me to move back to N.Y.?" Gloria looked at Stephanie. "That's not what Kindred said. He tried to get me to sell the house, telling me that Daddy wanted to sell. Oh, he's going to rot in hell. Liar!" Gloria exclaimed as she shook her head in disgust.

"God only knows how he got Uncle Archie's number."

"Mr. Rabinowitz, where did Daddy get all this money to buy all of this?"

"Well, Gloria as you know, I've been your attorney since y'all moved into this house, and I know all of your father's monetary affairs. I don't know if you knew this but when your mother passed on, there was an insurance policy—a substantial amount that your mother had taken out on herself if anything should happen to her. All of that money went to Archie. He never touched it. What he did with it was invest into the stock market. As you will find out, he was quite good at it. No, no, he was excellent at it. He bought a lot of stock that dealt with the family's initials. He has stock with a company called, 'Environmental Basic Trust' representing your mother's initials, E.B. 'American Building Inc.' is representing his own initials, 'A.B. Global Systems and 'Greater Securities' is representing you and each one of your marriages. He even has stock in a company called, 'Gemco Biogas' which represented the G.B. when you became a Bunker again. I can go on and on and you'll see it in the folder. It's quite an impressive and extensive portfolio with stocks representing Stephanie's and your twins, Matthew and Zoe, and Joey's initials. Your father bought these stocks for almost nothing and he never touched them. He bought a lot of shares in all these stocks. He bought a lot of shares in a stock representing your late husband Raymond, but Gloria, the most shares from one stock your father had a strong feeling about represented the initials of your first husband, Michael Stivic…and that stock was Microsoft." When he said that, the whole family looked at each other in utter shock and surprise. They lit up with excitement like an amusement park getting ready to open. They gasped, then screamed bloody murder, as if they were atop a rollercoaster that was about to plunge two hundred feet straight down. Rabinowitz braced himself by lifting his shoulders and lowering his neck and head. He squeezed his eyes shut and gritted his teeth while he covered his ears with his hands. While screaming, Gloria shouted, "We're rich!" as she put her hand on her chest.

"No Gloria, we are filthy rich!" exclaimed Stephanie, who jumped off the couch, then started jumping and spinning in place till she fell on the floor laughing.

"That was why Daddy was woopty-doing me but wouldn't tell me what the surprise was. He did all of this to get me back to N.Y. Oh Daddy, I love you," Gloria cried.

"And Gloria, he loved you too, and you are right. He hated having you so far away."

"Well, Mr. Rabinowitz, that explains the stocks but how was Uncle Archie able to buy all the real estate?" Stephanie had already gotten off the floor and was sitting back on the couch after regaining her composure.

"Well, this house has been paid for, for years, so he didn't have to worry about paying a mortgage, just the taxes. He just did a lot of saving and when he had an opportunity to buy real estate, he did. He got it cheap when the owner's husband died and she wanted to relocate back to Italy. The building that got burned up? I was the one to tell him to get that one. I wanted it for myself to open an office for my son, but I found another building with more foot traffic and I didn't have to worry about renovating it. He was able to purchase that by selling some shares in one of his stocks—the same with your old house."

Mr. Rabinowitz then handed her a sheet of paper. "Here Gloria, I want you to take a look at the number amount at the bottom of the paper."

As Gloria took hold of the paper, sobbing, and her hand nervously shaking, she sniffled a few times and looked at the amount. When she saw the amount, her head began spinning and her ears began popping. She was sure that if she was standing instead of sitting on the couch, she would've been floored.

"I just can't believe this." Gloria was exhausted from the surprise.

Mr. Rabinowitz leaned across the coffee table and shook Gloria's hand with a smile.

"Welcome to the millionaire's club. Y'all will never have to worry about money."

"With all these millions, neither will my great-great-great-grandchildren!" Gloria responded happily.

"As long as you handle it wisely. Remember Gloria, this can turn into a venomous snake. Be very careful how you handle it. Don't get too comfortable with it because it could bite you. Just deal with it cautiously, okay? And by the way, I hope that you will continue using me as your family attorney."

"Oh, of course, Mr. Rabinowitz. You don't have to worry about that," she assured him.

"When you are ready, I have the names of some excellent financial advisors who can help and teach you about handling your newfound wealth."

"I would appreciate that, Mr. Rabinowitz. Thank you for everything."

Mr. Rabinowitz pulled out another folder and took a quick glance at it. He then took out a pen and had the family sign their names, stating that they attended the reading of the will. He kept one sheet and the other went into Gloria's folder. He then handed the folder to her. When he was done, he stood up after closing his briefcase and exhaled.

"Well, that is it for now." He started bidding everyone farewell. "Please stay in touch."

He began making his way to the door when Stephanie who was closest opened it.

"Take care, Mr. Rabinowitz," she said with a smile. He nodded and left.

When Stephanie closed the door, they all began screaming and hugging each other.

"Hey! Let's go see the house next door!" Joey said excitedly. "I lived there as a baby for a short time but don't have the slightest idea what it looks like."

"Yeah, I can't wait to see it again myself!" Gloria began looking around but felt empty. "Hey, we don't have the keys!" she exclaimed in a slight panic. "Stephanie, stop Mr. Rabinowitz before he drives away!"

With that, Stephanie zoomed to the door and opened it. Rabinowitz was just about to drive away but Stephanie screamed out as if his car was on fire.

"Mr. Rabinowitz, stop!"

He stomped on the brake pedal so hard that his head nearly hit the dashboard.

"Child, what is the matter with you, scaring me half to heaven screaming like that! What's the emergency?" he yelled through the opened passenger side window.

Stephanie chuckled with embarrassment then cleared her throat. "Oh, ah, I'm so sorry, Mr. Rabinowitz, but, ah, you haven't given us the keys to the properties." Stephanie had made her way down the steps as the rest of the youth came down behind her.

"Oh," he chuckled. "I'm the one who should be sorry." He began digging in his blazer pocket then pulled out the keys. "These are the keys to the house next door. Unfortunately I don't have a key to the building next to the bar. Your uncle only had keys for it. It should be where all his important papers are kept."

"Okay, Mr. Rabinowitz," she said as she took the keys. He nodded then slowly drove away. Gloria then appeared at the door, looking down at them.

"Did you get them?" she asked.

"Well, I have the keys for next door but the other keys are where Uncle Archie kept his paperwork."

"Well, y'all go on over there without me. I wanna make a call." Stephanie nodded, then the four quickly and excitedly headed next door, hooting and hollering.

CHAPTER TWENTY-FOUR:
Searching for Mr. GoodBar-low

Gloria was happy, happy about everything, but for some reason, she could only think of finding and talking to Chris. She zoomed upstairs and started dialing Chris's number. She crossed her fingers as the phone rang…and rang…and rang, but he didn't pick up. She sucked her teeth in frustration as she sat on the bed.

"You are making this hard on me but I don't blame you," she said, "but I'm going to keep calling till I'm a pest."

Gloria then went to the closet to find the keys to the burned-up building. She went to the area where Archie kept all his important paperwork. Everything was in a big box. She brought the box over to the bed and dumped the contents out next to two envelopes, and there they were. She knew they were the keys because they were labeled with the addresses. She didn't know what was inside the envelopes because they were unmarked. She was about to open them, but from the side window she heard Stephanie calling her.

"Gloria! Gloria!" she yelled loudly from the second floor window next door.

Gloria opened up the window and stuck her head out. Stephanie was doing the same.

"What's going on, Stephanie?" she asked with concern.

"Hi ya, neighbor!" she greeted and laughed, causing Gloria to suck her teeth and roll her eyes.

"Oh Lord, there goes the neighborhood," Gloria jested

"Hey, hurry up and make your call then come over. Come and check out YOUR property!" she exclaimed eagerly.

"I'll be right over. I tried to call Chris but still no answer," she responded sadly.

"Okay, I'll meet you downstairs in YOUR house," she said again excitedly but it was not registering in Gloria's mind what had just transpired. She still was in shock.

Gloria headed back to the bed, totally disoriented, and started putting all the contents back into the box, forgetting to open the two envelopes that were next to the keys. Her mind was preoccupied about getting to see her old house again, which was now hers for good, and her mind was preoccupied in trying to get in contact with Chris.

Later, when the family returned from the house next door, they had time to digest everything that had happened to them. They all had calmed down and were slightly returning back to normal. The twins began joyfully heading downstairs but before they reached the stairs, Matthew turned to Gloria to inquire something.

"Hey Ma, can we call Grammy and tell her the news, or do you wanna?"

'Oh please, Matthew," Gloria said, plopping down on the couch. "You and Zoe do the honors. Please tell her everything." Stephanie, who was sitting next to Gloria, and Joey, who was sitting in Archie's old chair, started laughing. "Maybe now she'll stop annoying me concerning Ray's insurance policy," she mumbled to the two near her. Matthew nodded then they continued heading downstairs.

"Well, it's dinnertime. I am starving!" Joey commented as he slapped his knees.

"You gotta be out of your mind!" Stephanie exclaimed. "All that food you ate at the bar—I can't believe that you have room to eat more."

"Well today is a celebration. My Gramp's life was celebrated today by hundreds of people and we sent him to heaven in style. I also found out today that I am going to have another sibling arriving soon and I found out today that I am a millionaire. Why not eat? Boy! I can't wait to tell Dad!" He exclaimed excitedly. "Ma, do you wanna tell him?"

"No honey. You do the honors. Wait till he finds out about Daddy buying me our old house. Isn't this just a riot?!" She commented as she laughed. "Wait till I tell Lionel!"

"So, what do you think you are going to do with the house next door?"

"Well Stephanie, I was hoping now that you're well-to-do, one of you would take it."

"Sorry cousin. I'm staying with my man in Long Island City, plus it is closer to Manhattan. That's where all the auditions are."

"Joey?" Gloria asked.

"Sorry Ma. I love ya but right now I am leaning towards no. I am happy about the money but I just started the school year and, ah, I don't know, Ma. My heart is California……I think." Joey was sounding like he really didn't know what to do. "I'm going in the kitchen to eat." He jumped off the chair and headed quickly into the kitchen, leaving the two women laughing.

"Like father..."

"...Like son."

"So, ah, cousin, does this mean that you are going to stay in New York?"

Gloria hesitated, then rolled her eyes and smiled. "Yeah, I'm going to stay." When Gloria said yes, Stephanie jumped up and leaned across the couch and hugged her. "I don't need a boulder to drop on my head to get the hint that I should stay," she said, sounding muffled under Stephanie's embrace.

"Well, it's so good to have you back. So, now then," Stephanie slapped her knees as she changed the subject. "What are you going to do about Rupert and Chris?"

"Oh Stephanie, I made such a mistake. I don't know what to do. I gotta talk to Chris. I can't believe that I hurt him again." Instantly, Gloria was crying. "Believe it or not, and I mean this from the bottom of my heart, getting to see Chris and being able to explain everything to him is more important to me than the money."

"So are you saying that you love Chris?" When Stephanie asked this, Gloria hesitated a long time before answering.

"That's not what I'm saying. I-I I j-just wanna be able to, to..."

"To what, Gloria? Look, let's say that you see him and he is willing to speak to you. What are you going to say to him? 'Chris, I'm sorry that you caught me snuggling up with a handsome billionaire? I didn't mean it? I'm attracted to both of you?' If I was Chris, I would do either two things if you came to me like that. I would say, 'Take Rupert and I don't want to see you again', or if I really love you, like he says he does, I am going to want to know right then and there who you wanna be with. None of this dangling on a string business—me or him, I wanna know now."

"Stephanie, I don't know!" Gloria yelled in frustration.

"Well, you better know and you better know quickly or no matter how much you have, financially you will be happy, but personally, you will be poor, destitute and miserable."

Gloria just stared at her, unable to answer as the tears flowed.

"I wish that I could take your pain and hurt away, but this one you gotta do on your own. You already know the answer. I don't understand why you're beating yourself up. You are just prolonging your confusion and pain and postponing the inevitable." Stephanie was giving her a no-nonsense kind of look that Gloria didn't think that she had ever seen before. Gloria knew that she was right, but she still didn't answer.

"Well, while you think about what I said, I am going to call my man." Stephanie kissed Gloria then headed upstairs to talk to Jerry privately.

Gloria sat on the couch in her own world in silence till Joey finished eating and came out of the kitchen. He saw his mother in a daze and went to see if everything was okay.

"Ma, are you still on earth?"

"Yeah honey. Just thinking, that's all." "You want some company?"

"No honey, I'm fine. I'm just trying to sort out some things." "Okay, in that case, I'm gonna head downstairs."

"Okay honey."

With that, Joey was gone. Gloria then got her cell phone and started calling Chris again, but he didn't answer. She tried a few more times before she stopped. She then decided to go back over to the house next door. When she got there, she just walked around it slowly, going through each and every room, touching the walls and windows, smelling the air, listening for creaks, etc. She went up the stairs checking the banister, looking at the ceiling lights and looking in the closets then she went and sat at the bottom of the steps and cried.

After spending a long time in the house alone, she wiped away the tears then got up and headed out of the house. She looked down the block towards Chris's house to see if there were lights on. To her surprise, the lights were on. She quickly began walking down the street to his house, hoping that he would answer the door. When she got there, she ran up his steps and anxiously, she began knocking on the door. She waited awhile but no answer. With frustration, she walked down the steps then faced the house.

"Chris, I need to talk to you! Please come to your door!" she yelled. As she looked at the house she saw no movement. "Chris, I know that you are in there! Come to the door and hear what I have to say." Still nothing. She hit her hips with her balled up fists. "Oh, this man!" she exclaimed in frustration. "Chris, I don't know what else to do! Look, I know that I hurt you…twice, and I'm sorry! I'm sorry with all of my heart!"

As Gloria screamed up toward the house loudly, people on the street passing by stopped and looked and listened but Gloria didn't care. She sucked her teeth then put her hand on her forehead and paced back and forth a few times trying to think what to do.

"Chris, I never meant to hurt you. That was why I said that I needed time to think! Chris, I do care about you a lot and I don't care if everyone on the street knows!"

"Tell him, girl. Don't hold back your feelings," an elderly, heavyset woman commented.

"I don't think you should hunt him down. You are a woman. Let him make the first move," a woman carrying a huge bag with a beach blanket inside interjected.

"Shh!" exclaimed the guy with her. "Can't you see the pain on her face? She's hurting badly. You don't know the situation. Just stay out of it," he suggested. 'See, that's the bad thing about society. We are always waiting for the other person to make the first move. I made that mistake many decades ago, trying to be cute and pushing away this tall, dark and handsome young man. Society said to play hard to get, knowing that I liked him. I listened to what they said and ended up missing the opportunity to be with the man I still think was meant for me, but another woman has him now. Her name is Ruby Dee and his name is Ossie Davis. If he's worth it, fight for him. Do whatever it takes to get him back," the heavyset woman advised.

"Oh ma'am, I'm sorry, but you misunderstand. I just need to see him and say I'm sorry. We are not going out with each other," Gloria corrected as she turned to her to explain.

"But you want to, right?" asked the woman carrying the big bag.

"Of course she does," the man interjected before Gloria had a chance to respond.

"Yeah, she does," responded the heavyset woman at the same time. "She's in love with him. Ain't no woman gonna cry and have that kind of expression on her face if she didn't love him. Only someone who was worth it would get this kind of attention." She was nodding her head, satisfied with her prediction. The couple looked at Gloria's face and nodded in agreement with what she had said. Gloria felt a tad embarrassed talking about her situation with Chris out in the open with a bunch of strangers, but she had caused it all by shouting loudly towards the house. This kind of act would only encourage people to stop, stare and to comment. Gloria realized that her emotions had gotten the best of her. Now everyone had an opinion. She really didn't want to hear what they had to say, so she went to the sidewalk where the people were standing and began walking away.

"Hey lady, don't you give up now!" shouted the man.

"Don't worry, girl. He'll get over it and call you later. When he realizes that there's nothing next to him to keep him warm at night, he'll come calling. Trust me," said the woman with the big bag as she nodded.

"But is it worth it to take that chance?" asked the older lady to the lady with the big bag. She then yelled to Gloria, who had her back to her walking away. "Don't give up, honey. There is a stupid saying from that movie *Love Story* that says, 'Love doesn't have to say you're sorry.' That is a joke. If you love them and you've hurt them, do whatever you have to do to let them know how you feel. Love DOES mean that you have to say you are sorry, even if you have to embarrass yourself to do it."

Gloria heard what she said, but she didn't respond. The only thing Gloria wanted to do was to get away just to get her head right. It had gotten dark and a tad chilly, but she didn't care or she just didn't notice. She had so many other things to worry about, which were much more important than some darkness and cold. After about an hour being out, she walked back into the house and was greeted by Matthew and Joey, who were watching a show on cable.

"Where ya been, Ma?" Matthew asked while sitting on the floor up against the couch.

"Just walking and trying to absorb the day." She was sitting on the edge of the couch. "Where are the women?" Gloria exhaled with frustration, as her mind was on Chris.

"Stephanie went to her place with Jerry and Zoe is taking some 'me time.' Downstairs."

"I don't blame her. I'm getting ready to do a little 'me time' right now." Gloria commented as she arose off the arm of the couch.

"Whatcha gonna do, lie down?" Joey asked, while still focusing on the tube.

"No. I'm going to Mexico with Rupert." She braced herself for the explosion.

"Mexico with Rupert?!" they yelled in unison and looked at her with confused eyes.

"Yepper," she responded proudly, with a smile on her face.

"But Ma, what about Chris?" Matthew asked as he rose from the floor and plopped on the couch. Joey turned around to face her to hear what she had to say.

"I've been calling Chris since I got home but he won't pick up his phone or answer his door. While on my way back here, Rupert called me to see how I was doing. We had a very long conversation; me crying and laughing and so on. He understood. I even told him about the will and he was head over heels happy. That's when he said that we should go out and celebrate the good news. He wanted to take us all out but I told him that I just wanted to be alone with him."

"But Mexico?!"

"Yes Mexico," she responded as she nodded. "He had promised to take me after the funeral. Well, it is after the funeral. We're just going out to eat and dance. We'll make sure that I'm back by morning," Gloria assured them.

"I hope so. Remember that Joey, Zoe and I promised Reverend Felcher that we would be at church tomorrow," Matthew reminded her.

"Don't worry Matthew, Rupert knows that already. He is a respectful man," she assured him. "Well, let me go and get ready. He'll be here in a little while."

A half hour later, Gloria came down the stairs smiling and looking ready for her trip, then noticed that Zoe had made her way up the stairs.

"You really look like a rich woman, Ma," Zoe commented as she checked her mother from head to toe with a smile.

Gloria had her hair up and had two bangs hanging down in the front. She had pearls on, although they weren't real, and a white pants outfit with gold edges. The pants were bell bottomed and the top was V-shaped showing cleavage. It was short sleeved but she had a white shawl to drape her shoulder.

"And you look beautiful too," Joey added as Matthew nodded.

"Thank you, guys," she said appreciatively as Zoe was now rubbing the material.

Five minutes later, Rupert was at the door, looking handsome and dashing as usual. He greeted the kids and even remembered their names. They all talked for a few minutes then they headed for the door to leave. Rupert assured the family that he'd have her back safely. Joey was the one who opened the door as Rupert put his hand on her back and walked out of the house, down the stairs, and straight to the limo, where the chauffeur stood waiting till they came out of the house. Once they got to the limo door, he nodded to Gloria with a smile, then helped her and Rupert into the back. He quickly made his way to the driver's seat then began driving away.

Unbeknownst to Gloria, Chris had seen the white stretch limo zooming toward her house a few minutes before, when he had gotten home from hanging out with some buddies. When he had left the bar after he saw Gloria with Rupert, he went home and changed his clothes, leaving his beeper and other things in the pockets. He had become hungry and went to the fridge but there was no bread for him to make a sandwich, so he zoomed down the stairs, leaving the answering machine off, and forgot to turn off the timer, thinking that he would be right back after coming from the store, but while on the way to the store he ran into some buddies and they asked him if he wanted to hang out with them and he said sure. He was just returning to the house when he saw the limo go to Gloria's house. Angrily and quickly, he went into the house to the front bedroom window on the second floor and looked out towards the Bunker house to see Gloria, looking ever so beautiful, being led into the limousine by the world famous Rupert H. Hanley. He stood by the window watching till the limousine made a U-turn and drove past his house. The only thing that Chris could do was shake his head in disgust.

At three-thirty in the morning, Gloria was making her way into the house, which was nice and quiet, when she turned on the living room light and saw Stephanie lying on the couch asleep. Stephanie began to wake up, then sat up and rubbed her eyes.

"Oh, I must've fallen asleep watching television," she said with a deep yawn.

"Nice try, liar," Gloria responded doubtfully. "You have to have the television on."

Stephanie put an embarrassed smile on her face then chuckled. "So, I'm a bad liar. Sue me." She then shrugged her shoulders. Stephanie moved over on the couch to make room for Gloria to sit, then she patted the spot with an eager smile. "Tell me all about it."

Gloria shook her head tiredly. "You know that we promised to go to church today. I'm pooped. I just flew in from Mexico and boy, are my arms tired. I'll tell you all about it in a few hours. We really did squeeze in a lot of fun and madness in the short time that we spent together." Gloria took off her shoes, then slowly walked up the stairs.

"Oh great!" Stephanie commented in a frustrated manner. "You made me stay up all this time for some juicy details and all I get is some squeaky fun and madness?" Gloria chuckled when Stephanie said this as she turned off the living room light and headed up the stairs behind Gloria, sucking her teeth.

CHAPTER TWENTY-FIVE:
Gloria Reveals Her True Feelings

Gloria woke up to the aroma of bacon and eggs and fresh brewed coffee slapping her nose. She wiped the dry tear drops from her eyes, then she put on her robe and headed downstairs to be surprised to see the family sitting around the dining room table. When they spotted her as she approached, they all began chuckling. Matthew stood up and did the Mexican hat dance.

"Hola y muy Buenos Dias, Mamita Gloria," Matthew spat out as he teased her.

"Ma is the only woman I know who could fly to Mexico at night and come back with a tan," Zoe commented as Joey and Stephanie pointed and laughed more. Gloria then touched her face and waved the family off. She tried to laugh but only was able to smile.

"Oh you guys..." she said as she began to sit down. "What's wrong? No one wanted to wake Senora Gloria for some breakfast?" Gloria asked as she reached for the coffee and coffee cup. Everyone looked at each other, then looked at Gloria like she was nuts.

"We've been calling you for a good fifteen minutes. I even called you before breakfast."

"Yeah Ma," Joey added. "I even went up to your room and came in, but you were snoring and sounding like the MGM lion."

"Well, I must admit that I did have an interesting sleep, a revelational sleep." Gloria said as she continued fixing her coffee. The family noticed that despite her trip to Mexico, Gloria didn't look very serene or happy.

"Oh?" Stephanie asked as she spread some jelly on her toast and began eating it. "Why was it so revelation-y?"

The Life and Times of Gloria Bunker

"Well, remember the other night when I had the dream about Chris and Rupert hanging on a tree about to fall into what looked to be quicksand and I had to save them but the catch was that the first person that I save is the person that I want to spend the rest of my life with?" Stephanie nodded when Gloria asked this as she stared intensely at her. "Well, I had the same weird dream again."

"What's so revelation-y about a dream that you've already had? Not to wear a long strapless red gown with gold trimming with a matching shawl with opened-toed shoes when you are about to save someone you love?" The twins and Joey chuckled when she said this. "As a matter of fact, in the dream you didn't save either one. You woke up."

"Well, the difference this time I did get a chance to complete the dream..."

Gloria began telling the story from where she had left off from the last time she had the dream. Miles was sitting in a movie chair with the popcorn in one hand and with the other hand he was banging on the chair in a rhythmic beat chanting, "Follow your heart!" over and over again. Gloria looked at both men that she loved hanging from the branches and their bodies getting lowered closer to the quicksand, and there she was in the middle of the two, not knowing which one to save. She had to hurry or both would die.

"Hurry girlfriend, you don't have a lot of time!" screamed Miles from the chair as popcorn filled his mouth.

"I can't! I-I- don't know who is the right choice!"

Gloria then fell to her knees, crying and panicking as the two bodies lowered. She looked at Rupert then at Chris, Rupert then Chris, Rupert then Chris. Neither could move too much from exhaustion. Neither could scream because of the taped mouths. Even their cries were muffled. The only thing Gloria was able to see that showed some kind of emotion was their eyes—their pleading eyes. Their pleading, terrified eyes.

Gloria began thinking quickly in her head, then turned and looked at Miles, who was sitting at the edge of his seat eating the popcorn quickly, his eyes bulging out with intense excitement. Gloria looked at Rupert one more time, then she looked at Chris. After that, she knew what she had to do. She looked at Chris and shook her head.

"I'm sorry, Chris!" Gloria cried as the tears flowed down her face hard. When Chris heard her, he exhaled deeply in disappointment and frustration, then lowered his head in surrender. Gloria ran to the outer edge of the quicksand towards Rupert. When she got to the tree, she began to climb it. She had her eyes on the long branch that was lowering her two loves into the pit of death. Once she got to the huge branch, she shimmied across it carefully, almost slipping a few times, till she was right above Rupert. Gloria had to move quickly because her added weight was causing the branch to snap quicker, leading it to lower faster. Gloria didn't know how to save him. She didn't have a knife to cut the rope. Even if she did, she couldn't use it because he would plunge into the hole and die. She started thinking quickly, then she had an idea. She first ripped off the tape around his mouth, but he was so exhausted he couldn't even talk. The only thing that he was able to mutter was her name and that she had saved him again, over and over again. She grabbed him by the front of his pants and with all the adrenaline that she could muster, began pulling him up. Rupert was about two hundred or so pounds, but she was able to do it in the dream. It wasn't easy, but she pulled and pulled his dead weight upwards. He couldn't help because his hands and feet had been tied. She pulled and tugged till he was on the huge branch with her that was continually snapping. Gloria then quickly began to back up, pulling and dragging Rupert across the branch as he moaned. After she was so close to saving him, she couldn't pull him anymore because of the thickness of the branch and the fact that the rope was tied where the branch was thin. She was close but still so far away. Gloria then realized that she had a diamond ankle bracelet on. She figured that if diamonds could cut glass, why not see if it could cut through rope. She quickly took off the ankle bracelet and held it tightly in her hand like a weapon. Rupert was hanging over the branch the way a person would lie on the horse; feet hanging one side and hands hanging the other side. Gloria grabbed the rope and hoped that the diamond would cut it, and since it was her dream, it began cutting the rope like it was a sharp knife. Once the rope was cut, she continued pulling till he was out of harm's way. Since the branch was very low now, she was able to lower Rupert to the ground without him getting hurt. She jumped out of the tree just in time to see the huge branch snap off the tree and fall into middle of the pit, disappearing. She went to Rupert to finish cutting the rope to set his hands and feet free. When done, she leaned over him and looked him in the face and smiled.

"You ok?" she asked with concern. Gloria turned to Miles, who was clapping frantically.

Rupert looked at her with tired and weak eyes and nodded with a smile "I love you." He was able to get out of his dry mouth as he reached his head towards her and gave her a long kiss. When finished, Gloria smiled at him.

"Rupert, I love you, too."

To Rupert's surprise, Gloria suddenly stood back up and zoomed towards Chris, who was sinking fast. He looked dead as he hung there, motionless.

"Chris!" Gloria screamed in panic, then ran as fast as she could to the tree and climbed up. Miles was screaming from his seat and stood up angrily as the popcorn fell on the floor.

"Gloria, what are you doing? It is over! You've made your choice!"

Gloria continued after Chris, not paying any mind to Miles.

"Chris! Chris! I'm coming to save you! Just hold on, okay?" she yelled as she made her way across the snapped tree branch which was much more slippery than Rupert's. Chris did lift his head towards her and tried to show life in his eyes but all the energy had been drained from his body, causing his head to go limp again on his neck. Suddenly the branch made a huge cracking noise, causing the big branch to really bend and sending Gloria slipping headfirst downward. Gloria had an opportunity to go back but she refused. Chris was close to death but Gloria wasn't giving up even though she was in a bad spot. All the weight was causing her to lean forward; she lost her balance and flipped under the branch. She then shimmied hand over hand, as if she was on the monkey bars. Once she got to Chris, she swung her body over him and wrapped her legs around him. With one hand she pulled off the tape around his mouth and Chris looked at her as she began holding the branch with two hands again.

"You came for me after all," he exclaimed trying to smile. "Gloria, why did you come to me? You already saved the one that you love," he said sadly.

"It is true, Chris. I do love Rupert, but my love for him is different. I am in love with you. I have always been in love with you, but I've been too much a coward to admit it," she exclaimed with tears in her eyes.

"B-but I don't understand. Why did you save him first, then?"

"Chris, I couldn't live with myself seeing him die, but I love you so much that I am and was willing to die for and with you. Remember, just like I told you about the movie *Earthquake*—I love you to death." Gloria then kissed Chris passionately as the tears came pouring down. Gloria and Chris started hearing clapping again. It was Miles, who was now clapping frantically and standing up, his popcorn now on the ground.

"Bravo! Bravo!" Miles shouted as the tears rolled down his cheeks.

Gloria and Chris just smiled at each other as they hung from the tree, then all of a sudden they both started sniffling and licking their lips.

"Hey, do you smell bacon and eggs?" Gloria asked Chris as she looked around.

"Yeah," he responded as he nodded his head. "And fresh brewed coffee." Chris's voice was the last thing she had heard before she woke up. This is what Gloria told the family.

"Wow, Gloria. That was some dream. It seems like you have that dream every time you have spicy sauce. Whatever sauce you had last night came home with you this morning."

"So Ma, do you love C.B. or do you love Rupert?" Joey asked.

"I already gave you the answer. I love Rupert but I am in love with your C.B., Chris." When she said this, the whole family started screaming and shouting for joy just like when they found out that they were rich.

"Each one of you owes me a million dollars!" Stephanie ordered. "I told you, I told you that she loved Chris more than Rupert!" Stephanie held out her hand for the loot.

"Ma, we all wanted you to pick C.B. but yesterday when you went out with Rupert, we thought that you gave up on him," Joey mentioned.

"Well, I think that he has given up on me," she said sadly then she slumped her shoulders.

"So what does that mean? Are you going to stay with Rupert?"

"No honey. I have to see Chris and tell him how I feel. I want him to know that I love him and wanna be only with him."

"So when are you going to tell Rupert the bad news for him?" "Stephanie, he already knows," Gloria said as she sniffled.

"What?" they all said in unison.

"Yep, I told him yesterday."

"Yesterday? What? When? How? And he still drove you home this morning?"

"Well, he didn't drive me home."

"That low down bastard!" Stephanie exclaimed angrily as she shook her head.

"Listen, let me explain," she said as she slightly chuckled. "First of all, Rupert knew before I went out with him last night."

"And he still went out with you?"

"Yep, I was walking down the street moping because I was trying to see or talk to Chris. As I thought long and hard, I realized that I was in love with him. My cell phone rang and I quickly answered it, hoping that it was him but instead it was Rupert. He was checking on me. That's when I told him about Chris and how I felt about him. He took it badly, of course, but he still wanted to cheer me up. We talked for a long time and he even made me laugh. I told him about the will and how Kindred had lied about Daddy wanting to sell the house. I told him about the building next to the alley and I told him about the house next door. He was so happy for me concerning the will and the property, plus he kept telling me how I saved him because I told him about Kindred. That was when he said that we should get together and celebrate in Mexico. He said that he still wants to be friends and he said going to Mexico would be his way of showing his appreciation for all I've done for him. When I told him about Chris being the main person who knew all about cheating Kindred, he didn't know how to thank him enough. At first I didn't want to go but then I said, 'What the hell; why not?' I did tell him that I wanted to go with him and had an awesome time, just like when we went to Florida. We did the limo to the private plane to his resort. Since he had to do important business there this morning and the only reason he had left Mexico anyway was to surprise me at the bar yesterday, I couldn't have him bring me all the way back to NY then turn around and fly right back, so I told him just to send me back alone. He was reluctant but finally agreed to it."

"See I told you; just like I said. That Rupert is just the salt of the earth; the salt of the earth, I tell ya," Stephanie commented as she nodded and looked around the table. Gloria just smiled at her, then shook her head while drinking her coffee.

"You are chock full of jokes, you know that, Stephanie?" Gloria commented then her eyes lit up like a Macy's display window on Christmas. "Oh that reminds me; I gotta call Faye and tell her about my keeping the bar open. We have to restock the place. Now that we have money, we can have the bar stocked up on Monday. Let me call Faye now. Maybe we can get together this early." Gloria glanced at her watch. "Who knows? Today is Sunday. She just might be busy."

"Yeah, she's been spending all her time with us and with Teresa and her family. She probably hadn't had time to do anything for herself; God bless her—her and Teresa, and she has been through so much building mess. She told all of us about what you'd done for her and how Rupert saved the day."

"Yeah, but they still don't have a place to stay. They are…They are…" Gloria's mind started to wander and the family started to notice this and became worried about her.

"Ma, what is wrong?" Zoe asked.

"You know something, guys? God works in mysterious ways. It's been staring me in the face and I've been looking around it. Teresa and her family need a place to stay …"

"And we have the house next door!" They interjected with glee as Gloria nodded.

"That's an excellent idea, Ma!" Zoe agreed as Matthew and Joey nodded.

"Oh Gloria, that would really help them a lot, plus I'm sure that Teresa wouldn't mind being back in the neighborhood."

Gloria jumped up and went to the phone quickly. She still looked preoccupied and miles away. Even the family murmured that she looked spaced out, sad and depressed.

Gloria was able to get in contact with Faye. Faye agreed to meet her at the bar. Gloria also asked Faye if she would bring Teresa with her. Gloria told her that she would explain all when they arrived. Gloria said that an hour would be good and Faye agreed.

When Gloria got off the phone, she immediately called Chris. The phone rang but this time the answering machine came on. Gloria knew that he was home. When it beeped to leave a message, she got nervous and didn't know what to do. Should she talk or should she hang up? She decided to talk but didn't know what to say so she said something brief.

"Ah, hello Chris, it is Gloria. I know that you are there screening your calls, but I need to talk to you. I..." Before she had a chance to finish, the machine cut her off. She was hoping that it was the machine and not Chris. Gloria walked back to the table more depressed than she was before she left.

"Oh Gloria, I don't like seeing you like this. We are all hurting with you," Stephanie said sympathetically as she and the others started to look depressed.

"This should be the happiest time in my life. My dad went out on top and his legacy will continue forever, so why do I just feel so—so much like sh..."

"Sh-sh-should I fix you another cup of coffee there, Gloria? You know something? I'm coming with you down to the bar. Jerry is supposed to meet me this morning. I'll just tell him to meet me over at the bar." Stephanie interjected quickly.

"Ma, we would love to stay with you but we promised Reverend Felcher that..."

"It is okay honey, I know. You three go and enjoy the service. Say a prayer for me while you're at it." Gloria held out her coffee cup as Stephanie poured, then she fixed herself a plate of food before she went upstairs to get ready to go to the bar.

The family continued in light conversation and occasionally Gloria quipped and even laughed to lighten the mood. No need to make the family unhappy because of her mistake. But her mind was far away, wondering how Chris was and wondering what he was doing and if he could find it in his heart to forgive her for what she had done.

CHAPTER TWENTY-SIX:
Real Estate, Pastries, and Pies—Oh My!

Gloria and Stephanie ate quickly then made it to the bar within the hour. They had stopped first at Chris's house, but he didn't answer. After that, they had a casual walk down the street to the bar. When they got to the avenue, they window-shopped and commented at all the items that they could afford now because of the money. They even had time to check out the building next to the alleyway. Gloria saw that it was gutted but with the money, she would be able to fix it. She saw potential in it once it was renovated, and that's what they were talking about in the bar as they waited for the two women to arrive. Stephanie went and made some coffee for the ladies and brought some pastries.

Gloria kept dialing Chris to see if he'd pick up the phone. When Stephanie came and sat, she looked at Gloria's face to discover that she looked like she hadn't slept in days.

"Gloria, this just is not healthy, you being like this; I'm really worried about you."

"Stephanie I'm fine, really," she assured her.

"Yeah uh huh, your face says one thing but you tell me something else. Just give him time to calm down. I'm sure that everything will work out. He's an intelligent, good man..."

"Yes he is Stephanie, which is why I can't get over the pain from hurting him twice. I wonder if there was any other way to have avoided this. I tried, Stephanie. I kept telling him that I needed more time."

"Look, stop beating yourself up over it now. It happened. You cannot change what happened. But the good thing about it is that you are going to be able to fix it. There is a reason why after all these years he has come back into your life. Everything is going to work itself out," Stephanie assured her with much confidence.

As they continued talking, coming through the door with the keys were Faye, Teresa and surprisingly, her daughters.

"Hey you brought the whole crew!" Gloria said excitedly as the three girls went to her and greeted her with a hug. "Well, I'm glad that you all came." The girls then went and greeted Stephanie in the same manner.

"What's up, Gloria and Stephanie?" the two adults asked as they came and sat down.

"Hey girls, help yourselves to the pastries on the bar," Gloria offered, then faced the two.

"There is some coffee if you all want," she said then Stephanie got up to get it for them, plus some pastries. "I just wanna tell all of you how I love you for your help yesterday. I could not have made it if I hadn't had your help." She had a sincere look on her face.

"You're welcome, girl," Faye replied.

"Yeah, it was our pleasure; anything for a friend," Teresa added.

"I would've told you all this yesterday but, you know." Gloria then started to chuckle.

"Yeah we understand, girl; it is okay. We already know that you appreciated it."

"Sure do, and we were so concerned. You look much better than you did yesterday."

"Well, a lot of stuff has happened since yesterday that we wanna share with you all."

"Oh?" Teresa asked.

"Yes. First of all, I want you all to know that we are staying in New York." When she said this, the two women started joyously cheering, causing the girls to look and smile.

"Oh Gloria, that is good news!" Teresa said excitedly. "Girls, they are going to stay!"

Stephanie was making her way back to the table with the coffee, milk and sugar, plus some Danishes. She gave it to them, then sat back down. They graciously accepted it.

"Yeah girl, I'm happy for you."

"Well, that makes me feel good because Faye, that means that the bar is going to reopen."

"That is great!" she exclaimed happily. "I didn't want to go and work for those other restaurants anyway—too Boo-gee."

Gloria reached into her purse and pulled out some money in an envelope and presented it to Faye. Faye then looked at it, then at Gloria, then she shook her head.

"Sorry Gloria, I cannot accept that. I helped because I cared and loved Archie just like you. I felt your pain and I cried, too. I won't accept money for what I did."

"I knew that you wouldn't. This money is not for that. This money is because you worked. You cooked and you served drinks and you hosted, plus there's a gas allowance for picking up Teresa and her family and taking them back home. So now, you have to take it." Gloria said sneakily. "Faye, just take the damn money!" Gloria playfully demanded while Faye stared at the envelope and was reluctant to take it. "Look Faye, you haven't worked and I know that bills have to be paid. Daddy would want you to." When she said that, Faye finally took it as tears filled her eyes. Gloria looked satisfied.

"Now then, the lawyer came by yesterday evening to read Daddy's will. To our surprise, Daddy bought the building next to the alleyway and he bought this building." Gloria then looked at Teresa, who was looking at her happily. "And that's not all. Daddy also bought my old house next door. Stephanie doesn't want to stay there and Joey doesn't want to stay there either…" Gloria could already see Teresa's eyes swell up. "So I was wondering if you and your family would like to move into my house rather than that apartment. It might not have an indoor pool but at least you'll have your own private backyard," she said excitedly.

Teresa stood up and went over to Gloria and Stephanie and hugged them both at the same time, as she cried tears of joy.

"I love you two so very much. God bless you both and God bless Mr. Bunkers."

Teresa's daughters saw their mother crying and came over to see what was going on. When Teresa told them the good news, they hugged Stephanie and Gloria too.

"Oh girls, mi novio Hector is going to do flip flops when we tell him the good news!"

"Mom, you mean, back flips," Carlotta corrected as she smiled.

Teresa waved the comment away and just sucked her teeth. "Well, at least I had one of the flips right. No matter which one it was, that's what he is going to do when he finds out!" Teresa leaned towards the women at the table when the three girls went back to the bar where they were sitting eating the pastries. "You know girls, I think that my youngest, Yazmin, has a crush on your twin, Matthew." When she said that, they all started giggling very low and sneakily.

"Isn't that cute?" Faye commented.

"What's even cuter is that Matthew, I think, feels the same way." The low laughter just continued as the women continued in light conversation.

"So when do we reopen the bar?" Faye asked.

"Well I was thinking that if we..." Gloria said before Teresa interrupted.

"Are you going to keep the name Archie Bunker's place?" Teresa asked.

"Wow good question. I never thought about that. Yeah Gloria, what about the name?"

"Wow guys, now you all have me thinking, too."

The women started giving their opinions on what they thought Gloria should do concerning the name, then all of a sudden Faye got up and headed over to the bar.

"Excuse me guys, I just gotta have more of these pastries. You did a killing on them."

"Thanks Faye, but did you hear all the compliments about the fruit design yesterday and all the salads and meats?"

"Yeah, and I don't know how many people came back for thirds," Stephanie added.

"They even liked the finger food, like the deviled eggs, weenie wraps and mini sandwiches. Gloria, they also commented a lot on what you prepared."

"Yeah well, they commented a lot on what we ALL did. All you guys had a hand in the cooking. No one is excluded and every person seemed fulfilled in the stomach department. I think that we all make a good team—you know why? Because we enjoyed what we did. It was fun; no pressure and no hassle. We knew what we had to do and we did it, and the fact that our family helped out made it even more fun. Almost like a family business, huh?"

"Wasn't it a great feeling when everyone at first thought the food was professionally catered then, thanks to Iggy, found out that we ladies planned and catered the food? They couldn't believe it!" Faye commented excitedly, making the women laugh proudly.

"We were so good that I bet if we went into our own catering business, we could give those fancy-shmancy catering companies a run for their money," Faye commented jokingly while everyone continued laughing proudly, when all of a sudden, Gloria stopped laughing and sat there almost in a trance, but her eyes were blinking rapidly.

"I got it!" she exclaimed. "I got it! Why not guys, why not?"

"Why not what, Gloria?" Stephanie asked.

"Why not open up a catering place?" Gloria asked excitedly and with much enthusiasm.

"Whatchu tawkin 'bout, Willis?" Faye asked as she imitated Gary Coleman from *Different Strokes*.

"Guys, I have that building next to the alleyway which has two levels plus a basement. The building is huge. I don't see any reason why we couldn't do it up right."

All the women began looking around the table at each other, waiting for someone to say that it was a bad idea, but no one did.

"Well, I'm in. I'm already here working," Faye said with a nod

"Plus, you'll get tons of more money." Gloria reminded her. "Stephanie, when you are not auditioning, you can come and work here; and Teresa, it is second nature to you. Our kids could help out or we could hire a temp. Also, there is no bakery in the area. We could have walk-in traffic for the bakery in the front and in the back of the bakery, prepare the big stuff and..."

"Now, how would I be able to work both kitchens at the same time?" Faye asked.

"Listen, I'm just throwing out ideas here. Some things will work and other things we are going to have to rework, but it can be done. What do you all think?"

"I like it. I want my own money instead of always depending on Hector."

Gloria then turned and looked at Stephanie. "And you, cousin?" she asked to see if she was in agreement with it.

"Hmm, I think that it is a great idea." She nodded her head with a positive, agreeing smile.

The four ladies began to cheer happily over the plan as they slapped each other high fives and congratulated Gloria on a great idea.

"Now then," Teresa said once everyone calmed down. "What are we going to call the catering place?" When she asked that, all the women jeered, then playfully hit her.

As time passed, everyone had different ideas and something to say about the bar, the catering place and the names of both places. All thought that the name should be changed. Out of the four adults and three children, seven all together, four said it should be made into a family-type restaurant where a kid could come in just to get a hot dog. That would draw in a bigger crowd. There were two floors above the bar that weren't being used. That could be used for something, also. Everyone was excited with their ideas and Gloria was listening to all of them and taking mental notes.

While the women continued to talk, Jerry came knocking at the door and Stephanie's eyes lit up as she ran to open up the door to let him in. That was Gloria's chance to call the women into a huddle and sneakily gossip quickly about Stephanie.

"Do you all wanna hear something really cute? Stephanie finally admitted to us yesterday that Jerry and she are in love."

"Oh, that is very sweet," Faye commented as she smiled and looked in their direction.

"Well, they make a great couple, if I do say so myself."

"I bet you that he's the reason why Stephanie didn't move into the house next door."

"Yep, she wanted to be near her man." Gloria stared at them as both headed to the table.

"Hi ladies," Jerry greeted and they all greeted him back courteously. "Gloria, congrats on inheriting a great business. I wish you all the blessings in the world that it will also prosper and that you will leave an inheritance for your children, too," he said sincerely.

"Well, thank you so much, Jerry. That's so nice of you to say."

"Well, we're off. I just wanted to say hello to you beautiful ladies, all seven of you," he said as she looked around the bar.

"Well, you are welcome to come over to us anytime you want, especially if you are going to talk like that!"

"Amen, Teresa, amen!" responded Faye.

"So where are you two off to?" Gloria asked.

"Well," Stephanie added. "We're going home for awhile. I wanna give him an update on what's been going on here."

"Then later, one of my acts will be performing this afternoon and we wanna be there for support. It's a little club but it is good exposure. We need little places, little venues like these where people could go and watch a good performance you know, like when Stephanie performed here yesterday. Didn't you see everyone's face? They enjoyed it immensely and there were a lot of people in here, too. It was packed to the rafters. Just imagine if this bar had been bigger and all of those people were paying customers. You would make literally a killing—cover charge, a two drink minimum plus food. Wow!" Jerry said excitedly as he imagined this.

While Jerry was talking, Gloria's mind was going a million miles an hour. "Jerry you don't know this, but you also just gave me an idea."

"I did?" he asked with surprise. "What did I do?"

"Come on, you." Stephanie ordered as she grabbed him by his arm. "I'll explain. See you ladies."

"I know exactly what you're thinking, Gloria, and I think that it is a great idea."

"Me too, girl, once you sit down and get everything organized, you are going to be rich!" Faye said enthusiastically while Teresa nodded, not knowing about everything concerning her inheritance. Gloria started laughing and nodded her head with them.

"Wow, wouldn't that be something!" she exclaimed.

"And what's also great is that Chris and Iggy could do the contracting work on fixing the buildings up. I'm sure that Chris would... give... you ...a...good price."

When Teresa said this, she began looking at Faye who was throwing darts at her with her eyes, but it was too late for her to stop what she was saying. She was too excited and forgot about the incident yesterday with Gloria and Chris.

"Oops!" cried Teresa as she lowered her head in embarrassment. "I'm sorry, Gloria."

"It is okay, Teresa. No harm done," Gloria said in a low voice. "I saw Rupert last night and told him that I am in love with Chris. I've been trying to get in contact with Chris to talk with him, but he won't return my calls or answer his door." Gloria's eyes started tearing as she slumped her shoulders. The two women looked at each other sadly because they didn't know what to do or how to help. "I love him, girls, but he won't see me so I can tell him how sorry I am and let him know how I really feel." She started sniffling and wiping her eyes.

"I have so much good news that I wanna share with him. I want him in my life but I hurt him, girls. I hurt him badly."

"Okay Gloria, I'm so sorry. I wish that I knew how to help you."

"Me too, Gloria. I don't have a clue."

"It is okay, girls," she said somberly as she stood up. "Just the fact that you are here to hear me rant and rave." Gloria dug down in her pocket and took out the keys then gave one set to Teresa. "This is for you, neighbor." The tears were now coming down harder.

"Faye, call our liquor distributor and stock up on everything, okay? Then call the distributor and order the meats. I just wanna go home now and just lie down and think."

Faye, Teresa and the girls arose and started to get ready to leave when all of a sudden they heard a knock at the door. It was Iggy. Yazmin opened the door and Iggy greeted her as he came in. Everyone noticed that he had a suit on.

"Hey everyone!" yelled Yazmin as she tried to get their attention. "There is a giant muscle in a suit approaching!" When Yazmin teased, everyone laughed including Iggy.

"What are you all dressed up for, Iggy?" Gloria asked as she and the women checked him out from head to toe.

"Well, today is Sunday. I always go to church to give thanks to the big guy upstairs for changing me. I saw the bar gates open, peeked in and decided just to say a quick hello."

"Hello to you too," everyone responded in unison as some waved at him.

"The last time I saw you, you were looking pretty bad, Gloria. How ya feeling today?"

"She was feeling better before I upset her," Teresa said guiltily. "Reminding her about her and Chris."

"That is not true, Iggy. Don't listen to her. I am fine," she assured him.

"Did I miss something?" he asked, standing there looking confused. "What about her and Chris? Was that why he left so abruptly yesterday?"

"The first time, no; the second time, yes."

"Oh," he said somberly. "You two are such nice people, really."

"I've been trying to speak with him. I've been calling constantly since yesterday, but he won't answer his phone, plus I've gone to his house but he won't open his door."

"Then, Gloria, you need to go to church."

"Oh thanks, but I don't wanna bring my depressed, unhappy self into the house of God."

"Well, I can give you two reasons why if you go to church you will feel much better."

"And what's that, Iggy?" she asked

"Number one, God's spirit and his words will lift you up and make you feel like new."

"And what's number two, Iggy?" Faye interjected.

"Chris will be there," he answered nonchalantly, causing Gloria to perk up excitedly.

"What!" Gloria opened her eyes wide as tears really started to flow.

"Yeah, Chris was the one who got me going years ago. Chris never misses a service. If you didn't see him anywhere else, you will definitely find him in Rev. Felcher's church."

"I'm going," Gloria said as she began quickly walking to the front door to leave.

"Gloria, wait!" Faye ordered. "Let me drive you there!" Then she looked at Iggy. "And you too, Refrigerator." Faye then hit him in his chest, making him smile.

"I knew you loved me," he quipped, causing her to suck her teeth and roll her eyes.

Within minutes, Gloria was exiting Faye's late model Cadillac and was zooming up the church steps, leaving Iggy behind. People were still making their way into the church.

"Gloria, Faye, the girls and I are going to go to the house and check it out!" Teresa yelled.

"Do whatever you want!" she yelled back. "The house is officially yours. See y'all!"

By this time, Gloria was already at the top of the church's cement steps and was going through the big wooden church doors. Gloria walked into the church quickly to the sound of the choir. The service hadn't started yet because Reverend Felcher wasn't up in front interceding. The sound of timbrels and tambourines filled the church, along with claps, praises and singing from the congregation to the uplifting song. Gloria noticed that the church was filling up quickly, with all the seats nearly taken. Gloria didn't know what aisle to go down first. She sucked her teeth wishing that she had waited for Iggy. He would've told her where Chris sat. There were two aisles to choose between. There were seats that were on each side of the walls and in the middle. There were a lot of rows of chairs facing the middle of the stage. Gloria started walking randomly down the right aisle anxiously looking from side to side calling out his name loudly.

"Chris! Chris! Where are you?" she cried as she examined each row she passed. By this time, the choir had finished the song that they had been singing and were getting ready to continue till they heard Gloria's voice, which made everyone face her as they murmured.

"Chris?" she yelled again as her tears continued rolling down her face, not caring.

"Ma!" Gloria heard in a loud whisper. When Gloria looked to where the voice was coming from she spotted Joey, Zoe and Matthew sitting in the fourth aisle middle row. They were looking at her with concern. They didn't give her time to respond. They just nodded to where Chris was, who was behind them, four rows back in the aisle seat.

When Gloria turned to look at him, she yelled across to him as she started to walk towards him, but to her surprise he stood up and started walking away, shaking his head.

"Chris please let me talk to you!" she begged as she still tried to get to him but every time she went one way, he went in the opposite direction.

"Gloria, please, I don't want to discuss this right now. We are in a church, you know!"

By this time, someone had quickly gone to get Reverend Felcher, who came out quickly to see what was going on. When he came out on the stage, all the murmuring instantly stopped, but Gloria was still yelling across the church toward Chris, who was trying not to make a scene.

Reverend Felcher squinted his eyes making sure he saw what he thought he saw.

"Is that little Gloria Bunker and Chris Barlow?" he asked, not really talking to anyone.

The person who had gone to get him to tell him about the commotion approached the podium, then looked up to the reverend.

"Do you want me to escort them both outside, Reverend?" he asked valiantly.

The reverend held a hand out towards the person as if to say hold on.

"No, I don't want you to do or say anything, thank you," he said as he watched.

"Chris, you gotta be fair. Let me explain. Let me have a chance to say what I gotta say!"

"Gloria, I do not have anything to say to you!"

"Then let me talk. Be fair and let me do that!" Gloria pleaded as she tried to get to him.

"Fair?" Chris yelled then chuckled. "That's all I've been with you, nothing but fair. Ever since we've been kids I've loved you." This comment made everyone ooh and aah.

"You'd been my life. If I had been able to marry you back then, I would have. We would come to this very church and we would always ask Reverend Felcher to marry us but he would just laugh at our game, our pretending, but I was serious. We promised each other to always love one another and be there for each other. Do you know how many girls hit on me just to get you out of the picture?" This comment caused the women to murmur.

"Yep, that's true," someone commented loudly, causing people to look around nosily.

"I remember," another said. All heads turned to see who then commented.

"He is not lying," another added, as she nodded and looked around. She didn't care.

"But I played fair. I only had eyes for you. All through elementary, JHS and high school I played fair; not wanting to go to a college far away, knowing that I wouldn't have been able to be by you. When you talk about fair, you should look in the mirror and ask that question because you are the one who didn't play fair. You just one day decided to dump me without giving me an explanation—no warning, nothing. Not even a note. You made me think I did something wrong. You didn't return my calls; you didn't answer the door when I came to see you and when I did see you, you made up some excuse, making me feel confused and horrible. The next thing I knew, you were with someone else; just like that." He laughed embarrassedly as he looked around, trying to focus only on Gloria.

"Chris, please. Let me..." Gloria was slowly trying to get close to him.

"No, let me talk. You had a chance to tell me this almost 30 years ago, so now I'm going to do the talking," he demanded. When he said that, the congregation started shouting.

"Hallelujah!" one man yelled as he threw his hand up in victory.

"Tell her, Chris!" another exclaimed as he clapped rapidly.

"About time!" He held his hand up in a fist, before the woman next to him pulled it down.

"Man! 30 years?" Another man just shook his head in disbelief.

"You didn't care about me or my feelings, but I cared for you enough to let you go without a fight. I wanted you happy, and if happy was with someone else besides me, I was willing to accept that. I wasn't happy about it, but I figured why fight a losing battle. You would just end up hating me and I didn't want that to happen, so I just shut my mouth while you got married and went on with your life, knowing in my heart that you should've been with me. Then you come back to New York for your father's funeral and fate had you cross my path. The sparks were rekindled, so I thought,

The Life and Times of Gloria Bunker

but something kept telling me, 'Remember what happened last time.' That went over and over in my head, but because I was so happy to see you again, all those thoughts just disappeared. You had told me that you were single and not seeing anyone, so that was why I told you how I felt, laying everything on the table. I didn't wanna lose you again, even though I knew that I never should have lost you the first time."

As Chris continued to yell angrily across the church, there was a lot of sobbing and sniffling going on, but it wasn't just coming from Gloria. People in the congregation were feeling his pain and were outwardly expressing it.

"I told you how much I loved you and still love you and wanted to marry you. I even told you that I was willing to die for you." He laughed uncomfortably. "Unbeknownst to me that I was going to walk into your father's bar watching you kiss another man!" When he said that, people started gasping in shock and surprise. That is when the murmuring started all over again.

"She was caught kissing another man!" echoed through the whole church.

"Yeah, um-hmm," he said as he nodded. "And the man is none other than R.H Hanley!"

"Rupert H. Hanley!" reverberated off everyone's lips as everyone looked at each other like they couldn't believe what they heard. One lady looked like she had passed out. Her head went back as her eyes rolled in the back of her head, and her mouth flew open. The people around her began to fan her face. While all of this was going on, Reverend Felcher just stood there like a stone pillar, not saying a word.

"Do you know how it makes me feel that the woman that I love and have always loved is playing with my heart like it was a computer game?!"

"Chris, I told you that I needed more time. I had a lot on my mind."

"Of course, being flown in his private plane then helicopter to his resort in Miami, then back all in one night would really lay heavy on my mind too," he said sarcastically.

"Chris, when you left yesterday, I was dying. I tried to explain everything to you."

"Was that before he picked you up at your house in his white stretch limo when you and he were both dressed up to go out on the town? Where did you go last night, to Mexico?" When he asked this, everyone quickly turned and looked at her for an answer, even though he was being sarcastic.

Gloria started looking guilty even though she didn't do anything wrong.

"Ah, er, well, yeah, it was Mexico, b-b-but Chris, let me explain!" she pleaded again to the sound of jeers and people sucking their teeth and shaking their heads.

"Wow! Mexico!" someone shouted out. "Ssshh!" someone immediately yelled.

"See Gloria, that is what I'm talking about. There really is no need to say any more," he said, holding his hands up in surrender.

"Chris, give me a chance to ask for forgiveness!" Gloria demanded. When she asked this, Reverend Felcher stepped forward to speak into his mic. He didn't yell and his voice was calm, as if there were only the three of them in the whole building.

"Chris and Gloria, this is the house of God, a church, and the church was created on forgiveness. I want you both to remember that." When the reverend finished with that statement, everyone in the congregation began clapping. "Say what you have to say, Gloria," the reverend said patiently. while Gloria wiped at her eyes and the congregation gave her encouragement.

"Chris, I can never take back what I did when we were younger. I was dumb and stupid and selfish. I never should've gotten married. The only good thing that came out of that marriage was my beautiful boy, Joey." When Gloria said this, Zoe put her hand on his leg and smiled. Matthew hugged him, too, making Joey smile proudly. "And a good friendship with his father. Chris, when sweethearts declare their love so very early for one another, desire and lust for each other, sometimes one is not as strong as the other had thought. In our case, it was me. Their own desires and wants become more important, then it is too late to get back to the way it was. You're too ashamed. I've always loved you and I should've had the strength to tell you this so long ago but I didn't have the courage. It was easier to stay away and avoid it than just to say those few words, 'I am sorry' and 'I love you.' But it took yesterday to really see what I really wanted, and that was you. The scene in the bar was because I was just overwhelmed with it all. I had told you that I needed more time and Rupert was the reason why, but he wasn't what I wanted. He was more like an exciting best friend. When you saw me yesterday getting into the limo, I had already told him how I felt about you. He was unhappy about my decision, even though he never knew about you until I told him. We just flew to Mexico for one more time together just as friends. We just had dinner, talked and I came back alone. As a matter of fact, his personal assistant Miles was there all the time with us. Nothing happened, I assure you." Gloria was slowly making her way around to him but this time he wasn't avoiding her or trying to run away. He stood there as he watched her approach. Even though he wanted to flee from her, his love for her was preventing him from moving from his spot. He loved her and he couldn't deny it. She was and had always been his masterpiece, his precious stone, and his ultimate desire. Nothing else compared to her.

Gloria walked down the right aisle, turned left, passing the front rows in the middle facing the stage, then made a left again, going up the aisle toward him.

"Go get your man, girl!" one of the females yelled as she clapped and wiped her tears.

A man in another row yelled out, "If you don't take her, I will!" But his wife, who was sitting next to him, hit him with her purse angrily while he teased and everyone laughed.

"They really do make a beautiful couple, don't they?" another replied.

A little boy who was sitting with his mother asked, "Mommy, is this part of the service or is this for real?" After he asked this from his mother, she told him to shh while she watched intently, as if it was a Broadway show.

Once Gloria reached Chris, she bravely took hold of his two hands, then stared into his eyes that could always make her soften up and melt.

"Chris, I made a mistake many years ago by stupidly and cowardly getting out of our relationship. I won't do that again. I have always loved you, too, and yes Chris, I have always been in love with you and have never stopped being in love with you. Could you ever forget about that other Gloria?" she asked as she stared intently into his eyes.

"Yes Chris," Reverend Felcher asked as the organ player hit a high note. "Do you forget about the mistakes that Gloria made in the past, just like you want God to forget about the mistakes that you made in the past?"

Chris looked up to Reverend Felcher then to Gloria. "I do."

"And can you forgive her for the hurts and pains and confusions that you've suffered, never to bring it up, starting over fresh?" he asked as the organist hit another high key.

Chris kept his eyes on Gloria who was still crying. He wiped the tears from her eye with one hand then smiled lovingly to her. "I do."

"And Gloria, do you promise to be open from now on, never holding back secrets that could jeopardize Chris's feelings toward you, and forgive yourself for the way you acted?"

"I do do do do and do!" she exclaimed, causing everyone to start laughing.

"Good. Well, by the power vested by God almighty himself. Gloria, you have been forgiven," he exclaimed joyfully.

When the reverend said that, it was like chains that weighed Gloria down in an ocean of sadness, depression, guilt, confusion, pain and self pity were suddenly loosened and allowed her to float to the surface to breathe. She breathed in deeply as she felt lighter, more free, more at peace, then started crying tears of joy as Chris looked at her and she looked at him with loving and adoring eyes, then they told each other that they loved one another and hugged one another. While they embraced, the whole congregation started cheering and clapping as they cried tears of joy along with Gloria, then they stood to their feet. Chris then whispered into her ear.

"You know, Gloria, if we weren't in church now, I would be kissing you passionately."

"Don't worry, Mr. Barlow," she responded. "You'll have plenty of time to make it up."

All of a sudden, the reverend nodded his head to the organist, then turned to look at the choir, then festive music and song filled the church. Joey, Matthew and Zoe rose from their seat and went to Chris and Gloria and joined in the embrace happily. A few seconds later, even Iggy came and joined in, nearly engulfing them all in a huge hug as he cried. Everyone was happy for the whole family. The next thing everyone did was start singing and dancing in the aisles; even Iggy and the family began jumping, spinning and dancing. The little boy looked up to his mother with an excited and happy smile on his face and remarked, "Hey, Ma, this is the best show I've ever seen in my whole life!" He also was clapping and jumping to the beat of the music with his mother.

At that moment, Gloria had never felt so complete in her life. What happened afterward just fit right into her puzzle of life. Of course, she and Chris became heavily involved, spending all their time together. Unfortunately, Joey had to immediately head back to California to start school on Monday. He got picked up by the Jeffersons in their limo, along with Mike and his stepmom, Beth. The Jeffersons were thrilled for Gloria concerning the commercial property and getting Lionel's old house next door. So were Mike and Beth. Both families congratulated Gloria and Chris on their relationship and the two families promised to keep in touch. Joey told Gloria that he would pack everything up and have it all delivered. Gloria told him to only send the personal items. She was going to buy all new stuff and whatever he wanted he could take or give away. Teresa, her novio, Hector, and the girls moved in next door with help from Faye, Chris, Gloria and the twins. Come to find out, Stephanie and Carlotta had a lot in common with entertainment, so they quickly hit it off. So did Zoe and Teresa's other two, Izabel and Yazmin, but the two women kept their eyes on Matthew and Yazmin, who became quite a couple, always spending time together.

As for Stephanie, she moved back happily to Long Island City with Jerry and quickly started working again, doing background singing, voiceovers and commercials.

Monday morning was stocking up time at the bar. Teresa and Izabel were hired to work in the bar, hostessing till the bakery/catering business started. Faye, for the present time, was running the bar and the name would remain the same until they were completed with the building renovation, which she had been discussing with Chris and Iggy as they sat in the bar. Iggy had a big piece of paper and a pen while Chris sat next to Gloria.

"So Sunny, what do you have in mind, again? Iggy is the 'artiest' around here. He could draw an idea that you are thinking about."

"Well, I definitely don't want a diner or a luncheonette or a café. I want a family-type restaurant serving all of Faye's delicious dishes, but I also want a dance floor and a stage for performances. I don't just want the place to be a bar and grill. I want a place where a person could come in for one thing to a family who wants a feast; but I also want to be able to have a catered hall, too. I mean, if we are going to cater, we should have a hall, too." She said nodding towards Chris and Iggy.

"Well, construction-wise, that won't be a problem. We'll connect the two buildings together with beams going from this building through the alley then to the other building then close off the alleyway. That property is yours, too. The alleyway will give you an additional fourteen feet of open space, so you'll have the bar, the sealed-off alleyway and the new building. That'll be a nice size property."

"Yeah, plus if we dig the alleyway up, make it level with the basement of the bar and the basement of the new building, support it with additional columns, that could be your catered hall!." Iggy said excitedly with Chris nodding in agreement.

"So, where would the bakery and the kitchen to make all the food go?" Gloria asked.

"Well, you do have two floors above both buildings and with added beams; we could do the same over the alleyway." Chris suggested.

"I like that idea, but I don't want the bakery upstairs. I want it street level, where people can come in and eat and buy baked goodies. The catering could go on in the back."

All three became quiet as they thought about it. They began throwing ideas at each other but they really weren't great ideas until Gloria opened her eyes real wide and sat up straight as if she was a balloon and air was being blown into her.

"I got it!" she exclaimed with a smile. The two began looking at her inquisitively.

"Mrs. Ling next door will be moving out and relocating her Laundromat farther down Roosevelt. I'm sure that she'll give me the place. She might even let me rent it with an option to buy," she said enthusiastically. "I mean, the bar's kitchen is already on the laundromat's side of the building. Instead of us making another kitchen, I'll get Mrs. Ling' building and we could knock down the bar's kitchen wall and just add more ovens, so we'll use the kitchen for the new restaurant and the bakery and the catering. Faye would be in one spot instead of running to two or three kitchens!"

Gloria was excited about her idea. Chris and Iggy both looked at each other and nodded.

"That is an excellent idea, honey."

"I can go even further, and tell me how you'll feel about this," Iggy added. "We could dig underground here also to make the basement even bigger."

"I like that too," Gloria said as she nodded her head, really sounding like a real astute business woman. "Let's do it," she said as she slapped her leg one time.

"I'll find out how much material we need, then the cost, then we can start immediately."

"Sounds good" Gloria said. "Now, let's seal it with a kiss," she demanded with a smile.

"Well, madam, I was always taught that in business, always do what the client says." He then smiled and did the Groucho with his eyebrows. This made Iggy call out to Faye.

"Hey Faye, come here!" he ordered in a playful manner.

"What do you want, Musculasaurus! Can't you see I'm doing inventory of my deliveries?!" she yelled with her hands on her hips.

"Gloria over here told us to seal the deal with a kiss, so come over here and kiss me."

Faye stopped and looked at Iggy as he smiled then sassily replied, "Careful for what you ask for, because you just might get it. Once you get a taste of this chocolate kiss, you'll definitely go into a diabetic coma. I'm just that sweet." Then she snapped her finger in the air. Everyone started oohing and smiling when all of a sudden, Izabel went to him and gave him a kiss on his head, which made him blush.

"Watch it Iggy," Teresa warned with a smile. "Once you go Hispanic, you'll never be manic." After Teresa's comment, everyone started laughing, causing Iggy to really have a hard time hiding his crimson face. To save face, he just waved everyone off as he lowered his head bashfully.

"Is it getting hot in here?" he asked as he stood up. "Hey Chris, I'll see you at the shop."

Iggy quickly left as everyone teased him, then mother and daughter gave each other high fives and went back helping Faye.

"So Mr. Barlow, we're really gonna make this happen, huh?"

"Well, with your beauty and your ideas and my business and brawn...And Iggy's brawn, too," he laughed, "we're gonna make your dream, your idea a reality; and before you know it, it's gonna be completed, just like that," he assured her with a snap of his fingers, then the two embraced passionately.

One of the first things Gloria did to get the ball rolling was have a talk with Mrs. Ling about getting her building, and it was decided that Gloria could in fact obtain the building at a fair price, and that included renting it with an option to buy. Gloria knew all about this since she was a real estate broker in California.

Once construction started, everything flowed so well. When the Lings left the building, immediately the bar's kitchen wall came down and in a matter of just a few days, ovens were put in, displays for the cakes, cookies, pies and bagels were added, a counter and tables and chairs and cash registers were all they needed for the birth of Edith's Edibles, in remembrance of and dedication to Gloria's mother, Edith. There was even a picture of Edith in the logo that hung over the bakery. Teresa and her daughter transferred from the bar to the bakery. Edith's Edibles was an instant success, keeping Gloria busy going from the bakery in the morning then to the bar later. Gloria gave Teresa the authority to hire a part timer only, which she quickly did, leaving Gloria to have to deal with the bar with Faye. The family agreed to help in the bakery after school, which they didn't mind doing.

The bar stayed in business up till a week before the grand opening, then it closed so they could take out the bar and booths and tables and chairs to remodel. The floor design that Iggy drew was to Gloria's specifications. It was completed two days before the grand opening. Chris had told Gloria that everything would be completed in a snap of a finger. It was faster than she thought, but it was still more of a snap of a finger and a slap of a leg. Goodbye went Archie Bunker's Place' and hello to Bunker's, two levels of fine dining, from inexpensive to elaborate, with live music and performances with a stage. There even was a VIP lounge for private parties, from children's parties to adults, and on the lower level, which was no longer called the basement, was the catering hall with tables, chairs and a dance floor.

CHAPTER TWENTY-SEVEN:
Having It All

Opening night, Gloria was a wreck. She had advertised in all the major papers and invited everyone that she knew, but she had no idea that it would be so big of an opening, with Iggy out in the front keeping order. Bunker's was an girls. Faye was running the kitchen like she was only dealing with about three customers. Even Chris helped out and lent a hand wherever needed. Stephanie and Jerry were doing their part. The live entertainment featured many of Jerry's clients, his groups, but opening night headlined Stephanie. She was going to sing and dance later. Reverend Felcher and his family showed up and gave their support and surprisingly, Rupert H. Hanley showed up and took pictures with everyone. He and a group of people took the VIP room. Even Miles showed up and congratulated her.

Gloria walked around doing everything, from waiting to help with the drinks when she received a tap on her shoulder, so loving and gentle. Before she turned to see who it was, she smiled and said, "Sir, you better take your hand off of me. I have a big strong hunk of a fiancée who wouldn't take kindly to you touching his fair maiden."

"Oh it's okay, ma'am because I know this here fair maiden's beau. It's me," Chris said as she turned to face him. "Well, Ms. Bunker, you are a success. I knew you'd be," he commented proudly. "Your father would be proud. He left you ten minas and you made so much more from it. The Bunker name will be around for a very long time."

"Well Chris," she said, moving closer to him. "I am living proof that dreams can come true. I would not want any of this if you weren't in my life. I would still be the happiest woman in the world if I didn't have this but had you."

"There is a saying, 'Good things are worth waiting for,' and I can vouch for that. Sometimes it doesn't happen overnight, but if you pray and believe in your heart, those good things will eventually come to you....or hunt you down," he said then they both laughed.

While Gloria and Chris stared in each other's eyes lovingly, they heard someone cough from behind them and comment rudely.

"These people these days have no respect," he remarked angrily. "They'd rather kiss and hug than work!" The two lovebirds turned around and looked to see who made this statement. When they saw who it was, they both started laughing. Standing behind them were the Jeffersons, the Stivics, and Joey and his lovely date.

"Hello, you guys!" Gloria greeted excitedly as she began hugging them and Joey's date.. "Oh Billy, it's so good to see you again. You look absolutely gorgeous!"

"Thank you, Gloria," she responded, while everyone greeted Chris, then Billy greeted him.

"You guys tricked me," Gloria commented angrily in a playful manner. "You told me that you wouldn't be able to make it." Gloria then put her hands on her hips.

"Well, it's Friday night. What else was there to do?" Jerry said.

"Yeah, we decided to surprise you," Lionel added as he put his arm around Jenny.

"So.....surprise!" Beth exclaimed while showing signs that she was pregnant and about to burst. They all laughed when she said, "Surprise!"

"Well, you all are just in time, because Stephanie is about to perform," she said excitedly.

Gloria and everyone headed upstairs, then she sat them at a 'Reserved' table close to the stage. As soon as everyone got comfortable and the band finished their last song, Jerry came out on stage to a packed house. Gloria and Chris stood at the back of the hall, facing the stage. When he finished introducing Stephanie, the band began playing, then Stephanie came out, looking stunning in her opening outfit. A roar of applause, cheers and whistles echoed through the place as she started to hype up the crowd.

"Did y'all come to party and have some fun?" she asked to the beat of the drums.

"Yeah!" the crowd responded with enthusiastic screams and cheers.

"I said, did y'all come to party and have some fun?!" she asked again but more hyped.

"Yeah!" the crowd responded again, even louder. That was the cue for the music to start.

Stephanie started singing, Melissa Sue Anderson's song *Turn the Beat Around*, which got everyone into the mood for partying. Stephanie owned the stage and her audience. Gloria knew from experience that Stephanie loved to put on a show. She liked to keep the people dancing and on their toes.

Keeping them on their toes, Gloria thought to herself. *Like uncle, like niece.*

Gloria looked around the second floor at all the people who came, all the happy excited faces. She thought about where Stephanie, that little girl who was left at her father's door so many years ago, would have gone if he hadn't taken her in and if she would have turned out to be this star, performing in front of Gloria's face. She thought about all the property, the investments and the money that Archie, her father, had left her and how some way, somehow, he knew that her life would be completed once she came back to New York. She also thought about his passing had brought her into the arms of her first real and true love, Chris.

As Gloria watched Stephanie work the stage, her mind imagined herself as that little girl who was sick and lying in bed and her daddy came home from work and sang to her, making her feel so much better and safe. This put a huge smile on her face.

"Daddy," Gloria said with a smile, "as usual, you made me feel so much better. Even in your death, you refused to leave me. You are still here all around us, and everything that you wanted from me, you got. I got my man and I'm back, Daddy, to stay; Stephanie and the twins, too. I'm working on Joey, too, and with Billy in his life, I believe that he'll come back to New York." She chuckled low. "As long as I have them, plus you, forever in my heart and soul, it will still always be ALL IN THE FAMILY."

The End
Finished March 24, 2007

Epilogue

It was a Saturday afternoon and the whole family was together at the house on Hauser Street. Joey had flown in from Cali Friday night to see Billy and to bring the family photos of his little sister, who was born prematurely but was healthy as a horse. He, Chris, Stephanie and the twins were helping Gloria move all the furniture down to the living room because she had donated almost everything besides her mother's old chair and Archie's old chair to the Jefferson/Willis Help Center and a truck was going to come and pick everything up. Gloria had been so busy with the running of the catering hall, restaurant and bakery, along with Jerry promoting acts to perform on the second floor, she hadn't had a chance to redecorate the Hauser house. She was going to start getting all of that done once the house was empty then repainted.

While Gloria was up in her parents' room, she started packing up Archie's closet, which she hadn't been in since his burial. She had been using her mother's closet. After putting all of her father's clothes into boxes, she started on the second shelf, where all of Archie's important paperwork was, when she finally remembered that there were two huge manila envelopes in there that she had never opened up to see what was inside. Not thinking too much about it, she took them and went to sit on the bed to open them up. Once she opened up the two envelopes, she noticed that there were individual envelopes inside the big ones with Joey's, Stephanie's and the twins' plus her name on them. As she separated them, then placed them atop one another, she headed downstairs to hand them to her family.

"Hey guys, I have an envelope for each one of ya's from your Uncle Archie and Grampa!" she exclaimed excitedly as she ran to the couch, and the family came excitedly to get an envelope. Chris wasn't too far behind as he went to sit next to Gloria as she handed out the envelopes.

"Ma, how did Grampa give you these envelopes?" Joey asked excitedly as he reached for his.

"Yeah Gloria, how did you get these?" Stephanie added as she waited to get hers after Joey.

"Well," Gloria responded as she gave Joey his, then Stephanie, then the twins. "I had meant to open up two envelopes that I had seen in Daddy's closet months ago but had gotten preoccupied and forgotten about it, putting them right back into the closet until now while I was packing up Daddy's clothes. When I opened them up, I saw the individual envelopes with your names on them, so I am giving them to you now." After Gloria said this, the family all looked at their names on the envelopes for a few seconds then quickly and excitedly began opening them up.

"This is so exciting!" Zoe exclaimed as she was about to open her contents.

"So what did Archie give you, Sunny?" Chris asked as he smiled and leaned toward her.

"Oh, it is just a nice letter," Gloria said as she welled up with tears then put her head on his shoulder. Chris kissed the top of her head as he stared at the letter with her but didn't read it.

Everyone was quiet for a few minutes as they opened their envelopes. Gloria noticed that everyone had tears in their eyes especially Stephanie, who was really opening up the floodgates.

"So Joey, what is going on with your envelope?" Gloria asked inquisitively as he sat at the end of the couch.

"Wow, Ma. Gramps just told me how much he loved me and that he was very proud of me. He told me that he wanted me to find a woman and not to be afraid to let my guard down. Wow Ma, I wonder if Gramps knew that he was about to pass?" He sniffled a few times then held the letter up against his heart then lowered his head. "Hey Gramps, I think that I might've found one," he said in a low whisper, but Gloria was looking at him and understood what he had said.

"What about you, Zoe?" she asked as she turned toward Edith's chair, where she was sitting.

"I got a letter from Grampa but he put inside the envelope an embroidered stitch with his name. Grampa knew that I love to design and sew clothes. I am going to design something special so I can put his stitch on it, then I am going to keep it forever." Zoe also did the same thing that Joey did. "This is the best gift that Grampa has ever given me," she said as she wiped the tears.

Gloria turned to Matthew, then smiled as he sat on the bottom step with a smile on his face.

"Mattster, what about you? Anything you wanna share?"

Matthew kept staring at the letter. It took a few moments before he was even able to lift up his head and speak.

"Besides a beautiful love letter from Grampa," Matthew then held up a piece of paper so everyone could see, "it is an autograph signature of Prince, one of my Idols."

"Wow, Daddy knew a little more about you all than you thought, huh guys?" Gloria exclaimed proudly, causing them all to nod and causing Stephanie to shout out with a laugh as the tears flowed hard as she gasped and her chest heaved in and out.

"Yeah, you got that right, Gloria!" Stephanie yelled loudly, causing everyone to look concerned.

"Stephanie, is there something wrong?" Zoe asked as she reached across her chair to Stephanie who was sitting in Archie's old chair.

"Yeah honey. What does your letter say?" Gloria asked as she lifted her head off Chris's shoulder and stared in her direction.

Stephanie kept staring at her letter as she took her finger and ran it across the writing on the paper, then she wiped her eyes a few times before she was able to speak. When she finally spoke, she took a deep breath and she exhaled, then responded to the question.

"I just found out through Uncle Archie that I am adopted!"